TIPPING POINT

RAIN STICKLAND

Paperback ISBN-13: 978-0-9949500-0-0
Paperback ISBN-10: 0994950004
Kindle ISBN-13: 978-0-9949500-1-7

DEDICATION

To my daughter, without whom I would be living a less-than-stellar life.

To my friends, whose encouragement has been life-altering.

To my current and future readers, who make it possible for me to be a writer.

And for the people of Muskoka and Parry Sound, who will be the first to tell you that there is a great deal of artistic licence taken with the towns in this book, though the stunning natural beauty is an undeniable fact.

CONTENTS

Acknowledgments

Many thanks go out to the following people, for their advice and assistance:

Amanda K. Woods, for a cover that was so much more than I could ever hope to achieve.

Steve Kovacs, for his expertise in firearms that steered me away from a really big mistake.

Marlin Woosley, for his willingness to critique and scrutinize with complete honesty.

Sarah Lyons Fleming, for additional advice on covers and writing in general.

Bruce and Jean Horst, for giving me a place to begin my writing journey in the public eye.

There are many, many people who deserve a place on this list. There may not be room for them all here, but there's plenty of room in my heart for my gratitude. Thank you all.

1

UNRAVELING

They might not have been zombies in the truest sense of the word since they hadn't died and risen from the grave, but they were damn close as far as Mackenzie was concerned. The ignorant and uninformed hadn't even noticed the disaster that was about to take place around them.

But Mac had been watching, and planning, and she was not going down with that particular ship. She gave it a week, max, before the shit really hit the fan, and she wasn't going to be stuck in a city with half a million people when it went dark for the last time.

"Cam, we're out of time. We have to go." Cameron didn't argue.

Cam helped her mother pack up the only important things that were still in the apartment, which included their two ferrets. An hour later, they were heading north, already hitting rush hour traffic on the 401. It was the middle of the week, and most commuters were going in the opposite direction, but Mac was still jittery. There were a lot of lights out along the way.

Another hour saw them as far as Barrie, coasting on the 400. Once the signs started displaying the Highway 11 logo, she took a deep breath and let it out. Whatever happened to their old city now, they were ahead of it. She was glad she'd dropped off a big donation of ferret food at the shelter just outside Toronto. They would be okay for a little while.

Mac engaged the voice-to-text feature on her BlackBerry.

"Text to Mitch Corelli," she said, enunciating clearly, and giving the phone a moment to process.

"Mitch, you need to leave Hamilton. Pack what you can in your car. Only what's important, where you can't stand to leave it behind. Head for my home town. Please don't stay in the city. I don't think you know what's happening. Text me back and let me know you're on your way."

She told the phone to send it. It was the best she could do for her ex for the time being. If she spoke to him on the phone he would try to argue, or worse, laugh her off. He'd never taken her concerns seriously, and she didn't think he would now. Mac may not have been in love with him for many years, but she still cared what happened to him.

A few minutes later her phone read out his response.

"Give me a break. I'm not going anywhere tonight. I'm working." She engaged her voice-to-text again to respond.

"Okay. Good luck. You'll need it. Bye."

Apparently Mitch rethought his decision to brush her off, because there was a different tenor to his next text half an hour later.

"What the hell is going on, Mac?"

She shared a look with Cam. Something must have happened in Hamilton to modify his attitude so drastically. Instead of texting back and forth with him, Mac decided to hit the next off-ramp. If he was willing to listen, she needed to call him. Besides, she wanted to know what was going on. She held her breath as she waited for him to pick up.

"Hey, Mac. What the hell? Things are fucked up here!"

"First tell me what's going on there right now. You changed your mind pretty suddenly, so something must have happened."

"People are completely fucking crazy right now, that's what's going on. They're nuts! The power went out again just after I got your last text. Didn't think much about it, since it's been so shitty lately. I'm making deliveries so it doesn't really matter to me unless people can't pay, but then I just don't drop off their stuff. No biggie.

"Then I get to one place and this guy starts in on me like it's my fault the power is fucked up. When there's no power the Interac machine isn't always able to take payments. Probably their internet is down, right? The next place I get to it's the same thing, and these people are even crazier. If I wasn't such a big guy I'd have been very worried. Fucking guy was carrying a baseball bat when he answered the door. What's this all about?" Mac nodded to herself. It was what she'd expected.

"Do you remember Pierre, the guy I used to work with? He was my boss for a while."

"Yeah, the dick that laid you off, right?"

"That's him. Anyway, he told me something when I worked there. He worked for Ontario Hydro during the Northeastern Blackout. Some sort of planning executive.

"Anyway, one of the reasons he left was because of his disagreements with them regarding coal and nuclear plants. They were supposed to bring the nuclear plants online and shut off the coal, but they went ahead with the shut-downs without ramping up the nuclear. He told me back then that the brown-outs and rolling blackouts would get progressively worse until the whole system collapsed. That blackout was nothing compared to what we should expect, according to him." She took a deep breath for the rest of it. This was where the conversation could turn, so she chose her words carefully.

"Pierre basically told me the whole system was going to go down, and it might very well be permanent. He told me what to watch for, and that's what I've been doing. I'm not talking about some drunk plowing into a transformer and knocking out a few blocks or whatever. Those are meaningless. What's happening are outages that have no reasonable explanation other than a system overload. Every week it's getting worse and people are starting to go nuts, as you just saw for yourself."

"Yeah, okay, but you're telling me I should get out of the city entirely. I don't get the connection."

"Okay, follow me here. The outages are increasing in frequency and duration, right? Refrigerators can't even keep food from spoiling now. With no power, most gas stations aren't able to pump fuel. No fuel means no food delivery to replace what's gone bad. You're delivering booze, which isn't something people actually need, and people are already getting pissed when you can't give it to them. What do you think is going to happen in the next few days if the power supply gets worse? I would bet you don't even have a week's worth of food in your cupboards, right?"

"About that, yeah. So you're saying there isn't going to be any food in the city? That's a little paranoid don't you think? They must have some sort of contingency plan to keep the supply runs going."

"Are you sure you want to rely on our government to take care of you? How much confidence do you have in them after the number of times they've screwed you over? Bureaucracies don't operate well in emergency situations. You know that. It takes forever to do the smallest thing. People usually die before they get their shit together. I'm giving you another option, but it's your decision."

"What kind of option? What's up north?"

"Remember my plans for a big hunk of property and the whole

off-grid thing?"

"Yeah. You talked about it enough."

"Well, we pulled it together mostly. We've got everything up there waiting. It's not finished, or pretty, but I didn't want to wait anymore. You don't want to be in Hamilton when the shit hits the fan, Mitch. Seriously. With the number of people already living in poverty there, it's going to crash and burn faster than most places. Poor people are going to have a lot less food stocked up in their pantries. The drug supply is going to run out, and any addicts will be jonesing."

Mac could hear the skepticism and hesitation in his silence. She knew if she said anything else, though, it would work against her argument. She had to let him absorb and think about it.

"Fuck, Mac. If I leave the city I'll lose my job. If you're wrong about this, my boss is not going to be understanding if I tell him I walked away on the word of my ex-wife's conspiracy theories. He's gonna slam the door in my face."

"Mitch, if I'm wrong you're not exactly going to be on the street. Even without the shit hitting the fan, your life will actually be better off if you come up north with us. We're going to be completely self-sustaining, and until we are we've got all the supplies we need to tide all of us over. I was hoping to have everything done before we went up there, because that was always the plan, but circumstances being what they are..." She trailed off, not bothering to reiterate her concerns.

"We need to get moving. You too. It's going to be hard for you to get out of the city if things start going bad. We've got all the comforts of home up there, and lots of little toys you're going to love. No bills, nothing but privacy. I'll send you the directions. Make sure you have your phone and GPS completely charged for the trip."

At this point Mac was almost sure Mitch was convinced. He was an intelligent man, and lately he'd been expressing the desire for a life of peace and quiet. If that was the case, and the world was going to hell, the last thing he would want would be to get stuck in the middle of it. Still, she wasn't going to beg him to save his own ass.

"Fuck it. It's not like I'm working my dream job anyway. Send me the directions."

"I'll text them to you as soon as we're off the phone. You'll have to call me when you get close, though. Even with full directions you'd never find the driveway. I need to be at the road to guide you in."

If Mitch actually followed through, it'd be one less thing to worry about. She knew what he was like, though. He might intend to do something, but things always seemed to come up. She exchanged a glance with Cam and put the car in gear.

The old BMW 3-series was her long-distance and running-around car. She had a truck up north for any heavy-duty stuff. A four-wheel-drive with a winch and all other vital equipment, including a supply trailer. It would come in handy setting up the new building. They had a building there for temporary shelter, but it was meant to be a garage. The prep work had been done for the main house, but it wasn't up yet.

As they drove past Gravenhurst, Mac felt happier. She'd been looking forward to this. Cam's job was the only reason they had remained in Hamilton. Mac worked online, which she could do anywhere, but making money had become unnecessary.

"Do you think he'll come?" Mac was jarred a bit by her daughter's abrupt question. The silence in the car had been going on for a while.

"Damned if I know. You know what he's like. Says one thing, does another, in one ear, and out the other," she rhymed in a sing-song voice. Cam snorted.

"No kidding. Well, it's not like I want him to die or anything, but we're better off without him." Mac nodded in agreement.

"What made you decide that we had to leave today? I mean, I heard you muttering, and you warned me it might happen soon, but did something major happen on the news or something?"

Mac chewed her lip, trying to find a way to explain it without it turning into the usual educational two-hour lecture she tended to indulge in.

"With the outages, people are already protesting. These aren't activists working for the greater good. They're people who only care about their own inconvenience and discomfort. Then you've got the people who have loved ones with health conditions adversely affected by the heat and humidity. You heard what I said to Mitch about food. The whole situation is about to turn."

"So, basically people are turning into animals, and you think it'll get a lot worse, really fast. What's the plan then? We're not going back are we?"

"Not this time."

"What about my friends?"

"I don't want to see them get hurt or starve to death. We just need to make sure the garden and bulk supplies are okay first. A quick check should be enough, and then you can give Kirk a call." Kirk was Cameron's best friend from high school.

Mac's own best friend was in the States, and he had a pretty good situation there. She was thankful she'd managed to talk him into setting up an amateur radio station. Even when their phones went down, they might still be able to talk to one another.

"It's too bad we couldn't wait until fall before we had to leave. It would have been nice to see the leaves turning as we got into Muskoka." Mac smiled. She knew how her daughter felt. It was their favourite season.

"Well we'll be up here for the whole season, so if we want to see the leaves we won't have to miss a single day. Why do you think I planted so many maple trees? Best fall colours, ever."

The closer they got to Rosseau Falls, the narrower the road became. It was just barely enough for two cars to pass one another. As soon as they pulled off the main road, however, it became pretty much a single lane.

The road they were on didn't actually have anyone living on it. Their driveway was the only one. All other properties in the area had their driveways on a different side road. It had truly been the ideal parcel for them. They wanted no interaction with neighbours.

Having Cam's best friend and his girlfriend come stay with them might be a risk, but it was a calculated one. They were social only with people they liked, much like Mac and her daughter, and she got along with them very well for the most part.

They were getting close to the property, and she'd long since removed the telltale reflective number marking the property entrance, so she had Cameron direct their high-powered UV light ahead of them on the road. Finally she saw the marked tree. She slowed to a stop and got out of the car.

Mac walked over and placed her thumb on the biometric pad concealed in a hole at the back of the tree. The two halves of the bush-covered gate swung open. She was careful to brush the crisp dead leaves back over the pad, and walked back to the car when she was done.

The scent of pine and spruce saturated her olfactory senses as she inhaled deeply. To her it was the smell of home. She could also smell the water from the small river that cut through their land. It hadn't been hard to find a property with surface water in Ontario.

White willows grew past the riverbank opposite the building sites. She knew they were there because she'd been the one to plant them. They might need a source for salicylic acid.

The buildings weren't visible from the road. There was a veritable forest between the road and the current building. She'd spent a lot of time on Google Earth and Google Maps, deciding exactly how to place things, so nothing was left to chance.

She drove through the gate and slowed the car once she'd crossed the pressure plate. Mac waited until the gate closed completely behind her, and then continued on to their temporary home.

It was ugly from the outside. There was no getting around it. She hadn't bought a steel building that was designed to look like a regular home. She'd bought the A-style that was vaguely house-shaped, but didn't fool anyone. The two garage doors didn't help.

"Stay in the car for a minute, Cam. I want to back the truck out, and I'm sure we'd both be happier if I didn't back into you." Cameron laughed.

"I'd certainly be happier, and you don't enjoy playing nursemaid." Mackenzie laughed. That was certainly true.

Once the truck and car were parked behind the building, out of sight from their overgrown driveway, they started unloading the car. It didn't take them long. Aside from the ferrets, all they had was some food, a couple of bug out bags, and their laptops.

"Hey babies," she cooed into their carrier. Unsurprisingly they had fallen asleep. They slept a lot anyway, and when they were confined they took it as an opportunity to get even more sleep.

Her temporary bedroom was the only safe place for them, so she took them straight there and let them out. The bedroom would later be turned into a tool crib, so it had a two-part door. The bottom could be kept closed while the top remained open. It kept the ferrets confined while allowing the air to circulate.

The boys were familiar with the place so the stress on them was limited, but they hadn't been there in a few weeks and it was exciting to them again. They bounced around, doing their weasel war dance and pouncing on one another.

Squeaker displayed the characteristic that had given him his name, and made chirpy sounds. Pickle let out the odd noise, but mostly splayed his toes and bounced in his extreme happiness, his fur standing on end.

Mac spread some waste pads for them, before she snuck out the half-door to avoid them racing out past her feet. They needed fresh food and water dishes. The ones in their carrier had wet food in both of them from the movement of the car.

"How are they doing?"

"Crazy, as usual. We'd better go take a look at the garden as soon as I get their bowls in place. I'm glad I'm not leaving them alone in an unfamiliar room to get all this stuff done." Cameron patted her mother's shoulder.

"There, there. You'll be okay."

"Okay, shut up. You're an adult now. It's no longer child abuse if I beat you up." They both laughed, and Mac finished with the ferret bowls. Pickle went straight for the water, but Squeaker had to be nudged away from the door for her to pass through.

"No, you're not coming out now. Sorry, but you're stuck in here for a bit." He tilted his head way back in order to look toward her face. Even though she knew there was no real expression on his face, she still felt like he was guilt-tripping her. They were supposed to be smarter than dogs and cats, so she wouldn't be surprised if they were capable of manipulation tactics. They'd played tricks on her before, usually to get through closed doors.

"Mom! Are you coming?" Mac rolled her eyes.

"Who's the parent in this relationship," she yelled back.

"It's certainly not you! Let's get this done so we can relax for the night." Mackenzie just laughed. She'd raised a kid with sass, and she liked that just fine.

2

TAKING STOCK

Mac set up a couple of portable lights by the garden. Aside from some damage most likely caused by rabbits, a quick visual scan told her their situation was still good. Blackberry and raspberry bushes circling the perimeter of their cleared property kept most animals from wandering in and eating their food.

Mac walked through the rows. There was a lot they could pick tomorrow. For now she snacked on snow peas, and stuffed some tomatoes and carrots into the canvas bag she carried. She wasn't going to dig for potatoes or try to snag enough beans until she could really see what she was doing.

"Everything looks pretty good. We can have these tomatoes for sandwiches once we finish for the night. I'll just wash up these carrots to munch on until then." Cam shrugged. Mac knew she wasn't as keen on raw carrots as she was herself, but it was better than nothing, and they hadn't eaten since about noon.

"Okay, I think we've seen as much as we can see until daylight. Let's pack up the lights and head inside. While I'm washing the carrots, you can get in touch with your friends. So long as we have our garden, we're fine for next year, and anything that's gone bad in the long-term items we can replace tomorrow. It's all basics that are readily available."

It was one of many benefits to living in an area with numerous farms. People had livestock and produce for sale, and agricultural supply stores had giant bags of grain. It would probably be best if she took a trip to the feed supplier anyway. She wanted to buy at least a goat or two, and some chickens.

Fencing material was something else she could get tomorrow. She couldn't circle the whole property in fencing for the moment, but she wanted to at least enclose the animal pens. Mac was a huge believer in respect for animals, so she wanted the goats and chickens to have as much free range as possible, but she knew goats would eat the berry bushes and ruin what was a great natural fence. She also needed to keep the smells away from the area where the main building would be erected.

Once the lights were put away and the carrots scrubbed, she waited for Cam to finish chatting with Kirk, and pondered how to set up the livestock areas. Suddenly Mac was exhausted. Between the animal pens and all the work that would need to be done on their new house, there was a lot to be done.

Technically they didn't need another building in any desperate way, but whatever happened in the rest of the world it was how she'd always planned things. In recent years she'd kicked her efforts up a notch, feeling like time was slipping away.

She needed to grab a notebook to jot things down, because there were too many things to remember. She had lots of lists on her laptop, but a spiral notebook was easier to carry around.

She was just taking a step toward her daughter's bedroom, planning to give her a poke to hurry things up, when Cam came shuffling out with her eyes red.

"Hey! What is it?"

"They're not coming. At least not yet. I feel like I'm never going to see him again."

"Do you want me to talk to him? Explain why we left when we did?"

"No, it's not that. He believes me. He's seeing it in Oakville even. They're not having quite as much trouble with their power as Hamilton, but people are assholes. Already!" Mackenzie wasn't at all surprised. Oakville was full of some pretty snotty people, and they didn't like to be inconvenienced.

"So why aren't they coming?"

"Their car broke down. They have no way to get here."

"Fuck. Fuck, fuck, fuck. Now I feel like a shit for not getting in touch with them right away."

"It's not your fault, mom. I'm pretty sure he mentioned it to me about a week ago, and I didn't even think of it. I just figured they would have taken care of it by now. Leigh doesn't usually let things go when it comes to her car. She does *not* like riding the bus. They're on a waiting list for the repairs. Their usual garage is backed up, and when they called around they couldn't find anyone who could do it any faster."

"No, they wouldn't. The power outages would mean there's a lot of work that couldn't be done, so they'd be way behind. Did they say what was wrong with it?"

"Yeah, but I don't understand what it means. Here, take a look." Mackenzie took the laptop from Cam and skimmed the message.

"They need the timing chain replaced. They can't even turn their car on, or they risk blowing the motor. Don't worry, Cam. I'll figure something out. If I have to drive back as far as Oakville, I will. Just let them know I'm working on a solution for now, and I'll get in touch with them in the morning.

"What about your dad? Have you tried talking to him yet? You know he's welcome to come."

Allan was technically Cameron's step-dad. Mackenzie had never married him, but they'd been together about eight years while Cameron was growing up. She had always called him her dad. Mackenzie had nothing against him, and it had been good between them for a while, but then Mac had wanted more out of life, while Allan was content to coast through it.

"I wasn't sure if it would be okay. I wanted to, but you guys haven't talked much for a long time."

"The only reason we don't talk is that we have little in common now. We don't dislike each other. I mean, if he were here he'd be someone I'd have a lot of fun with, but in general that's kind of all he does. We used to play cards and shoot pool together almost constantly, so long as we weren't working, which we'd be able to do once everything is set up here. I just have to assemble the pool table in the new building. *That* should be interesting."

"Okay, I'll ask him then. It would be good for you to have someone to do stuff with. When Leigh and Kirk get here, I'll have friends to game with, but you might get bored or lonely."

"Oh, please. When have I ever been bored? Or lonely for that matter? When I get listless I find things to do. Projects, books to read, PC games, ferrets, you name it. Still, I would love to be able to play Canasta again, and he's the only person I know who actually plays it."

"Okay, hang on then. I'll go send him the message now. I don't think he's going to take me seriously, but I'm going to try."

Once Cam had messaged Allan they checked on all the canned and dried goods. Mac chewed her lip worriedly. They had money. She could send Kirk enough to rent a car if it came down to that. Rather than taking the time and risk of going back there herself, they could head straight out.

Money would only be good for so long, so they might as well use it up for things that mattered, like getting people to safety. That and whatever supplies and livestock they could get their hands on. She wanted animal-based protein, like milk, cheese, and eggs, even if the current science was right about vegetable protein being healthy.

Mac also wanted mushrooms. She needed to buy fresh ones to collect the spores, so she could grow them herself. Mac grabbed her notebook and added them to her purchase list for tomorrow. There were just certain things she wasn't willing to live without.

With that in mind she glanced at the coffee supplies. They would need more if Leigh drank it. Mitch certainly did. Coffee made the list, too.

She'd be planting winter wheat, some hard and some soft, once the first frost hit, so if things went well their flour supply would be replenished by June. In the spring she'd plant oats.

Abruptly she sat down and rubbed her brow. She couldn't help feeling as though there was something she was really going to miss one day. Something she'd forgotten about at the time, because it wasn't something they regularly bought or used.

She'd taken care of the chocolate issue, of course. That was vital. They had stacks of dark chocolate bars, a case each of their favourite candy bars, and cans of powdered hot chocolate. It might have to be rationed with the number of people they would have there, but they wouldn't do without.

They were set for any medicines they had legal access to. There was a case of FishMox and one of Bird-Sulfa. The sulpha-based antibiotic was for Cam, who had a mild penicillin allergy. The other one was for anyone who wasn't sensitive to it.

They had generic Tylenol Ones for pain relief, because they contained codeine and were available without a prescription. Same with Gravol and Benadryl. Allergic reactions were not something she wanted to be unprepared for. She'd also picked up standard hay fever allergy relief meds. There was extra-strength acetaminophen for anyone who didn't want codeine.

They'd put in a large stock of Imodium, too. It was on the WHO list of necessary drugs for a reason, and Mac often had more reason than most.

Mac stared at the shelves. There was something she was missing. She knew it. Even with all her planning, she was bound to forget that one thing, and she was sure it would end up being like an itch she couldn't scratch.

Tens of thousands of dollars had gone into what was on those shelves already. Same with the various fuels and chemicals they stored in a cheap garden shed surrounded by trees to insulate it from high temperatures.

She'd even bought sulphuric acid. They might need to make both batteries and ether one day. Anesthetics and major pain medicines would be one of the first things that got looted. Not just by desperate people who needed them, but addicts and users, too. If any kind of surgery needed to be performed, she wanted anesthetic to be available.

Mac had a couple of boxes containing chemistry equipment. To make the ether, of course, but she also had it for another reason. She had to be sure there was a way to make insulin. Her best friend was a type one diabetic. Even if he hoarded a supply, it expired within a year and became toxic.

Mac would check the fuel and chemical stocks when it was time to head out for the supplies she had on her list. She'd also pour her oldest fuel into both the car and truck tanks, and take the truck in with any empty containers to refill them, adding a stabilizer so the fuel wouldn't degrade.

When they were finished checking all the bulk storage bins, and had eaten their sandwiches, Mac dragged herself off toward her room. She wouldn't sleep just yet, but she wanted to lie down and relax with her boys. She needed the energy boost.

"Mom, wait."

"Yeah?" Mac swung her head toward Cameron.

"Have you thought of anything to help Kirk yet?" Mac nodded at her.

"Yeah, if it's possible. I've also got an alternate plan. Are their phones working? I'll need to discuss it with them to see what they're willing to do..." She trailed off. She had to find a way to convince them to leave their car. They couldn't afford to wait for it to be fixed, when it probably never would be.

"I think he uses the same carrier we do, and our phone still works."

"Okay, let him know I have a solution. If he's still awake I'll call him." Cam turned into her room and Mackenzie went into hers.

The ferrets were sleeping, which made her feel guilty for leaving them alone when they might be feeling stressed. They were snuggled up together in what was supposed to be a cat bed.

Mackenzie leaned over to pet the ferrets as softly as she could to avoid waking them. They both shifted, and Squeaker grunted as usual, but then they snuggled up closer to one another and continued snoozing. She chuckled a bit when she heard the soft snores coming from Squeaker.

"He's still awake," Cameron yelled from her room. Mac picked up her phone and pulled Kirk up on her contact list. He answered right away.

"Hey, Mac. What have you got?"

"I have a couple of options for you, and I don't think you'll like either of them, but I can't think of anything else.

"I'm assuming the mechanic had to order your timing chain, and the supply chain is already stuttering. Have they said anything about an ETA on your car?" Kirk laughed quietly, but she could hear the sardonic tone to it just the same.

"Yeah. A week to never. At first it was a couple of days, but when a couple of days went by and he hadn't called us we started to bitch. That's when he told us it would be at least a week because they were still waiting on the part. They have the motor apart but no timing chain, and no way to set it up once they get it if the power doesn't become more reliable. Without power they're as fucked as we are."

"That's kind of what I figured. So are you willing to leave your car there and rent a car to come up? If money is an issue, I can send it to you. It should still get there. Hopefully the rental agency can do a contract without their computers.

"If that's not an option, you might be able to get as far as Barrie using the transit system. It would be safer to do that than for me to drive back through to Oakville. I don't know when this is going to break, but in the cities it'll be soon."

"It's already started. Those rich assholes have been stepping all over everyone, trying to clean out the grocery stores. It took us forever to get any supplies today, and we made sure we went in there with cash only.

"We're okay for money. If we can find a car to rent, we'll do that. The car is a lease anyway. If they ever get it fixed it can go back to the dealer. Piece of shit."

"Look, if you can't get a rental, try to get to Barrie. Let me know what's happening and I'll be down there in a heartbeat. If neither option works, I'll come to Oakville. If I'd known you were having this issue, we would have called you before leaving Hamilton. You would've had to share the back seat with the ferrets, but you'd be here with us now." Kirk laughed.

"Leigh would have loved that. She couldn't put Squeaker down when we were over there the last time."

"Well, she'll see them soon enough. Take whatever money you have out of the bank, if you haven't already. You might not be able to later."

"Already done. Won't know until morning if there are rentals available, so I'll call back then."

"Okay, I'll shoot you all the directions to get here, but you might need to be talked in the rest of the way once you get to a certain point. We're purposely way out of the way here, and everything about it is as concealed as possible."

"Cool! When Cam told me you were getting into the whole survival thing, I had no idea it was that major. Zombie apocalypse be damned!" Mac laughed.

"Well, like you always say, 'People are assholes.' You're right. Hence those group archery lessons, and the steps I took to keep things extremely quiet around here. Okay, get your rest. We'll talk tomorrow."

"Alright, and thanks. You didn't have to help us like this, so it's really cool what you're doing."

"Of course I have to. We care about you. And we need as many non-assholes as we can get! Be warned, though. There's a lot of work to do around here right now. We'll get into that when you're safe, though."

They said goodbye, and Mac turned her head. Cam stood in the doorway, resting her elbows on the closed half of the door.

"You could have come in, you know. If I wanted privacy the door would be closed." Cam shook her head.

"I just wanted to see what was happening and then I'm going to bed. I'm really tired. He's going to make it here, right?" Mac could see that her daughter was really worried.

"Cam, whatever I have to do I'll make sure of it. If things get absolutely crazy they can defend themselves, but it isn't that bad yet. It's mostly the rich people acting like assholes from what I can see. The only issue I think they'll have there is if the agency's computers are down, and the agency can't do a manual contract.

"He said they're fine for money, and I know they both have credit cards. I should have suggested they take out whatever cash they can from their credit cards, too. I don't know why I didn't think of that before." Mackenzie flopped back on her bed, irritated with herself.

"Well, gee, mom. Why on earth aren't you perfect? I expected better from you!"

"Ha ha. Smartass. Go to bed before I feel I have to come over there and hit you."

Cam slipped away with a quick laugh, and Mackenzie just stared up at the ten-foot ceiling, trying to shut off her brain. She was never going to get any sleep this way.

She leaned over the side of the bed to snag Pickle from his blankets. Squeaker grunted in protest, but was too tired to make a stink about it.

The best stress relief in the world, as far as she was concerned, was snuggling a ferret. Pickle woke up just enough to lick her cheek a couple of times, but then he let out his own grunt and ignored her. She stroked his thick, silky fur. Pickle started to squirm after a few minutes. He didn't really like being held while he slept, so she put him back in bed and snuggled Squeaker until he also decided he'd had enough.

Well, if she wasn't going to sleep, Mac figured she might as well add to the list in her notebook. She'd calculated all the hygiene stuff they would need for two women, but that would change with Leigh and Kirk coming up. Tampons, deodorant, and toilet paper were high on the list.

Razors also made the list, though she wondered about getting a couple of straight razors. She did a quick online search and downloaded a tutorial on using one, and then found a knife shop. She wasn't sure if they had anything other than hunting or kitchen knives, but she'd check it out. Mac and Cameron needed good survival knives anyway.

Shaving cream popped into her head suddenly. Neither Mackenzie nor Cameron used it, but she imagined Kirk would have to. Aerosol cans would expire after a certain time, so she found recipes for homemade shaving soap. When she saw lye was one of the ingredients, she stopped and almost smacked herself in the forehead.

"Well, I'll be damned," she exclaimed softly. She'd finally figured out one of the things she had forgotten. Eventually they would have to make soap, and she was pretty sure every recipe she had for soap made from basic ingredients required lye. Now she had to figure out where she could get it in large quantities without making someone wonder if she was dissolving a body.

3

MAKING A POINT

Once Kirk called back late in the morning to say that they'd found a car and would be on their way shortly, Mac hitched their small supply trailer to the back of the truck and headed into Rosseau. She'd originally intended to go to Huntsville, since they had a lot more stores and selection, but the knife store was in Rosseau.

Additional research had netted her the information that there were indeed soap recipes that didn't require lye. Same with shaving cream. Laundry soap needed ingredients that had some lye *in* them, but she could easily pick up that kind of thing in bulk.

Her real worry was that there might be other things she was forgetting. Things she might have a hard time getting later. She'd stock up on whatever tampons and toilet paper she could find in Rosseau for the time being, because she wasn't heading back to the

Costco in Barrie. Later she'd hit every grocery store in the surrounding towns for more.

She was probably being an idiot with all her worrying, because the stuff that was most likely to fly off the shelves in the heat of a societal breakdown was stuff she already had. The obvious stuff, in other words. Toilet paper was something she'd gone overboard on, but she'd pick up more anyway. She wasn't running out of toilet paper. She didn't care if it *was* the end of the world.

Costco had been her close, personal friend for a while now. Gigantic purchases never looked out of place there, especially when you had a business membership. She had gone through their aisles countless times over the years, looking at every single item available for purchase, and making sure she did that for every shopping season. Different things were available at different times, and that had helped her make sure she wasn't overlooking anything important.

Many cartons of supplies had found their way to them via Amazon and eBay, too. Thankfully the landlord hadn't been the nosy kind, and she knew Mackenzie had her own business that involved shipping things. It helped when Mac opened the package of adult-sized footie pyjamas in front of her.

At the thought of clothing, Mac started to wonder if she should buy a couple of Angora goats. Angora might come in very handy for making clothes.

It didn't take long to buy out the stores in Rosseau, since there weren't many of them. Then she headed to the knife store. She saw the sign and chuckled, even though she already knew what it was called. *Sharper Image*, indeed. Good thing the big boys in New York weren't likely to come to this neck of the woods.

She walked into *Sharper Image* and waited until her eyes adjusted and the bell over the door stopped clanging. Then she moved over to a display that caught her eye. She was a bit of a sucker for weapons of all types. They had archery equipment, in addition to some firearms. What they didn't have were survival knives.

A clerk sidestepped to the display she was eyeballing and asked if she was looking for a gift. She stared right at him, holding his gaze until he was thoroughly uncomfortable. Then she gave her usual sort of sarcastic response to a perceived sexist remark.

"Right. Because I couldn't possibly have a use for one of these. Is that what you mean?" She raised her brows at him, not breaking eye contact, and awaited his response.

"Uh. No?" His questioning tone almost made her laugh, but she was more interested in pointing out the flaw in his assumption that she couldn't possibly be buying a survival knife for herself.

"Right. No, I'm not buying anyone a gift, except maybe my daughter." Finally she relented.

"I was actually looking for a straight razor to replace disposable blades." Now the young man was looking at her all googly-eyed, like he couldn't believe she would want to risk her lady parts with something so dangerous as a straight razor. In truth she didn't, but now she was stuck letting him make the assumption.

"Granted, these caught my eye, so I may get one or two. I don't have nearly enough knives." Now she was just playing with him.

"A filleting knife or two would be good, don't you think? Really good for getting the skin off, right?" This kid obviously didn't understand how his preconceived notions were doing him in, because he turned pasty white. She *would* need good filleting knives, and knives of every other kind, but if she bought too many he might just have a heart attack, and he looked to be all of seventeen or eighteen years old.

"What I'm really interested in are a couple of survival knives, but they have to be good ones. I want full tang only, so don't show me anything else. I don't want one of those flashy Rambo knives. I need to be able to use it. Oh, and the straight razors of course. I don't know much about them, so I'd appreciate any suggestions you might have, assuming you know more about them than I do."

As she waited for him to bring over some straight razors, she perused the selection of knives he'd pulled out for her. Mac had done her research on knives a long time ago, but had been hemming and hawing over her choice ever since. Now she was down to the wire, so it would serve her right if they didn't have anything she felt was good enough. She wasn't sure when she'd be able to go somewhere else, or if she even *would* be able to.

She stared at what he had pulled out, flipping over the tags to be sure of what she was seeing. The tags listed the makes and models, along with their prices. It didn't take long to discover that none of them were going to do the job.

He shifted back over, having never left her sight. After all, he had to be sure she wasn't going to walk off with the cheap merchandise.

"Look, kid," she said, "I don't have time for joking around with you. Is this the best you've got?" He blushed a bit.

"Well, we do have some others, ma'am, but they're pretty expensive. I thought you might want to see these first."

"I really don't. Have you got any KA-BARs? Maybe Ontario, Buck, Gerber, ESEE, something like that? I'm not interested in buying anything that's going to let me down when I really need it. You don't want me coming back here because I'm unhappy do you?" She paused for effect.

"With a knife?" His previous colour leeched from his skin, turning it pasty again. She grinned toothily and waited for him to come to the conclusion that he should probably show her some decent knives.

"Maybe I should go get my dad, huh? It's his shop. I'm still learning all this stuff, so I don't really know what's good and what isn't." With that he pretty much bolted, not even bothering to clear the knives off the counter. She could hear voices in the back, the teenager injecting a pleading quality into the conversation.

"Jesus, Mary and Joseph, Billy! She's not gonna jump over the counter and sink fangs into your neck. You gotta learn how to handle the customers. This'll be your shop one day." With that the stockroom door opened, and a man walked out who could have graced the cover of *Outdoor Life* magazine. She'd certainly seen enough of those covers to be able to judge.

The shaggy cut looked good with his wavy brown hair, and his goatee was well-trimmed. The laugh-lines creasing the corners of his eyes made him seem friendly and approachable. His smile showed he wasn't a stranger to oral hygiene.

"Hello, ma'am. My son says you're looking for a good survival knife." He looked down at the pile on the counter and nodded.

"You know your knives. You're right. These aren't even meant for survival. These are mostly for show like what the city boys like wearing on their hip to try to fit in. Only makes 'em look stupid. Do you know what make you want, or are you wanting to see a few different kinds?"

Mac was relieved to be dealing with someone who seemed to understand that she wasn't there on a lark. She told him some of the knives she'd been considering, along with the various features she was looking for.

"Well, we don't carry ESEE, but I do have some KA-BAR and Gerber I think you'll like. I'd recommend them to anyone. I'll get you a couple of models of each brand, and see if they're what you want. As for these here straight razors, are you looking for something specific there?" There was a bit of a twinkle in his eye when he asked.

"Well, to be perfectly honest, I'm just looking for backup, in case I ever run out of disposable razors one day. And I like to have backups of backups. I just want them to last, and preferably not kill myself with them. The disposables are such cheap pieces of crap, and I tend to isolate myself for long periods of time." *Jesus, Mac! Shut the hell up!* She could not believe she was talking so much. The twinkle had only grown into a little smile on the guy's face.

"Well, what about an old-fashioned safety-razor then, where you just replace the blades. A box of blades doesn't cost too much, and they can technically be re-sharpened if you're in dire need of a shave. Uh..." He didn't seem to know where to go from there, and Mac immediately started to blush.

"Or maybe one of each, just in case," he went on in a rush. Mac nodded and cleared her throat.

"Yeah, okay. That's probably a good idea. Just in case."

"Alright, I'll be right back with the other knives, the safety razor, blades, and a better straight razor than what my boy showed you here. It's okay, but if you're looking for real quality over the long haul, there are better. Most guys buy one as a sort of a phase or trend, and aren't serious about committing to it. They soon fall back to using a Mach 3 or whatever it is they've got in their medicine cabinet." Mac could see he was trying to reduce their momentary discomfort from the reference to her personal shaving habits, so she nodded and smiled to let him know she was okay with it.

The moment her lips curved, he snapped his mouth closed and just looked at her for a few seconds, before he shook it off and abruptly walked away. She couldn't help wondering if she had something nasty in her teeth. She picked up one of the cheap knives on the counter and took a quick look at the reflection of her mouth. Seemed fine to her, and she'd brushed her teeth before leaving the house. She shrugged it off. Whatever it was, it wasn't her problem.

When he came back he used his forearm to push aside the stuff on the glass counter, and then placed the new items on the freshly cleared surface. He had big hands, she noticed, and no wedding ring. Mac nearly sucked in her breath in shock when she realized what she'd been focusing on. She coughed to cover the slight gasp that had managed to escape.

"Sorry," she said when he glanced up at her. "I inhaled a little funny."

"You want some water? I've got some bottles in the back."

"No, really, I'm fine. Just a momentary thing, like inhaling a dust particle or something. Not that your store is dusty or anything," she blurted. She could feel the colour rush back to her cheeks, and wanted to roll her eyes at her reversion to high-school level communication skills. Mac had no idea why she was behaving this way. The guy was certainly attractive, but she had other priorities.

"So, I'm guessing you don't get anyone coming here from New York to complain about the name of your store, eh?" He snorted out a bit of a laugh.

"Not so far. Rosseau gets a lot more tourists than it used to, since we're getting a bit of a reputation as a resort town, so you never know. I've actually been considering changing it, because I don't want to deal with any legal crap. Just haven't come up with anything better. I'm not creative like that. I bought the store outright a few years back, name and all."

"Probably all the really appropriate ones have been used, since it's the sort of business that tends to use puns a lot. *A Cut Above*, *Close Shave*, that sort of thing. Maybe *Slice of Life* is available?" Mac rattled them off while he just sort of stared at her.

"You mind if I write those down?" She shook her head.

"How do you come up with stuff like that?" His expression was close to wonderment.

"In that case I don't know that I really did. They may even be names I've seen in the past and they're just kind of floating around in my head. I used to do some start-up consulting, and was always having to come up with names for clients' new businesses. A lot of people came to me wanting to run a simple shop, rather than having new inventions or anything, so they needed someone else to do the creative legwork for them. I've always had a bit of a knack for it.

"I'd do a name search for Ontario first, before going to the expense of changing your signage and all that. I'd also suggest checking for domain names online. That's often a good way to check for internationally used names. Like *The Sharper Image*. Then do a Google search using the key words *knife store* and then whatever name you're thinking of changing it to."

"Wow, thanks! You're not at all what I was expecting when Billy said I needed to come help you. He seemed kind of scared actually. What'd you do to him?" Mac knew he wasn't being belligerent by the return of his twinkle, and when she noticed his eyes were green she wanted to give her head a shake.

"Well, he sort of assumed I was looking for a gift, and I don't like assumptions. Particularly ones with a gender-based slant. It's not the kind of question that would have been asked if a male walked in, so I twisted him up a bit." He laughed.

"Yeah, you certainly did that. I thought I was going to come out and find She-Ra in my store. Or a serial killer. Though it's always pretty hard to tell with one of those, I guess." He gave her a look, like he just might be pondering it, and she laughed. Given that the twinkle hadn't gone anywhere, she knew he was yanking her chain.

"Nah. Just thought it would be a good idea to challenge his assumptions a bit." He nodded at her.

"Good. His mother's not winning any awards for independence and self-reliance. I heard she just hooked husband number five a couple of months ago, and this one doesn't appear to be any better than the last four. We were never married," he added.

"I think he may have gotten a bad impression of women from all that. And I haven't exactly been bringing a lot of women around, so he hasn't seen anything else."

Mac was absolutely certain that he had purposely steered the conversation in that direction. She was also certain that she didn't mind pointing it there herself.

"I know what you mean. I stopped trying to provide good male role models for my daughter a few years ago. Other things became priorities. I'm Mac by the way," she said, and held out her hand to shake his. She drew her hand back when he started laughing outright. He held up his own hand when she made it obvious she wasn't thrilled with his response.

"Mine too," he managed, laughing even harder once he'd choked that out. Her jaw dropped.

"You're kidding me!" She had to chuckle herself at that one.

"Okay, well, technically it's Neil McKinnon, but people in town have been calling me Mac for so many years I've just gotten used to it. Maybe you should just call me Neil. Might be less confusing that way."

"You're probably right. And technically, mine's Mackenzie. Uh, Thane."

"You don't seem so sure of that," he said, with a big grin.

"Yeah, I'm sure. I just don't usually give it out to people I've just met. I tend to be a lot more cautious about that sort of thing, and I've taught my daughter to be the same way."

She really *hadn't* hesitated because she was lying. In fact, even the property they lived on was owned by an umbrella corporation, rather than being listed under her own name, as was everything else that required an address.

The company was legitimate, but it made things difficult for everyday citizens to trace unofficially. It was owned by several business entities, which of course were owned by herself and Cam. An official inquiry would bring that up in a heartbeat, but she wasn't worried about those kinds of questions. She paid her taxes like everyone else, and she wasn't breaking any law that she was aware of.

"Alright, then, 'Mackenzie-uh-Thane,' why don't we take a look at some of these and see what you think?"

4

ONE STRANGE ENCOUNTER AFTER ANOTHER

As much as she might wish she could spend all day gazing at knives, not to mention a certain green-eyed creature who looked nothing like a monster, Mac had too many other things to do. For the first time she found that a little irritating, which she knew wasn't smart. She really didn't have the time.

"Okay, I'll take the Gerber LMF II and the KA-BAR Becker 22. My daughter will need a knife anyway, and I'll get a chance to play around with both of them. I'm happy with the KA-BAR and Coyote Brown for the Gerber. They both have non-reflective blades and all the other features I was looking for. Frankly, except for the partially serrated edge on the Gerber, and the different glass break points, they're very similar.

"And I'll take the razors and all that, too, of course," she said, making her decision.

"These are display models, so I'll get you the ones that are still in their packaging. I'm guessing you don't want any engraving or anything done."

"Honestly, I almost wish I could, because they're so beautiful, and a knife is such a personal thing, but no. It's just not practical. These will be getting good use, though you can assure your son that they won't be used on people. Most likely anyway. They're for survival in the bush, not combat." Neil smiled a bit, though he appeared preoccupied.

"Be right back with your stuff," he said a bit quietly, and turned away. Mac attempted to lecture herself, even as she pondered his behaviour and what it might mean. She was forty years old, shit was hitting the fan, and here she was wondering if a guy liked her or not. This was not how she usually interacted with men.

Suddenly she was sad, though. If things were going the way she figured they were, she didn't like to think of him and his son not making it through. By the time he came back, she'd figured out what she wanted to say.

"Look, Neil, you might think I'm some sort of crazy psycho after I say this, or maybe just misinterpreting things, but I felt like you should know what's going on. Or at least what I believe is happening." His face brightened, and she realized he thought she meant something else entirely.

"Well, that too, but that wasn't what I was referring to at the moment. Things are getting bad in the cities. I'm not sure what the news has been reporting up here, even news from the cities that you probably get. People are going without hydro about half the time now, and it's causing serious problems.

"Those problems are bound to bleed into other areas. Not just because power outages can have a cascade effect, and outages are likely to start happening here, but because people will start leaving the cities looking for a better situation. Nobody wants to be in an urban environment when things go bad. Just thought maybe you'd want to keep yourself safe and lay in some supplies. The supply chain in the GTA has already been disrupted, so it'll happen here very soon."

"Where are you from, if you don't mind me asking?" He seemed to be taking her seriously, thankfully, so she breathed a sigh of relief.

"I was living in Hamilton when it started, though I was actually raised around Huntsville. I've been watching for it, however. Most people aren't. Most people think everything will be fixed if only they get mad enough, and I don't think that's what's going to happen.

"I was warned a long time ago by someone who worked as an executive for Ontario Hydro. He told me this would happen based on what they were planning for the nuclear and coal plants. He said it was unsustainable and our outages would only get worse. It was after that big blackout I started getting concerned. That was caused by a stupid tree in Cleveland, and millions of people were affected. Like I said, a cascade effect.

"Anyway, I hope I don't sound like a survivalist nut. I just thought you might want to know what's probably coming."

"We're actually pretty set. It's one of the reasons we're up here. You're a prepper aren't you?" Mac smiled.

"Guilty. I see you're familiar with the term."

"Oh yeah. Charge me with the same crime. About that other thing you mentioned?"

"Yeah?" Her heart stopped as she waited for him to speak.

"You said, 'that, too.'" He waited for her to speak.

This time her breath caught in her throat. This guy could be the death of her if he could stop her heart and keep her from breathing at the same time. All she could do was nod.

"I'll bet you're pretty busy right now if you just came up from the city, so here...I wrote my cell number on the back. Call me when you get some time." He held out his business card. She moved closer to the counter to take it, unable to stop looking into those bright green eyes. When she reached for the card, he pulled back at the last second.

"Wait. I'm guessing you have a radio setup, right?" When she nodded again, he flipped the card over and wrote down his call sign and a frequency.

"Just in case," he said, and held out the card again. This time he let her take it from him, and she just barely resisted the urge to run her thumb over his. That was just a little too cliché for her, though. She flipped over the card and stared at the short note she hadn't even seen him write down. *Absolutely anytime. Be careful.*

"Do me a favour then," she said, smiling a bit. "Please let your son know I really was just teasing him." He winked at her, and it took everything she had not to lean over the counter and just mash her mouth against his. Instead she did what she had to do and walked out of the store with her sexy new cutlery.

Knowing he was still watching her from inside the store, she refrained from doing anything as undignified as a hip-shaking boogie, but there was definitely a bounce in her step as she headed for the truck. When she pulled past the store window, she waved. Through the glare she thought he waved back at her, but she wasn't sure.

Jesus, she was giddy. What a weird way to start what she'd assumed was going to be nothing more than a productive day. Of course, she'd managed to get what she'd been looking for, so it was still productive. Just more...eventful. She knew she was going to be thinking about him all day. Probably for a lot of days, because she wasn't sure when she'd get the chance to call him.

Still, she planned to the first chance she got. Mac didn't play idiotic games. He liked her, she liked him. Basic. Which was how she liked it. She actually let out a sigh, which made her laugh at herself, but her mood had certainly improved.

The trip to the hardware store turned out to be eventful, as well, but not in a pleasant way. The slimy twerp behind the counter kept insisting he needed her address to ring up her purchases, even though she was paying cash and bringing everything home on the trailer. She knew full well there was no such policy. The third time he said he needed it she told him to call his manager over.

"Now now, we don't need to disturb her. Even though I'm not supposed to do it this way, I'll put it through for ya."

"Either get your manager down here or I'm going to start causing a scene so that everyone in this store knows *exactly* what you're trying to pull. You need to be reprimanded, and I'm going to make sure that it happens. If I have to go so far as to make a ruckus, I'm going to go even further and make sure that they fire you. Call her. Now." Mac was beyond furious.

Obviously this guy figured she had to be living alone if she was going to the hardware store by herself. She wouldn't be surprised if he was either a peeping tom or rapist, and something needed to be done about it.

Once the situation was explained to the manager, Mac could tell the woman was pretty angry. She was tactful about it, though.

As a result of the situation, Mac ended up getting twenty-percent off her purchases that day. Happily it had been a big haul, so that twenty-percent amounted to a good chunk of change.

Things had worked out for the best, but she was still leery of what the guy might do. He could still lose his job, even though she hadn't pushed that.

She kept an eye on the vehicles in her rearview mirror as she finished up her business in town, which involved a stop at the gas station. As luck would have it, by the time she hit the main inter-section out of town she had seen the same green Civic a few times. If that was the guy from the hardware store, she was going to have to deal with him long before she got anywhere near the house. In fact, it might be a good idea to take a little detour. A bit of misdirection never hurt.

She took a turn-off heading toward Bala instead. There were a lot of near-vacant side-roads here, and sometimes no homes or farms for miles.

Mackenzie was heading in the direction she would need to take when it came time to get her goats and chickens, so she'd already mapped it out in her mind and wouldn't likely get lost. She wasn't sure about the asshole who was still following her, but it would probably be best for everyone if he did get himself lost out here.

Mac reached into the bag on the passenger seat and opened up the first knife box her hand came in contact with. The knife and sheath she pulled out were all black, so it was the KA-BAR. She shoved the blade into the sheath and pushed the sheath down the back of her jeans. Then she grabbed her phone.

She hated to operate her cell while she was driving. She knew damn well it was a good way to get herself killed, but in this case she really needed to do it. She opened Facebook as she slowed the truck and pulled over to the shoulder. By the time he caught up with her, she would be ready.

Once the truck rolled to a stop she put it in park, removed the seat belt and ran her search for the Ontario Provincial Police page. Way out here the OPP was the only law enforcement organization that applied. Then she opened a message box, typed in a short message, and made sure her location flag was turned on.

Once that was ready she opened a second Facebook page. This time she ran a search for the hardware store. She opened a message box to that one, too, typed another quick message without sending, and then switched back to the app version where the OPP message box awaited further input.

Mac got out of the truck, twisting in such a way that he wouldn't see the knife sheath. Surreptitiously she clicked the little camera icon in the message box. He pulled to a stop, and slowly got out of the car, obviously attempting to appear threatening, and savouring the moment when he thought he had the upper hand.

She snapped a picture, making sure to get both him and his licence plate in the frame, and pressed the enter key on her touch-screen. She had her head bent down as though she were merely checking her phone. Then she switched over to the hardware store message box and did the same.

She turned on her UStream app to broadcast a live feed, mostly to capture any audio, and watched him approach with a sly smile on his exceedingly ugly face.

"So, did your boss fire you? Is that why you're out here now?" He leered at her. It was the only thing she could call that expression in her mind.

"My boss don't know shit from Shinola. Just told me not to do it again." Mac laughed.

"Well, she sure as hell knows 'shit from Shinola' now, seeing as I just sent your location, as well as the image of you and your licence plate, directly to your employer's Facebook account. In addition to the OPP's. I can guarantee you just lost your job, if nothing else, and the police are going to be very interested in you if I disappear or get hurt. You do know it's a crime to stalk someone, right? That sexual harassment is a crime? I don't suppose you were ever privy to the 'No Means No' campaign, huh?" She glanced at the name tag still pinned to his work shirt, and noted the gradual reddening of his skin.

"Look, Gerry. You've got one option if you don't want to end up in jail for a very long time. Turn around and walk away, right this second. You haven't done anything too extreme, and if I don't press charges you're not even going to miss your dinner. If you insist on seeing this through, despite the fact that I'm broadcasting this over the internet, it will not be worth whatever satisfaction you get out of trying to hurt me.

"As it is, I would really like to get home without you following me there, and I don't have time to fuck around with you. Otherwise, the very next place I'm going to drive is to the Huntsville OPP station. Believe me when I tell you, if you push this you're going to regret it for the rest of your life. However long I allow that to be."

Mac watched him struggle with his decision, her right hand clasped around the hilt of her brand new knife, and her left holding her phone up so the camera could pick up everything.

"Look, kid. At the moment you only look a little too enthusiastic. It's not legal to do what you did, but a lot of people don't know that. There's very little that can be done if there's no

47

evidence of intent to harm."

She couldn't be sure, but it seemed as though his jaw wasn't clenched quite so tightly. Part of her was seriously itching to go after him, but she just had too much to do. Otherwise she would never have notified anyone of her location. Now that she had, her only options were to either talk him out of it, or take him down in self-defense.

"Bitch," he muttered, and backed toward his car. Mackenzie sighed. *People are assholes*, she thought, which reminded her of Kirk. She resisted the urge to call and find out where they were, because she wanted to keep her video streaming a little bit longer. She watched the compact shoot past her and drive off with a squeal of tires, and hoped she never saw him again.

She zoomed in on the video as he got further away, and watched his retreat for as long as possible. She wasn't too thrilled with herself for not having binoculars and emergency gear. She hadn't packed the truck with that stuff yet. Once she got it home again, she wasn't taking it anywhere else without the basics.

Eventually she got into the truck and did a U-turn to head back home. She was almost there when her phone rang. She used the hands-free to answer it.

"Hey Kirk. I was just wondering if you were okay. What's going on?"

"We ran out of gas. They couldn't fill the tank at the rental agency, and we haven't been able to find a station that's working. We're in some place called 'Gravetown' or something. Everyone says they've run out because of all of the people coming up from Orillia and Barrie. I guess those places are in shutdown now too."

Mac almost laughed. 'Gravetown,' indeed.

"Okay, find a restaurant that's open and then call me with the cross street. I'll bring you some gas. At least you're in a relatively safe place. It's called Gravenhurst, by the way. I'm about ten minutes from home. I need to switch vehicles and put the jerrycans in the trunk. I can be there in probably an hour. Grab a coffee or something to eat and just relax.

"While you're stranded, try to borrow whatever cash you can get from your credit cards. Normally I wouldn't recommend that as financial advice, but those cards won't be working for long, and there's a good chance you'll never have to pay it back."

"Yeah, okay. Makes sense. I'll tell Leigh. See you soon. And thanks again."

"It's not a problem, Kirk. We want you guys up here with us where you'll be safe. Or as safe as possible. See you in an hour or so."

Shortly after the conversation ended, Mac was pulling into the driveway. Cameron came out to see what was happening, and helped her load the car as Mac explained about the phone call from Kirk.

"Do me a favour while I'm gone. I had a little altercation with some ass-wipe who tried to follow me home. I really hate leaving you here alone, even though I did everything in my power to make sure he couldn't follow me back here.

"I'll probably go in to the cop shop tomorrow to fill them in on what happened, but I couldn't afford to take the time today.

"Anyway, what I want you to do is activate the sensors. I won't be gone long, but it's probably going to annoy the ever-loving hell out of you. We haven't had a chance to set it up properly, so I don't doubt that it's going to be set off constantly by every little bush and blade of grass, but you have to monitor every beep.

"Load one of the Glocks, put it in a holster, and wear it on you every minute that I'm gone. This guy is seriously off, and he's a sneaky bastard. Chances are, if he saw me come this way, I'll see him on my way to Gravenhurst. He won't know it's me, because I'll be in a different vehicle. If I see him, I'll call you and turn right back around to deal with him. A short delay in picking up Kirk and Leigh isn't going to hurt them. They're in a safe place.

"Damn. And I was in *such* a good mood, too!" Cameron gave her a look.

"You were?"

"I'll tell you about it when we're all tucked in for the night. Oh, speaking of which, I got you a sort of present. I was going to test out both of the ones that I bought, but I've developed an attachment to one of them already." She handed Cam the Gerber, still in its box.

"Oh cool! What's yours like?" Mac flipped up the tail of her shirt and pulled it out.

"Wow. These are both awesome. I prefer the black, though. Why couldn't I get mine in black?"

"He only had that model in the Coyote Brown and Olive Drab. It's got its own sharpener right in the sheath, though. You get a feature I don't have. Well, crap! I just realized I didn't buy anything to sharpen the rest of this stuff. Guess I'm going to have to go back. Maybe I should call him first."

"You have his number?" Cameron was obviously surprised.

"What? Your mother can't get hit on?" Cam rolled her eyes.

"That is *not* what I meant. You get hit on all the time, even when you're dressed like a slob. Most women do. What I meant was, you actually still have it? You don't usually even let a guy *hand* you his number. You're pretty blunt about it."

"Well, this was a bit different." Mac couldn't help the look that crossed her face.

"He had green eyes," she continued. "What can I say?" Cameron's mouth dropped open in complete shock.

"I'll tell you about it later." With that she pulled away.

Mac chuckled the whole length of the driveway, pleased at dropping a bombshell on her daughter. It had certainly been an eventful day. Now all she could do was hope that the major events were over with. *God*, she thought, *two hours. Just let me get this over and done with in two hours!*

Then she rolled her eyes. It wasn't that simple. She was probably going to have to go into Bracebridge to refill whatever gas they used. Hopefully she could just hit a station on the highway, but somehow she doubted it. Those would be the first hit by anyone travelling north.

It might be better just to head back to Rosseau. It was closer to home, and she knew it had fuel. It also gave her the opportunity to get the other stuff from Neil's store. She'd take a look at his card again when she got to Gravenhurst, and see what his regular hours were.

The trip away from the house was uneventful, and she made it to the highway without seeing Gerry's vehicle, or any other vehicle for that matter. Kirk texted her with the street crossing they were closest to, and by then she was only twenty minutes away. She called Cameron's VoIP line using the hands-free, and everything was still fine there.

When she did get in touch with Neil, she intended to ask him if he knew the kid from the hardware store. He might have a line on some leverage she could use against him in the future, though if he was new to the area he might not be in touch with the surrounding families. Gerry gave off the impression he was a local, and possibly from one of the big, white-trash families that populated certain areas. She might even recognize the name, since families tended to sprawl a fair distance in Muskoka and Parry Sound.

She ought to know. She came from one of those families. She just had no intention of rejoining them. Thankfully the only people who would recognize her now were people she could trust. Once she let them know she was around, she intended to make sure they knew she didn't want her family members aware of her presence. Most of her friends wouldn't associate with her family anyway. She came from a long line of scum, and had walked away to create her own family. She'd been gone so long she doubted they'd remember her first name, but why take chances?

5

EXPLANATIONS ARE IN ORDER

Mac pulled up to the restaurant closest to the street corner Kirk had mentioned. It was apparent they'd been watching for her, because they popped out less than thirty seconds later.

"Hey guys. Did you run out completely, or is the car here? I don't want to be filling a tank in front of a bunch of people hungry for gasoline if I can help it." Kirk and Leigh got into the car and gave her directions to where they'd had to abandon their vehicle. It wasn't far away, and it was off the highway.

"It was actually starting to sputter," Leigh said, a little breathless. Today had apparently been an adventure for her, too.

"Yeah. We kind of just let it look as though we were parking it when we went to look for gas. We figured if anyone thought we'd run out, they might break into the car thinking we'd be gone a while. I came back here to check on things a couple of times just to be sure."

"Probably for the best. This isn't exactly a crime-ridden town, but by the same token there are still people who steal, and teenagers are teenagers everywhere." She opened up her trunk and handed Kirk a full jerrycan.

"You might need to put in a second one later, but maybe we can stop somewhere else to do that. We can get on the road now, and if you start getting too low shoot me a text. I'll get us into an area where we can safely add another can. We definitely do not want to be doing this on the main road.

"We're going to stop in Rosseau and see about getting fuel there. It's a town that's not on the main highway. Not even close. It's actually the back way to our place. I have to stop to see a man about a whetstone, too.

"No, that wasn't a joke. I'll fill you in at the same time I fill in Cameron, but we really have to get everything done and get back to the house as soon as possible. I had a bit of a situation with a local boy earlier today that still needs to be dealt with, and I don't like leaving Cameron alone there without having everything set up and properly tested.

"Not to mention the fact that I haven't had a chance to tell her the whole story yet, so she's probably freaking out a little bit."

Mac took out Neil's card and entered all his info into her cell phone so she could call from the road. His hours showed that they would make it back in plenty of time. The store would be open for a while yet.

"You guys ready?" Kirk nodded as he handed her the empty jerrycan.

"Alright. Follow me. I suggest staying pretty close, seeing as it's dusk now, heading for full dark. Terrible time to be driving, but better than hanging around here." She waited for them to get buckled in, and then headed out for home.

She used voice-dialling to call Neil's business line, and a ridiculous flutter started up in her belly. When his voice came on the line, she grinned.

"Sharper Image," he said abruptly.

"Hi Neil. It's Mac. If this weren't a business call I'd be talking to you on your cell, but I have to stop in and pick up some sharpening supplies."

"The other Mac! No problem. I'm open for another couple of hours yet, and I'm always here to close things down."

"Great! Can you have a couple whetstones and maybe a kitchen sharpener or whatever ready? I don't know when I can get back to your store for other things we might need, but we can't do without those, and I'm in a sort of rush. I had a situation with a local boy today, and I want to get back to the house to keep my eye on things."

"Can do. Do you know who it was?" Mac suddenly noticed how good it felt to talk to him.

"His name is Gerry and he works as a cashier at the hardware place just down the road from your store. He kept trying to get me to give him my address, and I finally called down the manager. That wasn't enough to deter him. He tried to follow me home. Didn't work so well, whatever his intentions might have been. I shot a picture of him with his car's licence plate in it, along with my location, to both the OPP and his employer. A short message was attached." Neil whistled.

"How did you manage that one?"

"Facebook, if you can believe it. Of course, I also started video-streaming my conversation with him via UStream. Managed to talk him down, and waited until he completely disappeared from sight before I headed back to my place. It's doubtful he'll find it, but things aren't set up the way I want just yet, so I'm stuck worrying until I'm sure I can protect Cameron."

"Of course you are. I would be too. I'm pretty sure I know who you're talking about, and who his father is. If he's who I think he is he's not from bad stock, but he's a worthless shit despite that. Excuse my French." Mac had to laugh.

"No worries. I'll warn you now. I swear like a drunken sailor half the time." Neil's laugh just rolled out of him.

"Well, thank Christ! A woman after my own heart."

"Could be," she said bluntly.

"And up-front, too. I knew there was a reason I liked you. Okay, you'll probably be here soon, so I'll get everything ready for you. Can you call me later tonight? I'd like to know about this crazy, prepping, potentially psycho, fouled-mouth, honest woman I'm seeing so much of today." Her grin spread from ear to ear as she laughed along with him.

"Be careful what you wish for, cowboy."

"Oh, I'm wishin', I'm wishin'. See you soon, Mac."

Twenty minutes after hanging up with him, Mackenzie was pulling into the parking lot of his store, and she wasn't surprised to find she hadn't caught her breath yet. He just kept sending her into a tailspin.

Kirk snorted at the sign when he got out of the rental, and Mac smiled at him.

"Don't worry. He knows. He bought the store as-is, but he knows his stuff. You should come in. You're both going to need top-of-the-line survival knives. And I don't mean the kind with a compass on the end that carries waterproof matches. Those are okay for everyday stuff in the city or whatever, but they won't stand up to the kinds of things you'll end up having to do with them." Mac could see Kirk hunch his shoulders slightly. She'd hit that nail on the head. Every young man wanted a Rambo knife.

"You'll love these, Kirk, believe me. He's got KA-BARs." At that he brightened, as she'd known he would. A decade of playing video games had taught him to love military equipment, and to find out he would soon have access to a KA-BAR was like telling a kid he'd have free rein in the candy store.

"When we get home and get things settled a bit, I'll tell you a story I read about how it got its name, unless you've already heard it." Kirk looked at her with new respect. It was obvious he'd never had an inkling how deeply she'd gotten into the whole prepping thing.

"He has real ones?" Mac laughed.

"They're not rare or anything. I've got one on me right now, in fact. Bought it today along with a Gerber. I'll have him show you what I gave Cameron. The Gerber will puncture plane fuselage," she was saying, as she stepped through the door.

Neil's head snapped around and his eyes locked with hers as soon as she walked in and he heard her voice. Now *that* was worth coming into the store for, she realized.

"Hey," he said gruffly, then cleared his throat.

"I've got your stuff ready."

"Great. And now that I asked you to have everything ready, I have to ask if you have any knives that are comparable to what I bought today, but different enough in appearance that we can all tell our knives apart. Another colour of the Gerber would do the trick, but I'm pretty sure that KA-BAR only comes in black, so we'll need something else there."

"No problem. How are you liking yours so far, or have you even had the chance to take them out of the boxes?"

"I've developed an attachment to the KA-BAR. Almost became familiar with its use, actually." Neil gave her a worried look.

"That bad, huh? Alright. Let's get you set up so you can get home to your daughter. You can finish filling me in later tonight. I'm usually up 'til about three anyway, so call me even if it's late." She nodded.

He was back right away with the longer KA-BAR Becker BK-7,

which was perfect for Kirk. Leigh chose the Olive Drab, or OD, Gerber identical to the one Mackenzie had given to Cameron earlier.

Kirk protested when she went to pay for the items, but Mac had the last laugh.

"Don't worry. You may end up getting stuck buying the goats tomorrow." The look on his face was priceless. Neil wagged his finger at her.

"You're a tricky one, Mac. I'll have to keep an eye on you." She smirked.

"Both of them, I hope!" She thanked him for his help, told him she'd talk to him in a few hours, and headed back out to the car with a quick wink, leaving him to shake his head.

"How long have you known that guy?" Kirk's question made her laugh again. She calculated in her head.

"About six hours maybe." She swiveled down into her car, pleased to have added another look of confusion to the young man's face. Leigh just glanced at Kirk, obviously not sure what to make of the situation. She spoke out the window to them, all traces of teasing having left her voice.

"Keep your eye on the rearview mirror. Make sure we aren't followed." Kirk glanced at the store window, his question obvious.

"No. A different guy. We need to stop at the gas station and fill up both our tanks and the jerrycan we just emptied. Watch for a green Honda Civic. It's a hatchback, and pretty recent. I've lost touch with the newer cars, so I don't know exactly what year it is, but you guys probably wouldn't be able to tell either. Keep your eyes peeled in all directions. Pretend you don't know me, and follow at a distance, but not far enough that you get lost.

"This car isn't familiar to him, and if I don't get out it's because I see him somewhere. I'll pop my trunk so you can refill the empty jerrycan. When you're finished, we'll head straight to the house."

She rolled up her window and they drove over to the station, Leigh heading inside the convenience store so she could pay. Kirk started pumping their gas. He was definitely looking around him. Mac had pulled up on the other side and done her own visual search. No sign of him. Still, she snugged a baseball cap on over her long hair, and pulled on a windbreaker she kept in the car for emergencies.

She kept her head down while she finished the filling-up she had to do, and when she went in to place the cash on the counter. Aside from Leigh there was no one else in the store, so she felt safe telling the clerk it was pump three she was paying on. She went straight back to her car.

Mac was just about to pull away from the station, with Leigh and Kirk planning to follow, when a green Civic pulled up to the pump behind her. Her heart began to pound, and she tilted her face away from him when he stepped up to the pump beside his car.

She was pretty sure she heard him complain about 'fucking rich people,' but that was the extent of it. Apparently the old Beemer had offended him somehow, but at least he didn't see her.

The rest of the drive home was uneventful, giving her a chance to calm down again. That had been close. A deep sigh helped release the pent-up tension in her body. This was not a good situation. She may have gotten the better of Gerry in their little skirmish today, but she didn't think he was going to forget about her. She had no choice but to talk to the police tomorrow.

Mac slowed her car to a crawl and started using the UV light on the trees. She knew she was close, but she still hadn't driven this road enough to find the marked tree without the use of the light, and there was nothing visibly distinctive about it on the side facing the road. It made it easier to hide the driveway. Even from herself.

The purplish white glow finally appeared, so Mac pulled up level with it and rolled to a stop. She walked back to Kirk and Leigh's rental, and waited until Leigh rolled down the window.

"The gate will open in a second. I need to stop once I get past the pressure plate to make sure it closes properly, so just pull around me and head up the driveway to the house as soon as it opens. The passage through the trees will curve to the left, which is the direction of the house. It takes a bit before you actually see it."

Leigh replied that she understood, and rolled her window back up. Mac moved behind the tree and pressed her thumb to the reader inside the hollow. She waited for Leigh to drive past her, and then followed them through.

It wasn't long before the gate finished closing and Mac was following them to the house. The relief made her tired, and she wanted her ferrets and her pyjamas, and then probably her ferrets again.

In the meantime she had some explaining to do. She didn't know if she had the energy to go through it right now, but she had to. It wasn't just the danger presented by Gerry, and the instinctive knowledge he'd been planning to rape her. There was also the matter of her reaction to Neil. Cameron was going to want information.

Her daughter walked out when they pulled up. She'd have been alerted as soon as Mac approached the gate control, because there were sensors in front of it and she would have seen both cars on the monitors.

Mac walked toward her, holding her hand up.

"Give me a few minutes. I need to decompress." She didn't have to explain. Cameron knew her stress habits. She left them to chat and exchange relieved greetings, while she went across the open space to her bedroom. The scratching started as soon as her shadow crossed the gap beneath the door, making her smile.

The boys weren't used to spending so much time without her. Mac listened to the scratching for a moment. It sounded as if both of them were up and around. When she opened the door she leaned down to pick them up.

"Hey guys! I guess you missed me, huh?" They were both licking her face and sniffing her hair in between licks.

"Yeah, I've been through some strange smells today. One of those is probably stress, and another is a bit of fear, but that's okay. I've got you two." Eventually they both had enough attention, and she went straight for her dresser after putting them down. Sweat-shorts and a support-tank were the runway fare for tonight, along with bare feet. As soon as she'd changed she felt the weight lift off her shoulders. She was home.

She grabbed the boys again and carried them with her down the hall so Leigh and Kirk could see them for a bit.

"Okay, I'd better put them back in my room so we can hash all this stuff out, make whatever plans, adjustments, and arrangements that need to be made, and I can finally relax and go make a highly anticipated phone call."

Once she'd confined the ferrets again, she grabbed some snack food from the cupboards in case anyone wanted anything. It wasn't until then that she realized how hungry she was herself. She hadn't stopped to eat since she'd left the house around noon, and it was nearly nine. If she didn't have some protein, her blood sugar would start to drop. She added a hunk of cheese and a kitchen knife to the tray she was loading up, along with some small bottles of orange juice, and took it over to the six-seater table they were using.

"Alright. I'll tell y'all everything that happened today, and then you can ask your questions. I'm incredibly exhausted, so just let me finish before you ask me anything. I want to get it out in the right order. You can eat while I talk."

Thankfully they remained silent throughout her recitation, everyone nibbling on their own thing. When she was done, she cut off a large block of cheese and started chewing on it. Kirk spoke first.

"Why don't I go with you for whatever running around you

have to do from now on? Maybe it's sexist, but most guys will leave a woman alone if there's another male with her. You can defend yourself better than I ever could, but it's all about perception." Mac nodded and took a swallow of her orange juice.

"You're right. In an ideal world a woman wouldn't have to do that, but the world is far from ideal. Besides, I could use the help. Some of the stuff we're going to need will likely be heavy or awkward, requiring two people to lift it.

"How much of the garden stuff did you get done today, Cameron? Is there enough to keep you and Leigh busy for the day tomorrow?" Cam nodded.

"I grabbed all the stuff that was ripe, and started pulling some weeds, but I think it's going to take two of us a couple of hours for that. I didn't start until about four, since it was so hot. I only got the trailer partly unloaded, though. I couldn't really get in there to lift the cement bags. We'll have to empty it before you leave tomorrow, if you're planning to use it."

"I'll need it. I'm heading in to Huntsville to the OPP, and then I'm going to clear out whatever toilet paper and tampons I can find. I have feed, chickens, and goats to buy, too.

"If you have favourite brands of stuff, Leigh, make sure Kirk knows what they are so he can pick up as much of that as possible. I doubt you guys are as stringent on animal-testing as we are, so we probably don't have what you like, but you can take a look at the supply areas and see.

"Maybe make a list as you go through, because seeing

everything will probably remind you of things. If I wasn't so freakin' tired right now, I'd go through it all with you, but I got almost no sleep before I headed out today. Now I just wanna talk to that hunky stud with the green eyes and go to sleep." She cut off more cheese to take to her room.

If she thought she was going to get away with that, however, Cameron disabused her of that notion.

"Yeah, speaking of which, you sort if skimmed that part when you were telling us what happened today."

Mackenzie flopped back in the chair, sighed, and stuffed more cheese in her mouth. Cam was right about their need to know. They were heading into a dangerous situation, both with the power outages and the nut-job from the hardware store. So Mackenzie swallowed her food and told them what she knew.

"Well, he's a prepper, so that should reassure you. We won't have to worry about him stealing from us later, even if he's shown where we live. He has a son I wound up for a bit before he went to get Neil from the back. He's been up here a few years, owns the knife store, seems to know his way around them pretty well, has a ham radio, and took me seriously when I warned him about the outages.

"I really don't know much more than that, but I'd say that's a good start after three short conversations. Most of which revolved around sharp objects." That garnered a bit of a laugh from everyone.

"Is that it? Are you done grilling me?"

"You really like him, don't you?" Mac smiled.

"Yeah, I do. Surprised me. Not that I would like him, because he seems pretty great, but that I would meet someone like him at all right now. Weird timing, but whatever works." She was about to get up and leave when she realized they had no idea what the plans were for the future, so she turned to Kirk and Leigh and spoke to them directly.

"You guys are going to be stuck with the futon for now, and you won't have your own room yet. I'm sorry about the lack of privacy. We can get started on the main house in a few days. We'll have to do the interior framing, wiring, walls, plumbing, et cetera, before we'll be able to really live in it, but just getting the building up means we can spread out a bit.

"The next few days we'll need to get every bit of our main running around done. Anything that requires using gasoline, so that we can refuel all our tanks and jerrycans when we empty them. If we wait, we may not be able to stock up again.

"Our very first priority is to get things ready for livestock. They're absolutely vital." She paused for a minute, thinking, grabbing a handful of almonds to gnaw on while she considered the situation.

"Cam, maybe you guys should just forget about the weeding to-morrow. After I'm done talking to Neil, I'll draw up the plans for the enclosures, and you guys can start getting them set up. I just need you to do minor stuff, and then I can finish with the construction when I get back. You've got some experience with tools and stuff, right Kirk?" He nodded.

"Yeah. Even where I work, or *worked* I guess, I was using power tools all the time."

"So, what I'll ask you two to do, is dig some post holes and a shallow area that I mark out." Leigh spoke up then.

"We're going to have to learn all this stuff anyway, so is there anything else we can do other than digging holes, or even weeding?" Mac shook her head.

"Not without being taught how to use the tools. You could get seriously hurt. Have you ever used a cement mixer, or table saw?"

"No. Kinda regretting not taking that shop class now, though," Leigh said sardonically.

"Mom, I can use some of the tools. You taught me some stuff already, and I did actually take shop in high school."

Mackenzie took a moment to think about it. The last thing she wanted was for anyone to get injured, but time was short.

"Okay, it's probably worth the little bit of time it would take to get you two set up." She got up from the table, grabbing another juice and a big hunk of cheese to take with her.

"Alright, I'm going to go call him and subject him to my own form of grilling. He made it obvious he was interested in the ride, so now he'll have to pay the price of admission."

6

CONFESSIONS AND COMBUSTION

Mackenzie grabbed her cell, experiencing the same fluttering sensation she had earlier as she dialled Neil's cell phone.

"Mac?" She laughed.

"Yeah, it's me. I guess you weren't expecting anyone else, huh? Are you at home now?"

"Sure am. I take it you've finally made it home for the night yourself?" Mac practically groaned in relief now that she really was done for the day and could enjoy this conversation.

"I am, thankfully. It's been a very long, very trying day. We just got here last night from Hamilton. I didn't get much sleep because I had to be up early enough to run errands today, and I don't usually sleep at night. Between the psycho kid with his nefarious intentions, and having to run down to Gravenhurst to get Kirk and

Leigh fuelled up, I didn't manage to get as much done as I intended to.

"The upshot is that we now have four hands to do the work instead of two, so hopefully things will go pretty quick now." It was weird to her that she could talk to him like this, as a kind of how-was-your-day type deal, but she felt comfortable with him for some reason.

"Fill me in on the details with Gerry. I think if I know what happened I can talk to his dad and maybe calm the situation down. His dad won't take kindly to that sort of behaviour from his son."

She'd already told him the highlights, but she filled him in on the rest of the details. It didn't take long, since it had all happened so fast.

"Hence the quick attachment to your new knife," he finished for her.

"Yup. It really is a pretty little thing. Doesn't have the range of a firearm, but it would make an impression if needed."

"Would I be off the mark if I guessed you were equipped to handle yourself there as well?"

"You'd be right on the mark. I can handle that kind of equipment very well." It wasn't until she heard the teasing humming sound from him that she realized what she'd said, and what he had inferred from it aside from firearms.

"Uh, well, that too I suppose," she said, just to tease him back.

"I'm not sure I should run any further down that line of thought tonight. Might be more than I can handle. It's the one kind of imagination I've got." Mac laughed softly.

"Okay, I might let you off the hook if you talk about yourself for a little while. You've learned a lot about me already, and I hardly know you at all it seems."

"That's fair. Well, I'm forty-five. Just the one kid, and you've already met Billy. Never married, though I wasn't afraid of it. More that I was afraid of it with the wrong woman. Worked as a machinist for a number of years, but I didn't like working for other people.

"Billy started getting into mild trouble at school about eight years ago, and I was fed up with letting his mother get away with not doing any actual parenting. Diane kept getting married over and over, hoping someone would take care of her, instead of taking care of Billy.

"When I told her I wanted full custody, she didn't even question it. Just told him to pack a bag. Pissed me off, to be frank. No one should be like that with their own kid. She wasn't like that when we met, but shortly after she had Billy something happened. We lived in Vancouver for a while, and we weren't in the best neighbourhood. Some thugs broke in while I was at work, and Diane was home with the baby. They trashed everything that wasn't fit to sell, and stole everything that was.

"What I didn't find out until later was that they beat her while she was tied up, to force her to tell them where we kept our non-existent valuables. Her face was fine, and she hadn't told me or the cops that part, so I didn't find out until I grabbed her wrist a couple days later and she freaked out.

"I guess Billy was pretty much screaming the entire time they were there, so every time she heard him cry after that she couldn't stand to go near him. I had to put him in daycare while I worked, because it was like she hated him. I felt bad for her. It tore me up that I hadn't been able to protect her, and at the time I loved her. The damage was done, though.

"I stayed, and tried to help her, but she'd had a very sheltered life up to that point and just didn't have the coping mechanisms. Diane started hating me because I hadn't been there to protect her. She said she'd never feel safe with me again, and she left. Billy was with me for a couple of years before she asked for joint custody, but she was never a real mother to him again. I tried to understand, but when you're a parent you have to do what it takes to be there for your kid."

"I'm so sorry. Some people never get over being violated, whatever form it takes, and it's extremely difficult for people to watch a loved one go through it. You have to bury your own anger and pain for their sake, but from what you've said you did everything that could possibly be done. Her recovery was never your responsibility. She has to do that herself."

"When you told me about Gerry, I felt pretty much the same thing. The fact that you were able to handle yourself is a big relief to me, and yet I want to go after him because I don't think his nature is going to improve over the years. One day, if he hasn't already, he's going to seriously hurt someone. A woman more than likely. You said you're going to the OPP station in Huntsville tomorrow?"

"Yeah. If I don't talk to them now, they're going to come looking for me, so I might as well get it over with. I probably got him fired by sending that message to his boss. I doubt she would find it acceptable for an employee to follow a customer home." Neil gave a small chuckle.

"Probably not, no. Not real good for business. So, why don't you tell me your life story, since I've told you the highlights of mine. Bet ya didn't think you were gonna get a whole book worth when you asked," he added.

"I'm glad you told me as much as you did. I want to hear about your life. Hard to get to know someone otherwise." As much as she hated discussing her past, it would always come down to trust. It came a lot easier this time.

She filled him in on the family she had walked away from, and the two ex-husbands she hoped he didn't judge her for, or worse, compare her to Billy's mother. She told him about having her daughter when she was seventeen, and gave a glossed-over view of the mental problems of her daughter's birth father.

She waited for his verdict.

"There's only one thing I really want to know right now," he said softly.

"Yes?"

"When can I see you?" Mac took all of three seconds to consider her response.

"As soon as possible...if you tell me where, and when you can be there." She could hear him suck in his breath.

"Jesus Mac. I'll see you right now if you want. Look, I'm south of Rosseau. I don't know what direction you're in, but maybe if we're close enough..." He trailed off. This was where the real trust began, and she hadn't even known him for half a day.

"I'm near Rosseau Falls, Neil. You'd never find my place even if I gave you the address. I'd have to give you GPS coordinates, and even then I'd have to meet you out at the damn-near-abandoned road that leads to my driveway. I'm really paranoid," she explained with a laugh.

"Good. It'll keep you safe. In the meantime, what do you wanna bet that we're neighbours. Probably within walking distance."

When he told her where he lived, she just laughed.

"I'm so glad I didn't take that bet. I wonder if we share a property line. I'm pretty sure we're back-to-back here, though I wouldn't want to travel through that way in the middle of the night, not knowing exactly where I was going."

"We're really that close then?"

"We are. If you really want to come see me, I'll tell you how to get here. What do you think?"

"I think I'm already there." She gave him directions, brushed her teeth, put on her sandals, and headed out the door. She could hear Cameron calling out behind her, so she turned around.

"I'm just going to the road. Neil's going to be here in a minute."

"Are you kidding me? Just like that?"

"We probably would have run into him anyway. Turns out we're neighbours." For the second time that day, Cam's mouth hung open. Not the most becoming expression, of course, but Mac was enjoying it. She'd been far too predictable for years now, so when the opportunity came to give her daughter a bit of a jolt, she just couldn't resist.

"Seriously?"

"Yeah. I guess it's not that surprising. We're both into the whole prepping thing, so I'm sure he was looking for the same things that we were looking for, when he bought his property. Anyway, I have to get out there or he's going to drive right by it. I'll be back in a bit and you can meet him. Then you can judge for yourself if I'm crazy or not."

"Mom, I already know you're crazy. This is not news. I'm just wondering what happened to your lovable cynicism." Mac smirked and stepped outside.

She made it out to the tree and leaned against it, waiting for his lights to appear so she could flag him down. When he got there, she stepped out. He stopped the car and got out. She walked straight to him. When she was a foot away his right hand came up to brush her cheek.

"Yup, still beautiful," he said. She stepped a little closer, feeling the heat radiating from his body. His thumb just barely grazed her bottom lip, and she inched forward again.

"I think maybe you should try doing that with something else." His left eyebrow shot up at the multiple implications.

"I guess I'll try this for now." His left arm slid around her waist and he lowered his head very, very slowly. Mac stood on her toes and pressed herself full length against him. He groaned hoarsely and covered her mouth with his. Mac whimpered as a spear of heat pierced her through the middle.

Within seconds she was reduced to a mass of seared nerve endings. His tongue slid against hers while his lips moulded hers with pure heat. His erection pressing against her made her writhe. Finally she remembered the cameras, and had to pull away, panting.

"We're probably being watched right now. I've got night-vision cameras on the gate. We cannot keep doing this here." Neil swallowed, nodded, and then rested his forehead against hers.

"Yeah, okay. If there's a time and place where we *can* keep doing this, though, you gotta let me know, because I am *there*." Mac let out a weak laugh.

"You and me both," she said hoarsely, trying to resist the temptation to start using her mouth on his neck.

"Give me a second to get the gate open, and then you can pull your car into the driveway." He looked around.

"Concealed, huh?"

"You know it. You're gonna love this, cowboy." She slid behind the tree to put her thumb on the plate, and then heard his low whistle as he watched the bushes split and swing backward. She stepped back out to his car.

"After you," she said, gesturing to the driveway.

"You *are* good, honey. And I do mean that in every possible way." With that he got back in his car and pulled through the gate. She followed him through and waited for them to close. This was not the time to take a chance. Well, any *more* chances, she amended mentally.

Neil stopped his car and waited for her to catch up. She leaned in his open window to talk to him for a second. Before she could speak, he cupped the back of her head and kissed her deeply once again. She was straining to get at him through the door by the time he released her mouth. It took her a moment to remember what she'd been planning to say.

"I was going to ask if you wanted to drive up, or we could walk part of the way. I was thinking it would give me a chance to catch my breath and cool down a bit, but now I've got serious doubts about that."

Neil just laughed and indicated the passenger seat with his head. She sauntered around the hood of his car, and slid in beside him. She closed the door and buckled her seatbelt out of habit, which made him laugh again.

"How fast did you think I was planning to go on this driveway of yours, Mac? It's not exactly conducive to top-fuel, funny-car racing." She smiled at her actions.

"Habit, of course, but you never know. You're pretty slick." His smile slipped into a more sober expression.

"Mac, about that? I sure as hell can't lie and say I don't want you something fierce, but I want the whole package, not just sex."

He turned to look her directly in the eye. Her breath caught once again.

"Neil, are you having as hard a time as I am, remembering that we only met about ten hours ago?"

"Pretty much, but I don't care either. It is what it is, and I'm not interested in pretending it's not. The second I walked out of that room today and saw you standing there with that irritated look on your face, you snapped front and centre for me. I just wanted you to know that."

"The way you looked at me did something to me. I'm the cautious type these days, so it's hard for me to trust, but it seems to be a lot easier with you."

"Okay, let's go see your daughter before she loses her mind and thinks I'm attacking or abducting you." Mackenzie gave a rueful chuckle and took his hand as soon as he'd shifted back into drive.

He pulled in behind the BMW a minute later, and Mac saw that he'd been right about Cameron. She was waiting in the doorway, poised like an avenging angel. Mac got out of Neil's car and approached her.

"Jesus, Cam. You don't have to defend my honour. Get back in the house so we can come in too." As soon as they were all in the open space, Mackenzie turned to Neil.

"Neil, I'd like you to meet my ornery and cynical offspring, Cameron. Cameron, this is Neil, who likes to play with sharp objects." Neil choked out a laugh and extended his hand to Cam.

"Nice to meet you, oh ornery and cynical one." Cameron gave a reluctant smile and accepted the offer of a handshake.

"Same here. Nice to see you're still able to shake hands with a habit as dangerous as yours." Neil grinned at her response.

"Alright you two. You've met. Are we all happy? Cam?" Cameron rolled her eyes and moved further into the open space.

"I'm afraid we're not exactly set up here yet, so things are kind of a disaster at the moment. Not that I'm any kind of neat freak or anything, but this isn't the building we're going to be living in. The other one isn't up yet. Not that it'll be any prettier from the outside, since it's the same sort of building, but it will be a lot bigger.

"This will be the garage, workshop, and hydroponic greenhouse once we're set up. I still have to install the insulation before I can grow anything in it in the winter, but it keeps us dry for now." Neil nodded intently, obviously listening to everything she was saying.

"Was that a solar set-up I saw on the roof?" She nodded.

"Yeah. The two buildings will have separate systems, though they can be patched together if necessary, so both buildings can be powered by the larger set-up. This one wouldn't do both buildings. I meant to improve it, but things moved faster than *I* could."

"Speaking of which, have you heard anything new about what's happening down there?"

"Well, Kirk and Leigh got as far as Gravenhurst and ran out of gas. The stations there are already empty, from the people in the cities heading north looking for fuel. That will spread to Bracebridge and Huntsville soon. I don't think it'll be long before people start to understand what all this means."

Mac shook her head to dispel the gloom, and Neil kept his thoughts to himself for the time being. Kirk was drifting over with Leigh. They'd already seen Neil at the store, of course, but had never really been introduced.

"Neil, this is Kirk and Leigh. They came from Oakville. Kirk has been Cam's best friend since her second year of high school in Burlington, and Leigh's his girlfriend, as well as a friend to Cam. They're basically family.

"We left without them yesterday, thinking they'd be fine to drive here, but it turned out their car was dead. They rented the blue car out there, which is the one that ran out of gas. At least they made it to Gravenhurst. A lot less dangerous right now than a city with a couple hundred thousand desperate people, anyway.

"As soon as Cam said their timing chain needed replacing I felt like a total shit. I knew there was no way they'd be able to get it fixed in time to get out."

"Mac, you still managed to get us here, safe and sound. We're grown-ups. It's not your job to take care of us." Mac would have argued the point on any other day, but today she was too tired.

"Hey, there's someone you haven't met yet. Two 'someones' in fact. This might be a weird surprise for you, or maybe you expect weirdness from me. Come on. Let me show you my chamber of horrors, also known as the future tool crib." Neil followed her, a bemused look on his face.

Mac opened the door quietly, figuring the boys were probably sleeping. She didn't really want to wake them up right now. Neil could meet them later. Out of all the things that could have made her nervous about Neil, this was the one that actually did. It was a deal-breaker for her.

"Uh, what are they?" She wasn't surprised he didn't know what they were at first, since their faces were sort of buried.

"They're ferrets. Pickle and Squeaker to be exact. They're my boon companions, and overlords of this particular castle. In other words, I spoil them rotten."

"Wow. I never thought I'd see ferrets up here. A friend of Billy's had one, but I never saw him when he was sleeping. Just when he was bouncing around like he was on a trampoline or something. One of the funniest things I ever saw."

"They'll put on a show for you later, I'm sure. They're pretty tuckered out for the moment." Her relief was dizzying. If he'd been one of those guys that called them rats, she'd have known she'd made a mistake in letting him into the house.

Mac sat on the edge of her bed. Neil took one look at her and started getting a worried look on his face.

"You're so tired, Mac. I have to let you get some sleep. Is there a way for me to get out the gate without you having to go down there?"

"There's a pressure plate that works like a remote." She paused a second.

"How would you feel about staying?" As soon as the words were out of her mouth, the twinkle was back in his eye.

"I'd say I feel pretty good about it." Mac smiled.

"That's good, because I'd really rather you stayed." Neil pulled her up against him.

"Oh yeah? Tell me what you want."

"You," she whispered. "I just want you."

7

THE GOOD, THE BAD, AND THE VERY BAD

She yielded to the temptation of using her mouth on his neck, the rough skin raspy against her tongue and lips.

"You go in for the kill, don't you?" His voice was so rough she could barely make out the words.

"Yes," she murmured. "Right for the throat." A tortured laugh rumbled in his chest.

"Alright, honey. Have it your way. This is one game I'm willing to play. And I play to win." Mac shuddered as another spear of pleasure pierced her belly. Neil picked her up and laid her on the bed so fast her head spun. He instantly covered her body with his. If he hadn't cut off her moan with his mouth, everyone in the house would have heard her.

"Shh, baby," he cautioned when he finally stopped kissing her.

Mac wanted to whimper in frustration, but he was right. Sounds carried in this building.

"We're going to take this nice and slow, so we don't keep everyone awake."

"Okay, you win. Whatever game we were playing, you win."

"It's not that simple, honey. I'm not going to accept victory by default. I want your A-game." Mac felt the challenge rise up inside her, her competitive nature raring to teach him a thing or two.

"Alright. You had your shot, cowboy. Now you're going down." She was about to roll them both over when he smirked at her.

"I sure am." He moved faster than a snake. One second they were face to face, and the next she was naked from the waist down with his mouth clamped over her. She couldn't even breathe, let alone scream. By the time she managed to draw air into her lungs, her first orgasm had her choking on it. There was no mistaking what he'd done to her, though. Her entire body convulsed with it.

Neil slid up next to her, and whispered in her ear.

"You taste good. I could do that all day, I think. For now, though..." he trailed off, his hand cupping her breast beneath the support tank. His thumb found the erect nipple and circled it, slowly. Her hands latched onto his shirt.

"Why are you still wearing so many clothes, cowboy?" She managed to pull herself together enough to get his shirt off. Then she moved her hands down to the button fly on his old, faded jeans. He was so hard beneath her hand, that she knew he had to be close to agony.

She shimmied down the bed while she popped all the buttons open with a quick flick of her wrist. Then she swallowed him whole. She could tell he was trying to be considerate by not gripping her head. When his fingers tangled in her hair, though, it turned her on almost as much as having his mouth on her.

With what looked like a Herculean effort, he tried to pull away from her mouth. She dug her nails in a little bit and continued. The sharp little bites in his skin seemed to set him off, because his own orgasm took him over almost instantly.

What sounded an awful lot like a growl escaped his mouth when he was done, and she chuckled as she licked her lips and slid back up beside him. They both lay there panting for several minutes.

"God, you're good at that!" It was Mac's turn to smirk.

"I'm not done with you yet, though. Won't be long before I'm ready for the next round, and then you'll be sorry. I can last all night if I want to now."

"I don't think that's going to make me sorry, Neil. *Sore* maybe, but not sorry." His laugh was low and dangerous.

"We'll see about that. I'd say right about now, in fact." Then he rolled her over and thrust inside her. The sudden shock started a scream in her throat, but he was ready for that. His tongue was tangling with hers, turning the scream to a squeak.

They made love until close to three in the morning, when Neil finally turned off the light beside the bed and pulled the blankets over them. As he pulled her back against his body, he whispered in her ear.

"Sleep, honey. I'll be here when you wake up." Something about those words had her whole body relaxing. If he said anything else she didn't hear it.

When she woke up, as promised he was still there. She checked her phone for the time. It was after eleven. Early enough for her, but she wondered if he needed to be at the store by now. He was a big boy, though. He was capable of handling his responsibilities without her input. Instead of waking him up, she rolled over to curl around him.

At some point in the night he'd turned over, and now she could see the tattoo on his back. She'd spent the entire time looking at his front throughout the night, so it wasn't surprising she hadn't seen it then. Her finger traced the lines of the compass rose. She'd always loved that symbol for some reason. Suddenly Neil rolled over, making her yelp.

"Jesus, you startled me."

"Mmm." He pulled her into his arms and held her there.

"Serves you right," he finally said.

"Oh yeah? What on earth did *I* do?" She tried to think for a minute, then was stymied by his answer.

"You touched me. I don't think you've paid a high enough price for your actions just yet, though." Before she could even worry about having dragon breath, he was kissing her deeply. She could feel him hard against her, and felt the sudden flood of dampness between her legs. She shifted so she could press against him. He didn't need any additional encouragement.

Her eyes fluttered closed as he thrust inside, and she wrapped her legs around his narrow hips. His hands pinned her wrists over her head, and his hips rocked with hers. An orgasm began pulsing through her in less than a minute, and when she felt him convulse against her, her own pleasure multiplied.

He looked into her eyes and brushed the hair from her face.

"I'm looking forward to the day when I can hear you scream." Mac took a moment to catch her breath, and then muttered indignantly that of course *she* would never scream. Neil just chuckled knowingly.

She sighed deeply. This might have been an extremely pleasant way to start the day, but the day did, indeed, need to get started. Far too many things needed doing. So, she gave his naked ass a smack, and told him to get his muscle-bound physique off her now-weakened frame.

"You're a feisty one, aren't ya?" Mackenzie laughed.

"I'm pretty sure you already know the answer to that one. Or you have problems with severe memory loss. In a couple of hours I'll have known you...gee, a whole day...and already you've forgotten who I am."

"Smartass. Fine, I'm getting up. You weren't complaining about my muscle-bound physique ten minutes ago."

"A time and place for everything, cowboy."

"Huh! That's pretty lousy appreciation you've got for some

mind-blowing sex, don't you think?"

"Was it?" Neil laughed at her.

"You know damn well it was. Admit it, or I'm going to have to remind you." Mac decided she'd just have to call his bluff.

Half an hour later, panting, she was forced to admit that he was right. About all of it. Actually forced to admit it. He wouldn't let up until she said it. When she relented, though, she did it without the humour.

"It was mind-blowing alright," she said softly, stroking his shoulder and back with lazy fingers.

"Yeah, it was."

By the time she'd showered and was starting to dress, Neil was getting ready to go. He didn't have any spare clothes with him, so he needed to get home to shower before going in to the store. He apparently didn't need to be there until two, since he had a part-time employee on from nine until three. Billy wasn't ready to be left alone in the store for obvious reasons. He'd only been working there since graduation at the end of June.

Neil stepped in front of Mackenzie, waiting for her to look up from zipping the fly of her boot-cut jeans. When she met his eyes he smiled.

"I guess you're getting a later start than you planned, huh?" Mackenzie grinned back at him.

"It's normal for me to get up later than this. 'I am the night,' as they say." Neil chuckled.

"I hear ya. It's the same for me. It's why I was happy to give

Samantha the morning hours to fit in with her being able to get daycare. I sure as hell don't want to get up at seven every morning. Her wife was so happy with me she sent me flowers when I gave Samantha the job."

"Her wife, huh? You're telling me this because you think I might be worried about you having a woman working for you. And if I'm reassured that she's married, to a woman no less, you won't get a bunch of stress over it. That about right?" She raised her brows at him.

"I suppose. I don't think it was a conscious thing on my part, but maybe."

"Neil, I'm not going to play mental games and go on about how you're still a free agent, because I don't believe that's what this is between us. You made it pretty clear you wanted more than that. I don't see you as a guy who likes to mess around. I'm not insecure about stuff like that. If you're mine, it's because you want to be, not because I own you."

"Well, I want to be."

"Good. You're mine then. Ditto. Now get your ass to work. I've got things to do." Then she smacked his butt and shooed him out the door of her bedroom.

"God, I love a woman with sass!" Mackenzie laughed and traipsed down the hall after him. The ferrets were still conked, so she had to assume they'd woken up during the night and played themselves out again. She'd come back and spend a bit of time with them after Neil was on his way.

"I'm just teasing about kicking you out, ya know. You need to be fed first? We've got a bunch of healthy shit. There's some sort of hay-like substance here." Neil just laughed.

"You sure know how to make a man feel welcome. I guess you don't subscribe to the theory of getting to a man's heart through his stomach, eh?"

"Not so much. I prefer a more direct route. Like through the rib cage."

"Well, thanks for the friendly offer, but I think I'll skip the horse feed just the same."

"Yeah, I know *I'm* going to. Sit. I'll make you an omelet. You okay with onions in it?" His eyes lit up.

"You're actually going to cook for me? Cool! I love onions. You'll just have to suffer when I say goodbye, that's all."

"We both will. I'll brush my teeth after you leave, just so you won't feel left out. Normally I'd prefer mushrooms, but I haven't bought them yet. I need to get some so I can have the spores. I've got what I need to grow them otherwise." She looked around the cavernous area that would eventually house equipment rather than people.

"You'll have to see it when it's all done. A few weeks and you won't recognize the place."

"Hell, I'll be lucky if I can even *find* this place again. You did a hell of a job concealing the entrance." She nodded her acknowledgement of the compliment.

"Thanks. I tried. Okay, let me get some breakfast for us. A long day like today means I'll need my protein. Toast?"

"I think I can handle the toast, honey."

"Okay. How about you do the coffee, too. It's over there, under the coffeemaker."

Cameron walked in as they were finishing up their meal.

"Shut up Cameron. I can hear you looking at me." Cameron gave a grunt, and grabbed an orange juice. She'd obviously just woken up, and she didn't like to eat first thing. It usually upset her stomach.

"You got the plans ready for the chickens and goats yet?" Mac cringed. She didn't, so she'd have to sketch something out really quick. She was holding everybody back from getting the work done.

"You've got your hands full today, I think. Give me a call when you can. Thanks for breakfast, honey." He gave her a quick kiss, and left her to her daughter's glare.

"Chicken," Mac yelled after his retreating form.

"Sure am," he called out as he opened the door.

As soon as he was gone, Cameron launched her offensive.

"'Honey?' Are you kidding me?"

"Well, yeah, so I've got something that looks vaguely like a boyfriend for the first time in years. Leave me alone." Mac hunched her shoulders.

"You guys sure moved fast, but never mind that. You need to deal with more important issues than a boyfriend right now. I can't believe you didn't draw up the plans yet. Where are Leigh and

Kirk?"

"No idea. They're used to daytime hours, so they probably fell asleep long before we did, and got up earlier, too."

"I sure hope so! I don't know if you noticed, but there's a bit of an echo in here. It's not even insulated yet. You were pretty quiet, but not enough to keep us all from hearing what was going on." Mac cringed in embarrassment, but she still wasn't putting up with a lecture on sex from her twenty-three-year-old daughter.

"Look, you. I'm a normal woman who has sex and enjoys it. I taught you better than that."

"You also taught me to be cautious about safety."

"That's a good point. You're not allowed to have good points. It's too early," Mac said grouchily. Cameron cracked a smile.

"Tough. You raised me."

"Yeah, yeah. I'll go draw up the plans and then show you around the stuff you'll be working with. Please be careful today. I'll go over the safety precautions when we start setting up. Be back in a few minutes." She swallowed the rest of her coffee, and went to her room to get her notebook.

Mac managed to squeeze in a little play time with the ferrets before she got down to business with the plans. As she sketched, she pondered the best way to teach a couple of young adults how to use power tools in as short a time as possible, without them killing themselves.

As soon as she had a diagram that looked like they might understand what everything was supposed to be, Mac went outside to find Cameron talking to Kirk and Leigh. They had emptied the trailer, so she backed the truck up to it and hitched it on.

"You guys ready?" They all said they were, so she got down to it.

Once she'd stressed all the finer points of safety, she showed them how to move the portable table saw around. She told them the lengths they'd need to cut, and then had them set it up so the wall of the building could be used as a fence, when the built-in fence wouldn't slide out far enough. The posts didn't need to be perfect, just approximate.

She'd listed all the lengths, along with the number of pieces they would need of each size, in a sort of parts list, so they wouldn't have to figure anything out from the sketch. Then she explained the mixing process for the cement, how to brace the posts they stuck into the wet cement in the holes, and marked out the areas where the holes would be dug.

It took more than an hour to explain everything, but it would still save her time if they did the work, rather than her doing it by herself when she got home. She showed them the sections to leave open for the gates. She'd build those herself when she got back. She wasn't sure they were ready for that just yet. She knew if she gave them too many instructions, they might forget the more important stuff.

Mac filled a supply pack, adding the binoculars she'd missed having the day before, and tossed it in the truck. She and Kirk hit the road by three. There was plenty of daylight left for Cameron and Leigh to get some serious work done, and the worst of the sunlight was easing off.

Their first stop was the OPP station. Thankfully the building was pretty much empty, and an officer was able to take her statement right away. Even better, he was an old friend of hers, though it took her a second to realize who it was.

"Chuckles? Is that you?" He looked up from the blank report he'd been trying to get started, and when he finally placed her he stood right up.

"Holy shit. Mac? Is that you? You haven't been around here for years, and *this* is how we have to meet up again? That sucks." He gave her a giant bear hug. Chuck Forrest had to duck to get through doorways, so she knew he was well over six-four, but he was one of those guys you couldn't help thinking of as a teddy bear. She'd almost had a thing with him once, but it had just sort of slipped away and passed into obscurity.

"When the hell did you get on with the OPP? Last I heard you were still bouncing at the bar." He filled her in a little bit on his life. He was married with three kids, and had been a full-fledged constable for about a year. She introduced Kirk and explained who he was.

"I was going to look you up once I was settled again. We just got up here two days ago, and we've got so much work to do. And then this shit happened." They finally got down to filing the report. She sent the picture and video from her phone directly to his e-mail so he could have the kid's plate number, and gave him all the information she had on him.

"It's in the Parry Sound district, but I'll get things rolling. If nothing else we can knock on his door and scare the crap out of him. We'll talk to his boss and stuff. It's not like we're swamped with serious crime here, so whoever does work on this will be interested at least."

Mac was pretty sure he wouldn't be saying that to most people who filed a complaint, but he was one of the few friends she had that would give her the shirt off his back if needed.

"The guy who owns the knife shop in Rosseau thinks he knows the kid's dad and was going to mention something to him about what his son was doing."

"That's not a bad idea. Normally we would tell people to let us handle it, but you know what some of the big families can be like in this area. Some are good, and tend to handle their own, while others can be worthless but loyal to one another. If he thinks the father will be willing to do something about the problem, you may not have to worry about it again. Let's hope so anyway." Mac told him a bit about Neil, and he laughed when she said everyone called him Mac, too.

"That's just like you to end up with someone so similar they even have the same name," he teased.

"Ha ha. You saying I'm in love with myself?" They both laughed and chatted for a few more minutes before Mac felt she had to get going.

"It's so good to be back here, Chuck, even with that little shit dogging me. I've missed you guys, and I've missed this place. Hard to breathe in a city full of steel plants." She had to stop and think about it, but then realized Chuck needed to know what was happening. Maybe he could convince his fellow cops to keep an eye out.

"There's a reason we left the city, Chuck. Maybe you know more about it than I do at this point, if you've got information coming in from other detachments. The big cities are experiencing major power outages, people are getting out of hand, and it's spreading.

"You guys used to tell me I was paranoid for planning to go off the grid, so hopefully you don't think I'm nuts now and brush me off. It's going to get bad. Now it's too late to do anything about it, other than ride out the storm.

"Take care of your family, Chuckles. Make sure you have plenty of non-perishable food and water, because the grocery stores will probably be running out in a couple of days. Check with the detachments in the GTA. They'll fill you in. Better than they will the public, I'm sure.

"You wouldn't happen to know where I can find Gilles, would you? I'd like to at least touch base with him now that I'm back in this neck of the woods."

"We haven't talked in quite a while. Basically since he was at my wedding, I think. Just sort of lost track, but I did hear he was over in Humphrey, almost all the way to Parry Sound. Not sure what he's doing now." Chuck shrugged his big shoulders, and then gave her a quick hug as she was leaving.

Mac gave a huff of breath when she was behind the wheel again. Chances were good she'd be able to find Gilles just through the rumour mills. It was certainly more likely than finding him in a phone book. As far back as she could remember, he'd always had a cell phone rather than a landline.

As for Chuck, she didn't doubt that he already knew what was happening around Toronto and all that, but he was a Pollyanna.

They stopped at all the stores that carried the kinds of things they still needed, and Mac got her stock of mushrooms to collect spores from. They would cook up whatever wasn't needed for the spores, and add them to tonight's dinner. She was looking forward to a real meal for tonight, though the omelet was holding her for now.

The plastic cargo bin that took up a portion of the truck bed was filled to capacity now. There was nothing more they could get for human supplies without it potentially blowing out of the back, and they needed the rest of the space for the chickens and their feed.

The goats would have to wait for another day, as much as she hated putting it off. She'd need to build something like stalls in the back of the truck, or maybe in the trailer, to keep them from getting hurt during the drive home.

They went to the feed store and filled up the trailer with different types of hay and chicken feed, and drove straight to Bala from there.

Thankfully the chicken rancher had cardboard transport boxes similar to what pet stores used for puppies and kittens, so they managed to fit two roosters and ten hens into the truck box, with enough room around them for air to get into the boxes. The entire time they traveled through the area near Bala, she was on the lookout for Gerry's green Civic, but there were no sightings, so they got home without incident.

They'd only been gone about three hours, but somehow Leigh and Cameron had really gotten on top of things, and from inside the truck it looked like they were both in one piece still. She was pretty sure all the posts had been put in already, so she got out to take a look at everything they had accomplished.

"Wow. You guys do good work! Come here for a second. I want to show you something," she called. When they came over she pointed at the flat cement around the post and showed them how to round the cement so water wouldn't pool and rot the wood.

While Cam and Leigh repeated the process with the other posts, Mac and Kirk laid out hardware cloth for the base of the chicken pen and covered it with dirt. They surrounded the enclosure with hardware cloth and then poured cement to join the bottom edges to the base.

To avoid waste, Mac made a shallow mould with a few slats of wood. Grabbing a trowel she scooped the hardening cement out of the mixer and pressed it into the mould. She'd judged the amount almost perfectly. When it dried they would have a stepping stone. Then she rinsed the mixer out and dumped the dirty water where they would eventually start the path from the animal pens. No point killing the grass anywhere else.

She got started on the gate for the chickens while Kirk helped Cameron and Leigh, putting together a corrugated plastic roof that would cover most of the enclosure, with hardware cloth covering the rest. They added more plastic to the back wall and half of two sides, while Mac installed the gate.

She had to keep the roosters separate, which meant dividing the enclosure into three sections before she'd be able to let them out of their boxes. Mac pounded some long stakes into the ground, and attached a section of hardware cloth. She divided the back area in two for the roosters.

When everything was built she put in the water troughs. She hated doing everything backwards, but at least they could release the chickens now.

Leigh took one look at a suddenly-freed chicken, and her opinion was made abundantly clear.

"Ewww! They're disgusting. Is that shit all over it?"

"Yup. They're not normally that bad, but it's not exactly her fault. Where else was she going to shit? We should wipe them all down as we go, before we stick them in the pens. I don't think they'll take too kindly to a hosing, and that just seems mean to me after they've been in a box for so long.

"I know none of us really wants to touch them, but we can clean off our hands and use the hand sanitizer before we go in and shower. We'll take turns there. You don't have to worry about running out of hot water or anything, either. We've got a tankless water heater which heats on-demand, instantly.

"Make sure you do use the hand sanitizer, though. Salmonella is not our friend."

Leigh looked like she was going to make a snotty remark, but one look from Mac was enough to keep her quiet. It was concerning, though. If she didn't like hard work, or getting her hands dirty once in a while, they were going to have a problem.

8

MUCH ADO, AND THEN LESS

Mac let everyone else head into the house while she continued to work around the yard. She scattered some more feed into the chicken pens, just to calm them down a bit. Then she got to work on a nesting box setup. The hens would need a place to lay eggs.

She'd forgotten a lot of stuff from her childhood farming experience, and even though she'd been reading through as much material as possible, there weren't enough hours in the day to learn everything a person needed to know to be self-sufficient.

Mac had spent years studying solar energy and electrical circuitry, and then she'd gotten her amateur radio licence and learned to set up a ham radio. She had relearned vegetable gardening, studied electromagnetic pulses, absorbed knowledge on medicine and human anatomy, and had boxes of books on every subject she could think of. It was overwhelming.

Part of her wanted to shut out the responsibilities she was faced with, and just drift. Mostly with thoughts of Neil. She was a practical woman, though, and romance wasn't her strong suit. They'd spend what time together they could, when she was able to take time away.

She was finishing up cutting the slats she needed when the phone in her pocket vibrated. She took off her gloves, removed the ear protectors, and pulled it out to look at the display. Neil.

"Was your brain burning?"

"Not that I could tell, no. Isn't that supposed to be my ears?"

"I'm not sure. I think that's when someone's talking about you, not thinking about you."

"Well, I've got a bit of heart-burn. I just thought that was lunch coming back to haunt me. Guess it must have been you."

"Food, huh? Guess I'll have to get to that."

"You haven't eaten yet?"

"No. Too busy with live chickens to deal with a dead one right now."

"How's that going?"

"Disgusting."

"You're really a glass-half-full kind of woman aren't ya? Well, this should cheer you up. I talked to Gerry's dad, and he didn't even try to pretend his kid wouldn't do something like that. Most parents would, but I'm sure he's been told time and again that his son's a little shit. It's a small town, and people are only too happy to shoot you down. I didn't tell him anything about us, because I didn't want his son to find out. If he thought you and I were seeing one another, he might try to stake out my place looking for you."

"You're a pretty smart cookie for such a stud. I ended up seeing an old friend when I went to make my report, so he'll make sure the complaint is taken seriously. Hopefully the kid will be scared shitless for the time being, and he'll cross to the other side of the street if he sees me again. I can deal with him if I have to, but I don't want it going that far. I don't want to be living with something I can't take back."

"No, you don't. For now, what are you doing about food? Can I bring you something after I close the store?" Mac groaned.

"I'd love that, but I've got so much to do, and stuff that really needs to be cooked tonight. It thawed on the way up here, so I can't refreeze it. I'll take a break when I go to make dinner and eat, but then I'm going right back to work. I should have proper nesting boxes for the hens in an hour, and little cubbies for each rooster, but I need to build something for the back of the truck for bringing the goats home. The more I think about them, the more goats I feel I'm going to need, too."

"Here's a thought. I've got a horse trailer you can borrow, instead of building something. I was able to bring home a dozen goats in it. I'll bring it over, and then cook up whatever you say needs to be made while you finish what you're doing. I'm closing up in an hour, so I can be there in about two."

"That sounds wonderful! Let me know when you need me to

come down and open the gate. A bit of a walk will feel good by then, and clear my head. I'm pretty filthy right now, though, and I probably smell a lot like chicken shit and sweat."

"Who could resist?" Mac started to laugh.

"You've sure got strange tastes, cowboy, but that works out well for me. You didn't run away from the ferrets, so I'm sure you'll do okay. I need to get back to work. See you soon."

"Later, honey." Mac heaved a sigh of relief. Her night wasn't going to be quite the hell she'd envisioned. In fact, it might turn out to be pretty damn good. If she finished the nesting boxes in time, she could shower before he arrived.

She got back to work with a new energy, and after ninety minutes she was done. The rooster boxes were filled with hay and placed inside their sections. Mac attached more hardware cloth to the roof and attached it to hooks on the dividing walls to keep the roosters in their pens. It was a temporary fix, but she wasn't ready to deal with fertilized eggs yet.

There were ten nesting boxes in the main structure she'd built, and it would be slid through the gate once she had someone outside to make sure no chickens got out.

Cam and Kirk came to help, while Leigh remained on the futon, reading her book. Mac wasn't happy about the attitude she was catching glimpses of, but there was still a possibility it would work itself out once things were settled.

Kirk helped her carry the nesting unit into the enclosure, while Cameron ran herd on the two that made an escape attempt. She was laughing when Mac and Kirk finished.

"Having fun?" Mackenzie wanted to know.

"They're just so ridiculous, aren't they? They have no clue what they're doing." Mac just shrugged, too tired to see the humour.

She grabbed the ramp she'd made for the chickens to get to the second level, and put it in place. Then she packed each of the cubbies with hay to make them comfortable.

"Neil will be here soon with a trailer I can use to get the goats, and he offered to cook up that chicken we've got in the fridge. While he's doing that I'll get the mushrooms going so we'll have the spores ready in a day or two."

"Kirk said you knew the cop today."

"Old friend. You knew him a long time ago. You might remember him if you saw him. Really, really tall guy. Chuck Forrest." They all headed back to the house.

"I'm not sure. The name doesn't sound familiar. I don't really remember your old friends."

"Doesn't matter. He was a good friend, though, and I trust him. He'll make sure the situation is handled. The only thing we have to worry about now, is if there's a breakdown in law and order. Neil also talked to Gerry's dad, who said he'd have a word with him."

"What about my dad? He refused when I asked him to come the first time, but maybe if you talked to him he'd change his mind. I don't know if he's got his own car, though. He has the cab, but I'm not sure if it's his or belongs to the cab company."

"I can try, but you know how stubborn he is. Easy-going,

maybe, but stubborn as hell. Or maybe it's too easy-going to want to go anywhere. Give me his number. I'll try to talk some sense into him. It's a much better life for him here than in town, but with his allergies he might disagree."

"Thanks mom. I'll send you his number and let him know you'll be getting in touch."

With that, Mackenzie went straight to the shower. She wasn't a two-shower-a-day kind of person, but she was disgusting right now. She pulled the phone out of her pocket and dumped her clothes straight into the washing machine as she pulled them off. Tomorrow she'd wash everything that was in there during peak sunshine hours, instead of using up their stored energy.

She turned on the water and stepped in. This was almost a luxury, and one she'd been looking forward to in their plans to move here. Instantly-hot water that never budged in temperature, no matter what else might be running in the building. She had a main tankless water heater for the house, but a separate one for the shower. She would only need one in this building once the house was built, so she'd move this one over, but she also had three more waiting in boxes. Every shower would have its own.

The water pressure was amazing, too. She hadn't scrimped on the pressure tank, but she'd also lucked out with a flowing artesian well. She planned to run two buildings, along with hydroponics and watering the outside garden and animals, so there needed to be enough pressure.

With the water spraying from every direction, she was able to get showered off in less than five minutes, even after standing in the spray for a full minute to let the jets massage her aching body. Not all of the aches were from the day's work, either, she realized with a smile.

Once she dried off she picked up her phone and sent a text to Neil, suggesting he bring Billy. It would be good for him to get to know her better after what had happened at the store.

Mac went to her room and got dressed while the ferrets circled her feet, licking her ankles. Pickle suddenly became very playful and nipped her foot, making her yelp.

"You little bugger!" She had to laugh. He was sort of bouncing with his toes splayed. He looked so happy with himself for catching her off-guard. She scooped him up from the floor and ruffled his silky fur.

"You think that's funny, don't you?" She pretended to bite his neck while he squirmed in her arms.

"Well, that's what you get for biting the ankle of the hand that feeds you. Okay, that really didn't make any sense, but you know what I mean." Meanwhile Squeaker was launching himself at her bare calf. He didn't like Pickle being out of his reach.

"Oh, here!" She picked him up, too, and bundled the two of them together. There was something so comforting about having their noses nuzzling her wet hair, and sniffing in her ear.

Mac had just managed to put on her deodorant when her phone vibrated, right before it started to ring. She snatched it up, sliding her thumb across the screen to take the call.

"Does this mean you're almost here?"

"Does this mean you never say hello when you answer the phone?"

"Does this mean you answer questions with questions?"

"Okay, you've got me there. Yeah, we'll be there in a minute or two."

"See ya soon, cowboy!" The ferrets were pouncing on one another now, which kept them busy enough for her to get out of her room.

Leigh was still reading on the futon when Mac ran through on her way out the door. Kirk was coming out of the bathroom. There was no sign of Cameron, but then Mackenzie knew she was likely in her room, playing a game on her computer or something. Once things were a bit more settled, she figured the three young adults would spend time playing console games together, but they weren't in a routine yet.

Mac slipped on her sandals and set out for the gate at a light jog. This running back and forth to the gate was going to get her in good shape one day. She liked running. Amongst all the building supplies there was a treadmill waiting to be moved into the main building, along with a Bowflex, and in the winter there would be plenty of time to use the equipment.

She was at the gate wondering what Neil's place was like, when she saw the headlights of a truck. She figured it was him, but waited until he rolled down the window and stuck his head out to look for her before she pressed her thumb to the plate.

She watched him pull the trailer through, and then sidled up to his waiting vehicle.

"Doth mine chariot await, good sir?" She could just see the crinkling around his eyes when he grinned at her.

"It most certainly doth, mine lady faire." Billy gave his dad an incredulous look.

"Dad?" He sounded almost worried.

"It's okay, Billy. I've only driven your father slightly mad. He may recover yet." Neil barked out a laugh.

"I think it's fair to say it's more than 'slightly,' honey, but it's a trip I'm happy to take. Hop in buttercup."

"Buttercup, dad? Sheesh. When did you get so weird?" Mac could see him smile, though, so it looked like everything would be fine on that front. It would certainly make things easier if he considered this a positive thing.

"Hi ho Silver. Away!" Mac started laughing.

"That was really sad, cowboy."

"It's what you get for calling me a cowboy."

"You just have that way about you. Like an 'Aw, shucks and howdy ma'am' vibe. It's not a bad thing. Lots of women go for that. When it's coming from someone who's sincere about it anyway." Mac shrugged her shoulders.

"I don't care about lots of women going for it, as long as you do."

"Okay then. Never change. Pretty simple." Mac couldn't help herself. She reached forward and started playing with the hair lying on his neck, threading her fingers through it. When he pulled up to the house and stopped, she saw him shiver. As soon as they were standing together beside the vehicle, however, he seized her and started kissing her. She collapsed against the truck when he was done.

"I like when you do that, honey. Probably not the best time for it though."

"Do what? What did I do?"

"The neck thing."

"Oh yeah? Alright. I've got a good memory, and I'll be keeping track." He groaned. Billy came around the truck just then.

"Dad? Are we unhitching the trailer or what?"

"Yeah, alright. You okay with it here, Mac, or do you want it moved somewhere?"

"Here's fine, so long as you're okay to pull your truck out. I can back up to it easy enough."

Neil went around and got the trailer jack set up, while Billy unhitched. Once the trailer was lifted off the ball hitch, Billy went around and pulled the truck up out of the way.

"He got his licence?"

"Yeah. Couldn't stop him once he turned sixteen. He had to have it."

"I wish my daughter had been like that. I had to push her to get it last year."

"By the way, that has got to be the strangest smelling chicken shit I've run into in my entire life. You buy some fancy chickens that shit flowers or something? You smell really good."

"Amazing what a shower will do, isn't it? I managed to finish the nesting boxes a while ago, and decided I'd shower since I wasn't going to have to build anything else and could relax. You want to see it? The chicken pen I mean, not the shower. Shower's for another time." She winked, and he followed her over to the enclosure.

"That's a lot done in one day."

"Helps to have a couple of people working on things while you're gone. I came back and did the gate, and divided it into temporary pens. Mostly it was the nesting box setup I did around here. Everything else was Leigh and Cameron. They've got all the wood cut for the goat pen, too. I was pretty impressed when we got back. Now I'll have to set an alarm to remind myself there are live animals out here. They might never get fed otherwise."

"You seem to manage with your ferrets, so I don't think you'll forget." Billy overheard the last remark and perked right up.

"You've got ferrets? Can I see them?"

"Sure, as long as they're awake. You like ferrets?"

"They're awesome. A friend of mine had one." The enthusiasm on his face was unmistakable, and he seemed like a nice kid.

"Great! Looks like we've got something in common, Billy. I'm crazy about my boys. Let's go see if they're still playing."

"Why don't you point out the stuff you want cooked up, honey, so I can get dinner ready while you're doing that?"

"Perfect. I just have to grab some mushroom caps before I let you cook up the rest. Then Billy and I can go play." Neil laughed at her eager tone.

"What do you need the caps for?" It was Billy asking her. Mac explained as she pulled out the food from the fridge for Neil, and got her caps.

"I'll be growing them, and underneath the caps is where the spores are stored. Most of the time people just eat them. If you put the caps face down, though, and leave them out for a day or so, they drop their spores onto whatever surface you put them on. Then you can put the spores in a growing medium like soil and peat moss and grow your own. I'm growing Portobello and button mushrooms because they're the easiest."

Mac walked off with Billy, him keeping up a steady stream of questions, while she answered. He obviously had a lot of curiosity about things, which was another trait they shared, so it looked like she would get along with Billy just fine.

At the sound of a strange voice, Kirk and Leigh both looked up. Mac introduced them to Billy. Leigh looked a little pouty, but Kirk was his usual gregarious self.

"Let me introduce you to Cameron while you're here. That's my daughter. She's a few years older than you." Cam opened the door before Mac even had a chance to knock. Obviously she'd overheard her mother as she was coming to her door.

"Hey," she said to Billy. "I'm Cam. Neil's your dad?" When Billy swallowed and nodded, Cam started talking again.

"He seems nice. My mom sure seems to like him." Billy was

showing every sign of being lost in space at the sight of Cameron, so Mac just watched the show. He nodded at everything Cam was saying, until Mackenzie wanted to laugh. She wouldn't embarrass him like that, of course. She still had to make up for terrifying him at the store yesterday.

"I was going to let Billy see the ferrets. Maybe you can take him. I want to get these mushrooms set up for the spores. If you've got the PS4 set up, maybe all four of you can play if he's into that kind of thing."

"I haven't set it up yet, but it'll only take me a minute." Billy just stared at Cameron, apparently blown away by a girl who could do that, and Mac gave a sly smile. If anyone could show a man female ability, it was her daughter.

By the time she had the mushrooms done she started smelling something amazing coming from the kitchen. Her stomach growled angrily at being made to wait. She walked into the kitchen area and watched Neil as he worked. It was enough to make her mouth water, even if she hadn't been hungry.

Mine, she thought. Some of what she was thinking must have shown on her face. When Neil looked over at her, he started giving her the same look. She walked toward him, the pull stronger than gravity. He leaned over and whispered in her ear.

"You're looking pretty hungry, honey. Anyone I know?" She had to swallow her saliva.

"I'm not sure I know this guy's name," she said, and bent down to stare through the window of the oven.

"And he's got an awful lot of legs if it's only one chicken." He burst out laughing.

"You're gonna pay for that one, sweetheart. Just you wait." She winked at him and spun away.

"I can afford it."

9

TRIPPING THE MOONLIGHT FANTASTIC

The food was amazing, and the conversation was great, too, though things got awkward when Leigh made snide remarks. Mac wanted to tell her she hadn't been forced to come, but she refrained. She needed to talk to Leigh and find out what was going on.

Everyone else pushed the conversation forward and left the strange comments behind. Mac didn't think it was just the chicken shit she'd had to contend with. She was eating like she was starving and Mac was starting to get suspicious. She wouldn't bring it up with everybody else around, though.

"Hey, Mac. You said you were going to tell us a story about those knives. What was it?" Mac smiled at Kirk, unsurprised that he would remember her promise.

"Well, it's what I was reading online about the history of the name of the KA-BAR. I can't remember what the company was originally called, but they changed it. A hunter had his gun jam, and had to kill a bear with his knife. He sent the company a letter thanking them for making a quality knife that allowed him to kill a bear, but the lettering was smeared. 'Kill a bear' came out looking like 'K a b ar' with all the other letters missing. They changed the name of the company to honour his testimonial."

"Seriously?" Kirk's eyes were wide.

"As far as I'm aware. It's on their website. For all I know they could have concocted the story as a PR thing, but it's what they say about it anyway. I found out when I was looking for reviews on survival knives."

The food and conversation seemed to put everyone in a good mood, including Leigh, so the younger generation moved to the TV to play some *Black Ops*. Once the dishes were cleared, Mac could see a certain look in Neil's eyes, and knew he was entertaining the same thoughts she was.

"You know, I've got some great camping equipment in all this stuff. What do you say we go, uh, look at the stars." His smile was slow and seductive, flirting with sinister.

"I thought you'd never ask." The others were all being so loud they didn't notice Mac rooting through the supplies.

Once she had everything piled together, they filled their arms and snuck out. She led him toward the small river, and dropped her armload of gear on the ground. They were out of sight of the house now, with plenty of trees blocking anyone's view of the river, and she wasted no time in stripping off.

"Well that was fast! I thought I'd have to do some sweet-talkin' to get you out of those clothes." When he reach for her, though, she slipped away.

"Not just yet, cowboy. I haven't had a chance to go skinny-dipping in this river, and I'm not missing the opportunity. You have to take them when they come."

"Do you?" His voice was like silk, and she froze while he stalked slowly toward her.

*   *   *

"Well, *that* was a hell of a thing," Neil asserted, twenty minutes later, clearly not complaining. He blew out a breath as he eased his weight over.

"Those mad skills of yours have left us both sticky as hell," he observed.

"*My* mad skills? I think it's the other way around."

"Let's go fulfill that skinny-dipping fantasy of yours." She burst out laughing, jumped up, and raced him to the river. Suddenly she had all the energy in the world.

The water was cold, of course, but that didn't make it any less enjoyable. They splashed each other like little kids and then made love again in the water, her legs wrapped around him as he held her up against his slick flesh.

When they were finished they dragged their weakened bodies to the bank, both of them shivering.

"You eat a lot of oysters or something? Or do you just have an excess of testosterone that keeps you at full-mast?" She could barely get the words out through her chattering teeth. Neil smacked the extremely cold skin of her ass, making her yelp.

"There's that sass again. You can't help it even when you're practically freezing to death. Might be your best quality." Her mouth dropped open, and he relented slightly.

"Well," he drawled suggestively as he leered at her naked body. "Maybe not *the* best, but it ranks right up there.

"Look here, boyo," she began, and cocked her hip.

"Boyo?" His question interrupted what might have been an interesting tirade, but she was cold and let it go.

"Yes, boyo. Every once in a while my Irish pops out." She grabbed her clothes and pulled them on.

"Irish, huh? Well that explains a few things."

"Probably explains most things about me," she said. She looked around at the scattered camping supplies.

"I'm not sure that we really needed any of this stuff. How late is Billy going to want to stay up?"

"He's playing Black Ops. He'll stay up all night if the rest of them are into it."

"Why don't we make this fun for everyone? We can camp out here if you'd like to stay. I've got really good sleeping bags, and that air mattress is perfectly comfortable. Cameron can take my room. Leigh and Kirk can take Cameron's, and Billy can crash on the futon whenever he's ready to go down. Of all of us I think Leigh will be the first one wanting to go to bed. I need to talk to her, though."

"Okay, let's go sort everyone out, so you and I can come back here and just enjoy each other's company."

"Sounds faahhbulous, dahlink!" Her German accent was completely hideous, since it was vaguely British and Russian at the same time. Neil chuckled and grabbed her hand.

"I'm not sure you've got a career in theatre, honey. Stand-up maybe."

"Yeah, I'm hilarious when I'm terrified and standing frozen in front of a bunch of people. Something about it just makes people giggle uncontrollably."

"Fear of public speaking?"

"Not so much. More performance anxiety." They were walking through the door when Neil suggested she get some music for them to listen to, but since the open living area was right there, they dealt with the kids first.

Neil explained the situation, and the four of them just continued playing their game, nodding vaguely in amongst the swearing and laughing as they killed Nazi zombies.

"Fuck, I'm dead. Son of a bitch sniped me!" Billy shook his head in a dazed fashion.

"Wait. What did you say, dad?" Neil growled good-naturedly and repeated himself. Even if the others didn't hear him, at least one of them knew and could tell the others when the subject came up.

Mackenzie waited until Leigh got killed in the game, and quickly spoke in her ear.

"I should have made it clear to you, Leigh, so I'm really sorry. You're entitled to eat anything you like, or use whatever facilities we have in this place. It's not much right now, but it'll get better, okay?

"Seriously, never feel as though you have to wait for someone to offer you food, blankets, shampoo, you name it. It's here for everyone. And just so you know, you're welcome here. You're not an outsider. This is your home for as long as you need or want it to be. That offer even includes the chocolate we've got stashed. Alright?" Leigh nodded, and Mac could see there was a sheen to her eyes.

"We've got some hard work ahead of us, but once it's done we can start having some fun with it. Regular chores won't be a big deal, and we'll find stuff that each of us is good at and enjoys. We'll just have to share the stuff everyone hates. Like chicken shit."

As she'd hoped, the last comment put a smile on Leigh's face. Leigh got off the futon and stepped to the side, making it clear she wanted to speak privately.

"It wasn't just that, Mac. Something happened in Oakville that threw me. I didn't tell Kirk about it, because he would've flipped. A little kid got trampled in the grocery store by some snotty bitch, and when I helped him up she turned around and told me to keep my brat under control. I don't even like kids, and don't plan to have any, but I'd never treat a kid like that.

"His mother found us a minute later, and I told her what happened. The kid was still crying and holding his arm, so I think it might've been broken. I was so pissed at the bitch that stomped on him, but it scared me, too. That's a big reason I was so happy to leave the city when Kirk told me about coming here. I could see where things were headed."

"Jesus, Leigh. I'm surprised you didn't clock her." Leigh gave a weak smile.

"I wish I had, but I was completely stunned. It happened so fast, and then she disappeared into the crowd. I actually looked for her after, but couldn't find her. Kirk likes kids, and he'd have lost his shit if he'd known. It would've taken hours to convince him to stop looking for the woman and leave the store. I knew she'd be gone, after bullying her way through like that."

"Hey, Leigh," Kirk shouted. "What the hell? You playing or not?" Leigh shrugged at Mac and went back to the game.

The ferrets were awake when they went into Mac's room for the laptop she had her music on. It was the first time Neil really had a chance to see what they were like.

"Watch your ankles," she warned.

Neil engaged in a scaled-down wrestling match with Pickle, using his hand, which was almost as big as the ferret. Mac couldn't resist making a comment.

"My, what big hands you have!" Neil glanced up at her and

stared into her eyes. She sucked in her breath. She knew very well how proportionally accurate his hand size was with other parts of his anatomy, and she was suddenly itching to get her hands on him again. Apparently she had the libido of a rabbit these days, and he was the one with the carrot.

Hurriedly she gathered up her laptop and the accessories she might need, stowing them in a backpack-style computer case. She spent a few minutes cleaning up after the ferrets, and making sure their food and water were fresh.

Neil continued to play with the little monsters. Squeaker had joined in by way of gently gnawing his wrist bones. Mac watched and thought about all the ferrets in shelters she hoped to bring to the farm. She would need to do something about that soon. It meant going into cities to do it, but she'd risk it.

Apparently she'd been standing still for a while, lost in thought, because she suddenly felt Neil's arms wrap around her waist from behind. He nuzzled the hair away from the side of her neck, and began using his lips and tongue on the sensitive skin there. Every thought flew out of her brain, and her head tilted to the side to allow him access. Then he whispered in her ear.

"You ready to go, honey?" She shivered.

"Uh, yeah. Right. I think so?" The questioning tone had him laughing. He was apparently enjoying the effect he had on her.

"Good, because the view I've been getting of your backside with you bending over so much has triggered a certain level of interest that I'd like to do something about. If you're so inclined," he added softly. She was definitely inclined, but she laughed.

"You're getting turned on watching me change ferret waste pads? Huh. That's gotta be a first for me." Then she pressed back against him, making him groan in her ear. He spun her around suddenly, plastering her full-length against him, and captured her mouth in an almost brutal kiss. Lust slammed through her in wave after wave of spearing need.

"Let's go," he said hoarsely when he released her. Tingling from head to toe, Mac mechanically picked up her pack. The only reason she remembered the extension cord on their way out, was because it was bright red and directly in her line of sight near the door. Her hands were shaking as she plugged it into the outdoor outlet closest to the river.

When they got back to the riverbank, Mac just dropped her stuff on the ground. In less than a breath of time, Neil had her in his arms again. She let him take her over, and allowed the waves of heat to carry her away.

It was a good while later that Mac was staring down at herself in what little there was of the moonlight. She was naked again, she noted. She was spending a lot of time that way with Neil around. Not that she minded. She'd been celibate for a number of years, so this sudden abundance of sex was doing her body good. As well as her state of mind.

Despite everything that was about to go wrong with the world, and what she needed to accomplish in the interim, she wasn't worried.

"Penny for your thoughts?" Mac started at his voice. She'd really zoned out.

"I'm not sure I'm willing to share at that price." He snorted at her pithy response.

"Actually, I was just marveling at the number of times I've found myself naked with you, and how good you are for my stress levels."

"Mmm. I offer twenty-four-hour service, 365 days a year." Mac smirked at him.

"I'm sure you do. In the meantime, maybe we should get some clothes on. I'll boot up the laptop so you can go through my music files. Be warned. I think I've got about five thousand songs, though there are some duplicates. I've been meaning to properly sort and tag everything, but haven't gotten around to it. Presumably a day will come when I've got time to kill."

"Oh, I don't know about that. I can probably keep you pretty busy for a good many years."

"Years, huh?" Mac's heart was thumping erratically at the thought.

"Decades, in fact," he stated emphatically. Mac sucked in a lungful of air.

"You don't mess around, do you?"

"Been known to in the past, perhaps, but with you? Most definitely not." Neil was blatantly and utterly serious, and Mac knew in that moment that her heart wasn't getting out of this unscathed.

"Okay." It was all she could think to say.

"Mac," he began, but she put her fingers over his mouth.

"Neil, I'm not going anywhere for now. If that changes you'll be the first to know. Other than that, neither of us can give any guarantees. I won't take the time we share for granted, or waste a chance to be with you, but that's all I can say for now."

"Alright." He wanted to say more. She could see it on his face, and she wasn't ready to hear it. If she let him speak his mind, it would spiral out of control. He made her feel powerful things, which she suspected would be very difficult to resist if the temptation was put in front of her.

Mac had already plugged in the laptop's adapter, and was entering her password by the time Neil finished dressing again.

"Here. Media Player is open. Scroll to your heart's content and I'll set up the tent." Mac threw on her clothes and got busy with the small pop-up. It took less than ten seconds to set up once it was in the right spot. Then she stuck the inflatable mattress inside, spreading it out a bit before pressing the button.

Mackenzie zipped a couple of individual sleeping bags together to make one big one, and once the mattress was finished inflating she threw the sleeping bags on top.

"Maybe bring the laptop in here," she suggested. "We can make a playlist. You like to dance?"

"To some stuff. I like older music and dance styles. Stuff like Sinatra and Nat King Cole."

"Awesome. I've got a yen for some moon-themed dancing." In minutes they had Sinatra's *Fly Me to the Moon* playing. The laptop speakers weren't the best, but they did the job. It made her think she should build a gazebo with a couple of speakers in it. It hadn't occurred to her before, but then she hadn't been expecting to find a dancing partner.

Neil moved her over the soft grass to the rhythm of the music, making her heart sing. Everything about the moment felt wonderful. She'd resisted romance since her last marriage had fallen apart, knowing it led her into making bad decisions. Now that she was letting those feelings inside her, she realized how much had been missing from her life.

The smell of the light cologne Neil was wearing, mingled with the clear water and natural pine scents. Mac swayed wherever Neil led her, and it felt so beautiful she wanted to cry. The sensation shocked her. There had been a loneliness in her she hadn't known existed.

Something must have shown on her face, because Neil pulled her a little bit closer without breaking the silence between them.

When Nat King Cole came on, singing *Unforgettable*, Neil pulled her completely into his arms. Mac wallowed in the warmth he radiated, both physically and emotionally.

When the playlist was finished, they curled up together inside the sleeping bags. They talked for hours, and Mac got to know the man she knew she was falling in love with.

Mac woke to the sound of the alarm on Neil's phone. She'd asked him to set it for ten so she could get to a few places that closed early. She was cranky about it, though. She grunted and stuffed her head back under his arm.

"Oh, no you don't! You made me set this infernal thing. You're getting up." He jostled her shoulder until she pulled her head back out and glared at him.

"You're lucky I like you, cowboy. One day the rose-coloured glasses won't be there to protect your fine ass."

"You like my ass?"

"Well, for now anyway. Who knows if it'll look as good to me when those glasses disappear?"

"Guess I'd better take advantage of your temporary lapse in judgment then."

*   *   *

"I've never liked morning sex," she said fifteen minutes later, when she could finally speak again.

"Yeah, I could tell. All that screaming and moaning and carrying on."

"Shut up. A gentleman wouldn't mention such things."

"I'm no gentleman, I'm your lover," he purred into her ear. "And one day I'm going to be more than that."

"What the hell is more than a lover?" Mac wanted to bite her tongue. She knew what he meant, and tried to tell herself she wasn't ready to hear it.

"Wait and see. Assuming there's someone still around for all that." That was enough for her. She covered her ears.

"I can't hear you!" Then she made some obnoxious sounds to drown him out. He yanked her hands away from the sides of her head, and kissed her to shut her up.

"You hear me just fine, honey. Loud and clear, in fact." Then he ducked out of the tent to start pulling on his jeans, leaving her to sit there, completely befuddled.

"You gonna sulk in that tent all day?" Outrage got her moving. They got everything packed up and both had their arms full when they headed for the house. They dropped the stuff inside.

"You can join me in the shower if you want. It's a good one," she said.

"Works for me."

"Okie dokie. I'll just grab what I need from my room."

Mac made sure she locked the bathroom door before they started stripping off. By the time they were finished, she was feeling unusually limber. They dressed and went out to make breakfast. A loud sawing noise emanated from the futon.

"You sure he doesn't have some sort of sinus issue?" Neil grinned at her.

"I know, right? He's been like that his whole life. Doctors said he was fine, though. He never stops breathing or anything. I used to sit there and watch him sleep, just to be sure. Took me a while to stop worrying about it."

"No doubt. Well, this time we have the usual specialty. Mushroom omelets. Fuck!" Her loud curse cause Billy to snort.

"I just remembered the damn chickens. I gotta feed the poor

things. Be right back."

"No worries. I know how to make omelets, honey." She grinned over her shoulder at him and dashed out.

None of the chickens appeared to have starved in the meantime, so she scattered their feed and checked to see if there were eggs. She didn't find any. Their water was still full, so she left them to their clucking and pecking, and went back to the house. Neil was just pouring the makings of an omelet into a pan.

"I guess you found everything okay."

"You have no doors on your cabinets. Kinda hard to miss the pans, even if I wanted to pretend ignorance and wait until you got back to cook for me."

"That's because they're workbenches. This area will be for woodworking and repairs once we move out of here, but it was the most appropriate place to put a temporary kitchen. It has the big outlet for the stove, which I'll use for the small sawmill later."

"What kind of woodworking?"

"Whatever we need, basically. I like inventing stuff, and building furniture, which is a good thing. There's a lot of furniture to be built. Plenty of trees on the property to make whatever I want."

"You've been planning this for a while," he said, managing to flip the omelet with far more expertise than she could claim.

"Yeah, I have. Long before I could afford to do any of it. I may have to make you my love slave-slash-housekeeper, though. You're a much better cook than I am. Probably a lot tidier, too.

You wouldn't even have to do windows. I don't have any."

"I had another position in mind, but thanks. The first part sounded really interesting at least. Speaking of the windows, though. How the hell do you get it so bright in here?"

"See the tube over your head? It's called a Solatube. At night they switch to LED lights, but during the day they act kind of like a light periscope, amplifying and distributing the sunlight without putting big holes in the building." Neil nodded and glanced at her.

Mac was *not* responding to his reference to the other position. That conversation needed to wait. As romantic as it might seem on some level, she had to wonder if he was getting too attached too fast. Maybe it wasn't a problem, because she was feeling the same feelings. If it was mutual, it might not be something to fear from him, but she was still wary of it.

"You're freaking out aren't you, Mac? Look, I'm not some crazy, obsessive stalker who won't take no for an answer. Mostly I'm just teasing you." Neil slid the first omelet onto a plate and put it in front of her. He went back to the bowl that was sitting on the workbench and began mixing up more eggs and sliced mushrooms. She grabbed a fork from the cutlery bin that was sitting on the table, and waited for him to continue.

"I can see that you're the cautious type who doesn't go all ga-ga over a man just because there's chemistry. You have your priorities straight, and I respect that. You've also had some bad experiences and disillusionment. How am I doing so far?"

"You're a sharpshooter, cowboy. And before you continue, this is really good." She took another bite, and he smiled at her.

"Thanks. Okay, I've got a couple of years on you. Not just in age, but in preparation. My set-up is done, and I'm pretty relaxed about the whole thing. I've got all the time in the world to spend with you even now. You don't, and you're spending a lot of the day dealing with things I'm not. I can futz around my store having romantic fantasies about you all day if I want to. You can't. So, I think it mostly boils down to me being about six or eight hours ahead of you in all this." Mac laughed.

"So, another day and you'll have me all sewn up, is that it? Hook, line and sinker?"

"Well, a man can dream can't he? Honestly? I'm at a point in my life where I'm more than willing to take a risk, even if it seems crazy, but I'm also not the kind of guy who wants a woman who doesn't want him. That's some psycho-bullshit. Not to mention a huge blow to a real man's pride if he's got to hog-tie a woman to keep her around. If I'm crowding you, I'll move away until you're ready to pull me back. You're not a woman who will play games with that, so you do whatever you're comfortable with."

He sat down with his own omelet and began to eat. Mac was just finishing hers.

"I had a stalker once. Aside from the more recent little shit-head, Gerry, I mean. I mentioned to you before that Cameron's birth father had mental problems. I just didn't tell you how bad they were."

10

BOUNDARIES, BUT NO GOATS

"Brad became obsessed with me when we were friends in high school. I was going out with someone that I really loved. We broke up, though, and Brad was waiting in the wings. Being an idiot teenager I figured he would never hurt me. He loved me. I'd be safe and he'd never break my heart.

"I got pregnant, intentionally. I really wanted to have a kid, despite how young I was. Not to live off some man, or welfare, but I wanted a kid. Brad was all for it, of course. It didn't occur to me that it would give him a way to tie me to him permanently.

"He wanted to get married. I said I had to think about it. He was pissed. He basically dumped me, yet he started to follow me. Finally he stopped. I attempted contact in the middle of my pregnancy, thinking he had certain rights, but when he wanted to put his hand on my belly I felt nauseous. I didn't want him touching me, and it wasn't really about him. I just hated being pregnant at that age. Looking at my own body made me feel sick and ashamed because I was no longer thin and sexy. Stupid shit, but I was twisted up regarding looks at that age.

"That pissed him off, too, thinking I was rejecting him, so we didn't talk again until after Cameron was born. I felt she should have her father, and he still had rights. I'd felt so vulnerable during pregnancy, but my confidence returned after she was born, so I called him. A month later we were married.

"It was tumultuous, to say the least. There were lots of threats, and eventually there came a night when he nearly killed me. I was watching for him all the time when I drove my car, I had to pull into the cop station a couple of times, that sort of thing. I became hyper-aware of any guy trying to stake a physical claim on me, and I watched for it in Cam's boyfriends.

"So many women are flattered when a guy is jealous, and they'll do things to provoke it. They don't know how dangerous it is. Cameron knows, because I made sure she knew the signs. To be honest, I've broken a few of my own rules with you, and that's what I really find scary. Not you."

Neil had pushed his empty plate away by then, though he'd remained attentive while Mackenzie spoke.

"Well, how about I be flattered you found me so inspiring?" A quick laugh made for good tension relief for Mac.

"On a more sober note, it's somewhat surprising that you

haven't run away from me. I promise, if you find you can't love me, I'll walk away. I don't want to be with someone who doesn't want me. It's demeaning to everyone. What I feel for you is the most powerful thing I've felt since I first laid eyes on my son, but if you don't feel it, it's nothing more than a fantasy on my part." Mac grabbed his hand.

"I feel it. I just don't trust my own judgment. Does that make sense? I made two big mistakes when I made relationship decisions. I could say it was youth and all that, which part of it was I'm sure, but it was also a need inside me to be loved, and I overlooked things out of that need. I think I've grown beyond that, but I'm not sure if I'm fooling myself."

"What was it that you overlooked?" Mac sat back and thought about his question.

"Deal-breakers. Temper tantrums, bigotry, controlling behaviour, dishonesty, and disloyalty. Most of those in both of them. There were warning signs, too. Big red flags that I saw and actively chose to ignore.

"And before you ask, what I see with you is intensity. It's hard to fault you on it when I feel the same. Of course, I don't know what you're like under stress, and that's something I won't know until it happens. It's not something that can be predicted or imitated in order to bring it on. It's not like I'm going to manufacture a stressful situation just to test you, seeing as you don't bear any resemblance to a lab rat."

"Thanks for that." Mac laughed again.

"Cowboy, we wouldn't be having this conversation if you did. The whiskers would just be too much for me."

"And now we return to our regularly scheduled comedy program." Mac shrugged her shoulders.

"It's what I do. I can only hold a serious conversation about this kind of thing for so long."

"And they say men have a hard time communicating."

"It's still communicating even if someone is laughing. It's just a lot more fun."

"Not when someone is trying to hold a serious discussion and they think you're not being serious enough about it."

"Are we having our first fight?" Mac put on an excited, happy-face, and Neil couldn't hold back his laughter anymore.

"You're a pain in the ass with that, aren't you?"

"Little bit."

"More like a lotta bit, but I'll let it go for now. I was mostly done being serious anyway. I'll just say that the one and only tantrum I ever had was over in thirty seconds flat. My mother told me that if I ever did it again I wouldn't be allowed another candy bar for as long as I lived. Seeing as that's what I was throwing the tantrum over, you can imagine how effective her strategy was. I figured she had the power of God Almighty, and could actually make sure I never got a candy bar again."

"Sounds like your mother's a smart woman. Is she still alive?"

"Oh yeah. She lives near Banff. Has a mountain cabin. She's got a good set-up there. You remind me of her in a lot of ways.

Obviously not in certain ways, since I don't have that kind of thing for my mother, but you've got her good qualities."

"And what would those be?"

"Strong, feisty, smart, thinks ahead, and very capable."

"Huh. Well, I can't dispute any of that on my end. It is what it is." Neil laughed at her cocky response.

Mac liked the fact that he'd been raised by a strong woman. Both her former mothers-in-law had been weak, bending to the will of the men in their lives, including their sons. It made a difference when a man was raised by a strong mother. Not a vicious one, but one that showed by example what women were capable of. It was another check in the column of positives.

She wasn't finding any negative checks. Despite knowing he didn't have a firm grip on a relationship with her, he wasn't displaying the typical behaviours associated with insecurity. Only time would show her what he was made of, however.

Mac got up from the table and loaded everything from their meal into the dishwasher.

"You put your pans in the dishwasher?"

"Oh yeah. Nearly everything goes in the dishwasher in this house. Crystal wine glasses are the only exception. I even put my china in the machine. I hate dishes. Grosses me out."

"Huh."

"What? The first chip in the image of perfection?"

"Exact opposite. I do the same thing. Don't tell me you worked as a dishwasher in a past life."

"You too, huh?" They both laughed.

"I remember those bus pans loaded with everything from coffee and ice water mixed with cigarette butts, to eggs, wet toast, milk, you name it. To this day I shudder," she said.

"God, the big pots that had to be soaked, and then you had to stick your hand in there. No rubber gloves in the world were long enough for that job." Mackenzie laughed at that, even as she shivered visibly.

"Blech!"

"I agree. I think we need a distraction." Then he kissed her and she forgot all about dirty dishes.

"Jesus, mom!" Mac turned around and eyeballed her daughter.

"Don't tell me to get a room. You were in mine."

"More like, lock yourself up with the animals. I didn't think we were keeping rabbits. Sheesh!" Mac was already having a hard time maintaining a straight face, and she could actually *feel* Neil laughing silently behind her. His chest was jerking slightly with the effort of holding back.

"Anyhoo, what are we doing today?" Mac continued to stare at her daughter for a minute before answering.

"I have to go get the goats, so you and Leigh will need to get that pen finished while we're gone."

"Great. From one horny creature to another." That was it for Neil. It was all he could take before his laughter got the better of him. Mackenzie just choked on her surprise for a few moments, and waited for Neil to recover his composure.

"Get some breakfast ready for your friends. I've got stuff to do. In my room. With the other rabbit." With that deliberate taunt, Mackenzie dragged Neil away with her, trying not to hear her daughter make gagging noises in the background.

When they closed the door to her room, Mac checked to make sure the ferrets were still in their bed first, and then turned around and jumped on Neil. Surprised, he fell back onto the bed, grunting as her weight came down on top of him.

"Thought that was funny, did you Mr. Rabbit?" Then she started tickling him. To her delight she discovered he was highly susceptible. Suddenly a whole new avenue of fun and torment opened up for her. She was straddling him, and slowed down the strokes of her fingers, but she started to feel him harden beneath her instead. In a heartbeat the game had changed.

*   *   *

Goats, she thought. That was her first real thought after recovering enough to have any. She needed to go get goats. The day was slipping away from her again, and here she was having sex when she should be out buying goats.

"I'm a very bad prepper." He chuckled in her ear.

"Yes you are, and you should be punished for it." She swatted his arm for that.

"I don't mean I'm a naughty one, perv. I mean I'm not any good at it. If I were, the damn goats would already be here, and then I wouldn't have to feel like an idiot for lying around and having so much sex."

"Oh, *that* kind of bad prepper. I see. Well, I still think punishment might be in order. You'll have to be my love slave to make up for it. Shall I pick you up at eight?"

"Oh shut up. It's your fault I have no goats. There. You're the one who needs to be punished not me."

"I wholeheartedly agree. I'll have to be your love slave to make up for it. Shall I pick you up at eight?"

She could hardly keep a straight face anymore.

"Better make it ten. I still need goats."

"I didn't invite the goats."

"I sure hope not! I don't have those sorts of goats. In fact, I don't have any sorts of goats. Get your lazy ass out of bed. I'm gonna get my goats."

"You know what gets *my* goat?"

"Obviously it isn't me, because I'm not very good a goat-getting. I seem to have snagged a jackass, though." Mac finally managed to get off the bed and redress.

A sudden, sharp pain in her ankle made her yelp.

"Pickle! You little ankle-biter you!" She picked him up and brought him eyeball to eyeball. He was making huffy, chuckling sounds, so she just giggled.

"You're too freakin' cute. That's your problem. I can't get mad at you."

"Why thanks!"

"Not you, though it's nothing a little cosmetic surgery couldn't fix." He pinched her butt, making her yelp for the second time. She couldn't put Pickle down, because he would only nip at her ankle again. He was obviously feeling playful, and the nipping was his way of making sure someone played with him.

"Here. Play with Pickle. He needs some attention, and you've obviously got some excess energy." He looked down at his semi-nude body.

"Not *that* pickle, for cryin' out loud!"

By the time they finished messing around with the ferrets and left her room, everyone else was awake and eating cereal.

"Hey, Kirk. You ready to go get some goats?"

"You know, I have to say I honestly never thought I would hear that question, much less as it pertains to me, but sure. Why not? Let's go get the goats." Neil started laughing, and Mackenzie was beyond explaining to anyone why he thought that was so funny. She was having to keep her mouth clamped shut as it was.

Neil finally managed to regain a sober mien, so Mackenzie arranged to drop off the trailer at his place that night. Cameron couldn't resist a dig, apparently.

"So, does that mean you'll be perverts there instead of here tonight?" Mackenzie looked around for something to bean her daughter in the head with, but nothing came to hand. Billy was kind of snickering, but being subtle about it. He was obviously something of a fan of Cameron's now.

"Hey, I don't mind coming back here and playing video games

if you guys want to have some time to yourselves," Billy chimed in suddenly. Neil and Mackenzie exchanged a look. Cameron didn't even seem to notice. Then again, five years was a big difference to someone who was twenty-three.

Billy likely wasn't even on her radar, so they probably didn't have anything to worry about there. In a few years that might change. They had no way of knowing what might happen in their own relationship, much less with their kids.

Mac shrugged her shoulders at Neil, to let him know it didn't matter to her if Billy wanted to come over. In turn he looked at Cameron, Kirk and Leigh.

"It's up to you if you feel like company. You're going to be pretty tired after having to work more today." All three of them rushed to assure Billy that he was welcome, so Mac figured they must have had a good time playing into the wee hours of the morning.

She knew Cameron sometimes felt like a bit of a third wheel with Leigh and Kirk. Kirk was her best friend, but when Leigh was around she was his priority. It was only natural at that age. After twenty years of marriage that might change a bit, but for now they were still pretty into each other. At least with Billy around, Cameron would have someone to talk to if Kirk and Leigh went off to spend some time alone together.

"Well, the camping equipment is all there, if anyone wants to be outdoors tonight, or you can keep the same sleeping arrangements as last night. Cameron, just make sure you spend some time with the boys, okay? I don't think they're getting the level of attention that they're used to. Pickle nipped my ankle a few minutes ago." Cameron nodded that she would, and it wasn't exactly a hardship for her. She was almost as crazy about the little carpet sharks as Mackenzie was.

"Okay, we all need to get to work. Billy's off to the store with his dad for the afternoon. Kirk's with me and the goats." Mac tried to give a convincing glare at Neil's snort.

"And Cameron and Leigh will be putting together the goat pen in the meantime," she continued determinedly, before Neil could get her going again.

"We're going to have to set up a schedule for feeding the animals, because I forgot about the chickens until ten thirty. I don't want to stress them any further and force them into a moult. We need the eggs, and being moved seems to have affected them already."

Neil needed to get going, so Billy ran out to turn the truck around and give them a minute to say their goodbyes. Neil ran his hand down her blond hair, his thumb caressing her cheek.

"I'm going to miss you something fierce today, I think." She leaned her face into his hand.

"I know the feeling. I'm having a ridiculously hard time saying goodbye to you right now for some reason. Must be the cowboy in you." He chuckled.

"It's because you've had the cowboy in *you*," he whispered in her ear. She cleared her throat.

"That might be a factor," she admitted.

"You know how to get there tonight, right? Should be easy enough for you, since I never bothered to conceal my driveway. I knew nobody traveled that road. I may reconsider, though. Especially if Gerry finds out you're seeing me. I don't want to have to hide what you are to me, and we'll see how things go with the police and all that, but your safety is the real priority.

"Alright, I have to get going. Samantha is going to be spitting kittens if we're not there on time, and I have an errand to run this afternoon, so I need to make sure Billy's okay for the short time I'm gone. That means doing some more training. Training family members is a pain in the ass, I have to say."

Mac nodded in sympathy. She knew all about that from her attempts to have her daughter do work for her, instead of her having to work at the factory. It hadn't gone well.

"Have a good day, cowboy. I'll be thinking about you plenty, I'm sure."

"I'll definitely be thinking of you. Probably forget all about some poor customer at closing time, and lock them in the store like I'm some dreamy high-school kid. Be careful today, honey. I guarantee that kid will be even more pissed off now." He gave her a long, slow kiss, looked into her eyes for another moment, and then shook it off to walk out the door. Mac went back to the table.

"I forgot to mention to you yesterday that we need to clean out the cement mixer when we're done with it for the day. I made a mould last night for a stepping stone. If you make a couple different shapes, we can have a nice walkway. Just keep the depth consistent.

"When you rinse the mixer, dump the dirty water where the path will be, so we can keep the rest of the grass nice. We'll put in flowers in the spring to attract bees for pollination, and if we can get enough, we'll build some hives for honey. It's good for wound care, in addition to being a healthier sweetener than sugar.

"Either of you have a bee allergy?" She directed the question at Kirk and Leigh, since she already knew Cameron didn't have one. When they said they didn't, Mac continued.

"If Kirk and I aren't back by about six, please scatter some chicken feed and change out their water. Check for eggs while you're at it. Don't forget the roosters. We'll probably be back before then, but I'm heading to the land registry office in Parry Sound first. I want to see who owns the land around here. It gives us a tactical advantage if we have detailed maps. After that we're off to the goat farm."

Five minutes later, Mac and Kirk were in the truck once again, the horse trailer hitched to the back. Within half an hour they were talking to a clerk at the land registry office. There had been no line, so they were served right away. Mac got multiple copies of the maps she needed.

Since things had proceeded so smoothly, Mac decided to grab more of the basic essentials. They filled up the cargo bin again. This time she managed to find the soap base she'd been looking for, so she was content. Finally it was time to track down her elusive goats.

11

PEOPLE STARING AT GOATS

The goat rancher had chickens, too, which pleased Mac. They were Wyandotte, rather than the Sussex she'd purchased from the other farm, though both were good for egg production and harsher winters. She bought twelve, this time only getting a single rooster with the eleven hens. Kirk shook his head.

"They're going to have to create a new reality TV show called 'Chicken Hoarders' just for you."

"Funny. I'm paranoid, not a hoarder. There's a difference. I just want to be sure we have enough diversity. Another rooster could make all the difference, despite the difficulties it might cause. Then we won't have first cousins being mated later on. We can always build a second coop. I'm going to need to start a logbook for breeding.

"Neil having goats is a bonus. We can exchange bucks if we need to, at least for breeding. I think he has chickens, too. Much healthier to be able to swap roosters. Genetic diversity is going to be a serious problem down the road."

"You know, you guys are the weirdest swingers I've ever known. Instead of swapping partners, you swap chickens and goats." Now Mackenzie did laugh.

She had always liked Kirk. Cameron had tried to date him for a while, but things just weren't like that between them so they'd mutually called it off. Thankfully it didn't seem to bother Leigh. It was too bad, though. She hoped to one day have Cam marry someone she actually liked, male or female, though it looked as though Cameron leaned toward men.

Mac opened up the horse trailer and tried to judge how many goats she could safely put into it. Then she glanced back at the little things inside their pens. Maybe they were kids, though. She'd done tons of research on goats, but it was a lot different being next to them, and some were smaller than others. She couldn't tell most breeds apart yet. She'd been focusing on proper care, and which ones produced the most milk.

While she waited for the farm's owner to make her way back over to them with the flattened chicken boxes, Mac grabbed her notebook from the glove compartment of the truck, and jotted a few notes for herself about the chicken feeders they were using. She wanted to make things as simple as possible for everyone. Then she went back to the goat pen where Kirk was watching them romp.

"Neil said he moved twelve goats in that trailer, but I have no idea what size they were. Can we fit that many, do you think?" Kirk shrugged.

"Probably. You said you were planning to get that other kind, too, right? The ones with the long hair?"

"The Angora, yeah. These could be the Alpines, but I'll have to check. I don't even know if they're fully grown. They seem so small. Milk goats can give up to six litres of milk per day. The math just doesn't seem right." Rose reached them just then.

"Those Alpines will do a little less than that. I've got Saanens if you really want good milk production, but it depends on your needs. Are you looking to sell the milk, or is it just for your family?"

"We've got four of us on the property, and we were planning to get more than one goat for milk, so four to six litres from each one might be more than we can use. I also want to make lots of cheese. I particularly like the lower lactose part of the deal. I love milk, but lactose doesn't love me.

"What's really important to me is genetic diversity. I want to be sure that whatever goats I get, none of them are related to one another in any way, and I want enough to keep the ranch going for a while so I'm not line-breeding." Rose nodded her head.

"We've got many distinct lines here, so that won't be a problem. As you can see, there are hundreds of goats, and a number of different breeds. You could actually cross-breed some dairy goats, too, rather than get all the same kind."

"That's a thought. Maybe a buck and two does for each breed. I know that's a large ratio of bucks, but that diversity thing is a big deal for me. Can you take a look at the trailer to be sure I can transport them safely, and maybe give me an idea how many I can fit in there? I'll take a couple of trips if I have to. I don't want to hurt them." Rose seemed pleased that she'd be selling to someone who actually cared, so she gave what advice she could.

"That's a three-horse slant trailer, looks like, so I'd say if you're making a short trip within the area, you'd be fine with taking anywhere from nine to twelve. You could have maybe four different breeds if you wanted. How far do you need to travel?"

"Not too far. Thirty to forty-five minutes. It usually only takes about half an hour to make this trip, but that's without being particularly cautious. We're near Rosseau Falls, so we have to drive up and around Lake Rosseau. I'm sure it will still be stressful for them." Rose appeared to consider it for a moment.

"It can take a few days before they fully recover from being moved. I can give them a shot of oxytetracycline to combat shipping fever if you're worried about it, but they'll be with some of their own herd which will make a big difference there. You've already got bedding on the floor of the trailer, so there's no reason you can't take the lot of them today. It's only an issue if they're still weaning."

"Alright. I want three of them to be the Angora ones. I'll just be keeping the wool to mess around with spinning and weaving stuff, so I don't think I need those long-term. It's the dairy ones I want to be sure I have a long time. We'll start with some Alpines and Saanens, and if there's room I'd like maybe a third breed. What would you recommend for the third, considering the first two dairy breeds?"

"We have Nubians and La Mancha. Both of them have high butterfat content in their milk and are good producers, so it's really a matter of personal preference there. Why don't we take a look?"

Mac and Kirk wandered with Rose around the different pens. When it came down to a choice, aesthetics were the only things she could go by. She didn't really like the small ears of the La Manchas, and the Roman noses of the Nubians appealed to her.

She picked out the goats that looked the healthiest to her from each herd. They all had energy and bright intelligence in their eyes, and she had a fondness for animals that had brains. Of course, she knew that would also mean having to outsmart the goats more often than not, but she liked mental stimulation. They would keep her on her toes, much like the ferrets did.

She managed to finagle some milking equipment as part of the deal since she was buying so many of them. It would save them some time and effort.

There was enough room for all of the goats to lie down, including the Nubians, so off they went.

"Wow. You just spent thousands of dollars like it was nothing!" Mac shrugged, concentrating on the road so she didn't hit any potholes.

"No choice really. I pulled everything we had out of the bank, and I'm investing it in things that will soon be all that really matter. Bank balances are going to disappear, and what use are the strips of plastic we use for cash now?" Kirk looked uncomfortable.

"It's just that we've hardly contributed anything. I feel like a mooch."

"Kirk, please don't think like that. It's a huge relief to me that I'm able to bring you guys to a place where you'll be safe.

"You being with us is actually a huge help. There's so much work to be done, but it will be a lot easier with four of us doing it. With just the two of us, things would have been very hard to pull off. It's also nice to have someone tall in the place. Being short can suck sometimes." Kirk gave a quick snort.

"I haven't been your height since I was about ten years old. I don't know how you manage."

"Yuk it up. You'll get your comeuppance one day. Just you wait. You with all your tallness." They shared a laugh.

"How's Leigh doing? Why didn't you tell her she could just grab whatever food she wanted?"

"I did. She wouldn't do it if she didn't have your permission. I told her she was being an idiot, but she got all weird about it."

"You should have said something to me, then. I would have told her right away. I didn't think I had to. I mean, what was she supposed to do? Just not eat?"

"She said something about getting groceries here. We had a few things with us in the car, but that was gone before the end of the first day, and so she was really hungry by the time we had dinner last night. It didn't make sense, because whatever groceries we got weren't going to last long anyway. We weren't prepared for this in any way."

"Not independently maybe, but as a group the four of us can do this. Cameron and I need the extra hands. I've never given a damn about money. Nobody becomes anything in this world without the help of others. It takes a village, and all that..."

"Well, nobody is raising kids, but I get what you mean. I'm good with electronics and stuff, so maybe I can be a help there. I'd be better at building stuff than Leigh, but she wouldn't be a visible deterrent with that guy you're having problems with. I feel like I'm getting the easy part of all of this."

"Oh, don't worry. We have almost everything we need now, so that means we're going to be working right alongside Cameron and Leigh with all future projects on the property. We need to get the garden sorted out, so they can do that while you and I expand the goat pen. What I designed was meant for maybe six goats. I want to triple it.

"The goats will be allowed to graze later on. We'll also let the chickens out in groups then, but until we get proper fencing up we need to keep them penned at all times. We'll have to keep males and females separated except for breeding.

"The blackberry and raspberry bushes that surround the cleared section will be a huge temptation for the goats, and they'll basically clear-cut them so we end up with no berries left. I need to

152

get a fence up inside that perimeter.

"I'll have to set up the sawmill. I can completely avoid buying lumber that way. Once we've got that fence, I'm not going to need to cut down too many more trees. Mostly just for furniture."

"You're seriously going to do all that yourself? That seems like a lot of work! I mean, I'll help with whatever you need, but that's massive."

"I love carpentry. It's not so massive when you've got proper tools, either. I've got all the toys I need. Everything that's in the current building is stuff I built, except for what's obviously store-bought. I didn't make the mattresses, but I made the bed frames, futon, workbenches, and walls.

"Some jobs can be combined. You're cutting pieces of the same lengths for certain things, because there are standard measurements, like with the beds and futon. All of them are queen-size, which meant using a lot of wood cut to specific lengths. It's almost like assembly-line work then, and it can be done really fast.

"I added to that because I made the workbenches the same lengths, too. Gives me lots of space to do stuff on them later, and they're good for food prep in the meantime. More than one person can be helping in the kitchen area and have plenty of room to spread out.

"I've got giant lists of parts needed for assembling things, and then I combined those lists for any commonalities. I've pre-cut most of what's needed for the new building's interior stuff because of that. I was ridiculously anal about it, but it saved me from setting up over and over again. I just hadn't done the plans for the exterior stuff yet. There wasn't enough time."

"Hey, whatever works. I was wondering what all those weirdly-shaped piles of wood were for. I mean, the steel studs and two-by-fours I could see, along with the drywall, but there's all that smaller stuff." Mac nodded.

"The stairs and risers are cut, and all the parts that go into assembling them. There's a straight staircase as well as a spiral. There are actual kitchen cabinets, rather than what we're using now, along with the doors and countertops.

"We'll continue to use the table we're using now, and the beds and futon, but we were always going to have a third bedroom, so the extra mattress is there. I need to assemble the bed frame that's pre-cut. We just don't have room for it with everything that's stored in there.

"We stuck the third mattress up in the overhead storage, as you may have noticed when you were going through the supplies. Along with the fifty-million cases of toilet paper. I'd tell you guys to use that area for privacy, but I'm not sure enough regarding its safety. Everything we stored up there is light, except for the mattress."

"We're fine where we are for now. We can do the camping thing if we need to get away from everything for a night. It might be fun, actually. We've only been here a couple of days, so it's not like it's been long enough to feel crowded or anything."

Mac pulled into the gas station in Rosseau to top up the truck's tank. She wasn't surprised when the green Civic drove by. It was a small community and Gerry was probably unemployed. For much of the younger generation in the area, cruising was a favoured pastime. There wasn't anything else to do.

She was even less surprised when she saw the car heading back to the station a few seconds later.

"Kirk, Gerry is on his way. I'm going to pay for the gas so we can take off." As quickly as she tried to move, it wasn't fast enough. Gerry walked into the store and headed straight for her. Kirk came in behind him.

Gerry sized up Kirk and sneered.

"That your boyfriend, bitch?" The clerk behind the counter spoke up.

"Gerry, get out of here before I give you a lifetime ban. You don't talk to my customers that way."

"Fuck you, Jim. Stay outta this." Gerry walked up to Mac, violating her personal space, and stared down at her.

"You think you can get away with getting me fired? Just wait until I get you alone, bitch."

"Gerry, you do realize there's a camera in here, right? And witnesses?" Mac turned to look at the clerk.

"Jim is it?" When he nodded she continued.

"Jim, Gerry here has already been warned by the police and lost his job for harassing me. Could you please call the police?"

"Happy to." Jim had a smug look on his face. He didn't seem to like Gerry very much.

"Oh, fuck you, Jim. Don't you call the fucking pigs on me." When Jim continued to tap out the number on the cordless phone, Gerry snarled in rage and overturned a stand full of candy bars and gum.

"Hey!" The loud, sharp sound Mac made when she yelled at Gerry was very effective at getting his attention.

"Look you piece of crap. Don't ever come near me again. A restraining order will be in force, but I guarantee it'll be me that's enforcing it. Now get the fuck out of this guy's store or the three of us are going to start tearing you apart. You're a puny little shit, and it will not go well for you." Jim had already come around the counter to keep Gerry from destroying his store. Kirk was standing beside her with his fists clenched at his sides. Gerry cursed and kicked some of the chocolate bars when he slammed the glass door open. The pane cracked when it hit the railing beside it.

Mac didn't take her eyes off Gerry until his car peeled away from the station. She'd been very concerned that he might take out his anger on the goats or chickens, or even just her truck. Her fingers were stiff by the time she release the handle of her knife. She hadn't pulled it out, not wanting anyone to know she was carrying a concealed weapon, but it had been close.

She was shaking with anger as she flexed her fingers. Gerry had no idea how close he'd come to seeing her wrath up close and personal. There was a good reason she'd been keeping an eye out for a video camera.

Since they had to wait for the police now, Mac took some

pictures of the mess Gerry had left behind. She wasn't sure if they should touch the stuff, but Jim wanted to pick up the stock from the floor, so she and Kirk helped him. There was footage of what had happened anyway, so she didn't think it would matter. It was a simple vandalism issue in Jim's case.

"I'm Mac and that's Kirk, by the way," she said belatedly. Jim laughed.

"Nice to meet you. Just not under these circumstances. Sorry I couldn't get him out of the store sooner. That kid has never been anything but trouble. There's nothing wrong with the rest of the Newman clan, but that kid's like a changeling or something. He keeps getting into trouble like this, his dad's gonna wind up kicking him out. He doesn't seem to have any friends that would take him in either."

The cops arrived within fifteen minutes, so they had to have been in the area. Mac smiled when she saw the second one get out of the car.

"What is it with my old friends these days? All y'all are turning into cops!" She smirked until Gilles recognized her and let out a yell.

"Well, what the fuck are you doing here Mac? You back for good, or just visiting? And why the hell haven't I seen you before now?" Mac just grinned and walked up to give him a hug.

"You know very well I had no idea where you were. You're as bad as me! Chuck said he lost touch a long time ago, but the last he heard you were in Humphrey." Gilles nodded.

"Yup. Married, too."

"Oh my God! It's a freakin' epidemic with you guys, all this growing up and shit. So much for hanging out and drinking until dawn, eh?" Gilles laughed.

"I stopped doing that years before I met Felicia. I'd never have met her otherwise. Or at least she'd never have given me the time of day."

"I don't doubt it. Well, you're whoring days are over, I guess. Then again, we all knew that wasn't what you were looking for. God, those were the days! Anyway, your partner there is looking a bit annoyed, so I guess we should get down to business here. This is a bit more complicated than it looks."

It was another thirty minutes before all the details were out. Gilles was shaking his head at her.

"What is it about you? You're always attracting trouble."

"Very funny. I'm not putting up with victim blaming and shaming, thanks. Chuck's got the details at the Huntsville station, but I think it was someone from Parry Sound who would have visited Gerry to issue the warning." Gilles sobered.

"I'll find out and make sure this is dealt with. We don't have much use for men who pull that kind of shit around here." When the incident report was filled out, a copy was given to Jim so he could file his insurance claim for the door and the little bit of damage to his stock.

"I'm required to press charges against him now, even if you don't, Mac, so don't be surprised to get a subpoena." Mac just nodded. She knew they'd never be able to serve it to her. Gilles gave her his cell number so they could catch up at a later date, and then he and his partner had to leave on another call.

Mac drove up their driveway ten minutes later. The goats were finally home. She looked around at what had been done in their absence. The enclosure was looking good, but she realized she needed to keep the does separated from the bucks now.

Then there were the new chickens. The hens would be fine with the others, but the rooster needed a home of its own. Mac dragged her fingers through her hair and scratched vigorously at her scalp.

This was the problem when she made plans, and then kept changing them on herself. The closer they got to disaster, the more worried she became. The more worried she was, the more she tried to compensate, which resulted in more work.

There was no sign of Cameron or Leigh, so Mac figured they were inside. The garden looked like it was already done, which thrilled her. One less thing on the list. Cameron popped out of the building suddenly.

"Mom, something's happening on the news or whatever. It's trending on Facebook, and it looks major."

"Fuck. It's starting."

12

ZERO DARK SEVEN MILLION

Mac and Kirk quickly herded the goats into the small pen to graze and tied a rope back and forth around the opening. As soon as they had let the hens out of their boxes and into the chicken enclosure, Mac took off for the house and went straight to her laptop. Facebook wasn't a news source, exactly, but it pointed her in the direction she needed to go. She opened that first.

Rather than a single item trending, there were several that were related. The Greater Toronto Area, or GTA as it was called, had gone dark. It accounted for nearly half the population of Ontario. At least seven million people were without power, and there was no estimate on when it would be back up again.

The second item appeared more alarming than a power outage to anyone who didn't understand how problematic that outage was.

Looting and rioting had started in Hamilton, Oakville and Mississauga. The damage in Burlington wasn't as severe yet, but she didn't expect that to last.

Toronto was the worst. Already the police and military had been called in to do what damage control they could, but it looked like a lost cause to her. There just weren't enough cops or military police to handle millions of panicking citizens. Justin Trudeau had followed in his father's footsteps and invoked the War Measures Act, basically stripping everyone of their rights.

The third item mentioned the empty grocery store shelves, which had most likely been the impetus for the rioting and looting. The food was already gone, because they'd stopped delivering. The truckers had refused to go to a city where they knew they would end up trapped. All shipments had been rerouted to cities that still had power.

As much as she wanted to talk to Neil right then, she had another obligation. She needed to try to get Allan to come to the farm, and she'd take the opportunity to get more feed.

Mac called him and got his voicemail. As soon as he called back, she'd head to his place. It wasn't that far, since he lived in Bracebridge, but she was pretty sure things would be getting bad there very soon.

The truck was only a two-seater, so she wouldn't have room for anyone to go with her if she was going to bring him back. It was a risk she was willing to take, however, when she thought of the pain Cameron would suffer if anything happened to her dad.

Her phone rang. It was Allan.

"Hey! It's Mac. Long time no talk. Are you busy tonight?"

"Hey back! It's been years, probably, and no, I don't have any plans. Why?"

"I've got to go to the feed store so I thought I'd stop in for a quick visit."

"From Hamilton?" Mac was surprised.

"Didn't Cameron tell you we're outside Rosseau now?" She could hear him take a quick puff from a cigarette, and then cough after he finished inhaling. He had allergies and asthma, used two inhalers, and still smoked. One of many things he did that used to drive her nuts.

"Well, shit! If I'd known I'd have come and seen ya. I drive all over the place with the cab. I could've stopped in any time."

"We've only been here since Tuesday night, trying to get the farm setup finished. We've got goats and chickens now, and the garden is doing pretty well. You really should see the place."

"Holy crap! I still can't get over how close you guys are. Cameron never told me where you were. Just said something about a farm. I figured it was down south somewhere."

"I need to get going for now, but then I'll stop by. What's your address?" Allan inhaled from his cigarette, and promptly coughed once again.

"I'm on a main drag. Wellington. Hey maybe we can go shoot some pool or something. I haven't had much chance to do that lately." He gave her his house number.

"I have a pool table here. I just haven't set it up yet. I figure that's going to be a pain in the ass, but soon I'll have all the time in the world for all that anyway."

"Really? Holy shit. You always said you wanted to get one, but I never thought you'd do it." That was the other thing that had turned her away from Allan. His complete lack of faith in anything she said. He either thought she was lying, or he just didn't believe she could do it.

"I already know where Wellington is, so it's not like I'll get lost. I should be there in an hour." When she hung up a few minutes later, she saw she had chewed off part of her thumbnail. Allan was fun to hang out with, but he was annoying, too.

Thinking it through, she grabbed her phone and called Neil.

"If you haven't seen it already, check out what's happening in the GTA," she said, as soon as she heard his voice.

"I'm guessing it's bad. Hang on. I need to go back to the office computer. Give me the short and sweet version, and I'll get the details once I'm online."

"The entire GTA is dark, and nobody is saying anything about it coming back. Rioting, looting, etc. Military police are already in Toronto to support the city and provincial police."

"And so it begins," he said softly. She could tell he was looking at some of the information online, so she remained silent for a few moments, letting him read the various reports.

"God. It's so strange," she said reflectively. "You and I both believed it would happen, but now that it's starting it's so surreal.

Part of me still thinks it's not. Plus, this is Canada. We don't usually have riots. When they happen they're a very big deal."

"Yeah. I can guarantee if we check back with the news sites later, people will be dead. And I don't think it'll be one or two, either. They'll get trampled, police officers will shoot out of panic or necessity, and panicked civilians are going to be killing other people. Toronto is the fourth largest city in North America. There will be no good news tonight."

"Maybe we should rethink tonight's plan, Neil. Neither of us will want to be away from our kids. We can do what we did last night. We'll still be close enough, and everyone will have somewhere to sleep. Maybe just come over when you've done whatever you need to do at home after you close up the store. What do you think?"

"You're right. The animals don't need constant attention with the way I set things up, but I should check on them before I leave them alone again. I think we're all going to be a little shaken up, that's for sure. Billy doesn't know yet, but I'll tell him as soon as I get off the phone. He needs to know the seriousness of the situation. How are you holding up?" Mac almost burst into tears, but she managed to control it. Her voice was a little rough when she answered him, though.

"I'm definitely shaken. It's one thing to know something is coming, and another thing entirely when it shows up at your door. The entire foundation of our society just cracked, and most people won't even know that until it's too late.

"I think part of me looked forward to it, as bad as that sounds, because we've overpopulated the planet and ruined it. But now I'm mostly just scared, because things just got really dangerous for all of us. It doesn't help that I ran into Gerry again today." She filled him in.

"I'll be there in an hour," he said.

"Wait. What? Your store doesn't close until nine. You can't get here until at least nine thirty."

"Honey, the store doesn't need me. You do. I'll check on the animals and then we'll be right over, okay?"

"I wish I could take you up on that, but I have to go somewhere first. Cameron's step-dad is in Bracebridge. As far as she's concerned, he's her dad. I need to try to convince him to come back here. Cam's worried about him, and she's going to start getting frantic now. Why don't you just close your store at the usual time? I've got to go to Allan's and then stop at the feed store. I have no idea how long it'll take me to get his ass in gear, or if it's even possible."

"Alright, but as a compromise why don't you call me when you're on your way home. Then I'll close up. Okay?"

"Fair enough. I'll talk to you then."

When they ended the call the tears that were burning in her eyes rolled down her cheeks.

She hadn't known until that moment what it would feel like to have absolute faith in someone. She was not the kind of woman who leaned on a man for support, but then she'd never found one she *could* lean on. It didn't make her feel weak or stupid. It made her feel like she was a part of something that built her up and made her stronger. Now, when the world was starting to fall apart, she'd been given an incomparable gift.

She was seeing what he was like under stress far sooner than she'd expected, and it hadn't changed anything for her. She believed in him. There was something so solid and steady about him, and he was making her a priority.

He'd been willing to drop everything. For her. That might not have seemed like a big deal to most people. She didn't know. Maybe they already had that in their lives, but for her it was a brand new experience. Having someone who had her back when it mattered most was almost devastating in its poignancy.

Mackenzie wiped her eyes and smiled. She needed to go soon, but she still had animals and three young adults to deal with. She was about to head out to join them, and thought better of it. She had two more phone calls to make.

She called Mitch first. She knew she wouldn't get an answer, but it still shook her when the mailbox was full. She couldn't even leave him a message. He might still be able to charge his phone in his car, but there was a good possibility he'd already run out of gas.

Her next call was to Ian. He was her closest friend, with the possible exception now of Neil. He lived outside Cleveland, and they hadn't been in touch since she'd left Hamilton. He didn't pick up, either, but she left a message for him to call her back.

She'd probably hear back from Ian later that night, if he still had a working phone. If not she was going to have to get on the radio and try to contact him that way. She wanted to make sure he was okay. She'd been storing the radio in a Faraday box to protect it from potential EMPs for as long as they didn't need it. It looked like it was time to pull it out and set it up, though. The internet could go down soon, and they needed their communications set up so they could find out what was going on in the rest of the world.

Mackenzie went back to her laptop and checked the hours for the feed store. They were open until seven, so she had plenty of time to see Allan first. By the time she went for the feed she'd know how much of the truck and trailer she could fill with it.

She did a quick search on Cleveland to check their news sites. Only some minor outages so far, so she figured Ian was probably just busy with his usual crazy schedule.

Kirk, Leigh, and Cameron were crowding around Leigh's MacBook at the table. Every one of them looked terrified. She didn't blame them. It was probably for the best that she was interrupting them. She cleared her throat to announce her presence. They all looked up at her, and she realized they were going to need reassurances from her.

"I know you're worried. One of the best cures for fear is information. Not only are we going to keep up with the news in the rest of the world, but we've got a zillion books on how to do everything we might need to do.

"If you know exactly how to grow food and take care of

livestock, then you won't be afraid of starving. We could probably support twenty people just on what we've got set up now, and we'll improve on that. When the shit hits the fan, and we're surrounded by people who are starving, I'm going to do what I can to help them, but it will be done quietly. If people find out what we have here, we're screwed.

"Before we all head off to our different tasks, there's one thing I should mention now. There's no way for us to know how things will shake out around here, so we need to be prepared for the possibility that law enforcement will no longer exist. I'm sure you realize I'm not happy to say that, since I now know of two friends who are cops.

"They may just decide to go and protect their families, so it won't necessarily mean anything bad. It'll just mean we're on our own when it comes to self-defense. We'll need to get the rest of our sensors set up, and then have them turned on at all times. If someone steps onto the property, we can warn them off.

"Once people stop being able to use their cars, we won't be able to run ours except in an emergency. Things will be very quiet. A car can be heard from miles away, and people will come looking for it. We'll need to insulate this building and run power tools indoors, too.

"I'm going to try to spend some time with Neil tonight, looking over the land registry maps for this area. I want to know who our neighbours are, what kind of set-up they might have, and what kind of threat they pose. I'm hoping Neil knows something about them, though he might have kept to himself out here. I'll find out soon enough. He's bringing Billy here in a few hours.

"Plans for tonight have changed a bit. Neither of us wants to leave you guys alone for the night right after getting this kind of news. I think we're all pretty shaken. We knew this would happen, but seeing it happen is different."

"I'll say," Cameron spoke up. "I don't exactly like people, generally speaking, but it's still scary, and it won't be fun to watch."

"An abstract wish that the rest of human civilization would just go away, doesn't look anywhere near as attractive when you have to watch the actual suffering take place. Believe me, I know how you're feeling right now.

"Okay, there's not much point in continuing to rehash this. It's happening, and we need to make sure we finish setting up. We need a second goat pen a fair distance away from the first. Believe it or not, the smell of the bucks can ruin the milk, and it'll get worse when they're in rut."

"We need to set up food and water troughs, and they need to be high enough that they can't piss or shit in them." Mac looked around at her three partners-in-crime.

"Man, am I ever glad I'm not doing this alone. Cameron's stuck with me, but you two are far more welcome here than you realize. I promise, the workload isn't going to be like this forever. It'll never be a vacation, exactly, but if there's a way I can get rid of a chore, believe me I'll implement it as quickly as possible. Hopefully we'll each find stuff we enjoy doing out of all this work, so it won't seem so bad. Better than starving, though."

Mac pulled out the maps from the land registry office, and spread them on the table. Leigh closed her MacBook and moved it onto her lap out of the way.

"I made a bunch of copies of the map that details this property. This gives us the boundaries, where Google Maps and Google Earth can't tell me that. This should help us plan any future buildings. This side of the river is actually a pretty small section of our land, and my original plans call for most of the buildings to be here, if not all.

"However, if I'm right and Neil's property backs onto this one, we have nothing to worry about when it comes to protecting that side. Leaving aside the little detail that I wouldn't be messing around with him if I thought he was like that, there's the fact that he made his own preparations well in advance of ours. He's not going to be stealing other people's food."

Mac picked up the papers and fanned through them until she found the one she was looking for.

"Yes! I gotta say, we got lucky here. We already live in an area where people tend to have gardens and livestock, so that helps in the grand scheme of things, but this is a major bonus. Holy shit. His property is huge. The river bends just past our parcel, and then runs through the entire length of his. We can use the river to get there. I should buy a couple canoes.

"We need to build a bridge anyway. It's a good way to block off river traffic, or at least monitor it. It's easy to swim across the river for small stuff, like when I planted the willow saplings, but if we have to move anything big over there, or try to build on that section, we need a bridge."

She scanned the various maps, looking at the path the river took, checking property ownerships to see if there might be a threat from that direction. There were five unknowns, really. One on each side of them, and then three across the road. Neil's property covered their back side completely. Without Neil's help, however, she was spit-balling regarding the other owners, so she went back to a copy of the map for her own property.

"Those arches you've seen outside, stacked on their sides, are for a building forty by eighty feet. The peak reaches eighteen feet, which allowed me to plan a couple of upstairs rooms, so it's certainly going to be big enough for all of us. The building we're in now is only twenty by sixty. I intended to store the vehicles in here, but I'm debating now.

"That's the extent of the material we have for steel buildings. Everything else we put up is going to be a wood structure by necessity, unless we buy some garden sheds at the hardware store today or something. There's no way I can order another big building. These two took a while to be made, and then had to be airlifted in because the road was too narrow.

"We should probably get what we can today. Goats need shelter, and I'm already really fucking tired. I'm probably too old for this shit." That got a chuckle out of the three younger people at the table.

"Laugh now. One day you'll be on this end with a bunch of kids laughing at you," she asserted, smirking at them.

"Mac, we've got about five thousand on us. We didn't have much. Even our credit cards had pretty small limits. Throw that in with whatever you've got left. I mean, you spent more than that on goats today. It's the least we can do." Kirk pulled everything out of his wallet, and Leigh grabbed her purse to do the same.

"It'll help," Mac said. "I would rather you weren't giving me everything you have left, but I know it'll be far more valuable spent on supplies than sitting in someone's pocket. It won't be long now before it's worthless.

"My plans have changed a bit for the rest of the afternoon. I'm going to the feed store. Kirk, you'll have to stay here for this trip. I'm hoping to convince Cam's dad to come back here with me, so I'm stopping in to see him first. There's only room for two in the truck. I will not be going unarmed, so even if I run into any trouble, I've got it handled. I'll risk the possibility of having to deal with Gerry myself, but I won't risk Cam's dad starving to death if there's any way I can help it."

"Thanks, mom," Cameron said quietly. Mac could see the worry on her face.

"He probably won't want to come, and there isn't much I can do to sway him, so I can't make you any promises. I can give him directions, but it's a long walk if he runs out of gas. Well, we'll see what happens. Let's get our shit done so one day we can actually stop and breathe for a while."

13

Nostalgia and Gerrymandering

Mac put a bucket of water in with the goats for the time being. They already had grass to eat, but she tossed in some green hay to make sure they were okay. They would have to provide elevated troughs for food and water later.

Cameron moved the rooster partition and added another one, so she could get the new rooster settled in, while Leigh and Kirk started on a second goat pen. Mac decided to deal with the gates when she got home, and instead left for Allan's place.

The first thing Allan did when she got there was ask her if she wanted a beer. Mac smiled at him. He hadn't changed a bit. She was happy to accept it, though. It had already been a long day. They sat and chatted sociably for a little while before Mac brought up the reason for her visit. As she expected, he had no intention of going anywhere.

"Power is fine. Even if it goes down they'll get it fixed. Whatever is happening in Toronto doesn't mean jack shit up here. Just like when we lose power, it doesn't hit them."

No matter what arguments she presented, he didn't budge. There was no way he was coming back to the farm with her that night, though he promised to come for a visit if he was out that way with his cab.

"Allan, try to keep your fuel tank full if nothing else. Once you see them run out of fuel here, you might start to think differently about all this. If you change your mind, here's the directions. You'll need them anyway, if you plan to visit. The only problem is, you're not going to be able to see the damn driveway. Everything is concealed.

"If you get to the exact mileage I've written down in the directions, just walk onto the property. The sensors will cover a pretty big range once we have them set up in the next few days, so we'll be alerted that you're there. Expect a possibly-armed welcoming committee. If the cameras are in range, we'll know it's you, but if you're off on the mileage or something you might come in on an area that the cameras don't cover."

"Jesus, Mac. Getting a little paranoid in your old age, don't you think?"

"Bite me." He laughed.

"No way. I tried that once. Your reaction wasn't what I was hoping for. I'm still not sure my balls ever recovered."

"That's what you get for trying it while I was sleeping. I'm glad to see you learned your lesson. Alright. Even if you're not coming back with me, I'd still better get going. I really do hope I'll see you there one day. Once the pool table is set up, I'd love to shoot some rounds with you. It's been a long time. Some canasta would be good too. I can't find anyone else to play it with me, and I've forgotten the damn rules!"

"I'll come by." Mac gave him a hug as she was leaving, wondering if she'd ever see him again.

"Look, Allan, if you start to see signs that I'm right, and you don't have the gas to get to the farm, buy all the groceries you can and pack up some shit so you're ready to go. When the shit really hits the fan, I'll come back and check up on you. I've got fuel stockpiled with stabilizers added to it. I'll be mobile for a long time after everyone else runs out.

"You'll have to come back with me if that happens, because Cameron is already worried about you. Once she knows you've got no power, gas, and probably food, she's going to lose her mind. Okay?"

"Yeah, yeah. Get going. And tell Cameron I'm fine." Mac waved farewell as she climbed into the truck. She was glad she'd waited to go to the feed store until after seeing Allan. This way she'd be able to fill up both the truck bed and the trailer with green hay and everything.

When she was fully loaded she called Neil to let him know when she'd be home.

"Did he take you up on your offer of free room and board?" Mac had to laugh, since the hard work made the term 'free' a little bit loose.

"No, the stupid bastard did not. Drives me bonkers to see these people just stick their heads in the sand. I don't know how it is they can't see what's happening right in front of them."

"Well, that's the vast majority of the population, honey. As long as they're able to sit in their homes and watch TV, they think nothing is wrong. It's when that television no longer has an output that they go nuts." Mac sighed.

"When you're right, you're right. Okay, I should be there soon. God, I can't wait to see you. I've been going nuts all day thinking about you, and it only got worse with everything that happened this afternoon."

"Same here, honey. I'll probably get there about an hour after you. I'll see you then." Mac pressed the button on her steering wheel to end the call.

She was almost home when she saw the green Civic behind her. She'd gone back to the feed store in Huntsville, so she'd taken Aspdin road west from there. Now she was supposed to head south from Rosseau to get to the farm. Instead she took 141 west until she was able to turn south onto Clear Lake Road, which led her back to the main road heading toward Bala. *Right back where we started*, she thought.

It wasn't until she checked her phone and saw that she had no signal that she got a bit nervous. She wasn't sure if the cell towers were down, or if he had a signal jammer, but both possibilities re-sulted in the same issue. All he had to do was steal her phone if she managed to do anything with it.

It wasn't long before she had her answer regarding his plans for her. He pulled up alongside the trailer and slammed into it, jarring the truck a bit. Then he sped up and came up level with her rear wheels.

Mac was astonished that he would think his tiny little car could cause her real problems. She supposed if she didn't know how to deal proactively with an attempt to run her off the road, his maneuvers might be bothersome, but that was about it. As it was she slowed a bit and took the opportunity to steer into him, shoving him across the oncoming traffic lane. She managed to plow him off the road and straight into a tree.

She slowed the truck to a stop and got out, her gun in its holster nestled in the small of her back. Tucked in to the left of it, was the sheath of her knife. Her phone was discreetly concealed as well, though she had turned on the voice recorder. She might not be able to transmit, but she'd damn well record this conversation. Or part of it at any rate.

Her legs felt a bit shaky as she walked back towards the Civic. The front end was totalled. Hardly surprising considering the speed at which they had both been travelling. She walked cautiously around to the driver's side of the car. Mac could see the partially-deflated air bag in front of Gerry. She stepped forward and yanked open the door.

"Yo, shithead. You awake in there?" A groan came from the seat behind the wheel. She pulled out her knife and slashed at the airbag to get it away from his face. He seemed fine, except for the scrapes from his impact against the airbag.

"We need to have a little talk Gerry, so shake your head and listen up. You want to tell me why you thought it was necessary to try to run me off the road? Maybe you'd like to explain to the cops again, what you're doing following me and jamming my cellphone signal? I assume you realize those are highly illegal in this country." She had noted the presence of the jammer on the floor.

"Fuck you. I don't give a fuck if it's illegal. Now you're gonna pay for wrecking my fucking car, bitch." He tried to open his seatbelt, but apparently it had jammed.

"Get me outta here, ya cunt. I know you've got a knife. I saw it."

"I don't think so. You can just stay in there and hope it's not the cops who find you like this. That jammer violates federal law, not just local or provincial. Only feds are supposed to have them, and you sure as fuck don't qualify. Hmm. Maybe I should get my friends from the OPP to come and assess the scene. What do you think?"

"Fuck you."

"Wow. You truly have a way with words. No wonder the girls are falling all over themselves, trying to get into your pants." Her sarcasm obviously hit its mark, because he started trying to force his way through the seatbelt, jerking his body against it in his fury.

"I'm gonna fucking kill you if you don't get me out of this car right fucking now!"

"Uttering death threats. The hits just keep on comin', don't they? You really are a stupid motherfucker. I won't even have to bother reaching in and turning off that jammer, because I can walk away and drive out of range. Assuming you still have a working cell phone in there, you'll have to turn off the jammer to use it. Looks like you can't reach it from there, though.

"Thankfully there are no 'duty to rescue' laws in Canada like they have in France. I'm perfectly free to walk away and leave you here to rot. Especially considering the fact that you've already threatened to kill me. I wouldn't let you out now, even if it were a crime not to help you."

"You fucking cunt. I just wanted to fuck you before, which was better than you deserved. You shoulda just let me have my due, but now I'm gonna have to kill you when I'm done with you." By that point he had managed to pull out a pocket knife, and had started sawing away at the belt webbing. Mac turned off the recorder on her phone. No point in allowing the data to embed where it might be retrieved some day. Then she pulled the Glock from its holster, and pulled the slide back to chamber a round. She aimed it at Gerry and rested her finger alongside the trigger guard. Then she whistled sharply to get his attention.

"I think you should probably calm down, Gerry. Bullets are not something with which you should fuck. They tend to be somewhat faster than the average human." The stupid bastard decided to sneer at her.

"Look who's breaking the law now."

"Really? You sure about that? Occasionally a citizen is given authorization to carry if there is a verified threat to a person's life, based on a law enforcement officer's confirmation that they can't provide adequate protection. Seeing as two of my oldest friends are OPP constables, you can see where it might be possible that I would, indeed, have an ATC.

"Now, fold up that pocket knife, Gerry. That's it. Now toss it over here by me." He complied, in his own way, attempting to throw it at her head. From his seated position, however, it didn't accomplish much.

"You know, Gerry, just when I think I've seen the dumbest that life has to offer, someone comes along and changes my mind. You currently hold that record. Now, you've managed to saw through some of that webbing, so you should be able to break out of that seatbelt given enough time and effort. I just have no intention of being around when that happens.

"I told you this afternoon that I'd be the one enforcing any re-straining order, not the cops. The next time you come after me, I will not hesitate to put a bullet in you. You're a clear and present threat to my continued existence as far as the law is concerned. Your problem is that nobody realizes I'm more of a threat than you are. You know nothing about me, and going after someone you don't know is just stupid. This wouldn't be the first time I've had to protect myself, and as you can see, I'm the one who's still alive.

"Later Gerry," she sang out, as she backed away from him. Even when she had to head up the slight incline to the road, she didn't turn around until her heels touched the gravel. She pulled the slide back half-way, dumped the bullet into her hand, and re-holstered the weapon. When Mac got to her truck, she stored her weapon as per government requirements, removing the magazine, and installing the trigger guard. She put the knife in the moulded pocket of the driver's side door, just in case.

Technically speaking, she shouldn't have even had the gun with her. If it was found in her vehicle, she was in some major shit. She had authorization to transport only, and in Canada that meant going to and from a shooting range or competition, going by the most direct route possible. Nothing else.

All of what she'd told Gerry was the truth, so far as it went. She certainly hadn't told him she had an ATC. Only that it was plausible, and she was more than happy to let him go on thinking she would always be armed. In the near future that would be the case anyway.

Now she was stuck trying to figure out what to do about the collision. She had damage to her vehicle that would match the paint scrapes on the Civic. If he chose to whine about being knocked off the road, it would put her on the defensive. Not a position she intended to be in.

She could talk herself out of anything he might say about a gun, and she had the recording to prove his threats this time. It was entirely possible she *could* get authorization to carry at this point, if they didn't arrest the little shit.

Not that she really believed there would be time to process it. By the time she got approval for something like that, she could already be dead if she bothered to wait for it. One would hope the exceptions could be expedited. If not, it made the exceptions pointless.

She was going to have to contact Gilles. Maybe he could get someone out there right away so they could find the jammer. It was a serious violation of the Radiocommunication Act, and under normal circumstances she would hope it meant a long prison term. As it was, she was only doing it to keep her own ass out of the sling until such time as the sling no longer existed.

It had taken her a lot longer to get home than she'd planned for, what with the scenic drive and the incident with Gerry, so she didn't have much time before Neil would be there. She needed to call Gilles right away, and then let the kids know what was going on. They sure as hell didn't need this right now, but then nobody ever needed a psycho following them around.

Gilles tried to press her on meeting her at her place for a statement, but Mac promised him she would head to Parry Sound to deal with it as soon as possible. She sent him the recording to corroborate her phone statement, mollifying him somewhat. At first he'd been a little pissed at her for leaving the scene, until she told him about the cell jammer. She blatantly lied about the level of the threat she felt to her safety, seeing as she only mentioned the knife she had on her.

"I did tell him that if he came anywhere near my house he would be meeting Mr. Glock," she said, knowing that if he brought up a gun she was covered. They weren't going to take his word over hers. Not only was she friends with a cop, but he was already on file as being a threat to her.

"You want me to try for an authorization to carry for you? I might be able to swing it." Mac smiled. It was good to have friends.

"Not sure if it would do much good. They don't give a lot of those out, but maybe. Up to you." Mac knew it wasn't likely she would get it, but Gilles probably felt he should try to do something to help protect her, or help her protect herself. She gave him her licensing information so he could get the process started, just in case there was time to put it through. She did prefer to do things legally when possible, though she wasn't above an illegal maneuver or two.

As soon as she got off the phone with Gilles, she called in the other three and explained the situation to them.

"He's fucking insane!" This was Kirk's unbridled opinion, which Mac happened to agree with to some extent, though it wasn't something that would fall under the legal definition of insanity. He was lucid enough to understand the difference between right and wrong. He knew the rules, but he was obviously of the opinion he should be exempt from them.

That feeling of entitlement was endemic to the last few generations. In her case, Gerry felt entitled to a body that belonged to her, and she'd be damned if she gave him even a shred of it.

The other three continued to chat amongst themselves. It wasn't until she heard Cameron say something about hunting the guy down and making sure he wasn't a problem, that Mac stepped into the fray.

"No. That's not an option at this point. Gilles is going to try to get me authorization to carry, because there's a threat to my life that's on record. His statement that the cops can't provide adequate protection, seeing as we live way out in the middle of nowhere, might do the trick. That's assuming the ATC can be obtained before the shit hits the fan. I doubt it. I intend to have my Glock with me at all times anyway, legal or not. If it happens that I get the permit, it'll just make things cleaner.

"The last thing we want is to go after him when he and I have a known conflict. If he turns up dead, this is the first place they'll come looking. I know you're a little bloodthirsty, and I appreciate the sentiment, but it will bring down trouble on us in more ways than I can count. I'm trying to keep the police away from this place, along with everyone else. Gilles and Chuck are the only ones I would trust, and I won't even let *them* come here right now.

"Later, when things get bad I'll be happy to have them here, along with their families, but until then forget it. Their loyalties need to be to their jobs for the time being."

Her phone beeped, indicating a text.

"Okay, Neil's going to be at the gate in a minute. Before I forget, from this point forward you don't go anywhere without your knives. Whether it's on the property or not. We're on the verge of instability now, and...people are assholes," she said, nodding at Kirk to acknowledge his favourite expression.

"I'll be back in a bit."

14

ACCESS GRANTED

Mac ran down to the gate, anxious to get to Neil. Despite the surface composure she'd shown in front of Cameron, Kirk and Leigh, she wasn't feeling the least bit calm. She knew she should be worried about her sudden need for a shoulder to lean on, but couldn't bring herself to care. When the world was falling apart, and an ass-wipe psycho wanted to rape and kill you, a person was entitled to momentary weaknesses.

She thumbed the plate and then climbed in his truck once he'd pulled through the gate. He'd needed to bring the truck to take home his horse trailer, but it would be useful if he agreed to go with her to the hardware store later to get some sheds.

They were flat-packed if she remembered right, but even then she wasn't sure if she could fit more than one or two in the truck bed. She'd have to remove the cargo container as it was. She did have the supply trailer, though. The horse trailer could hold a few, too.

She remained silent until Billy had gone into the house to join the others. Neil seemed to be feeling the same thing, because he didn't say a word either. When they got out of the truck, Mac grabbed his hand, pulling him toward the river and out of sight of the house. Of one mind they stepped into each other's arms and just held on tight for a long time. Finally she leaned back a little to look at him.

"You just don't know. I can't even begin to tell you what it's like for me to have someone do what you've done."

"Hold you?" She shook her head.

"No. Well, sort of. It was that you offered to come running when I needed you. I haven't needed people too many times in my life, because I learned pretty early on that they couldn't be counted on to be there. My marriages were *not* a team effort. More like a competition, with both people trying to satisfy their own needs first. Never backing one another up. I couldn't trust them," she said simply.

"Ah. Well then. You know better with me."

"I do, yes."

"Not only *will* I be there, honey, but I *want* to be. I never want you to feel alone like that again. I'd rather you came to me than be hurt or scared, because knowing you felt that way would be painful for me. You matter to me, Mac. You're important to me, to my life, my future."

"I can see that. Obviously you've become important to me, too, because I never, ever turn to anyone the way I have with you. I just don't open myself up like that." She let out a deep sigh and leaned back into him.

"I've got other news, too. Ran into Gerry again, and it was a really nasty situation this time. If you'll look at the side of my truck and trailer you'll see that he tried to run me off the road. Good thing I didn't have your trailer with the goats inside it. Not only would the goats have been hurt, but your trailer would have been damaged."

"Like I would give a fuck about a trailer. That pissant, fuck-face son of a bitch!" She put her fingers over his mouth.

"Let me tell you the rest of it. He's going to be in serious trouble, I think, seeing as he had a jammer in his car. I made a recording of him threatening to kill me. His car is totalled, which is what happens when you put a Honda Civic against a big ol' four-by-four where the owner is happy to run you off the road in return. Truck wins, car meets tree."

She filled him in on the rest of the details. He still looked like he wanted to annihilate the guy, but he calmed down a little bit when he found out how well she'd taken care of the problem on her own. She knew he appreciated her self-reliance, despite the fact that his protective instincts were lit up like a Christmas tree. Then she filled him in on Gilles' offer to try and obtain an ATC.

"I doubt he'll get it in time." Mac nodded her agreement.

"Not likely, no, but if the application is in process, if I'm caught with a handgun it might be forgiven. I'll just try hard not to get caught with one. I lied to him, though. I couldn't put that on him where he would have to decide between his job and his friend. Well, also to protect myself, because I wouldn't blame him for throwing me in jail. It wouldn't be easy for him, but he might do it. I'll tell him later, when he no longer has his badge on. I hate lying to my friends."

"Well, I'd say you're justified under these circumstances. You're trying to protect yourself in the best possible way.

"So, you had a pretty shitty trip this afternoon then. First Cam's dad says he's not interested in coming here, and then Gerry. Any serious damage to your truck and trailer?"

"No. Dumbass cucumber-fucker." Neil laughed at her cursing.

"That's a new one."

"I doubt it. Plenty of cucumber fuckers out there. Women and men who don't have the courage to go to a sex shop for a dildo, usually." Neil raised his eyebrow at her in question. She snorted.

"Don't look at me. I don't bother trying to hide the fact that I enjoy orgasms on a regular basis. The most uptight people are the ones who have something to hide. Like male politicians who are anti-gay, and they're found with another man weeks after they've shot down civil rights legislation. I always suspect the most vocal anti-whatevers to actually be doing in deep, dark secret whatever they're campaigning against.

"The upshot of today's most recent entanglement is that I'm

going to Parry Sound on Monday to make a statement. I don't need that shit. I need to be doing shit around *here*. Maybe I can slip in some body work to fix the damage. If not, I can hammer it out and paint it myself, but it'll look like shit. I don't want it rusting, though."

Neil suddenly started laughing, which Mac figured was a strange reaction, so she looked around. There was a goat standing about five feet away. She joined in laughing.

"If she thinks I'm sharing you, she's going to be very disappointed."

"I don't know, Mac. She's pretty attractive. Ouch!" She'd pinched his ass in response to his remark.

"Sadly it looks as though our little bit of privacy comes to a close. Goats have needs. And far too much curiosity for their own good I think. Time to finish getting them settled. I didn't have a chance to find a way to lock them up properly. It looks like the rope I'd wrapped and criss-crossed around the opening didn't cut it. Hopefully this is the only one that's wandered out."

"I doubt it. They tend to follow each other once one of them demonstrates a successful escape."

They had to round up three others and convince them to go back through the opening in the enclosure.

"Why don't you finish building the gate, and I'll stand guard here?" Mac snorted.

"I'm not sure if I should trust you alone with such attractive specimens. God knows what I'll find when I get back." Neil laughed and shooed her away.

"Go on. I'll behave."

"Uh-huh." She flashed a smile over her shoulder and went inside to grab what she needed.

"Alright, you guys. We had some escapees, so we need to deal with the gates. Neil's making sure no more slip out for the time being. Once we get them all properly housed, we'll go get some sheds."

Mac was pleased to see Billy heading out with them. He seemed like a good kid. Having Neil for a father had done him a lot of good, whatever influence his mother might have had. When she got back outside, Billy was ready to work right alongside the others, not even questioning it.

Leigh and Cameron were building feed troughs for the goat pens, while Mac finished the gate for the first one, showing Billy and Kirk what to do for the second. Neil helped her install hers when it was done. Doing manual labour beside him was an interesting feeling, she realized. They were working as a team, and there was none of the bitching she was used to.

There was, however, the distraction of standing so close to him. Every once in a while their eyes would lock, and she wanted to jump on him. The proximity of the younger generation was the only thing that kept her in check. She was pretty sure it was the same for him, because the expression on his face was making her heart pound.

"You guys don't need to help us, you know. It's not really your problem or responsibility. Billy's obviously a good kid, though. He never even hesitated. He just expected to help, and jumped right up to do so. That's not typical for that age."

"He is a good kid. He's always been helpful. Any time he was around me, whenever I was doing something he always wanted to be doing it with me. If I'd allowed him to, he'd have been working in the store a long time ago, but I wanted him to have time for fun.

"His little bit of rebellion ended once he moved in with me, really. I think he just wanted his mother to pay attention to him. He worked with me to set up our cabin and all that stuff. We've been working on it for years, a bit at a time, until we had enough to get us through anything."

"You must be sick of all the set-up, though. You've earned a break and the time to enjoy what you have. I don't want you to feel like you have to do it all again."

"Mac," he warned, the flash in his eyes backing it up. "What did I tell you not half an hour ago?" For some reason everything in her softened to mush at his anger. She stroked his face, her thumb brushing his bottom lip.

"Okay, cowboy. My lack of experience with people who are truly interested in helping someone else is my issue to deal with. Sorry. I'll try not to be an asshole again. In that way at least. I can't guarantee anything otherwise."

Mac had no idea how it happened, but she was suddenly sitting on the top rail of the goat pen with Neil's mouth on hers, their tongues tangling. Instinctively her legs wrapped around his waist.

"Oh, Gawd. Stahhpp! My eyes. I cannot un-see this." Mac just waved a vague hand at her daughter, not giving a damn. Cameron snorted in disgust.

"How do you expect us to get any work done while we're gagging over here? I doubt the goats will want puke on their gate. Hell, the *goats* will probably throw up." The other three were laughing.

So much for romance, she thought, as Neil slowly pulled away from her, panting.

"I am not turning around right now to look, for what's probably a far-too-obvious reason, but has our audience gone back to work now?" Mac nodded and tried not to laugh.

"You're mighty purty when you're angry, though, cowboy." He snorted in her ear.

"John Wayne you are not. A fact for which I'll be eternally grateful." He picked her up off the rail and set her on her feet, deliberately at a bit of a distance from him.

"Now, let me clarify this for you. The world is about to go to shit. Are we agreed on that?" Mac nodded hesitantly.

"Alright, so follow me here. You paying attention, Mac?" She nodded again, abruptly, her own anger starting to rise.

"You're not ready, and that means you're vulnerable. Things can still go wrong for you. Your garden's a bit sickly because you weren't here to look after it, and you need this crop to survive if you want to have enough food to get through winter, as well as the seeds you'll need to re-plant your garden in the spring. You need your livestock to make it through the winter. You need a proper roof over your head, seeing as your current building has no insulation." Her shoulders sagged. He was right.

"You're overwhelmed with stress that you're pretending isn't under the surface," he continued relentlessly. "You're taking on the responsibility of everyone around you. From the plans I'm seeing around here, you're setting up something that could take care of a lot more than just the four of you.

"I'm not trying to tell you that you shouldn't help anyone else. It's who you are, and exactly the woman I admire so much, but you need some help. Not just the help of three twenty-somethings who don't know what they're doing. You need someone who cares just as much about your emotional and mental needs, as they do about your physical survival.

"You can walk away from *us*, and tell me to piss up a rope if you want, but so long as we're together I'm going to be *that guy*. If you accept me in your life, you have to accept that I need to give you what you need. I can't be anything else."

Mac looked away when her eyes burned.

"Honey, I'm not trying to shame you. Don't look away from me. I'm not trying to be right, or make you feel bad. You've done everything right. You're not wrong in anything you're doing. You're only wrong in what you're saying to me about me not needing to help you. I absolutely *do* have to do this. This is an extreme situation we're all facing. I can see how capable you are, and that you wouldn't need help if you weren't facing this kind of timeline."

"You done now?" He nodded with that damned twinkle in his eye again.

"Let me just correct one little misconception on your part there, cowboy. The garden may be sickly, but I've got a zillion back-up seeds and enough food to get us all through the winter even if none of the animals or vegetables produce anything edible. Our dry food and canned-good shelves are very well stocked, buster. And I've rescued sicker gardens than this one."

"I stand corrected then." The smirk on his face had her digging a finger into his ribs.

"Since you're mister helpful, help me unload all this feed and follow me to the hardware store. We'd just decided to buy some sheds before I left to get the feed and try to bring Allan back here. I might need your truck bed."

"My bed is always at your disposal."

"I'll bet. Hook up your horse trailer while you're at it. The more sheds we can get, the better. I have a feeling we're going to need them."

Mac checked to make sure her weight hadn't jostled the posts in the cement. It was pretty fast-drying stuff, but wasn't supposed to be load-bearing for about four hours. There was a small gap between the post and the cement now, which gave her another excuse to poke him.

"You said something about helping me? Fix those posts, would you? Seeing as you're the one who tossed me up there."

"Bossy. I like it. Gives me an excuse to toss you back up on the rail, just to prove I'm still a man." Mac sidled away from him warily, before risking another poke at his ego.

"You just do as you're told, mister. I won't have any backtalk from you on the job." He raised his eyebrow at her, and then moved too fast for her to dodge him.

"Not the rail this time," she yelped.

"Alright." He tossed her over his shoulder instead and smacked her ass.

"Hey! We've got work to do. Don't go getting me all excited with a spanking when we don't have time to follow through." Neil started laughing again and put her back on her feet.

"Not the response I was expecting from you, but one worthy of closer inspection."

"Uh, just kidding?" He looked at her face.

"We'll have to see I guess. Later."

"Much later, like maybe never. As in, 'Never, because I'm going to dump hair removal cream into your shampoo if you ever try it.' That kind of never."

"That's a hell of a threat, and most men would back down after that, but I'm not most men, honey. I think I'm going to have some fun with you." Mac planted her hands on her hips.

"You've already had plenty of fun with me. Get your ass in your truck so we can get this shit finished."

"Correction: I haven't begun to have my fun with you yet. I've got a lifetime of fun planned for you, and I haven't even dipped my toe into the water as far as I'm concerned." Mac groaned. She was feeling a great deal of sexual frustration at the moment, and there was going to be a long wait before any of that frustration could be eased.

Instead of retorting, Mac just spun on her heel and let the others know they were going to be leaving, while Neil fixed the little problem he'd created with the fence posts.

When they got to the hardware store she kept looking around, but didn't see Gerry. They managed to get six eight-by-ten sheds for just under five grand, so Mac decided to get a couple that could be used as single-car garages.

The young woman working the checkout was a little surprised when Mac handed her cash, and she had to call the manager over to double-count the hundreds, just to be safe. It was the same manager she'd spoken with about Gerry, and so Mac got the same discount she had the last time.

When the discount was entered and the money was finally accepted, the manager asked if she could speak with her. She happily complied. They stepped away from the till, Mac holding the receipt for the sheds she'd have to drive around to the side of the store to pick up.

"I wanted to apologize to you. I didn't fire Gerry when the first incident happened, because I thought it was possible it was a mis-understanding. I didn't really believe it was, but I had to be sure. I'm glad you sent that message. It gave me a fully justifiable reason to let him go. I know his dad, and it was a relief to know I could give him a good reason for the termination. He hasn't asked, so I assume he knows something about the situation already?"

"He does. A friend of mine let him know, and I'm sure another friend of mine, one with a badge, paid him a visit the same day. The kid doesn't know me, but I do know people in the area. He's actually caused problems since then, and either he's been arrested, or they're looking for him. If you see him you might want to let the police know. He could be angry with you, too, so you should be careful."

"I will be. Thanks for letting me know. I hope you'll be careful, too. Do you need these sheds delivered?"

"I've got a friend with a pick-up and trailer, in addition to mine. We'll be fine, but thanks. For everything. I knew what the situation was when you didn't let him go before. I spent a lot of years in the city, where a manager would never apologize to a customer under these circumstances. Too much risk of liability. I'm a small town woman, though. My name is Mac, by the way."

"Carol Swenson. Pleased to meet you. I'm sure I'll see you around town in the future." Mac could see Neil coming up to her. Carol turned a bit to look at him.

"Mac! How are you?" It took her a second, but then she looked back and forth between both Macs and started to laugh.

"Is this the Mac you were telling Samantha about? I didn't even make the connection for some reason. That must be pretty strange for you guys, being called the same thing."

"Nah," Mac said. "We've got it all worked out in code and hand signals." Carol laughed again and Neil shook his head.

"She calls me Neil, among other things."

"I'll just bet. Well, you two have a nice evening. I'm so glad I got to meet your Mac, Mac." Then she started laughing all over again as she walked back to her office.

"I guess I should expect a lot of that around town, huh?"

"That's assuming anyone knows your name, honey, and we're keeping that to a minimum at this point. Carol only knows about me and you because she's married to Sam, and she's not a gossip, though she does have a sense of humour."

"What I find interesting is that you told your employee about me. How come?"

"Oh, I told her she should probably expect to have her boss coming in as an old married man one day soon." Mac felt her jaw drop, only to have Neil chuck her under the chin and then kiss her as soon as her mouth was closed.

"Wait. What? What?" She was sputtering, so he helped her out with that problem too, by kissing her again, right in the middle of the store. She looked around, wild-eyed, but no one was paying them any attention, surprisingly. She figured Neil would be exactly the kind of man who would inspire gossip amongst the local ladies.

"Stop kissing me in public. I thought you didn't want the little shit to find out about us."

"I don't, but I don't know anyone that's in here right now. I run a knife store, and not too many women come in there. It's mostly women in here right now, in case you didn't notice. It's too late in the day for contractors, I think. Kind of surprising there aren't more men in here, though. It's one store where the men in this town don't mind going shopping with their wives. Now don't look at me like that. They live how they choose to live. I'm not the one following any stereotypes."

Mac glared at him for another ten seconds, just in case. Finally they headed to their trucks to get the sheds loaded at the shipping dock.

Driving her truck, with him following behind her in his, Mac had a bit of time to ponder her situation. *Old married man, indeed*, she thought huffily, though the insane side of her was waltzing around in a dreamy haze of happiness. He'd already intimated his interest in that direction, so she wasn't really surprised about that part of it, but the fact that he'd said something to his employee was rather dizzying.

Mac pulled to a stop beside the gate, motioning for him to stop, too.

"What is it?"

"Come with me for a minute. I need to get you set up."

"You're setting me up? For what? Target-practice? I think I'll just stay in the truck, thank you. Much harder for you to hide the blood evidence on upholstery."

"That's not entirely off the menu just yet, but no. I'm talking about the gate. It's ridiculous for you to not have gate access when you can just walk over from your property. Assuming you're not afraid to give me access to your fingerprints, of course."

"Well, you're pretty friendly with the local constabulary, so I doubt hiding my prints from you would do much good."

"Not really, no. And those aren't my only cop friends, either, which is somewhat surprising considering my checkered past, and a list of former associates that were outright criminals.

"Come on, you. Ya might as well get this over with. It only hurts for an hour or two."

"Very funny. Checkered past, huh? I'm intrigued."

"Don't be. It's not that interesting. More irritating than anything else. For now I'll just tell you that I don't have a criminal record, though I probably should." He followed her to the tree she was always stepping behind when she had to let him in. He smiled when she brushed some dead leaves from the top of a small biometric scanner.

"Man you're good. Natural hollow, and those leaves look like they've been there forever. Wireless?"

"Nope. Too risky. Detectable with a signal scanner, and easily duplicated, completely nullifying the moderately decent security of a fingerprint."

"Moderately decent?"

"Retinal scan is tens of thousands of times less likely to be copied or cracked. The units are too big to hide like this, though, and having it hidden is more valuable than having better security. You can't crack it if you don't know it's there. The wire goes down behind the bark, mostly. Then it's buried until it gets to the opener mechanism."

"Well, that's certainly one area where you kicked the snot out of my setup. So what do I do?"

"Hang on. I have to enter my prints and then open access for a new set of scans. We'll do all ten. It can get picky if there's dirt on a print, or you get a cut. People also lose their fingers, or even a hand, so they recommend doing the full set. Try not to lose your appendages, though. I'm developing an attachment to them."

"I'm already attached to them, or they are to me, so I certainly don't intend to. Nice to know you're *developing* an attachment to them, though." She smirked at him.

"Fine, I'm madly in love with your fingers. Happy? Now show off those beautiful digits to the scanner, so it can love them as much as I do."

Just as the last one finished scanning, Neil turned to her.

"Mac?"

"Hmm," she said absently as she shut down the scanning and returned it to its secured mode, covering it back up with the dead leaves.

"You're already madly in love with the rest of me, too. It's only a matter of time before you admit it to both of us." She turned to face him. Before she could speak a single word, his body pinned hers against the tree, and his mouth made sure she didn't.

15

REVELATIONS

With bark in her hair and a stuttering heart, Mac drove up the length of the driveway and then past their temporary home. She wanted to unload the sheds close to where they would likely need to be assembled. She parked and headed straight into the house to get herself cleaned up a bit. Adding sweat to the reek of sex certainly wouldn't make it any less noticeable, so a shower was vital.

It wasn't until she turned to close the bathroom door that she noticed Neil coming into the house.

"Gotta pee. You can shower with me after if you feel a need. I certainly do." Then she slammed the door to drown out anything he might say. She had just closed the lid and flushed when he strolled right in.

"Hey! I don't walk in on you when *you're* takin' a leak."

"First, how would I know? Maybe you will once you've known me for a week. We don't live in the same house, so you're not always around when I use the facilities. Second, why would you think I'd care? For that matter, why do you care?" Before she could even answer, he covered her mouth with his hand.

"I don't think you actually do care. You're not the type to worry about peeing in front of a guy you've been having all kinds of sex with. The other kind of bathroom break is another story, and I'll go so far as to say it's for the best if people retain a certain amount of mystery in a relationship. Sharing has limits." Mac almost smiled, but not quite.

"You don't care about me walking in here, but you're freaked out about something else right now, or I wouldn't have been so rude as to barge in on you."

"At least you admit that it *is* rude. Who says I'm freaked about anything?" He just stared at her, stone cold, and waited. Her stomach dropped.

"Shit. Fuck. Damn it! I am so totally an idiot for saying that. Sorry. I am *not* a dishonest or passive-aggressive woman. I'm so off-balance with you. You keep saying things that freak me out, and if I didn't feel anything they wouldn't bother me in the least. I'm fucking terrified of my own feelings, which is ridiculous. When did I become such a coward?"

"Coward, honey? I don't think so. Just off-balance, like you said. We talked about this before. You haven't had any time to think or absorb. I have. I'm being impatient and have no excuse for it. I shouldn't be pushing you.

"We're both feeling the intensity, and I don't believe there's a difference in how we feel. I just think I've had a bit more time to take a breath and accept it. I came in here to apologize, because I saw you freak out and I didn't want you feeling that way any longer than necessary. I want you to be happy with me, not feel pressured."

"I *do* feel happy. Even when I'm freaking out, it's not because I'm really upset. It's because I'm not. I'm freaking out because you're making me happy, and that is so totally stupid on my part. My brain tells me I have to be smart and cautious.

"Then you say stuff to me that should scare the ever loving shit out of that side of me, and it barely squeaks a protest, but the other part of me wants to wander around like that dreamy high-schooler you mentioned. I don't want to be the kind of woman who can go ga-ga over some guy, and gets all moony because he talks about marrying me."

Neil grinned at her.

"But you *are* the type of woman who does, apparently, or this wouldn't be coming up. Granted, it wasn't that part of it that really freaked you out. It was me pushing you on your feelings, and I find it so hard to stop myself even now, because I have no problem admitting how I feel. Doesn't scare me in the least. My only fear is that it will scare you, and I won't do that. I meant what I said out there, but I need to stop poking at you. It's not like you don't already know.

"Come on. Into the shower. I'll join you, since you offered already. I'm not about to turn down any opportunity you present that involves getting you naked." She stripped off, turned on the water, and stepped in.

"It really is a hell of a shower you've got here. I could learn to covet this thing."

"Believe it or not, this was important to me because I hate wasting time. I want to get clean as quickly as possible. People always have dribbles for showers to save water, but then you have to be in there for twenty minutes instead of five, using at least as much water, if not more."

"Mm. Well, there are two of us using it now, so I think it would be safe to go with ten minutes or so, don't you?

They used up far more than the allotted time, but Mac was practically purring when she stepped out. He toweled her off, but when she started to return the favour he touched her wrist to stop her.

"No. I can't take it. Lately I have the self-control of a drunken rabbit. It's humbling to admit, but there ya have it. It might be a good idea if you keep your distance until we finish for the night." Mac smiled knowingly.

"That's gonna work, is it?"

"No harm tryin' anyway, but if you're within reach I can't make any promises. Course, if you're not within reach I'll probably be looking to get you *within* reach. Oh well. You're a gorgeous woman. There's probably no help for me."

Mac snorted with laughter.

"Oh please. Gorgeous my ass. We need to get dressed so we can get some work done. Get a move on ya lazy git."

"Yes ma'am. Though I must protest the lazy part. You can't call someone lazy when they're banging you so often and so thoroughly. I mean, that's a hell of a workout."

"Just so long as you don't turn it into an exercise video. I might have a few choice words to say about being part of your floor work."

Mac traipsed into her bedroom, dressed, and fixed up the food and water dishes for the ferrets. Only one waste pad needed changing. She took the biodegradable bag from the garbage can outside with her. It was getting pretty aromatic, so she needed to set up the composting area for the animal waste.

Mac grabbed the shovel she used for digging in places that weren't part of the garden area. Neil stepped out of the house then, so she told him where she was going. He said he'd go back and help 'the kids' with whatever remained to be done on the second goat pen.

She chose an area somewhat in the corner of her property, but still out of sight from the road, and from the neighbouring land should someone decide to visit their property boundaries. She'd picked the spot because of a fallen tree that would be behind the bins, helping to conceal them. If they stepped far enough onto her property to see what would soon be a compost bin, the sensors would soon be in place to register the intrusion.

Mac intended for the bins to be fairly well camouflaged anyway. People might know that someone owned the property, of course, but she hoped to avoid them knowing anyone was actively working the land. She'd probably made lots of noise when she'd prepped the areas for the concrete pads, but that had been a long time ago.

When she got the chance to go over the land registry maps with Neil she could find out if he remembered hearing anything around the time she'd been doing the work. Hopefully he would also be able to tell her if the other owners had developed their land. Not everyone did. Sometimes it was just an investment.

Mac dug a wide trench for the compost boxes she intended to bury here. With the number of animals they had now, they'd need quite a few bins. By next spring they should have some good compost for the garden, but for safety sake it needed to brew for months to remove the risk of salmonella.

Mac went back to the house and built the first composting box. She wouldn't be building the rest today, so she left with it as soon as it was complete. All in all she had her composting area at least partially set up within the hour. She dropped in the small bag of ferret waste, scattered soil on top, and closed the lid with a sigh. Now to deal with the rest of the animals that would be filling up the bin.

The second goat pen was complete. It was a lot further from the house than the one they were leaving the does in, which was a damn good thing. If the bucks had that much of an aroma now, she wasn't looking forward to the smell when they were in rut.

"You just need two sheds put up for now, right?" Mac nodded at Neil.

"Right, but humour me and at least *pretend* to look at the directions first, would ya?" Neil laughed, and started fishing for the page that had wafted further into the box when he pulled out a few pieces.

Mac shook her head. They'd done everything bass-ackwards when it came to the animals, because there had been such a rush to get them and bring them home. At least when they built the third and fourth pens they'd be able to do things in order. Everything would be completely in place when they moved any goats into them.

By the time the sheds were assembled, Mac was in a foul mood. She was sure she could have built them from scratch, including cutting down the trees and using the sawmill to turn them into boards, faster than the sheds had gone up. If she'd had to do the job by herself, it would have taken her a month of Sundays.

It was a good thing Neil actually *had* read his directions, because the design was as counter-intuitive as she had ever seen. Although the panels were deeply corrugated, they still flopped around a fair bit just from their size. Any stability they attained came with the later installation of cross-braces and attachment to the other panels. They hadn't poured a concrete pad or anything. The goats were far too nosy for them to even attempt it.

They could move the building onto a pad later, once they had a place to shift the goats to, getting them out of the way. At least this way it gave the goats an opportunity to eat up all the grass. Maybe she'd also let them graze away the grass in the new pens before putting in the pads and sheds. Waste not, want not, she figured.

It wasn't until they were done for the night that a breeze finally kicked up, of course. Everyone was hot and tired, so the four younger adults started talking about going for a swim. Mac and Neil declined to join them, so they went off on their own to grab stuff like swimwear and towels. Billy and Neil had both grabbed overnight bags this time, so Billy had a change of clothes for after his swim.

Mostly Mac wanted some peace and quiet to relax and get a grip on what was happening in her life right now. She'd already done a fair bit of thinking while working on the compost bin, but she still had things to sort through in her head.

Mac was lifting her ponytail off the back of her neck to revel in the cool breeze when Neil came up behind her to rub her shoulders. A surprised moan came out of her mouth. She hadn't even noticed how tight her muscles were. The shoveling had warmed them up, making them loose, but her irritation with the sheds had turned the ones in her shoulders into knots.

"This is assault, sir. Please cease and desist all criminal activity. You have three hours to comply."

"Mm-hm. I'll get right on that. Got your cuffs with you? I'd like to be taken in for house arrest. Maybe go biblical with the whole eye-for-an-eye thing. What do you say?"

"You rub my back, I'll rub yours? That's a deal. My cuffs are in the house. If you come quietly I might use them on you."

"I can come quietly," he whispered in her ear. "You have a little more difficulty there as I recall." She stiffened as the spear of heat slammed through her body, and let out a soft gasp. *Ah, God,* she marveled, wondering when the man's potency would wear off for her. Hopefully never, because she was pretty sure she was looking at a very long-term commitment with him.

"If they're all out of the house swimming," she began, barely managing to speak. Neil didn't need her to finish the sentence. They went straight to the house and into her bedroom. Seconds after the outside door closed, signaling the exodus of the other four, Neil thrust inside her.

Once he was hilted, however, he stopped.

"I could spend the rest of my life right here." Mac looked into his eyes, but couldn't speak. A feeling so powerful washed over her that she shuddered. It spread through her chest and out into her limbs, until the words were pushing up through her throat. Until she couldn't have stopped them if her life depended on it. She tried to choke them off before they came out, she really did, but the whisper still traveled across her tongue and into the ether.

"I love you, Neil." She knew there was utter shock on her face as she looked into his brilliantly green eyes. She could feel it in every pore.

"You don't have to be scared, honey," he whispered. "You already know I love you, too. There isn't a doubt in my mind about you. I love you, baby," he repeated, and began to move inside her. By his third stroke, Mac was convulsing beneath him, the spasms in her vaginal muscles triggering his orgasm so that he spilled scalding heat inside her.

Mac was still in complete shock. She knew she shouldn't be, since she'd been honest enough with herself to admit her own feelings. Her shock came from having spoken the words aloud. Words she could not pull back inside herself, and pretend did not exist. It was too late for that now. Her feelings for him had cracked her heart wide open, until the emotions came pouring out in an endless torrent.

There was a heady sense of freedom in her vulnerability, however. Until then she hadn't noticed how much work it had taken to maintain the protective shell she kept around her heart. There was no fear in her now, though. Only wonder that she had found anything like this, after mostly writing off the possibility in her own mind.

"You don't have to run from this, Mac. It doesn't matter how crazy it might seem. It's what we feel."

"Neil," she whispered to him, her mouth finding his. This time it was intentional when she spoke the words she knew he needed to hear again.

As soon as the words left her mouth he began to move inside her once more, slow and gentle. He rolled them over until she was rising above him, holding to the torturous pace. When they came together an endless time later, they shattered completely, the pieces of them temporarily becoming a single being.

* * *

Ever so slowly Mac became aware of her surroundings again. Neil was stroking her hair as her head rested in the hollow between his shoulder and chest. It was certainly convenient to have a man that was so much taller than she was, she realized. Granted, everything about him seemed to fit her. His thoughts must have been running in a similar vein, because they spoke at the same time.

"I love you." At any other time it might have been funny, but right then it seemed more poignant to her than anything else. They both smiled. She could see the relaxed wonder on his face, as he moved his hand from her hair and brushed the backs of his fingers across her cheek.

"You've got such soft skin. You really are beautiful, you know. In fact..." He reached down to the jeans he'd dropped on the floor, and pulled out his phone to snap a selfie of the two of them. When she saw the result, she told him to send it to her phone.

When she didn't hear a corresponding notification beep she asked if he was sure he'd sent it to the right number. He showed her the MMS on his screen. Mac looked around for her phone. It was a BlackBerry Passport, which was large and oddly-shaped, and it also happened to be red so it should have been easy to spot.

"Well, hell. What have I done with the damn thing now?" The

last time she'd used it was when Neil's text had come in to tell her he was coming up to the gate. She'd only looked at the screen, but then she couldn't remember whether or not she'd put it back in her pocket. She moved her lazy carcass away from Neil's warmth and reached for her jeans. Nothing.

Feeling like an idiot, she asked Neil to call her phone so she could find it. When he did it went straight to voicemail.

"Well *that's* really strange. It must be turned off. I never turn off my phone now that they finally made it easy to switch to silent mode on the damn things."

"Maybe your battery died. When was the last time you charged it?" She had to think about it.

"Probably a couple of days before we left Tuesday night. Yeah. Five days is about right for the battery."

"Your phone lasts for five days without charging? Are you kidding me?"

"If I use it constantly for reading or using other apps, then no. It might last up to three days then. I've only really been using it for a few calls and texts here and there, though. It's a BlackBerry. Battery life is their best feature as far as I'm concerned. Every other phone I've had has needed to be charged every single day. Not ideal for a prepper. I'm surprised you don't have one."

"I have a satellite phone in addition to the iPhone. My other tech is pretty much all Apple stuff, so I went with them for the phone, too. Simple convenience more than anything," he said, giving a shrug.

"Not very convenient to have your battery run down all the time. Not that it really matters at this point. Like you I'll probably have to switch to satellite soon. Once the power is down in this area, the towers will go out here, too. Of course, there's also the radio.

"I'll be right back. I think my phone's probably on the table. I was talking to Cam, Leigh, and Kirk, when you texted you were at the gate."

Mac had put her clothes back on while she was babbling. Sure enough, when she got out to the table her phone was on top of the maps she'd left there earlier. She pressed and held the power button to no avail. She went back to her bedroom and dug into her computer's backpack for the adapter she'd stowed in there, then plugged it into the wall outlet. It took a few seconds before she could even get it to power up because it had been completely drained.

It finished its boot sequence, and moments later three different notification tones came out of the speaker.

"Well, there's your text anyway. What the hell else did I miss? Jesus." She didn't bother checking her e-mail for the time being. A lot of it would be activism stuff that could no longer make a difference. Anything of importance would be in her phone calls. She apparently had two messages waiting. The first was from Mitch.

"Hey. Man am I ever sorry I didn't come up there when you told me to. This is a fucking nightmare, and I don't have the fuel to get there now. Is there any way you can help me out here?" She'd had the phone pressed to her ear, but now she pulled it away with a disgusted grunt.

"Oh, for fuck's sake, Mitch!" Neil was looking at her, his brows raised in question.

"It's my second ex-husband. We're still friends. Get along fine usually, now that we're no longer trying to be married, but occasionally he seriously strains my patience." She let Neil listen to the message on the speakerphone.

"He expects you to solve his problem for him now, even though you already gave him a solution?"

"Yup, that's pretty much his pattern. Of course, I still care what happens to him. I mean, how can you not? You don't just love someone for years, and then stay friends with them if you don't give a shit."

"Hm."

"Don't. We've been apart for ten years now. If there was a hope in hell of a reconciliation, or any unresolved romantic feelings, then at least one of us would have made an attempt many years ago. It's just not there."

"No, it's not that. If you had wanted something you'd have gone after it and been honest about it. It's the fact that you offered him asylum, basically. You really are trying to take care of everyone. How can you be the way you are?"

"Huh?"

"After the life you've had, and some of the ways you've been treated, most people would be uncaring shits. You're something else entirely."

"Sure. Okay. Anyway, let me finish listening to my messages. Then you can pander to my ego a little more. I think I like it." Neil chuckled and pulled her down for a quick kiss. When she listened to the next voicemail on speaker, though, his expression darkened. Understandably.

"Hey my Canadian sex kitten. How are ya? Got your message. Call me back and talk dirty to me." Mac took one look at Neil's face and held up her hand.

"That is so totally not what you think."

16

THE SAILING OF THE FLIRTATIONSHIP

"What was it then?" The blunt question reminded her that there were a lot of things they hadn't been able to share with one another yet.

"I guess I'd better explain, huh? That was Ian, who's my closest friend. I met him through business stuff, online. He lives outside Cleveland, and I've never actually met him in person. We started talking a few years ago, I edited his book, and we later became business partners. I run all his websites, too.

"He's not actually interested in me, and never has been. Honesty compels me to admit that at one time I was interested in him. I made my interest known, and he was pretty blunt about not wanting to go there. In fact, I almost lost him as a business partner and client over it. Not to mention as a friend. I guess he didn't think I could handle rejection, though I was fine with it. I just misinterpreted things."

"*He* rejected *you*? You were fine with it. I see."

"I doubt very much that you do, because it's pretty hard to encapsulate several years' worth of friendship in a single conversation. We were flirting back and forth. He took it as a joke. I thought he was interested. When a guy isn't interested in me I don't hold a torch for them. I lose all interest myself. Probably a lot to do with self-esteem, and very much like what you were saying about me.

"At the time I thought I had some pretty deep feelings for him, other than friendship, but knowing he wasn't into me just killed it. I was a little depressed about it for a couple of weeks, and then I moved on."

"So why is he talking to you like that then? Wouldn't he realize that it might be hurtful to you?" Neil's jaw was rigid. She knew she wasn't explaining Ian very well, but then Ian was pretty hard to explain.

"I doubt it. He's forgetful with stuff like that. It's one of the reasons I wasn't embarrassed talking to him afterward. He just didn't seem to retain the conversation. He does that with other things, too. There's some stuff we've talked about that I swear we've had the same conversation ten times, and he just doesn't remember anything that was said before.

"And it isn't hurtful. I just find it funny now. I joke with him, too. He doesn't take me seriously either. If I hadn't been single, however, I wouldn't have been flirting, and I won't be doing it now. I'll let him know I'm with you. If he knows I'm not single he won't act like that. He's not that kind of guy.

"Look, I have to call him. It's important for me to talk to him. Listen if you want, but try to relax would you? You start acting like a jealous schmuck over something that doesn't mean anything, I'm going to be very disappointed in you."

"Mac, my first reaction might have been jealousy, which isn't so surprising considering his message, but that's not what I'm thinking now. Make your call and we can discuss it after."

Mac gave him a suspicious look.

"Just to let you know, cowboy, before you ever utter the words, there are four words that really do freak me out. See, if you ever do say them now, and I turn into a psychotic banshee, you can't say you weren't warned." Neil raised one eyebrow, which for some reason she'd always found insanely sexy on a man, and waited for her to continue.

"'We need to talk,' is the phrase I'm referring to. That's probably something most people expect a man to hate, but I find it almost always precipitates, 'I don't love you anymore,' or 'I'm sick of your fucking bullshit and I want out,' or..."

"I get it," he interrupted, looking at her strangely. He stood up and pulled her into his arms.

"How about I stick to three words? I love you." A lump formed in her throat. Maybe she'd been carrying around a little more pain than she'd realized, because it now occurred to her that even saying that much about it was painful.

"I love you, too," she said softly, and let him hold onto her for a minute.

When she'd shaken off the slightly melancholy mood, she pulled away to call Ian. This time he picked up.

"Hey hussy, how are you?" His usual cheerful tone made her smile. She didn't bother to tone it down for Neil's benefit. She loved Ian. He was her best friend, and she didn't give up her friends unless they did something to deserve it. Otherwise they had her loyalty.

"I can't be your hussy anymore. You'll have to find a new one. This one's off the auction block to a really high bidder."

"What do you mean?"

"I'm taken. *Finito.* I'm seeing someone, and I'm crazy about him."

"Oh, wow!" His response was exactly what she'd expected from him. More surprise than anything else, and she couldn't blame him. She'd been single a long time, and safe to flirt with.

"Your command of English has grown to two words, I see."

"Ha ha."

"And you've managed it again. Sort of. Anyway, that's not why I was calling you before, but considering your usual pervy message, I thought I'd save you the embarrassment of fawning over me anymore." Neil was grinning at her, but she ignored him.

"Okay, so what's up then, aside from the unusual state of your sex life?"

"Very funny. Bloody American. Actually, it's really important. I'm permanently up at my northern property now, and for good reason. Things are bad in the GTA. Toronto is dark, and so is Hamilton and every other city. They've instituted what you would call martial law, actually, and it's not going to be very effective. They've got military police along with federal, provincial, and city police, trying to keep millions of people under control."

"Holy shit! When did this happen?"

"We've been having bad outages for a while. I told you about them, remember?"

"Yeah, yeah I think so." Mac rolled her eyes. Typical Ian.

"Cameron and I left the city Tuesday, because people were starting to get seriously pissed. We just barely managed to get some friends of hers up here the next day. They had to rent a car, and ran out of gas partway here. I had to go bring them gas a couple of towns away. We've been working like crazy to get things ready here.

"Today we got the news that all the cities in the GTA are dark, and they're not even giving an estimate of when people will have power. It's already hit outlying areas. Barrie and Orillia were both without power on Wednesday, and there's no food left on store shelves in any of the cities near Toronto. Have you had any power issues there?"

"Yeah, off and on. You think it's the same thing?"

"Shit. Yeah, I do. It's a cascade effect. Okay, please, please go get as much insulin as you can right now, along with test strips.

I'm begging you to take this seriously. Remember we talked about this, where you might have to store the insulin deep in your well in a waterproof bag if your power goes out?"

"Yeah, okay. I might as well. It doesn't hurt to be careful." Mac wanted to sigh in relief, but she couldn't yet. He was still far too unprepared.

"I'm sending you a list. I formatted it so it shows on your phone as legibly as possible, so that you can go directly to the stores and get everything. I've even added the stores near you where the stuff is sold. You *need* to pick up every single item with an asterisk beside it, but pick up everything else if you can. It's the difference between being dead, being alive and shitty, and being alive and doing okay. Those will be the new levels of normal."

"You sure about this?"

"Look, I tried to get my ex to come up here, and he didn't take me seriously. I just got a message from him asking for help. He's still in Hamilton. I don't know if there's a way for me to do anything for him, but I haven't had time to think about it. I was more worried about you. You're the one who can't go three days without insulin. He can deal with his own shit for a few days while I come up with something. *If* I come up with something.

"I believe, a hundred percent, that everything I've been preparing for is about to happen. This is the shit-hits-the-fan scenario I keep saying is going to go down. It was inevitable. The power grids couldn't compensate for global warming.

"Even if I'm wrong, there's no harm in you having that stuff on hand. I'm not asking you to make a suicide pact with me. Just buy it. You can afford to buy it, but you can't afford not to. Thankfully you've got your radio already, and we can communicate that way when the towers go down. It's too bad you didn't hook up full solar already, but there's a makeshift kit on the list that you can use for small stuff.

"Now please go get your insulin right now. You can fish in your pond for food if you have to, so the list can wait until you have the insulin. Okay?"

"Okay," he said in a doubtful tone.

"I sure hope you managed to get in touch with that friend-of-a-friend who's a chemist, but if not you might have to find a pharmacist or something later."

"Wow, you're really sure this is the big one, huh?" Mac gritted her teeth.

"Ian, I'm not usually wrong about stuff this important, and I've been keeping an eye on this for a long time. You know that. I said it would happen eventually, but I never once told you that it *was* happening until right now. Don't make me shit kittens up here worrying about you. I've got enough on my plate to deal with. Like chickens. And goats."

"You got goats? Cool."

"Yes, I got goats. After much delay, blamed partially on Neil, I finally managed to get twelve of them. And twenty four chickens." Neil had started laughing at the mention of the goats.

"Wow. From urbanite to goat and chicken rancher. A bit of a

culture shock. Neil the new guy?"

"Yeah, that's him. The goats are the only culture shock, though. I had chickens growing up, remember?"

"Oh right. You told me that."

"Yes, I told you that. Are you heading to the pharmacy?" She could hear the wind blowing into his headset, so she figured he was driving.

"Well, I have to go teach a class right now." Mac wanted to scream.

"Ian, be ten minutes late. Tell the other guy you'll be there when you can get there. He can handle it for ten frickin' minutes. The two hours may not make any difference, but maybe they will. Don't take the chance. Once the cascade starts, it's going to happen very fast, and your pharmacy may not be willing to fill your script if they don't have power."

"Okay, okay. Jeez you're bossy."

"I have to be. Gotta keep all my self-destructive friends in line. You know I'm right, though, or you wouldn't agree to it. You'd brush me off. So, just follow your usual instincts and listen to me. Thank Christ Kirk and Leigh were a lot easier to convince, and they're supposed to be young and foolish. Then again, you're old and crotchety now."

"Ha! One of these days I'm coming up to Canada to kick your ass."

"Good luck with that. Especially now. Hey, at least you probably won't need a passport after this goes down. You'll just have to walk, that's all. Or sail a boat."

"You're kidding me! All the way up there?"

"It's not the north pole, Ian. Jesus. It's only about two and a half hours north of Toronto, and the way you drive I'd say more like ninety minutes."

"You saying I'm a reckless driver? I'll have you know, when I was a cop..."

"Yeah, yeah. Pizza, sirens, radio, high speed chase. I remember. The scary thing is, you were the cop in that scenario. I can only imagine how crazy your suspect was."

"Ha! No kidding. Alright. If I get all this crazy shit, and you turn out to be wrong, I'm seriously coming up there to kick your ass."

"Well, it would be about time you got off your ass and did something worthwhile with your life. I'm only the greatest thing in the world, and you haven't even bothered to come and meet me. I'm good enough to put up with all your weird website demands, but not good enough to be seen in public with. Yeah, I see how it is."

"Exactly. So tell me about this new guy. He some hot young stud you hooked up with in a bar or something? Half your age and you gotta wipe his nose for him and all that?" Mac was laughing.

"I can't talk about him right now. He standing beside me, so I can only tell you the good stuff. He might, you know, beat me or something if I tell you the truth about him."

"Uh-huh. I'll believe that when I see it. You tell him you're an honorary black-belt. I'll back you up on that."

"Because the 'honorary' means so much, right? Just like an honorary degree will get you what, exactly?"

"Yeah, pretty much. Might buy you a good ass-kicking from someone who actually has a black-belt, maybe."

"Probably. Anyway, I have to get going. I think I might go for a swim."

"What, you got a pool up there at your posh Canadian resort?"

"River, and yes, I told you about it. I have a river on my property. In fact, I share it with my sexy new neighbour."

"Hey, I thought you said you had a boyfriend. You cheating on him with your neighbour now?"

"Right. 'Cause that's just who I am. Jackass. No, my sexy new neighbour *is* the guy I've been seeing."

"Oh, okay. I thought you were being a hussy again."

"Uh-huh. I gotta go. You go get your insulin, okay? You said you would. I'm gonna hold you to that. If you don't and I have to come down there and rescue you, I'm gonna kick *your* ass. I don't care if you *are* some hotshot martial arts master. Talk to ya later." She felt Neil's arms slide around her waist as she hung up.

"You'd really do that, wouldn't you?"

"What? Kick his ass? I couldn't if he had three limbs tied to a telephone pole. Might be able to shoot him, though."

"You know I meant going down there to give him insulin." Mac shrugged.

"Honestly, I'm probably going to have to anyway, even if he

gets his insulin now."

"What do you mean?"

"He's fully insulin-dependent. He has a rare form of diabetes. If he goes three days without it, he's dead. Insulin has a maximum of a one-year shelf-life before it turns toxic. His test strips only last for so long, too, but they're not as important as the insulin. He'll need a fresh supply of insulin within a year, no matter how careful he is to stretch it out. Then it's a slow and painful death."

"Okay, I understand that part, but how do you intend to help him? Do you have a background in pharmaceuticals or chemistry?"

"No, but if I have to I'll learn to make it myself. It won't be what he has now, but it's better than nothing. I have the lab equipment and precise instructions on how it was first altered for use in humans. I do *not* want to be making this stuff. It means having to use animals in a way I'm not sure I can deal with, but I won't let him die either. We'll just call that plan C for now."

"What are plans A and B then?"

"Plan A is to find someone who knows how to operate the equipment at the plants that make synthetic insulin, and then provide a power source. Any type of insulin is better than nothing, though the long-acting stuff would be best.

"Plan B is to find a chemist, or a pharmacist since they understand chemistry better than I ever will, and have them make the insulin for me. There are going to be a lot of people who need it, and a lot of them will die, but maybe I can help some other people at the same time."

Neil sat down on the bed again, still not having bothered to dress, and shook his head.

"How do you plan to get to Cleveland?"

"I've got lots of stabilized fuel, which will be perfectly good in six months, and possibly years from now. I'm sure you have a bunch yourself. Half of it is treated with PRI-G and the other half with STA-BIL. I wasn't sure whose claims I believed more, so I used both. I've been cycling the cans for a while."

"Okay, but you know what's going to happen if you have to stop anywhere to put fuel in and there are people around."

"Oh yeah. I'm well aware. People are assholes, as Kirk is fond of saying. It's more like people are *murderous* assholes, but that's why I've learned archery and firearms, among other things. I won't be going unarmed if it comes to that. My other option is a sailboat. I can get from Skeleton Bay all the way to Cleveland by boat. That's the better plan, but it means learning to sail without anyone to teach me.

"If I can find someone in this area to make the insulin, I can show up there with it, and I won't need a vehicle to drive all over the place. He can just meet me. Before things got bad I was about to start looking around for someone who would agree to help me in exchange for whatever power generator I could sacrifice.

"In fact, instead of swimming I should do some research and maybe make some calls, for as long as I'm able to. There isn't much time left. I might not need the information for months, but pretty soon I won't be able to access it."

"First, come and sit beside me here for a second. You've got a bit of time, I think." Mac decided to humour him for the moment.

"I'm curious about his reaction when you told him you were seeing someone." He held up a hand before she could snap at him.

"Maybe I should explain why I want to know, so it makes more sense to you, and doesn't piss you off. I want to know if he's worth you risking your life to help him. Not to mention your daughter, whether she goes with you or stays here. I'd also like to see if he took you seriously, since it will give me an idea when you plan to leave."

"Why do you want to know when I'll be leaving?"

"Because I want to be prepared to come with you if it's possible." Mac almost choked, though she didn't know why she was surprised.

"What about Billy? He's only eighteen. You wouldn't leave him by himself, would you?"

"No. There are other options, but you and I can talk about that when it's time. Like you I'm preparing for a worst-case scenario, but I'm preparing for a best-case scenario, too. I've got some goals and dreams I'd like to fulfill if possible."

"I'm not going on a spirit-quest here. I'm only considering this because I don't want my best friend to die."

"I'm not referring to the boat trip. I'd only go because you're going. Staying behind, not knowing if you're safe, would be torture for me, and I'd rather spend that time with you. I want to hear your stories, and learn pretty much everything there is to know about you."

"Pretty much?"

"Well, yeah. I don't need to know every instance of you scratching your ass, for example, but I'd like to know what formed you into this amazing person you've become."

"Oh, okay. For the record, I don't need to know the ass-scratch-count either. We'll keep that information *off* the record. Word to the wise, as they say, be careful what you wish for. I've had a long forty years. Lots of stories, lots of boring shit, lots of pain. Sunshine and roses aren't what formed me, except maybe the burns and thorns.

"Why don't I just send you the recording of the call? Just keep in mind when you listen to it, that he cares a lot about me. He just knows better than to try to be parental about it. He acted like that a couple times and I bit his head off.

"The last thing I wanted, especially when I had an interest in him, was for him to think of me that way. He's quite a bit older than me, and I've never been interested in having a daddy-daughter relationship, so I made damn good and sure we would never have one, whatever happened.

"He cares about people a lot, just in general. So many people think of him as their mentor, and that's because they *know* he cares. It's only been in the last couple of years that I've let him nag me about things, but then he lets me nag him. Our business relationship meant it was still important that he saw me as an equal, even when the possibility of anything romantic was gone.

"I wasn't a cuddly kitten when it came to business, and being a woman I had a lot of guys trying to treat me that way. I made sure they learned differently right from the start, so they never tried to pull a fast one on me again. If you've ever seen or read *Ender's Game*, you'll probably remember the part where he kicks the shit out of the bully at the very beginning, and they ask him why he beat him so bad." Neil nodded.

"He says it's because he wanted to win all the fights after that one."

"Exactly. That's the corporate world. Hell, that's just the world. I worked my ass off to show it made no difference I was a woman. That's the kind of feminism I believe in. I also believe that damn near anything is possible, but you have to be willing to pay the price to have it."

"Alright, what price do you think I'm going to have to pay to have your love and companionship for the rest of my life? Because whatever it is I'm going to pay it." Mac smiled at him, as he reached for his jeans and rooted through his pocket as though he was trying to pull out his wallet.

"Well, you might have to sit through more of my ridiculous lectures that you don't actually need to hear because you're so strangely perfect for me. I don't charge for them, though. You can put your wallet away."

"Done. Here." He was holding out his loosely-fisted hand, palm down. She automatically held out her own, mystified. Then she felt something drop into it, and she stared in disbelief.

17

CARPE DIEM

"What... You can't... I can't..."

"...speak, apparently. It's okay Mac. It's for later, when you're ready, but with what's happening out there I wanted to make sure it fits you. It's better to find out while there's still a chance to get it sized. Just try it on."

Mac was sure her mouth had opened and closed like a guppy's several times already. Not the most attractive reaction to an engagement ring, but she couldn't help it. Neil started putting on his clothes.

"When *I'm* ready? And you are? Right this minute, you'd be willing to go through with this?"

"Hell, yes."

"It's the same colour as your eyes," she said, tears in her own as she watched him pull his t-shirt over his head.

"What?"

"Your eyes. They're emerald green. You have such beautiful eyes." Mac just stared at the flush-mounted, princess-cut stone in the centre of the ring, trying not to be an idiot. What he was suggesting was impossible.

Neil started humming the opening bars of *I Feel Pretty*, and Mackenzie started laughing. He sat beside her again.

"I chose it because it's your birthstone, not for my eye-colour, but I hear proper accessories can really make the outfit. You can dangle me off your arm like a purse, so long as I get to keep my eyes where they are, for whatever length of time I'm still using them. After all, I want to be able to see you. Especially when I'm able to call you my wife."

Mac's lungs burned in her chest, and her heart pounded. Just hearing him use the word was enough to conjure images of a life together. A small voice in her head wondered, *Why aren't we both terrified of this?*

"Neil, I cannot try this on if it's not official. It's bad luck. I'm sorry." She held out the ring to him. He blinked at her in confusion.

"You? You're superstitious? Level-headed, pragmatic, logical you?" Mac smiled at him and gave him a wink.

"No, not really, but if you want me to put it on you're still going to have to ask." The twinkle was back in his eyes when he looked into hers.

"Okay. Will you please try it on?" Mac rolled her eyes.

"You already asked me that." Neil sobered.

"Mackenzie, will you marry me?"

"Hell, yes."

"You're such a romantic, honey." Neil slid the ring onto her finger. A perfect fit. Mackenzie wasn't surprised. Everything about Neil was a perfect fit for her.

"You started the 'hell yes' thing, but you're right. I'm not particularly romantic, except in the sense that I'm willing to make a really big jump with you. Then again, you sure get me feeling all mushy a lot of the time. Like when we were dancing to all those old songs. I thought that part of me was dead and buried. Now it's awake and walking around as a zombie."

"Your zombie free on Monday?"

"The zombie *is* available, now that you ask, except for the little thing with the police. We'll be lucky if we're able to do it even then. Hopefully everything holds out for a little while."

"I think it will, honey. Just enough for us to get married. Somehow we seem to have had everything fall into place. Maybe other people would think the timing sucked, but I don't feel that way. To me it's like everything lined up just so we'd be together at exactly the right moment."

"Well, cowboy, you certainly know how to make a zombie heart go pitty-pat, don't you?" Neil chuckled at her, and then leaned down to give her a searing kiss.

"How's the zombie heart doing now?"

"Mm. Wow! I think you might be the cure for zombification or something." Mac patted her chest.

"Yup, definitely a cure. Okay, now that we've got all the mushy shit taken care of, and resolved whatever issue there may have been regarding Ian, I really do have to get some research done. He might be blasé about his situation right now, but he isn't interested in dying either. He just has a tendency to believe I exaggerate, or I've been listening to too much left-wing media or something."

"Okay, send me the recording. Speaking of which, why the hell did you record your call?"

"It's just the app I have on my phone. I have it set to automatically record calls. Sometimes there are details I might need later, and I won't know that until I'm in the middle of the call. Usually I delete the recordings later, if there's nothing I need on them.

"This coming from someone who's a paranoid prepper? I mean, you're more cautious than I am. I'd think you'd be the last person to record calls."

"I'm not a seditionist or anything, though there was a time when Harper was still prime minister that I seriously considered some activity on that front. As it is, even if my calls could be recovered without my permission, I've got nothing to fear. Not only am I careful about what I say on the phone, but my phone is encrypted. They can't force you to give them the codes to decrypt your phone if you're not crossing the border. Even there the legislation is being challenged."

"My faith in you is restored."

"Hardy-har-har," she drawled sarcastically. She unlocked her phone and texted him the mp3 recording.

"Okay, go play now. I've got a chemist to find."

"God, I love you." He kissed the top of her head, and left her with a bemused expression on her face, taking his phone into the open area of the building.

She shook her head and turned to her laptop to begin her search. Hours later Mac was hanging her head when Neil came back in to see how she was doing. Her head was pounding, and she felt like she hadn't gotten anywhere at all. She stretched her neck and back to try and back the headache off, but it only caused a piercing pain to shoot through her left occipital nerve. She winced and stood, feeling a sense of relief when his arms wound around her.

"There's no way I can get him the long-acting insulin. It's manufactured in Germany, for fuck's sake. It's repackaged and shipped all over the world under different names, but it's all made in one place from what I can tell.

"There's a company in Calgary that's working on insulin from safflowers, but that's nowhere near being on the market. It's apparently great stuff, but it has to go through all the approval shit. Granted, I don't think Ian would be that picky about approval from Health Canada or the FDA if there's no other insulin available to him, but there's no way I'm going to make it to Calgary and then get it down to him.

"Insulin production from bacteria appears to require a reactor, because it deals with replacement of DNA stuff that I can't even begin to understand at this point because I'm pretty sure I'm permanently cross-eyed.

"So, it's back to finding a chemist, or whatever, who can make it the old-fashioned way. They're going to think I'm nuts if I call them and ask, 'Could you make insulin from animal pancreas if it was the end of the world as we know it?' I have to figure out something to tell them, so that it seems like it's a theoretical deal."

Neil began rubbing her back and neck, obviously having noticed her previous attempts to ease her own discomfort. She whimpered at his touch, and couldn't help marveling at how much better it felt when someone else did the massaging. It didn't matter what body part it was.

"So, cowboy, how was *your* evening?" Neil gave a soft laugh.

"Not bad, though I missed you. Finally couldn't take it anymore and had to come see your gorgeous face."

"You zombie-seducer you. What did you get up to while I was melting my brains and turning myself into even more of a zombie? I suppose that's why they feel the need to eat brains."

"Well, I spent some time with the *young 'uns*, swimming and then just hanging out and looking at the stars. They're beautiful tonight, by the way. Then I had some fun with the goats."

"Oh, *really*? Hmm. You know that sexual intercourse with live-stock counts as cheating in my book, right? Will you really be able to restrain yourself after we're married? It would totally suck to have to divorce you, and then be denied because the world has fallen apart."

"Ah, the goats were just foreplay, honey. You're the main event." Mac turned around and covered him with her hand.

"Yeah? Well, this better be just for me. You start getting hard-ons like this for the goats I'm either going to have to get rid of them or you, and I need the goats."

"Don't you worry, honey. This is all for you." He grabbed her wrists and pinned her hands behind her back, pulling her forward against him. Then he pressed her upwards slightly, so that her mons was ground against his erection. His mouth pressed against her ear.

"Every...single...inch." Her strangled moan was muffled by his mouth. Suddenly her headache was gone, and she desperately wanted to get her hands on him.

*   *   *

"How?" She whispered the question.

"How what, honey?" His voice was rough as he panted.

"How do you do that to me? How do we have this...whatever it is?"

"You mean the insane chemistry that makes me want you every time I so much as look at you? That?"

"Yeah, that ol' thing." She could feel his chest move as he laughed.

"I don't know how, specifically, but I know it has a lot to do with the way I feel about you, and the way I know you feel about me. We wouldn't have this chemistry, if we didn't have that other stuff. Sure, people feel lust for one another, even without love, but it just never gets this potent when it's only physical.

"A lot of people don't think men get anything more from sex when there's love, but it's not true at all. Even when I want you so much it hurts, I still want to cherish and protect you. Maybe it's the tug-o-war between those two extremes that makes it so intense." He kissed her brow, and stroked her damp hair back from her forehead.

"I like to consider myself a sane man, but you've made me throw all caution to the wind and propose marriage in just over two days. And the truth is I just don't care if it's insane or not. I guess you must be feeling something similar, because you tossed out your own caution to be with me.

"Honestly, I never believed in love at first sight. In a way I still don't, because I feel you have to know someone to be able to love them, but I *knew* you at first sight. The love was a natural result of that. Loving you was just that easy. Maybe that's the answer. Knowing."

"You've got a real way with words, cowboy. I think you're right. I haven't believed in love at first sight for many years, but I did know you. Right from the first moment I looked into your twinkling green eyes." Neil snorted.

"Twinkling? You're making me sound like Santa Claus, for Christ's sake."

"Well, I can only be grateful that Christmas didn't come early, and managed to wait its turn." A shout of laughter nearly deafened her.

"A gentleman allows a lady to go first. It's just how it's done. Sometimes even first, second and third."

"Third? I don't think we've hit that one yet, but certainly second."

"Well, I do love a challenge as you might have noticed." The reminder had a quick arrow of lust pierce her belly.

"I double-dog dare ya."

*　　*　　*

Much later, a very contented smile on her face, Mac was reflecting on Neil's inability to refuse a challenge. *That could certainly be useful in the bedroom*, she thought. She figured the words, 'I bet ya can't...,' would be some of her favourites in the years ahead. Her smile turned wicked.

"Oh no. I'm done for at least another ten minutes. You'll just have to wait."

"What did *I* do?"

"I see that sexy look on your face. I need recovery time. Besides, we need to tell our kids we're getting married before you forget you're wearing a ring and someone sees it."

"Good point. What are they all up to anyway? They're obviously not in the house, because presumably we'd be hearing automatic gun-fire. *Battlefield* or *Black Ops* most likely."

"Campfire, marshmallows, and guitar. Billy and I both play, and we brought them with us, so he's probably trying to impress Cameron. Thankfully they weren't raised as brother and sister, because things could get really weird."

"I wouldn't worry about that for now. I guarantee Cam thinks she's far too old for him at the moment. That might change, but it'll take time. Poor Billy."

"You wouldn't have a problem with it?"

"Nope. She'll love where she wants, and your son is a good kid. I only care that she's happy. She's a natural cynic, though, and it takes a lot to impress her when it comes to guys."

"So are you. I managed, apparently."

"Not really. The natural cynic part, I mean. Obviously I was impressed. There's a lot that's impressive about you."

"You're not a cynic? You sure seem like one on the surface."

"Oh, I'm a cynic alright. Just not a *natural* one. It took years of dedicated practice, much like it takes with being a true bitch. I had to work at it, and I take pride in what I've achieved. I never quite managed to be a slut, though. An unattainable goal for me."

"You worked to become a cynic, a bitch, *and* a slut. Huh. Two out of three ain't bad, as Meatloaf would say."

"You seem to have gotten through my defenses quite handily. Sure you're not a spy or something? I hear they're pretty adept at seducing women."

"I'd be more like the comedic 'Spies Like Us' version, than James Bond. Still, I can do the Connery accent pretty well. High class stuff there." Mackenzie laughed at him.

"Oh, please. You can't tell me you've ever had a hard time seducing women. I'm sure they fell all over themselves trying to get into *your* pants, rather than the other way around." Neil looked at her incredulously.

"Hardly. I've always stepped somewhat wrong-footed when it came to talking to women. You've got some kind of magic when it comes to untying my tongue." Mac snorted.

"Okay, so I'll add tongue warlock to my resume. Might bring me some interesting clients if I'm ever back in business again."

"So, what all were you doing for a living? You've mentioned a few things."

"Editing books, web design, online courses with Ian, drop-ship sales, and start-up consulting mostly. All part-time, but I worked a lot and the variety was good for me."

"You get bored easily? You think that'll apply to me one day?"

"Not a chance. I don't get bored with real people, and when I say 'real people' I mean people that are *being* real. I hate using such a trendy phrase, but that's what it boils down to. There are a lot of people who live fake lives. It's always a mask you're talking to. They're pretty easy to spot, though.

"Sadly, real people seem to be few and far between. Until the shit hits the fan anyway, and the true person comes out. And that's when I start feeling bad for them, which always pisses me off."

"You're a total sucker for helping people aren't you? If only your business associates had known that, eh? They could have pled poverty, and you'd have fixed whatever problem they had."

"Possibly, but I was pretty astute when it came to people playing me. I had a couple of them try it, but to the best of my knowledge nobody made it work."

"Was that with your consulting stuff somehow?"

"Yup. Negotiating deals for my clients. However, most of the companies I dealt with were publicly traded, which meant their financial information was readily available online. Maybe they didn't think I would know how to read a quarterly report, but that was their mistake."

"Tough as nails, huh? That's the woman I fell in love with, but then I knew you were also a woman who'd be just as fierce in protecting the people she loves."

"You're gonna make me blush, cowboy."

"Gak!" Neil suddenly lurched forward. Mac folded her arms behind her head and stared at him complacently.

"Ah, the sound of a cold, wet ferret nose. Which one of my boys has come to greet you, I wonder?" Neil reached behind his naked back to pull out Squeaker.

"Jesus, short stuff! You sure know how to startle someone."

"Be grateful he didn't want to take a nip. You'd have landed on the floor on the other side of the bed. They've got amazingly tiny front teeth that deliver a hell of a pinch when they wanna play with you."

"I'll keep that in mind. I don't suppose pulling up the blankets would help?" Mac shook her head, wiping the hopeful look from his face.

"Not in the least. That makes it worse actually. They go under the sheets, thinking they're being sneaky...which of course they are. It's usually the feet they go for then, and they love it when you move your legs around. Makes it more of a challenge for them. It's their favourite form of entertainment, I think. They laugh. I swear they do."

Neil put Squeaker through a bout of hand-wrestling, and then plopped him on top of Mac's feet. She yelped when Squeaker nipped her ankle and then slid off the bed to head for the water dish.

"You did that on purpose!"

"Sure did. That'll teach ya for not protecting your future husband from the local beasts. You might respect me in the morning, but they sure as hell don't."

"Nope. They're spoiled rotten, and that'll never change. In fact, I need to go get more."

"More what? Ferrets?"

"Yeah. It'll take a couple of days, but I have to do it. I was always planning to. I dropped off food at the shelter near Toronto about a week before we left, but there are two more in Ontario that I know about. They have no idea what's coming, and those ferrets are going to starve to death. The shelters are all in the city.

"Which brings me to Mitch, actually. Now that I've had time to think about it, I have to go back to the Toronto area shelter anyway. I should go there first and pick up Mitch. He can make it that far, even if he has to steal a bike. I can go to Ottawa and the Sault right after."

"You never called him back after he left his message, did you?"

"No. There wasn't any point in calling him. I hadn't come up with a solution yet. He annoyed me, so I kind of put his problems out of my mind for the time being. It irritates the fuck out of me when I try to help someone, they ignore me, and then they end up calling me again for help. This wouldn't be the first time his life has been in danger because of it. Or mine."

"Yours. He's put *your* life in danger? Explain."

18

DRUM ROLLS AND FANFARE

Mackenzie wasn't surprised by Neil's reaction. She wasn't going to hide things from him, but her revelations wouldn't always be pleasant and she'd have to deal with the fallout.

"He ran with a rough crowd. It was stupid for me to get involved with him. When we met he lied and said he had a friend who was friendly with some bikers. He said the other guys were bad news, so he stayed away, but this guy was someone he'd gone to high school with."

"And you thought his loyalty was an admirable trait," he concluded.

"Maybe. I guess. I haven't led a blameless life myself, so I didn't want to judge anyone else, but maybe the loyalty thing had something to do with it. Of course, none of it was true. He wanted to join. Our relationship got serious enough that we began to live together, and then he started disappearing. At first I thought it was another woman, but I was wrong.

"I gave him an ultimatum when he came home with a leather vest and a patch. He surprised me by choosing me over the club, but by then it was too late. Thankfully it was a puppet club for the big boys, and it was so full of idiots that the whole thing fell apart. He disappeared quietly from the scene then.

"It doesn't end there, sadly. Multiple times he got into drugs. Selling and taking. I lost count of the number of times he needed to be bailed out of a jam, owing money to the wrong people. I'd get calls from scum while I was at work, and even then I didn't put up with shit. I told them not to call me ever again, and hung up. Yet I still helped him."

"And you're still going to help him? You're risking your life for someone who doesn't think twice about you doing so. Are you out of your fucking mind?" Mac closed her eyes, her temper warring with her sense of fair play. He was right, and she knew it. Compromise might be the only option here. She sure as hell wasn't going to fight with Neil over her ex-husband. The price she was willing to pay to help him only went so high these days.

"Okay. Believe me, I see your point. I agree with you. The best I can come up with is this, because anything else might be something I couldn't live with.

"I go down there..."

"You mean 'we,' don't you?" She raised her hands to stave off further argument, and nodded her agreement.

"Okay. *We* go down there, but only as far as the shelter. If he's not there by the time we've loaded the ferrets, he gets left behind. I have to get the ferrets anyway. I can't leave them to die. I may not be able to help all of the animals in the world, but I can save some, and I'm willing to risk my life for them. It might seem stupid, but I have to do it."

Neil relaxed and pulled her into his arms.

"It's not stupid. Scary, but not stupid. Alright, you've got a deal. We can go tomorrow. I've got a sign on the store saying it's closed for a family emergency and will reopen next week. I doubt it will, but I didn't want people thinking it would be empty for long stretches.

"I gave Samantha a paid, two-week vacation and grabbed all the stock from the back already. At some point I need to go back and get the display stock, though. I don't need anyone coming after me with my own inventory one day."

"Wouldn't make you the sharpest knife in the drawer, no."

"That was bad, Mac. You're usually funnier than that." She poked him in retaliation. Then she heard the kids coming in.

"That's our cue," she said. Neil grinned at her.

"Think Cameron's gonna lose her shit?" Mac returned his grin.

"She very well could, though she'll probably wait until she's alone with me before she has her say. It's one thing for her to tease me about sex and try to embarrass me, but this is something that might worry her. Or she could just shrug her shoulders at me. Of course, that'll mean she's pissed off."

"Guess we'd better get dressed and find out." Mac took a deep, cleansing breath and let it out. She hoped Cameron wasn't upset, but it wasn't up to her daughter. Mackenzie loved her kid, but her decisions had never been controlled by her. She'd made her choices based on what she thought was best for her child when she was young, but Cam was an adult now and would just have to deal.

It turned out that the four of them were getting food at the moment, which was good. That way they wouldn't have to compete with the sounds of a game.

"Hey, guys. We've got something to talk to you about." Mac barely managed to get the words out. Her mouth went dry as they all turned around to look at her. She'd never made a personal announcement in quite this way before. She usually just told her daughter stuff in private. Doing it this way made it seem huge and life altering. Which, of course, it was. Thankfully Neil took over the next bit.

"In fact, we've got more than one piece of news to deliver, but we'll start with the happy stuff."

"We're getting married on Monday," Mac blurted.

"Uh, okay, right." Cameron rolled her eyes and assumed it was all a joke. Billy, however, was smiling.

"She already said yes, huh? Didn't you say something about waiting to ask her later, dad?" Now it was Neil's turn to look a little awkward.

"Well, she made me!" Mac started laughing, and poked him in

the ribs again.

"I did not! I just said I wouldn't try on the ring until you were really asking me. It's bad luck, after all."

"And you don't even believe that, so tell them another one." Cameron was looking back and forth between Neil and her mother.

"You're not kidding? You're actually getting married on Monday?" Mackenzie nodded at her and held her breath.

"Holy shit. What the fuck, mom? You suffer a recent blow to the head? Hell of a way to go off the deep end." Finally she relented with a smirk.

"At least you've got some company, since he's obviously just as crazy as you are." She shook her head at both of them. Mac let out her breath in a rush of relief.

Neil looked at her in question, and she smiled at him to indicate it would be fine. He put an arm around her and squeezed.

Kirk and Leigh took the whole thing in stride, since they probably didn't really care. They didn't see how it would affect them. Billy, on the other hand, was keenly aware of what it could mean for him when a parent got married.

"So, what's going to happen then? You guys get married, and then does that mean you're going to want to be alone and stuff?" Mac knew what he was getting at.

"Billy, we want you around now, and that won't change. I like you quite a bit. We won't shuffle you around like unwanted baggage. It doesn't matter how old you are. I didn't get rid of Cam just because she was an adult." Neil looked at Cameron.

"You know that goes for me, too, right Cameron?" Cameron smirked.

"My mother would kick your ass if you tried." Mac grinned. At least she'd never made her daughter feel insecure about her living situation. She *wanted* her kid around. Especially now.

"Alright, that's the happy stuff. Then there's the not-so-happy stuff. Neil and I are going back to the city tomorrow. For two reasons. First the ferrets at the shelter there need to be removed from the situation. They've got some food for the time being, but it won't last."

"Let me guess. The other reason is Mitch." When Mac nodded at Cameron, she could see that her daughter really was pissed now. She didn't blame her.

"Before you blow a gasket, we're only going as far as the shelter. I'm going to tell him to meet us there. If he's not there by the time we have the ferrets loaded up, he's lost his ride. I won't risk anything more for him than I'm already risking for the ferrets, okay?

"There's as much chance that he won't show up this time, as there was when I told him to get his ass up here. He left a message today when my phone's battery was dead. I didn't get it until a couple hours later. I might not even be able to reach him now. I'll try once we've all finished yapping.

"There are two other shelters we have to go to later, but they're not in a complete blackout yet. We can hit them both in a two-day span with no trouble.

"Of course, this means more work. We need to create a space for that many ferrets, and some will need to be separated from the others. There will be some that are already used to one another, but that won't be true in all cases." Neil nudged her.

"It would help if we settled the living arrangements, honey. Then we'll know what space is available where, and how to divide them up." Mac considered it.

"I totally let that slip my mind. The two of you have been coming over here. Hell, I haven't even seen your house. I guess I just pictured you both living here. We're crowded right now, but that other building will be huge.

"This is meant to be a garage and workshop, so nothing was done to make it look decent. I've always had totally different plans for the other building. This can't be just my decision or my way of doing things, though. At this point we all need to have a say. Whatever bedroom I'm sleeping in, though, the ferrets come with me. Well, and Neil too I suppose."

This time Neil dug his finger into *her* ribs.

"You suppose? I'm pretty sure I'm a little more useful to you than that."

"Cocky, ain't ya cowboy?" He squeezed the back of her neck in a mild threat.

"I have reason to be. Anyway, I've got some ideas about housing, but there will be some shifting while things are being dealt with. Billy and I built a pretty small cabin and the two bedrooms are more the size of kids' rooms. Not really meant for more than a couple of bachelors. I don't think either one of us figured on something like this happening."

"Bah. You had women crawling all over you both, I'm sure. Didn't you Billy?" Mac's teasing question had him turning red and stammering a bit before answering.

"N-no. Dad wasn't exactly Mr. Smooth with the ladies. Didn't get out much. And I've never even had a girlfriend." He looked like he was hoping for the ground to swallow him up after saying that, and he refused to glance anywhere near Cameron.

"Well, it just goes to show. You never know what will happen. Now your dad's getting married, and one day I'm sure you'll have lots of women to choose from. You've got your dad's looks." When Billy's face turned scarlet at that, Mac relented and moved on.

"Anyway, it sounds like you've got some thoughts on all this, cowboy, so let's hear 'em."

"Does anyone want to take over the cabin maybe? I'll stay here with you, if we can make that work. A couple of weeks and we can get the other building up. If you walk me through the plans for it, I can help you carry them through. I'm curious how you intend to make a steel building look like a home, but logs don't make a comfortable place either, without something being done to the inside."

Mac saw Kirk glance at Leigh. She already knew where this was going. They had no privacy here, and even if they didn't stay at the cabin permanently, they could at least have some privacy while the new place was set up.

"You've got animals at the other place, don't you?" Neil nodded in answer to Kirk's question.

"Well, if you can show us what to do, we can take care of them for now. If that's okay." He looked uncertain.

"That's alright with me. What about you, Billy? Where do you want to be?" Of course, Billy glanced first at Cameron, but Mac knew what his answer would be without him doing that.

"I'm fine on the futon for a while. Dad said something about this place maybe joining up with ours. Do you know if it does?"

"It does. I got maps from the land registry office, and the properties are connected, which makes it easy no matter what happens in the rest of the world."

"So, basically we're not really moving anyway. It's more like we just have a bunch of different places. Like outbuildings on a farm."

"That's a good point, Billy. We also have the option of using the river to get back and forth, which may end up being very useful.

"For tonight and tomorrow let's leave things as they are. In case we're not here, I'd feel a lot better if you guys were all in one place. Cam can take over my room and be with the ferrets again, and Kirk and Leigh will still have privacy, even if it's not a whole house. Billy can have the futon. We can move things around when Neil and I get back from Toronto."

"Guess you better try to call Mitch, honey. We can deal with the rest of the stuff later." Mac's shoulders sagged.

"But I don't wanna," she whined, making Neil laugh, though it was more or less the truth. Talking to Mitch, if she could reach him, was going to be an aggravation. It always was. Even if their conversation was fine, she was always left feeling vaguely irritated. They had managed to become friends after splitting up, but the only reason for that was because they'd been together. He was not someone she would have made friends with normally.

"Yippee. Now I get to give him what-for and have him piss me off again, but it's still better than him dying in the city." The expression on Cameron's face indicated she might have an entirely different opinion on the matter, but Mac knew her daughter better than that. If Mitch came to their door in need, she'd let him in, just as Mac would. She'd just be more grudging about it.

Granted, Mackenzie was feeling pretty grudging about the whole thing, too. He was lucky there were ferrets to consider, though she wouldn't be so nasty as to tell him he was getting rescued only for that reason. Even if she wanted to. A lot.

Everyone else began rooting around in the kitchen for food again. Mac went to her bedroom and made her call.

"Thank fucking Christ! Where the fuck have you been? Why didn't you call me back?" Mac pulled her phone away from her ear and glared at it before responding in a scathing tone.

"Who the *fuck* do you think you're talking to Mitch? Shut the fuck up and listen, because I'm only going to say this once. This is how it's going to be."

"Alright, I'm listening."

"Thank you," she said crisply, before outlining the plan as precisely as possible, putting a great deal of emphasis on the fact that she was only giving him one shot to get picked up.

"Mitch, I'm not kidding when I say we'll leave without you. As soon as those ferrets are loaded, we're gone. I won't take the chance that we don't make it back, and I guarantee people will be coming after us when they see we have a vehicle with fuel.

"If you don't have enough gas to get to the shelter, you're going to have to find another way. It's less than an hour by car, so you have other options. I don't care if it's a bicycle, or you steal a motorcycle and siphon fuel from the tank of your car to put into it. I'm not going as far as Hamilton, so you need to work it out.

"We'll leave here at noon, so expect us to be there by three. I might have to find a way to convince Kelly I can care for the ferrets. That could take some time, but don't count on it. I'm going to try calling her before we go. If her phone is up, I'll be able to prepare her, and maybe she can pull things together before we arrive. That means we could be gone within the hour.

"Finally, if you come here now there are some changes since the last time we talked. First, I'm getting married on Monday if the offices are still up and running. Second, security is an absolute priority. If you fuck with the security I will shoot you myself. Third, there's more work to be done, so you'll need to help out. Is any of that unclear?"

"No. I'm good. Don't think you can shoot me without a gun, though." His smartass remark pushed her instant-bitch-button.

"Mitch, do you honestly think I don't have a fucking gun? I've had my PAL for the last five years, for Christ's sake! I got my restricted at the same time. Believe me, I have a gun and I've had a lot of practice with it. Do not fuck with me on this."

"Okay, okay. Calm down. I was just kidding. I'll be there tomorrow. If I don't have enough gas in the car, how long do you think it would take me on a bike? I'm not in the best of shape." Mac was only slightly mollified, but she looked at the map on her laptop and answered him calmly.

"It's sixty klicks. Google Maps says it's just over three hours on a bicycle, so you'll have to guesstimate from there."

"It actually gives the time on a bike?"

"Yeah. Where the fuck have *you* been? They do hiking trails and all that shit now. You still have internet on your phone?"

"Yeah, so far."

"They must have backup power on all the towers there then. That's good. Try and download the directions from the address I'm sending you right now. Save them in case the 4G network goes down between now and then, even if you have to do it by taking a screen shot. All you need are the text directions, but get the map too if it makes you feel better."

"I have to get going. I need to find Kelly's card from when I adopted Squeaker. I'm hoping it has her cell number on it. You clear on everything?"

"Yeah, I think so. I'll find a bike and stick it in the car. Hopefully the car will get me there, but if not I'll use the bike."

"Okay. Good luck. Be careful getting there." When she finally hung up, she was just as irritated as she'd expected, if not more so. He was going to push her. She knew it. And there was no way she was risking everyone else for him. If he fucked with her and it put anyone else's life in danger, he was gone, one way or another.

19

BREAKING SOME EGGS

"Well, that sounded pleasant. You okay?" Neil was standing at the door, leaning on the lower half. She spun in the desk chair to face him, and leaned back.

"I've been better, but then I've been far worse, too. He'll either be there or he won't. Now I have to see if I can make sure the ferrets will."

"Come and have something to eat before you go hunting for that business card. It's already really late, but I'm guessing you intend to call and leave a message anyway, so an hour and some food will put you in a better frame of mind." Mac bared her teeth at him.

"What makes you think there's something wrong with my frame of mind?" Neil laughed and opened the door to walk into the bedroom. He pulled her up out of her chair and kissed her softly on the mouth.

"Maybe it's because you just threatened to kill your ex-husband. Not that it's an uncommon occurrence, but I do believe you actually meant it." Mackenzie sighed.

"I did, actually. I won't put up with him risking all our lives. I'm sure the garden would be happy with the extra fertilizer." Neil gave a mock shudder.

"You're a cold one, honey. Sexy."

"Oh, shut up. I know damn well you'd do the same if someone put us at risk."

"Damn straight. Wouldn't be the first time I've taken the law into my own hands. Guess I'll probably have to tell you all about that, though I think the story can wait for a little while yet. There are other priorities."

"Oh sure. Pique my curiosity and then refuse to tell me."

"That's right. Food first, and some time spent with the rest of us so you can get your equilibrium back."

"You think time spent in a crowd of people puts me back on an even keel?"

"It's not just people, it's your family, and maybe not *entirely* on an even keel since you're big on solitude. Still, it'll take you out of your own head for a little bit if you're listening to the kids swearing and laughing for a while."

"I'm some kind of weirdo, aren't I? That I would enjoy listening to my kid swearing, I mean. Most mothers would be appalled."

"You're not most mothers. You're better than that."

"Okay, okay. You can stop with the flattery now. I'm going. What's for dinner?"

"I don't know. You haven't made it yet." She was pretty sure he was going to bruise from the fist she plowed into his upper arm. He was still rubbing it when they got to the kitchen and Mac saw the sandwiches sitting there for her.

"Aww. I'm almost sorry I punched you now."

"Shut up and eat, honey." She shut up and ate.

*　　*　　*

The swearing and laughing were still echoing in the room as she searched for the business card. She finally found it in the third filing cabinet. It was with Squeaker's adoption paperwork, along with all his vet records.

Mac went to the bedroom and called the number. As expected, she had to leave a message. She hoped Kelly would be able to check her voicemail, and that she would do so in the morning.

Neil sauntered into the room to let her know the camping gear was set up, but that Kirk and Leigh had offered to be the ones to sleep outdoors. Then he shut the top section of the door. Mac was so tired by this point that she was just grateful not to have to walk more than two steps to a bed. It had been a crazy day, both emotionally and physically. It would be nice to stay with the ferrets, too. They'd been wandering around her feet, sniffing at things as she made her call.

Mac picked up the only ferret within reach. Pickle immediately started licking her on the mouth. She pressed her lips together to keep it from getting too weird, and then snuggled him when he was done, rubbing her face against his silky fur.

Neil snagged Squeaker as he attempted to trot by, and held him up in front of his face.

"How come I don't get any love?" Mackenzie chuckled at him.

"He doesn't know you yet, except for the smell of your butt maybe. He's not quite as affectionate as Pickle, though. Maybe with all the ferrets we'll be bringing back, you'll find one that actually likes your face as much as it likes your ass, but I have my doubts. That's a pretty fine ass you've got there. The muscle probably makes it tough and chewy, though."

Pickle wanted down by then, and so did Squeaker, so they were both released to the wilds of the bedroom floor where they promptly pounced at one another and then started performing a war dance.

"That's normal behaviour for them, right? They don't need to see a shrink or something, do they?" She giggled, which told her exactly how tired she was.

"Yes, that's completely normal for them. It's their happy dance. And when you see the toes splayed out like that, it means they're really excited. They're just having a good time. Pickle also splays his toes like that after he nips my ankles, so that tells you how much enjoyment he gets out of doing it.

"Alright, I'm done for. It's almost four, and I told Mitch we'd leave at around noon. I said the same in my message to Kelly, but I don't know if she'll even get it."

"Here, honey. Stand up." When she took his hand and stood, he started stripping her.

"Hey now! Nobody said anything about doing that."

"Not saying doesn't mean not doing. If you're not interested we'll find out shortly, but I'm pretty sure you will be."

"Confident, aren't we? Not that it's a bad thing, but it sure is tempting to knock you down a peg or two just to see if I can." He stripped off his own clothes and turned her to face the bed so her back was to him. She could feel the heat of his skin behind her, even though he wasn't touching her yet, and suddenly she wasn't quite as tired anymore.

Neil gently pushed her forward onto the bed, until she was lying completely on her front. Mac waited for him to touch her, but was surprised when he started with her legs, massaging them. Undoubtedly she had just died, because nothing felt this good on earth. Fifteen minutes later, after every muscle in her body felt like liquid, he slid inside of her.

They made love soft and slow, but even then it wasn't long before she was biting her pillow to keep from crying out when she came. He followed her almost immediately, and then they drifted off still connected.

Mac woke to the feel of Neil stroking her hair. She rolled into his arms, not wanting to get out of bed.

"Why couldn't we have met at a time when we'd have had at least a week together without worrying about being somewhere or doing something that was of life-and-death importance?" Her complaint had him tsking at her.

"Because things wouldn't have worked out this way. We'd have been floundering for things to say probably. You wouldn't have warned me at the store about what was happening in the city, and we might never have had a real conversation.

"For that matter, you might never have come into the store at all. You could have ended up buying your stuff anywhere. Instead, we have this. So, even if it means some frustration, I'm grateful to be with you now, and to know that I'm most likely going to be your husband in a couple days."

"Mm. Husband. First time that's sounded good to me in many years. Alright, you win the debate. Claim your reward, cowboy."

"I want that massage from you at some point. I got ripped off yesterday. Now let's get ready."

"Deal." Mac fed the chickens, and checked the goats. There were six eggs from the hens, so it looked like they had most of their breakfast. They'd leave the cereal to the kids, who seemed perfectly content with that.

Neil was out of the shower by the time she came back in. She handed him the eggs and headed off for her own. Once she was dressed she took care of the boys and went to the kitchen area to find scrambled eggs and toast, along with orange juice and coffee.

"You put on a nice spread this morning."

"Figured we'd need it. This looks to be an interesting day today. You know things could get very bad, I assume, so are you planning to carry?"

"Already am. Fixed and projectile. The knife is on me, but my Glock is in the car."

"Good. Does Cameron still have protection other than the survival knife?"

"She has her own Glock, among other things. I'll have to show you when we have a bit of time. We need to set up your fingerprints on the gun safes anyway, as well as retinal for the doors. When they're locked it would pretty much take a truck to get through them, so it's an added layer of security."

"Yeah, I notice there weren't any deadbolts. What did you use?"

"Electromagnetic, with power-loss fail-safes. Industrial grade, so they'll take at least a thousand pounds of force, but I think they might actually be rated higher than that. I bought them so long ago I forget. Either way, there isn't a man alive who's going to get them open with a crowbar."

Mac dug into her eggs and closed her eyes in pleasure. Their very first eggs from their own chickens, and they were worth it. A totally different experience from what she'd had even from the farmer's market. Neil was also a damn good cook, and he did them justice.

"I still say you'd have done well as my love slave and housekeeper. I pay premium wages, you know."

"Consider me paid for the remainder of our lives, honey. Being your husband is by far the better end of the deal, so I can do the cooking thing and load a dishwasher. Assuming you don't change your mind before Monday."

He'd said it as a joke, but she could see the tiny grain of seriousness in it.

"Neil, I'm not changing my mind. I haven't had any doubts or second thoughts, and I'm not going to. You don't even have to keep distracting me or convincing me with sex, if you don't want to." He laughed.

"I don't think the 'want to' part is an issue, Mac, and it honestly never occurred to me that I might be able to distract *or* convince you with sex. I'm not quite that confident in my abilities, though I do seem to perform well enough with a woman who responds so beautifully."

"I have no idea what you're like with a woman who doesn't respond, and I doubt I'll have the opportunity to find out. I don't seem to have much say in the matter."

"Good. You done?" She nodded and swallowed the last of her coffee. He took her dishes and added them to the ones already in the dishwasher, while Mackenzie dialled Kelly's number again.

Thankfully the woman picked up the phone. Mac explained what she was doing. She wasn't really surprised when Kelly just asked her how soon she could get there. Mac could hear the fear in her voice, and the knowledge that someone was coming to help had to be a big relief.

"I'm leaving in twenty minutes. Depending on what I find along the way, I'm hoping to get there sometime between three and four."

"Oh, thank God. I didn't know what I was going to do. I kept charging my phone in the car, hoping to hear from someone who could help, but I didn't want to drive anywhere without knowing where to take them." Kelly had tears in her voice.

"Hold on, Kelly. We're on our way. A scary-looking guy named Mitch might show up. You don't have to let him in if you don't want to, but he's heading there to hook up with us. I just wanted you to know in case you saw a guy who looked like a biker hanging around your door. He's not going to hurt you or the ferrets. He loves animals."

"Oh, okay. Thanks. I might have been terrified otherwise. There's been a few jerks walking up and down the street, avoiding the cops, and they seem intent on causing trouble. I don't think they'd quibble at attacking a woman.

"You have no idea how grateful I am that the ferrets have a place to go. With them taken care of, I can concentrate on my own safety. I just couldn't leave them. I'll get them ready for you. We have twelve here right now, and I should be able to fit them into three or four carriers. Will you be able to transport that many?"

"No problem. If you have food or other supplies you want to send with them, I've got room for that too."

"Alright. I'll get that ready too, then. Thank you. See you in a few hours." Mac hung up, left a list of instructions for Cameron for getting things ready for the new arrivals, and then turned to Neil.

"Okay, cowboy. Saddle up. We're on a mission!"

The trip took just under three hours, even though there were partial blockages from abandoned vehicles on the highway. She was glad she'd chosen the BMW, because the truck might not have made it through, and the car was a hell of a lot better on fuel. It might have been over twenty years old, but its gas mileage and emissions were comparable to many of the new hybrid engines. BMW had made great cars back in the nineties.

She had a couple of full jerrycans strapped to the roof rack behind the sunroof, covered in a light tarp to disguise them. She couldn't risk the gasoline poisoning the air in the trunk, since she'd be flipping down the back seats to open the cargo area for the carriers.

When Mac drove into the area where the shelter was located, she kept her eyes peeled for the men Kelly had mentioned. There didn't appear to be anyone on the street, but she knew there had to be someone looking out their window right now. For all she knew people still drove their vehicles here, but optimism wasn't the smartest outlook right now.

There was no sign of Mitch when they got there. Surprise was not her first reaction, certainly. He still hadn't taken her seriously, and she wasn't in a playing mood. He should know better. When she gave him an ultimatum, she always meant it.

"Fucking asshole," she muttered. Mac pulled into the driveway, happy to see an open garage door. She took the car out of gear and coasted inside. She came to a stop and turned off the motor, yanking up the parking brake. Then they got out of the car and rolled down the garage door manually.

Neil was still smiling at her cursing her ex. He wasn't the only one who was relieved, though. She really hadn't wanted to bring Mitch up north with them, even though his demise was now practically guaranteed. He would make things more dangerous for everyone. She knew that. He had a big mouth and did stupid shit if he was pissed off, drunk, or stoned, and he would always find a way to be at least one of those things.

"I know. It's for the best. Let's just get the ferrets and go home."

"Well, it's not like we won't be bringing anyone home with us. So you won't be lonely any time soon."

"What are you talking about?"

"You were never going to leave that woman here by herself. She obviously had nowhere to go when she talked to you earlier, and she's scared and upset. You're going to walk away and leave with just the ferrets? Not in a million years, honey."

"If you know this, why are you so complacent?" He gave her a shrug and a sheepish smile.

"Because I'd never be able to leave her here either. So she'll come home with us, and be a big help with the ferrets." Mac tried on her own sheepish grin.

"We're both pathetic. How the hell are we ever going to survive this bullshit with that working against us?"

"We have each other, and there's strength in numbers. We need to band together. Well-fed people are loyal, and loyal people are a deterrent to anyone who wants to steal from us. Sort of like a very visible neighbourhood watch."

"There are only so many people we can help this way. I'd rather work out a system for giving food to people without them finding us, and possibly helping with other things. We don't need much help at this point. With six of us running two gardens and two sets of livestock, we're pretty set. Granted, if we increase production to help feed everyone we'll need more help, but other than that I'm happy to give it all away so long as we still have the food we need."

"What about bartering, though? Did you really never think that you might want some help with something you couldn't do yourself?"

"Not so much. I made sure I studied up on everything to be sure we wouldn't be stuck without something. The only thing I knew I'd need help with was the insulin. I'm not good with chemistry, and the very idea of digging into the pancreas of an animal to obtain insulin is abhorrent to me. I know people are going to die. A lot of people, and as hard as that might be to swallow, it's honestly what this planet needs. Once people are gone, it'll come back on its own."

"Well, leaving aside plumbing, electrical, sewage, medical, and dentistry for the time being, the fact is we'll all be safer if we're working together. That won't happen right away, because I think you're right. The world is going to tear itself apart at first, and then maybe we can do something to help."

Kelly came into the garage through the door that led into the house and shelter. She had tears streaming down her face.

"I started to get so scared you weren't coming. I don't know why exactly. Just that my girlfriend has been missing for a couple of days now. She runs a veterinary clinic on the edge of Brampton. I wanted to go looking for her, but I couldn't leave these guys, and then I knew I'd never be able to fill up the car again, so even if I did find her we wouldn't be able to get anywhere safe."

"Okay, we're here," Mac said soothingly. "We'll see if we can help you find your girlfriend." Neil held up two fingers and Mac had to choke back a laugh. He was right.

"Your girlfriend a vet, or is she the manager?"

"Vet. She's brilliant. Amazing with ferrets, but lots of other animals, too."

"She must be pretty damn smart. Hard to get into vet school in the first place, much less deal with such widely varying anatomies. People always complain about high vet bills, but they have no understanding of what it takes to get that knowledge."

Kelly looked at her and grinned, cheerful now that she had some hope things might work out.

"You're right. People don't stop to think that with humans they have specialists for individual body parts. Specialties within specialties even. When I tore my rotator cuff, which was an accident related to a ferret if you can believe it, I not only had to go to an orthopedic surgeon, but I had to see one that specialized in shoulders, and he also had to specialize in arthroscopic surgery. It took forever to get in to see him. There isn't much of a waiting list for vets."

"Well, that's what happens when people have to pay for their own services. With our healthcare, people go to the damn doctor for the sniffles or a pimple. Bogs down the system. Never mind the fact that it's been decimated by our government. Not that it really matters at this point. Healthcare is going to be pretty much non-existent now." Kelly looked up at her in alarm.

"What do you mean? What's going on? I didn't have time to watch the news on Wednesday night and we haven't had power since Thursday afternoon. I tried picking up a few items at the corner store Thursday night, and every shelf was wiped out, with nobody in the store and the door wide open. I knew something was wrong, but I didn't know what. Is this happening everywhere?"

"Not yet, but it's coming." Mac explained what she knew of the situation as quickly as possible.

"Alright, why don't we load up the ferrets and whatever you think they'll need? We have a way we can help you and your girlfriend. Assuming we find her and you're both willing." Mac told her about their ranch-like setup, and Kelly was only too happy to agree.

"Can I get there on a tank of gas? My car is full. I can bring more stuff for the ferrets, and some clothes."

"Alright, but make it as quick as you can. Any food, books, and medical supplies you have would be a huge help, and we'll see if your girlfriend is willing to let us loot the stash at the clinic. That could make a huge difference for all of us, particularly the animals, even if she doesn't want to come."

They were almost finished loading both vehicles when the garage door began to roll up with a loud rattle. Mac bent down to reach behind the driver's seat of her car, pressing her fingers against the biometric locks on her portable gun safe.

Mac yanked the gun out and stuffed it down the back of her jeans, holster and all, but unsnapped the holster to make it ready. The Safe Action trigger system made it unlikely it would go off without someone physically squeezing the trigger, so she had stored it fully loaded with a round chambered.

She was facing the garage door again before it was up high enough for anyone to see that she'd been bent over. Then she waited.

20

CRY HAVOC

"What's going on in here? Looks like you people got some gas that you can donate to the cause, or you wouldn't be driving around in that fancy car of yours." Mac almost rolled her eyes. Another idiot that thought a twenty-three-year-old BMW was expensive.

"No, we don't have anything to donate to your so-called cause. I'm afraid you'll have to go home empty-handed," Neil spoke coldly. Mac was impressed. He was pretty intimidating. She hadn't asked him if he was carrying, but at the very least he had to have a knife on him.

"You got *that* wrong, ya fuckin' goof. And now you've pissed me off, so we're going to take everything that we want. I'm thinking the redhead first, for me at least. Who wants the blond bitch?" Mac had already noted the other four scuzzy-looking twerps standing behind the first one.

The one with the big mouth was brandishing a baseball bat, while some had knives. One had a handgun that he'd stuffed in the front of his pants, which told her he actually knew very little about handling a weapon. He was lucky he hadn't already shot off his dick. He was fondling the grip, as if he'd like to pull it out but wanted to keep the threat vague. Mac had no such qualms. Her decision made, she aimed her Glock, two-handed, at the one with the gun in his pants.

"I don't be thinkin' so, boys. If you'd bothered to bathe I might see some sort of appeal, but as it stands I'm just not interested. I don't think my friend here is either. Or are you?" She was asking Kelly, but she didn't shift her eyes to look at her.

"Not really, no. The one with the gun for a dick strikes me as the type who has to compensate for something. And I'm not really into the sausage these days anyway." Mac had to grin at Kelly's sass, despite the tenuous situation. She was going to enjoy having her around.

"See? You don't have our permission, which means you don't get to have what you want. And I have the means to enforce those rules as you might have noticed." The idiot with the gun in his pants made a slight movement, and Mac shook her head at him.

"Really, just don't. I *will* shoot you, and chances are good it'll either be in the crotch or the gut. Neither of which are pleasant options for you. I really don't want you having that gun to play with. You might shoot off your dick, and try to blame me for it.

Pull it out with one finger and your thumb.

"How fucking stupid are you that you would keep a weapon like that in your pants? Probably for the best if you shot your dick off and couldn't reproduce, though. This world does not need your genetic sludge contaminating the gene pool. Put the gun on the ground. Thank you," she said, once he'd complied.

"Now *all* of you, very slowly back down the driveway about five feet. If you try to run I'll shoot you in the back for your cowardice. You want a new gun, cowboy?" She could see Neil smiling in her peripheral vision.

"Sure do. It's a nice piece. SIG Sauer 1911 Stainless Super Target, if I'm not mistaken. That's a pretty expensive gun here, though I prefer a .40 calibre to a forty-five. Forty-fives are better for show than results in my view, which is consistent with the mentality. What the hell is a piece of shit like you doing with a seventeen-hundred-dollar handgun? I'm guessing it wasn't a legitimate purchase."

The guy didn't respond, though his eyes looked longingly at his former piece. Obviously he was going to miss the status symbol that made him the envy of his friends.

"Now, who here is right-handed?" They looked confused by Mac's question, but four of them raised their hands confirming her original assessment.

"Okay, the rest of you put down your weapons and back away another five feet." When they had, they were all pretty much at the bottom of the driveway.

"Do you happen to have some duct tape in the house?" Mac purposely left off Kelly's name, even though she doubted there would be consequences to these jackasses learning it, but she liked to err on the side of caution. Kelly said she did, and ran in the house to get it.

Neil finished checking over the SIG, made sure a round was chambered, and moved over to her side.

"What do you have in mind?" He'd spoken quietly enough that his question couldn't be overheard.

"Dominant hands, finger tendons."

"Messy, but effective. Neighbourhood will be a little safer, and they'll be lucky to survive what's coming, but you won't have to live with actually killing them. Nice. Who gets the joy?"

"I figured you, since they might overpower me if I get close, and they're pissed that a woman has them covered. You're better equipped to handle them. If you don't want to cut them, that's fine. Just tape them up together, and I'll do that."

"Oh no. You've had all the fun so far. I'd like to play my own tune." Mackenzie grinned wickedly.

"You have no idea how much I love you right now," she whispered.

"That's a new one. You love me for being mean as a snake. Then again, I feel the same about you. You're pretty fucking hot, standing there holding a gun on a bunch of fuckwits."

"You'll have to bang me later. I'm a little busy right now." Neil just laughed. She had no doubt that he had every intention of doing so.

Kelly came back with the tape.

"Sorry. I couldn't find it at first with everything I was throwing around to pack the car."

"Alright. Do you know how to handle a gun?"

"No. I hate them, so I've never had one. Especially with the ferrets getting into things."

"Okay. Cowboy, can you make the gun safe for her to hold while you do what you have to do? Probably best if she doesn't have to watch any of this anyway." Kelly looked alarmed.

"What are you going to do to them?"

"We're just going to make it difficult for them to prey on anyone else. At least for a while. I don't know how permanent the damage will be, though. If you're squeamish about blood, you might not want to watch." Kelly was fine with the explanation, but turned away as Neil strapped two of the men back to back, explaining that he wasn't going to kill them. They were just making sure they couldn't follow. It was true as far as it went, and made them compliant.

He strapped a second pair together, and then the odd one out was taped to a pair with his back to their shoulders on the one side. They couldn't do much to move their hands by this point, but once he cut into the fingers of one of them, and the screaming started, the other four began putting up a fight even though they didn't fully understand what was happening.

"Why don't you get the rest of whatever you were getting,

Kelly? People are bound to start noticing something is going on and come out to see what it is." Kelly nodded her head and ran in, the empty gun still in her hand.

The cars were loaded by the time people found the courage to come out of their homes. They didn't look upset, though. Smug satisfaction was the only way she could describe the expression on one woman's face, as she watched Neil make the last cut.

"They try to rob you, too?" The woman was asking Mac.

"Sure did. And there was some nonsense about rape, too."

"Should cut off his fucking dick, then, but maybe this will be enough to teach them a lesson. Doubt it, but we'll keep an eye on them and see how it goes. Cops can't do shit right now, but at least we won't have to deal with them anymore."

Mac nodded at her and backed toward the BMW, not anxious to continue the conversation. The last thing she needed was to have to explain what they were doing there, and where they were going. They didn't have room in the cars for this many people.

Neil used the faucet on the side of Kelly's garage to wash off his hands, though he still had a little bit of blood on his clothes. Then he did the same with his knife, and dried it on a clean area of his shirt. Once he sheathed it, he walked back to the car and reclaimed the SIG from Kelly who had retrieved it from the house. They all ignored the whimpering of the men who were just now trying to move down the alley.

Mac had always known she had violence in her. She used it for what she considered good, so she wasn't alarmed by it, but it allowed her to recognize the same traits in Neil. She wasn't alarmed by his violence either, since he had the same moral compass she did. Maybe that had something to do with the tattoo on his back that she had yet to ask him about.

Kelly got into her car, and Mac and Neil got ready to follow her to the clinic. Thankfully the people still shoving at the taped-together gangsta wannabes seemed to have little interest in going anywhere. They probably figured everything would be fine in a few days. A whole bunch of Pollyannas.

As they slowly pulled through the crowd, Mac mentally wished them the best and hoped they would make it despite their naïveté. Then she heard some of the ferrets chattering in the carriers and she smiled. At least these guys would.

They made it to the clinic in thirty minutes. When they pulled in to park, the situation started looking bleak. Kelly pointed out Annette's car, but it was the broken glass entry window that Mac and Neil were looking at.

"Sure hope that fancy new gun of yours is loaded," Mac said quietly. Kelly had just seen the broken window, and was looking at them with terror in her eyes. Mac put her finger to her lips, hoping Kelly understood. If she panicked, they might lose any advantage they had.

Mac was no commando, and she was pretty sure Neil didn't have any military experience either, but between them she figured they could deal with whatever had happened inside. Especially if they had surprise on their side.

"It is fancy isn't it? Not as fancy a piece as you, but worth a spin." Mac rolled her eyes.

"Alright cowboy, I don't understand hand signals, so we need to have a plan for when we go in there. Hopefully Kelly knows the layout well enough to describe it to us."

Mac motioned Kelly over. Thankfully she seemed completely rational and level-headed, despite the situation, but then Kelly had been dealing with ferret emergencies for a number of years. Mac assumed she'd learned to distance herself from a situation.

"Tell me what to expect in there, Kelly."

"I don't know! Anything could have happened," she whispered.

"No, I mean the floor plan. Do you remember the way things are set up in there? Like which rooms are where?" Kelly nodded.

"I've been here a zillion times. Not just for the ferrets, but for Annette, too." Her voice wavered.

"It's okay, Kelly. We're going to go in there and see if we can find her, alright? But we need as much information as you can give us. If there's someone still in there, other than your girlfriend, we want to have the upper hand. It's the only way we can make this work." Kelly nodded again and began describing the interior of the clinic.

Mac closed her eyes during the recitation. She needed to visualize it as Kelly spoke, or she'd never remember what she'd said. By the time Kelly finished, Mac had a pretty good idea what she wanted to do.

"I'm guessing you don't have a key to the back door."

"I do, actually. I shouldn't, but Annette gave me one anyway. I even have the alarm code, though I don't guess that matters now."

"If it were still working, it would have gone off when the place was broken into the first time, so just give me the key." Once Kelly handed it to her, Mac turned to Neil.

"You take the front, but give me a thirty-second head start to get back there and unlock the door. We'll keep going until we hit trouble or meet up. Hopefully we'll be quiet enough about it that we surprise anyone inside."

Neil cupped the back of her head and kissed her. She could see he didn't want her doing this, any more than she wanted him going in there, but it needed to be done.

"Alright, honey. Please, please be careful. I don't want you using this as an excuse to miss our wedding on Monday." Kelly looked up in surprise at that.

"Don't worry, cowboy. I'll be there. Let's just hope the damn office is still open by then. Let's get this over with and get home so we can get these babies settled in.

"Kelly, why don't you watch over the fursnakes? Try to conceal yourself somewhat, but also keep an eye out for anyone coming this way. Honk the horn if anyone shows up. Take this, and protect yourself in whatever way you have to, but I'm going to want it back. I've got a fondness for it." Mac handed Kelly her survival knife, still in the sheath. Kelly pulled it out a little bit and stared at the blade.

"Chances are you'll be fine. We don't intend to be in there long.

We'll let you know what's happening in a few minutes."

Once Mac got to the back and unlocked the door, she took several cleansing breaths before quietly pulling it open. Only the emergency backup lights illuminated the hallway. She was in a section with exam rooms, and all four doors were open. She sidled up to each door frame, and aimed her Glock into the rooms as she checked them.

There was nothing in any of the small rooms, but she heard a clattering sound coming from the larger room that housed the cages. She couldn't see any animals being held there, so at least they wouldn't alert anyone to her presence.

Mac leaned a little bit further around the corner. She could just see Neil on the opposite side, indicating with his head the part of the room that was obscured by the wall she hid behind. She leaned out slowly, saw what Neil was looking at, and then nodded at him. He counted off to three on his fingers, and then jerked his head. They both moved into the room.

The man standing by the broken drug cabinet was swaying slightly, struggling with a plastic-wrapped syringe. Mac assumed the woman lying in the corner was Kelly's girlfriend, and her face was badly bruised. It didn't look like she was conscious, though she appeared to be breathing. Mac figured that was for the best for the time being.

"Hey fuckface!" Mac yelled it at the obviously impaired man. He jumped and then spun around, dropping the syringe. He smirked at her and pulled a knife from the pocket of his jeans.

"What are you gonna do with that little toy?" He sneered as he spoke, apparently so stoned he didn't realize the Glock 22 was real. When he kept moving forward, she fired a round into his shoulder just as Neil hit him in the leg. He screamed and went down. Both the forty-calibre and the SIG had done their jobs nicely on their first real-world test.

"I'm guessing you cleared the other rooms and didn't find any-one," Mac said to Neal.

"Yeah, it was just this asshole. Getting stoned on animal tranquilizers, obviously. Looks like Ketamine in the vial on the floor, which is a dissociative drug. Too bad. He probably isn't as upset about being shot as he deserves to be. Let's get him tied up, just in case."

Mac found a roll of gauze and tied his ankles while Neil yanked his arms back and wrapped more gauze around his wrists. She grinned at the yowl of pain that came from the bound man.

"The one person in this room who's skilled at medical stuff will most likely be unable or unwilling to help this schmuck. That's probably ironic, but I've never been very good at defining irony. Can you go get Kelly while I see what I can do for Annette?" Neil nodded agreeably.

"It doesn't look like we hit any major arteries. He'll just have to do whatever he can for himself after we're gone, but we should probably get those slugs back. Think they went through him? Or will we have to dig into his wounds to get them?" Mac smiled grimly at Neil and bent down to collect her shell casing from the floor. She grabbed Neil's and stuffed them both in her pocket.

"I kinda hope he's still got them in him. Might be fun to torture him for a while after what he did to her." She holstered the Glock and stepped over to the woman sprawled on the floor.

"Annette? Is that you? You're safe now, okay? We're going to get you cleaned up, and maybe try to treat some of your injuries so you don't feel so bad." The woman blinked up at her.

"You're Annette, right?" When Mac received a short nod in response, she breathed a sigh of relief. The woman was coming back to herself and her surroundings. It was a good thing, because they needed to get whatever they were taking from the clinic and get moving.

"Alright Annette. You're going to be safe now. We've taken care of the man who was hurting you. He's not dead or anything, but he's no longer a danger to you. We need to get you up off the floor, though. Can you help me with that?"

Mac held out her hand, blocking the bleeding man from Annette's vision as much as she could with the angle of her body as she helped her to her feet. Mac kept a firm arm around Annette's shoulders and turned her away from her attacker.

"Do you have a shower in here, Annette?" She nodded again.

"Would you like to clean up?"

"What about evidence? I don't want to wash away evidence. I have to press charges!" Mac did her best to soothe her.

"Annette, there won't be any way to press charges. The police aren't really available for that kind of thing right now. Besides, he's definitely suffering for his actions."

"What did you do to him?" Annette's eyes were wide open.

"We put a couple of shots into him, that's all. He's been into the Ketamine very heavily, and he's tied up. I doubt he'll be able to identify us later, from what I understand about the effects of Ketamine." Annette's shoulders slumped in relief.

"Thank you. Thank you so much. I don't know who you are, or how you ended up helping me, but thank you. And yes, I'd like very much to clean up now." Mac helped her as Annette limped toward the bathroom near her office.

"I'm Mackenzie, though most people call me Mac. You may have noticed another man in the room with us, though maybe you didn't. Either way that was Neil, my fiancé. We went to the shelter to get the ferrets out of the city. Kelly told us you haven't been home for a while, so we all came looking for you."

"Kelly? Is she here? Oh, God, I need to get washed up before she sees me like this. She always worries so much."

"Well, I'm sure she's pretty worried right now and would at least like to know you're not badly injured. Do you have any broken bones or bad bruising? Something that might indicate internal bleeding?"

Annette shook her head.

"He backhanded me a couple of times when I wouldn't give him the key to the drug cabinet. When I was on the floor he kicked me a lot, but I was mostly able to protect myself with my arms and legs. I've got no abdominal distension that would indicate any major problems, and the pain is no more than I would expect. If there was serious internal damage, I'd likely already be dead. I'm not sure what day it is now, but he did this Thursday afternoon as soon as he broke in."

"Today's Saturday. If you do have any problems, be sure to let us know right away. We've got a situation that needs to be dealt with. In here *and* out there in the rest of the world. That means we have to keep things moving as much as possible.

"Let's get you cleaned up first. Hopefully the water is still running. Kelly can grab a change of clothes for you from her car." Annette nodded and went into her bathroom, locking the door.

21

FERRET BUSINESS AS USUAL

Kelly burst into the hallway seconds after the bathroom door closed, trying to get to Annette.

"Easy, Kelly. She's having a shower, and she's going to need a change of clothes. Something loose, preferably. She's pretty banged up, but says she doesn't have serious injuries." Kelly paced back and forth.

"Where is the son of a bitch?"

"In a lot of pain."

"Good." Mac's mouth twisted into a sardonic smile.

"It took a couple of minutes to get Annette out of the room, and he was still sobbing and moaning. I don't think the bullet holes agreed with him."

"Where did you shoot him?" Mac almost laughed at the grim satisfaction on Kelly's face.

"I got his shoulder, and Neil got his leg. He was coming after me with a knife, so stoned he thought I was holding a toy gun. I guess he didn't see Neil, or figure I would put up much of a fight."

"Are we going to have trouble over this?"

"Well, you certainly won't, since you didn't shoot anyone, but if a problem arises we'll deal with the consequences."

"We'll never tell anyone. Annette can just say it was a couple of Good Samaritans that came along and helped her."

"Not sure that would work. Especially if you both come with us, and it gets out we brought you to the farm. I still plan to get the slugs out of him. A little digging around would serve him right. Can you get some clothes for Annette while she's getting cleaned up?" She said she would and Mac went back into the larger room.

She was spared the mess of digging for slugs, though it took her a while to find them in the dim room. Hers was lodged inside the back of the drug cabinet. It was so badly mangled by that point, she doubted they'd get any rifling marks, but she stuck it in her pocket anyway. She found Neil's sticking out of the side of the man's leg, so she yanked it from the wound. Her actions provoked a few curses from the stoner.

"Shut the fuck up. You beat a defenseless woman for some drugs, you slimy piece of shit. You're lucky you didn't do anything else to her, or it would be your dick you'd be crying about."

"What the fuck do I want a nigger pussy for?" She could barely make out the words through the slurring, but that didn't change the level of her ire at hearing them. She stomped on his leg wound in response, making him scream.

"Scum. You're soon going to see just how hard life can get, even for a white boy, and I doubt very much you'll survive. I'll sit back and happily imagine your slow demise. For now, shut the fuck up or I'll shoot you again." When Neil walked back into the room, she happened to notice the blood on her hands.

"Gross. I have the scumbag's blood on me. I need a sink." Neil spun her toward the opposite wall. She began scrubbing her hands with antibacterial soap and a fingernail brush. She didn't speak again until she'd dried her hands on a paper towel.

"I'm going to check on the ferrets. Kelly needs some time to deal with Annette and explain the plan to leave the city. I suppose it's possible that Annette won't want to go, but after this I very much doubt it." Neil stroked her back and nodded.

"Okay, we'll both go. This guy isn't going anywhere, and I don't enjoy being near him."

They got to the side of the car, where Mac inhaled deeply.

"You don't have any gum on you, do you?" Neil shook his head.

"Never mind. I've got some in the glove compartment, I think. Hang on a second. I can't stand the taste in my mouth from the smell in there." She found a container of the hot and spicy cinnamon gum she liked, and pulled two pieces out to stick in her mouth. She held out the container to Neil who shook his head again.

Mac sank down into the car to check on the ferrets. The twelve little bundles snuggled together in groups made her smile. They had water bottles attached to the carriers, with scoops under the spouts to prevent water getting all over the place, and there were feeders in the carriers, too.

There was kibble on the floor of the carriers, but that was to be expected. She was surprised more water hadn't spilled out. Some of the city streets were pretty bad.

Mac stuck her fingers into all four carriers, one after another, letting the few ferrets that were still awake sniff the strange antiseptic smell on them. Of course, they were probably used to Annette smelling like that. A couple of them licked her fingers, and one decided a delicate gnawing was in order. It made her smile.

She got out of the car in a much better frame of mind, and looked over at Neil.

"You look like you feel better, honey." She gave him a relaxed smile.

"It's called *ferrapy*. Ferret therapy. There's something about them that pulls away all the stress. You hold them or touch them and you're suddenly filled with protectiveness and love, rather than whatever you were feeling before.

"That gives me an idea. I'll be right back." Neil shook his head at her and took his hand off the car's door frame so she could close it.

"I'm with you," he stated. Mac companionably took his hand and walked to the back door with him so they could go straight into the hallway. She went over to Kelly and whispered quietly in her ear.

"How is she with the ferrets? Does she have a favourite?" Kelly brightened at the idea.

"Yeah, she loves them as much as I do. Beanie Baby is almost like a familiar to her. We usually call her Beanie or Bean. She's the really tiny one with the blaze. Completely deaf, so you have to be careful not to startle her."

"I know which one you're talking about. She was one of the ones licking my fingers a few minutes ago. I'll go get her, as long as you don't think Beanie will freak out if I bring her in here."

"Not at all. She's used to the smells, and she's come in with Annette any number of times, just because Annette wanted her with her. She'll be fine. If she was licking your fingers, she isn't afraid of you. That's a wonderful idea. I should have thought of that myself. I don't know why I didn't."

"You have a lot of things on your mind. We'll be right back with Beanie."

They returned with the tiny little girl in less than a minute. Mac almost didn't want to let her go, she was so sweet. Mac reluctantly handed her to Kelly, though. She couldn't weigh more than three-quarters of a pound, and was the smallest ferret she'd ever seen. Of course, she'd only ever had male ferrets, and they could be twice the size.

"Annette, honey, I've got Beanie out here. Would you like to see her?" In an instant the door was open. She burst into tears the moment she laid eyes on the ferret, and her hands were shaking so bad she couldn't pick her up and hold her, but Kelly held her up to Annette's face.

With Beanie nuzzling into her springy hair, Annette began to calm down really fast. It was a good thing, because Mac was anxious to get on the road. Once Annette was able to hold the ferret herself, Mac started to speak.

"This may be bad timing, but we don't have a choice. We need to get going, so Annette needs to have the situation explained to her. I don't think there's going to be a better time." Kelly nodded, while Annette just allowed herself to stroke Beanie, not really even interested in the conversation.

"Annette, I need you to listen to this, because it directly impacts you. All of the greater Toronto area is in blackout, and martial law has been imposed. The blackout is spreading..." She continued to speak, while making sure Annette was really looking at her and listening.

"Kelly has already agreed to come with us, if you're willing to go. We have no time for a drawn-out debate here. What happened in your clinic is a direct result of what's going on in all the nearby cities. There is no longer any real law and order, so the assholes are coming out.

"There's the typical looting and all that stuff, but we ran into a situation at your place that resulted in some violence as well. No one was killed, but we made sure they couldn't continue to bully the neighbourhood. No matter where you go in the cities, it's really fucking dangerous. Especially for women, as you've been blatantly made aware of.

"We came down to get the ferrets out of the city. We can give them a safe place where they'll never run out of food. We've got a good set-up already, because we were preparing for this sort of thing."

Annette was starting to absorb what Mac was telling her, and she looked to Kelly for confirmation.

"She's right. We can't stay in the city. In any of them. There's no food in the stores. Please, tell me we can go with them. I want you safe, just as much as I want the ferrets safe." Annette blinked, her eyes damp. Mac knew she sure as hell wasn't feeling safe right now, and that was something any victim of violence desperately needed.

"You can keep us safe there? How?"

"It's not just that we have weapons and good security. We're very well-concealed, and with the two of you there will be eight of us. The more people we have, the less we're going to have to worry about anyone coming to hurt us." Mac looked at Neil when she said that. He'd been right as far as that went. If everyone was there, working together, they'd have so much less to fear than if it was every person for themselves. She didn't like the idea of being crowded, but safety was the priority.

"But, doesn't that mean more people to feed?" Annette directed her question at Mac. Instead of answering, Mac asked Neil how many goats and chickens he had.

"I've got twelve goats, same as you, so between us we have two-dozen. We have dozens of laying hens and a few roosters between us," he continued.

"Wow. You guys really took the whole preparedness thing seriously, didn't you?"

"Well, we were right, weren't we? And the last thing you can count on when the shit hits the fan is bureaucracy. They aren't very good at big emergencies. The first thing they did was scare the shit out of the citizens, instead of bringing in food and supplies. They've already invoked the War Measures Act, stripping people of their rights, and for what? They sure as hell can't control anything that way."

Mac was feeling a little pissy about Annette's remark, despite the fact that she should be used to that. She just wasn't expecting someone to think it was a joke when the evidence was all around them.

"Sorry. Really. I didn't mean that the way it sounded. It was more relief that I was feeling than anything else. I really want to get away from this place. Do we just go now, or is there something else we need to do?" Mac gave her a once-over.

"Drugs. For the livestock. I'm not asking you to bring anything for people to get high. Sure, antibiotics will work for people, as will some other drugs you probably have here, but we only want stuff that's necessary. I have FishMox and Bird-Sulfa, along with anything I could get OTC.

"The only prescription stuff I have is birth control for the younger generation, because it's really easy to pick up a big supply of it."

Mac saw a look flash across Neil's face at the mention of birth control. She was going to have to talk to him about that, but it could wait for later.

"Hopefully that asshole didn't destroy your entire supply of Ketamine getting high, because we might need it for the animals. Kelly tells me you're a good vet, and anyone who even got into veterinary school I know has to be damn smart, so I don't have to tell you what we need. To be honest, I have no idea. I have all kinds of books on chicken and goat diseases, anatomy, and treatments, but I haven't had the chance to read any, and certainly haven't got a clue what they might need to keep them healthy in the future.

"I've been preparing for a while, but time ran out on me. Neil might have a better grasp on some of that stuff, since he's been doing it longer, but he's more inclined toward developing a community aspect where we share our skills, so I doubt he knows how to perform goat surgery either." Neil chuckled.

"Hardly. I have a friend I figured I'd approach about it, if it came down to it, but I didn't do anywhere near the self-educating that you did." Annette looked back and forth between them, and then spoke up finally.

"Well, why don't I just bring everything? If there's no law and order, it hardly matters does it?"

"We're a little off the main highways, so hopefully Rosseau

won't have been hit yet. It was fine yesterday. When we get back we'll try to refuel. We may not be into the realm of lawlessness up there just yet, but you can see it spreading.

"Once we settle in there, we're going to spend as little time as possible off the property. I hope you can handle that. We've got a lot of land, but certainly no nightlife, unless you count stars and wild animals. Of course, there won't be any club hopping in the cities either, so it hardly matters." Annette smiled a little.

"We're not exactly into the bar-crawl scene, don't worry. We both love animals, obviously, and having so many around will be wonderful I think. I love goats, though I've never treated any. Not much opportunity here for that. Some backyard chickens mostly, though some cities around here have by-laws against having them."

"Tell me. Hamilton is one of them. I was living there when this started. Anyway, give us a minute to straighten up a bit by the drug cabinet, and then you can come in to pack whatever supplies you can fit in the cars. Kelly left some space in her car for stuff, and I still have a little room in the trunk behind the ferrets."

"You have them in your trunk?" Annette was shocked.

"No. My back seats fold down so there's trunk access from within the car. The very back of the carriers is just under where the trunk starts. I don't have anything in the trunk that would hurt them anyway. My extra fuel is on the roof rack. You'll see what I mean when you come out."

With that, Mac and Neil went to 'straighten up' by way of

dragging the whining drug thief out into the front hall area. Annette didn't need to come face to face with the guy. Getting knocked around when you were all alone was a pretty scary thing.

She was trying her damndest to be cool and collected about the whole situation, of course, but her hands started shaking.

"I think I need another ferret," she said, looking at the offending appendages. Neil shook his head before he spoke.

"Let's get Annette in there to gather her stuff, so we can leave this place and go home. The drugs will be good to have, but the longer we stay here, the more danger we're in." He grabbed her shaking hands, and warmed them between his own. The gesture soothed her much like her *ferrapy* did.

"Hey, you're almost as good as a ferret! Cool!" Neil rolled his eyes at her.

Once Beanie was back in the car, it took Annette less than fifteen minutes to organize all the things she wanted to take with her, including drugs, books, and surgical supplies. Mac had books, but the drugs and surgical supplies would be wonderful. She hadn't even thought of the surgical gear for the animals. Mostly she'd just hoped that kind of thing wouldn't be needed. She only had what was necessary for minor human stuff.

They all helped Annette load her supplies into the two cars, barely managing to squeeze everything in. Mac took the opportunity to add more fuel to their tanks, bringing both cars back up to full, and nearly emptying the jerrycans. She really hoped they would be able to top everything up when they got back to Rosseau.

Everyone still had power, but she was more concerned about whether or not they would still have any fuel.

"What happened to all the animals you'd normally have in there, Annette?" Annette gave a shrug.

"I couldn't perform surgery with the intermittent power, so I had to turn away anyone whose animals needed that kind of care. Eventually we called off all the appointments because we couldn't get anything done. Just in time, as it turns out. I saw my final patient right before the main lights died Thursday afternoon. I sent everyone home after that. I was just getting things closed up when that guy broke in."

Annette didn't want to talk about it anymore, and Mac wasn't going to push it. The timing would have been really bad right now anyway. They had to get back.

Suddenly it occurred to Annette that she would have to do something about her car. When she said she had a full tank of gas, Mac was fine with it being brought along, but she suggested Neil be the one to drive it. Annette was in no condition to be driving three hours straight.

"Do you have anything else that you want to bring along with you from the clinic, that maybe you didn't think would fit? With another car there's quite a bit of space that's suddenly available. We're not going to be able to come back here and everything helps."

It turned out that Annette had some portable diagnostic and exam equipment, which would be extremely useful, in addition to a countertop vaccine and medication refrigerator. She had a DC adapter to plug it into that she'd originally bought for her laptop. They had to adjust the front passenger seat so it was as level as possible, but it would be worth the trouble.

Some cages and incubators were coming along for the ride, too. It took them another hour, but Mac felt the benefits would outweigh the risk. Mac could build her a couple of exam tables later on, but so much of the stuff that Annette was grabbing were things she'd never have thought to buy.

When they were finished loading Annette's car, Mac and Neil went back to cut the ankle bindings on the scumbag. Movement would be awkward for him, but at least they weren't sentencing him to death that way. He could walk to find help.

"Okay, I'll head out first, followed by the two of you in Kelly's car. Neil can follow to make sure you don't get lost or left behind. It's almost seven, and as you can see it's getting dark, so I won't really be able to tell if you're behind me. Be honest with me here, though. Are you two going to be alright for the next couple of hours?" Kelly nodded.

"I can be a hard-ass about it. We need to be somewhere safe right now, and I'll make sure we get there."

"Alright. If for any reason you need to pull over, Neil will be behind you and will pull over with you. He can text me to let me know what's going on. Anyone have any questions, or other issues? Bathroom breaks?" They all shook their heads before Kelly and Annette got into Kelly's car.

Finally, it was time to go. They'd pushed their luck as far as they could without breaking it. Mac pulled out of the parking lot, already feeling better just being on the move.

Some of the ferrets made dooking sounds in the carriers. Poor things would need a bath when they got there. There was no way they'd been confined that long without a few of them sitting in poop. Oh well, it would give the kids plenty to do tonight. She'd done enough for one day, and she was in desperate need of some downtime.

22

HOME ON THE STRANGE

They were nearly home when she got a text from Mitch. She had the phone read it out to her.

"I'm okay. Just couldn't get there. Sorry." Mac realized he was a lost cause. She had no more fucks to give, as the expression went. She sent him back a terse message.

"Don't apologize to me. You're the one who's fucked now. I'm already back home. There's nothing else I can do to help you. Hope you make it." She wasn't risking anything more for him. Too many people and animals depended on her, and she could not focus her energies on saving one person who was determined to fuck himself over.

She wasn't surprised when she didn't hear from him again. She couldn't help him, so he had nothing to say.

Mac felt a little lighter, albeit sad, knowing Mitch was a non-issue now. She wanted to talk to Neil, but she didn't know if he could talk hands-free in Annette's car. She wasn't risking an accident for something that could wait thirty minutes.

It seemed to take forever for everyone to get through the gate tonight. It was just shy of ten, which was early for her, and she'd only been awake eleven hours, but she felt so bloody miserable she just wanted to go to bed. Of course, that only brought up another concern. Between the two houses and the tent, they didn't really have enough places for people to sleep.

There was the other mattress in the upper storage area, but no privacy even if they brought it down. She'd have to think of something, unless Neil beat her to it. Annette would want to feel safe, but she might also want solitude after such a stressful day.

Mac pulled up behind the other two cars, and saw her daughter framed in the spill of light from the doorway. She had to pull her misgivings back in. Cameron was still young enough to need her mother's strength. This was not the time to show weakness.

She got out and headed over to give her daughter a one-armed hug, which was all Cam tolerated these days, if that.

"Hey. Did you guys get the feeding, milking and egg-picking stuff done, in addition to that stuff I wrote down?"

"Yeah. Each goat only had a little bit of milk, and ewww, that was disgusting by the way." Mackenzie laughed at her daughter's expression.

"You'll get used to it."

"Because *that's* what I dreamed of being when I grew up. A goat farmer."

"Well, you might yet have a chance to grow up if you have stuff to keep you alive, so stop complaining. I need you to get those ferrets into the area I asked you to fence off inside the house. Wipe them all down first, and then they'll all need a full bath probably. They were stuck in those carriers for about six hours. Between the four of you, the work should go quickly.

"I need to eat and sleep, in that order. Find out from Kelly which ferrets have trouble getting along with the others so they can be separated. You guys will have to camp out in the living area, while Kelly and Annette take your room."

She was in the middle of explaining about Beanie when Neil walked up to them, irritation showing on his face in the light from the house.

"You done being boss-lady yet?" Mac gave him a confused look.

"What's wrong?"

"You. That's what's wrong. This has already been handled. You, on the other hand, have not. You've got a sandwich waiting. It's not a hot dinner, but it's quick. And then you can go relax."

"What the hell? What do you mean this has already been handled? Who handled it, and how? And what do you mean about *me* being handled?" Neil turned her toward the house and got her walking while he explained.

"I called Billy from the car. All you were doing was keeping your daughter from getting on with things."

"Were you driving while talking on the phone? Do you know how dangerous that is?" Mac could almost feel her eyes light up in righteous fury.

"I had my Bluetooth, Mac. Jesus." Mac shrunk down to her normal size again, and the fire and brimstone disappeared.

"Oh."

"Yeah, *oh*. You're not the only grown-up on the planet." Cameron disappeared as soon as Mac and Neil got to the kitchen area. Obviously she was staying away from this one. Mac was wishing she could do the same at this point. She decided to try a sheepish smile. Neil snorted in response.

"That's not gonna work on me tonight. Eat your sandwich, drink your juice, and then haul ass to the bedroom. Spend some time with your boys and I'll be there a few minutes after you." Mac couldn't help herself. She had a stubborn streak that chose the worst times to put itself on glorious display.

"I'm not going to bed until you do. I'm as capable of doing shit around here as you are." Neil's eyes narrowed dangerously. Mac was seriously regretting her display of temper now.

"I told you I'd be in a couple minutes after you, Mac, and I will be, because you and I have something to talk about that is in need of immediate attention. That's why I made the arrangements to have things taken care of before we got home. However, after we have that discussion I can see that you're in desperate need of a good night's sleep. Either that or a fistfight, and I'm not hitting my wife." Mac could tell that it had just slipped out, but it still made her close her eyes as the warmth of the words stole over her. She smiled. A genuine one this time.

"You mean to tell me I can't even have a *little* fistfight with my husband after we're married? That really blows. Could be fun," she teased. The corner of his mouth quirked up as she went on.

"We've still got time before the wedding, you know. We could have one now."

"Not a chance, honey. As far as I'm concerned you might as well be my wife *now*. You do look more stressed out than you were in Brampton, though. Did something happen on the way home?"

"Sad more than stressed. Had to say goodbye to a friend today, that's all. Mitch sent a text. I texted him back, wished him good luck and told him I couldn't do anything else to help him. That's all. It was right before we got home. I wanted to call you, just to hear your voice, but I didn't think you'd have hands-free. As you might have guessed I have rather strong feelings about driving while talking on a cell." Neil raised his eyebrow at her.

"Yes, despite the subtlety of your towering anger, I did catch the mild flavour of your opinion beneath all the layers obscuring it." Mac started laughing.

"You've got a hell of a way with words, cowboy. You're mother teach you to talk like that?" He smiled.

"She did, as a matter of fact. Damn good thing, because I'd never be able to keep up with your sharp tongue otherwise."

"I thought you liked my tongue, but I guess not. My mistake. I'll keep it to myself then." He growled in her ear.

"I don't think so, honey. I like your tongue just fine. I just have to keep my own flexible enough to deal with it."

"I've never voiced any complaints about *your* tongue. I'm pretty sure any vocalizations I might have made in that respect were more in the vein of complimentary noises." Neil was nuzzling her neck now, and he flicked his tongue out for just a quick taste behind her earlobe. She murmured in response.

"Well, that might have been a noise, and perhaps not a complaint, but you've definitely been more complimentary than that. Guess I'll have to try again." Mac suddenly let herself drop, sliding beneath his arm to wiggle away from him.

"Nuh-uh. Save that for later, cowboy. Now let me eat this dried-out old sandwich here, would ya?" Mac plopped onto the chair and took a very large bite. She didn't care if it was dry at this point. She was starving. Her stomach felt like it had been scraped out with a grapefruit spoon.

Since Neil was being quiet, she decided to be obnoxious and started chewing with her mouth wide open, making loud smacking sounds there was no way he could miss.

"What on earth are you doing, oh sexy one?" Mac almost choked on the food she'd been chomping at so grotesquely. It took her a minute before she could swallow, and then she had to take a drink of her juice to get it all down.

"I decided to hit you with all my dangerous feminine anti-wiles."

"I'm pretty sure you hit me with partially-masticated food a couple of times, too." Mac snorted and swallowed more juice.

"All part of my charm." She crossed her eyes, gave a sinister open-mouthed grin, wrinkled her nose and touched the tip of her tongue to the end of it.

"Wow. I'm completely swept away. Had I known such beauty awaited me, I'd have demanded you show me the real you right away. I can't stand it for another second. I *must* have you. Right now." His completely deadpan expression killed her. She was trying so hard not to laugh out loud, that it came out as a wheezing sound. Neil was soon chuckling with her.

"You're absolutely crazy. You know that? Now finish your partially-masticated, dried-out old sandwich so we can go to bed. Then we can have that discussion I'm so keen on right now."

"Well, you're lucky I'm in a receptive mood, and you refrained from using those four words."

"I have a pretty good memory when it comes to psychotic banshees, but then it wasn't that long ago that you warned me. I think I can remember something for a day or two. Don't worry, it's not that kind of talk. I'm settling rather nicely into the idea of being married to you, honey. The anticipation might actually kill me."

As soon as the dishes were in the dishwasher, they trotted off to her bedroom. Apparently he'd decided that his supervision wasn't necessary, or whatever it was he'd planned to do before following her. Mac sat beside Neil on the edge of the bed. She realized it had become *their* bedroom now, not just hers, since they'd be married soon. He showed no signs of wanting to spend the night elsewhere in the meantime. That gave her an idea.

"So, where do you plan to spend tomorrow night, the night before our wedding?" She could have fun with this one, she realized.

"Um, howling at the moon outside your non-existent bedroom window? I don't know. Was there somewhere I needed to be? Is there a ritual involving bootlaces, pine cones, and a dirty jock strap, where you invoke the demons of syllabub and tell me I have to lick the back of your knee six times in order to ensure lifelong happiness? Because we really don't have to go to all that trouble. I'm sure we can be at least *half* as happy without those elaborate preparations."

"Well, that'll never do. It's mint leaves, not pine cones, and you have to lick the back of my knee until I achieve *orgasm* six times."

"My apologies. I must have misplaced my copy of the ritual. I've got it here somewhere I'm sure."

"Alright, I give up. You can stay here that night, too."

"Can I? Well then. I'll have to lick the back of your knee tonight instead. Can't be too careful." Mackenzie was giggling helplessly by this point.

"Alright already! What was it you wanted to talk to me about? You can always lick my knee after we talk."

"Oh, good. I was afraid I was going to miss out. Anyway, at the clinic you said the birth control was for the younger crowd, and I wanted to know why."

"Ah, yes. I forgot I was going to talk to you about that. I saw your face when I said it, and realized you'd be concerned."

"Concerned? Hardly. Curious."

"Oh. Well, as far as I know I can't have any more kids. Plus I'm forty. Tried for a long time, and could never get pregnant. Or if I did it didn't take. It happened with both husbands, so I was the issue. I stopped trying."

"Yet you were able to have Cameron."

"I was seventeen, and that's about as fertile as it gets for a female. I just figured I got really lucky with her."

"You never went to a specialist?"

"I did, but they didn't know what was wrong. I didn't have any cysts or uterine abnormalities. Both times it got to the point where they were ordering deeper tests, which happened to coincide with the breakdowns of both my marriages, so those tests never got done."

"You had no other signs of illness or anything?" Mac shook her head.

"There are some causes of infertility that have no symptoms that I know of, but I'm no expert. Back when I would have wanted to do serious research on the topic, the internet wasn't really a thing. Anyway, my point is it's very unlikely there's even a snowball's chance in hell of me getting knocked up, so you're off the hook."

"You think I'd want to be?" Mac could see this was getting into some dangerous territory, and for no real reason.

"Maybe not, but the question is moot. As far as I'm aware I can't have children. Not anymore at any rate. I'm sorry. If you wanted more children, I'm *really* sorry, because you're a damn good father. You shouldn't have had to miss out on more kids if you wanted them.

"We probably should have talked about this *way* before we talked about getting married. Having kids can be a deal-breaker for some people. If it's like that for you, please tell me now. I'll understand. Really."

When Neil just looked at her, Mac wished she could swallow the words she'd spoken. The problem was, she wasn't sure if it was because she thought she'd hurt him by saying that, or because she was afraid he might back out now. If he did, she knew she would be devastated.

"You'll *understand*? Really? How could you possibly think I'd walk away from you over something you have no control over. I want to marry you because I love you, and because I want a wife not a brood mare. If it ever happened that you miraculously got pregnant, *and* you were willing to have the baby, I'd be happy as all hell. That doesn't change the fact that I'm already happy as all hell just being with you." Mac felt like a shit, and the only thing she could think to do was lighten the mood.

"Have you ever noticed how *irritated* we make each other over how much we *love* each other?" When he smiled she continued.

"Neil, I based what I was saying on how devastated *I* was that I couldn't conceive again, because I do know how badly a person can want a child. A couple of times I thought maybe I was pregnant. It was a feeling I couldn't explain. Then the feeling would pass, and there was another box of tampons to go through. Crude way of putting it, I guess, but I would look at that box at the start of a period and just start crying, knowing that I needed to use them yet again.

"Still, I had Cameron so I finally put away my hopes for more kids and moved on with my life. I got past it, but I'm not sure I ever got over it. Strangely, I never wanted either of my husbands, even then, to be real fathers to a child of mine.

"I still dreamed of having a child with someone I *did* want one with, and doing it right the second time. You know, where everything was a joy, and something to be shared, not an excuse for someone to tell me what to do. Or another living person for a guy to use in order to manipulate me.

"I used to have this fantasy of being pregnant, with the man I love holding me from behind. He would have his hands on my giant belly and he would be so in love with me. So happy about the child we'd made together. I wanted *that* family. The one where I was absolutely vital to someone. Someone who couldn't wait to make a child with me." Mac was startled when a tear slid down her cheek. She wanted to laugh it off, but she couldn't.

"Mac, honey, you *are* absolutely vital to me. No mere hope for a child that doesn't even exist could compete with that. Having a kid with someone is never a sure thing, even when there's nothing physically wrong with either person. It happens or it doesn't. You don't throw away the best thing that's ever happened to you over a maybe. And that's what you are to me. I've never found anyone to compare to you.

"Of course, we could try really, really hard. Over and over, like six times a night. I'm sure I could keep up my part of the bargain." Mackenzie gave him a watery smile.

"Oh, you can definitely keep it up, cowboy. In fact, I was wondering if your flag ever *stopped* flying. How do you walk around with the thing just waving around like that all the time? Doesn't it put your back out or something?" Then Mac found herself on *her* back once more.

"Why don't we keep trying until we put *both* our backs out?"

"Ride 'em, cowboy!"

23

BEYOND FULL CAPACITY

Mac was feeling a whole lot less stressed when she woke around noon. Neil had kept her up for a number of hours, in addition to waking her throughout the night for a few more bouts, but by dawn they had both completely crashed.

Thoughtful as always, Neil had made sure to include morning care for the animals in his instructions to Billy the night before, and Billy had also hiked over to the cabin to do his usual chores there. Mac couldn't get over how responsibly Neil's son behaved.

Not that Mac had any complaints with Cam. Far from it. As much as her daughter might be disgusted with some of the new experiences in her life, she still did whatever was necessary. She had worked hard her whole life. She'd had a part-time job in high school, and worked full time as an adult until they'd made the final trip up north that week. Mac knew some of that had been her own influence, but the traits were already there.

Neil wasn't in bed beside her, but the message light was flashing on her phone. She saw the text from him, saying that he'd gone out to make their new residents more comfortable. It occurred to her that she should get her ass out there and walk everyone around the place, explaining the set-up.

Mac wasn't sure she like the idea of bringing anyone else to their property, whatever Neil had said. She didn't feel they needed more help. She had a good handle on everything, and the more people they had, the more likely it was their location would get out. That was not something she was willing to risk.

She wanted a peaceful existence. Whether or not the end of the world was nigh, she liked spending time by herself, doing solitary activities. That hadn't been the case for the last several days, and she found herself pining for solitude. If they took on more residents, solitude would be a fond, fond memory.

Neil was a lot more extroverted than she was, that was for sure. Not that it was a bad thing. They could complement one another that way. There were things she'd be better with than he was, and vice versa. Any activity that required a solitary bent would likely be her province. Anything that required outgoing socialization would be left to him.

As much as she didn't feel like traipsing a few feet from her bedroom for a shower, Mac *really* wasn't ready to face the world without one. If she hadn't shot someone the day before, and spent the night having sex more times than she could count, she'd have just gotten dressed.

Neil was at the table with Kelly when she poked her head out of the bedroom wearing her bathrobe. He raised his head, but she shook hers. She didn't want to talk to anyone. The memory of shooting that guy had brought some unpleasant emotions to the surface. Emotions she'd been able to forget during the night, but at some point she'd have to sort through them and deal. This was as good a time as any. Neil seemed to understand, and stayed where he was.

She opened the bathroom door carefully. When Mac was sure it was empty, she went in and closed and locked the door behind her. One bathroom was *not* going to be enough for this group. They needed to get the house built, sooner rather than later.

She took a much longer shower than usual. She wasn't a cruel person, so now she was dealing with the disgust she felt for the pain she'd inflicted after collecting the slugs. She needed to get rid of those as soon as possible. Mac hurried up with the rest of her shower then, and headed to the bedroom as soon as she was dry, anxious to get them disposed of.

She dressed in a tank top and shorts, and grabbed her dirty clothes off the floor. She picked up the jeans by the waist so nothing could fall out of the pocket. When she went to take them out, however, both the casings and slugs were gone. Mac dropped the clothes on the floor and ran into the main area in a panic.

"Did you take them?" Neil stood up and kissed her on the forehead. She wanted to shake him off.

"Did you take them?!" She was nearly shouting now.

"Take what, honey?"

"From my pocket. The slugs and casings. They're not in there now. What did you do with them?"

"Oh, yes. I thought you might have forgotten they were in there, or maybe wouldn't want to deal with them. I kept the casings, since I wasn't sure if you had a reloading press or not, but the slugs went in the river after I smashed them a few times with a rock." Mac sagged against him.

"I thought one of the ferrets got to them or something. They might not be able to swallow a slug whole, and it would kill them if they tried, but even licking it would be bad. It was such a careless thing to do. Normally I'm a fanatic about things like that." Neil smiled and rubbed up and down her arms.

"Well, no worries then. They didn't get to them. You want some eggs? There are plenty of them this morning. We might end up with too many of them soon, so it looks like we have a lot of baking and dehydrating in the near future." Mac finally turned to Kelly.

"I'm sorry. I'm naturally rude, so I'm not sure there's even a point to apologizing for it, but there you have it. It probably won't get better. Before I forget, though, you're supposed to eat whatever you like, whenever you like. Just stick the dishes in the dishwasher, and we'll get along fine." Kelly smiled at her.

"Neil already told me that. No worries. In fact, he made

breakfast for me, and for Annette. She just went back to the bedroom for a while. It wasn't a good night for her, of course. She was stuck in the room with that guy for two days. At first because he had a knife, and later because she was too beat up to get away.

"Speaking of knives, I forgot to give this back to you last night." She gave Mac her KA-BAR, and Mac gazed at it lovingly. Kelly laughed at her expression.

"Thank you. I love my toy. It's how I met my soon-to-be husband." Neil interrupted briefly to find out from Mac how she wanted her eggs.

"Over easy it is, then," he said casually.

"You have a very unusual sense of sentimentality, don't you?"

"I suppose so," Mac answered Kelly. "Some women like flowers. I like a good old fashioned knife. Well, I suppose the engagement ring has its charms, too." Neil gave her a look at that, and so she stuck her tongue out at him.

"How long have you two been going out?" Mac kind of smirked at Kelly's question.

"I'm not sure you could call it 'going out,' but we met on Wednesday." Kelly choked on her coffee.

"Wow! I've never seen a whirlwind romance like that before. Annette and I have been together for a couple of years, and we just started talking about getting married. I'd never had a relationship with a woman until I started having feelings for Annette. Yet when it happened it felt like the most natural thing in the world. Is this bothering you that I'm talking about my sexuality?" Mac snorted.

"No. I don't care if you're into leprechauns, so long as they're capable of consent." Kelly laughed and went on.

"Okay. The marriage thing is going to have to wait now, anyway. There's just too much going on for me to deal with all that stuff. I don't know how you guys are managing."

"It's been pretty exciting around here, that's for sure. Neil was a huge exception for me. I've never been particularly impulsive with marriage, though I did make two really stupid choices. And I never had with my two ex-husbands what I have now with Neil." Neil looked up again and grinned.

Kelly nodded, but otherwise didn't respond. She just sat there stirring her coffee. Mac let her think while she ate the eggs Neil slid in front of her. He cleaned up the counter and stove and left the house. Mac dumped her plate in the dishwasher and poured some coffee into a travel mug to take outside with her, leaving Kelly to her musings.

As soon as Mac was outside she made arrangements to get Leigh and Kirk set up at the cabin. She had seen the mattress on the floor of the living area, so Cam had apparently taken her up on her suggestion. She'd take the tent with Neil tonight if the rain continued to hold off.

Whether Mac wanted a day off or not, things still needed to be done. They got the third and fourth goat pens done, but without any concrete pads or sheds. They had built one so that it was attached to the does' pen, and the other so it attached to the bucks' pen. Then they added a gate in between, instead of an exit gate. It saved on wood, since they only had to build three sides for each pen. Once the concrete was dry enough around the posts, they opened the new gates and let the goats wander back and forth. They had double the space, with no need for another shed just yet.

Mac went through the gardens, double-checking that the automated watering system was working properly, and searching for pests. If they ended up with snails or anything, she'd let the chickens into the gardens for a snack. That was why she'd chosen to put the coop so close to the gardens in the first place. All she had to do now was make sure the chickens couldn't escape the yard if she let them out of the coop. Annette came out of the house while she was standing there.

"I was wondering if you would show me your setup with the animals. I'd like to get familiar with things around here." Mac nodded and did as she'd asked. When they got to the goats Annette's face brightened right up.

"Oh, they're so adorable! I love goats, but I don't know much about breeds or anything. I'll have a lot of studying to do to catch up on their physiology, of course, but I'd like to familiarize myself with them from the outside in. Tell me what you know about them."

Mac explained the breeds she'd purchased, and her limited knowledge about breeding and milk production. She was even less knowledgeable about the angoras, so she was pretty vague when she talked about them. She'd let Neil fill her in on the goats he had at the cabin, since she hadn't asked him about them.

322

With the number of people at the farm now, combining her household with Neil's, she was thinking they should buy more of the angoras for breeding. They might actually need that much wool as time went on. She wasn't trying to save the world's goat population or anything, but self-sufficiency was important now.

Mac took Annette to the chicken pen, letting her know it was a temporary set-up due to their initial rush.

"In fact, all of this is temporary in a way. You can see the concrete pad over there with the capped pipes sticking out. That's for the new house. The design of the steel building makes it an easy set-up, and once we have the time it'll only take a couple of days for it to go up. With three bedrooms it'll be enough for our family.

"Leigh and Kirk have already gone with Neil over to his cabin, so they'll be living there for now and looking after the livestock. We're leaving the animals where they are. Mine are stressed from being moved, so their production isn't up to par yet. Until they are I don't want to stress the other ones, and it's good separation for later breeding.

"You and Kelly are an unexpected gift and surprise for us. Having someone who knows ferrets in addition to a real vet, could make a big difference in the future. You'd both be welcome here anyway, but this keeps us from the hope-and-pray kind of vet care we'd have been forced to resort to." Annette let out a small chuckle.

"I'm happy to be able to help. I want to thank you again for what you did at the clinic, and also for bringing us here."

"Thanks aren't necessary. We're all helping each other survive however we can."

When they were done with the short tour, Annette decided to head inside, so Mac asked her to let Kelly know the back door would be locked for a couple of days. She had to start on better ferret accommodations. With the twelve they already had, not including Pickle and Squeaker, and whatever number they would end up with from the other two shelters, the current situation would turn into a disaster.

Mac was finished digging by the time Neil's truck pulled up to the house. She left the shovel where she'd already plunged it into the dirt, and headed over to let the three of them know about the back door.

"Jesus, honey, don't you have a hat, or sunblock at least?" Mac touched her face. *Fuck*. No wonder her skin felt tight, even with all the sweat.

"I do, but apparently I'm a big idiot, so why don't we let that go for now? I didn't want to forget to tell you not to use the back door."

"Why? What on earth are you up to that you've forgotten any semblance of self-preservation?"

"Oh, for fuck's sake. It's not that bad. Is it?" From the looks on their collective faces, it apparently was.

"Shit. I guess I'd better get my ass inside then. Come on. I'll tell you what I'm doing when we all get into the house."

She was naturally very pale-skinned, and now she was being forced to spend a lot of time outside. When Mac checked her face in the bathroom mirror, it became obvious she would not be going outside much in the near future. She looked like a boiled lobster, and her sunblock could only do so much.

After applying burn gel to her face, her skin felt somewhat better and she headed back out to explain what she was doing with the ferret run. She wrote down the measurements for Neil so he could continue where she'd left off. He headed out with Billy right away to get started.

"Man, am I ever going to look stupid tomorrow when we get married," Mac said to Cameron.

"You kind of look stupid already, wedding or not."

"Very funny. I need to figure out what to wear tomorrow, though."

"I'm not sure why you're even bothering to get married." Mac looked up sharply at her daughter.

"Well, I am."

"That's not what I meant. Relax. Even if I think this is insane, I was talking about the possibility that the world is about to self-destruct. What difference will it make if you're married?"

"Hard to explain, but it feels important to me, and it's obviously important to Neil or he'd never have gone out and bought a ring. He wanted to make sure he could get it sized, because he didn't think there would be anyone around to do it later." Cameron thought about that for a minute.

"It's so weird to think about. All these things we can do now, and soon they won't be there. Things we maybe didn't think about, because it wasn't important to us, but might be later. If you'd met Neil a few weeks from now, he'd never have been able to get you that ring. Or maybe he'd have looted it, but it might not have fit, so you'd have to go through the store's inventory to find one that did."

"You're probably wondering what will happen if you end up finding someone you actually want to make a commitment to. Well, you know, Billy sure seems to be interested. Maybe you should tell him your ring size just in case."

"Mom! For God's sake. He's only eighteen."

"I was just teasing you, though he's a mature eighteen. A couple of years from now and he'll fill out enough that you'll be drooling over him. He'll get over some of his shyness, too. That doesn't mean you'll be interested, of course, but he sure won't seem so young then." Cam smiled wickedly.

"It's not that. He's already a total hottie. He's just too young for me. His shyness also makes him seem like he has no confidence, and that bugs me. I've noticed the way he looks at me, but I've been ignoring it. If I react in any way it will lead into the big talk I don't wanna have."

"I'm glad I'm not either one of you. Those conversations suck from both ends.

"Can you run out and ask Neil what his ring size is? Maybe I can find something online and call to have it sized and ready for pick-up tomorrow. He put some thought into my ring, so I want to give him something other than a plain gold band."

Cameron ran out and Mac went into her bedroom. She found a single jewelry store in town, which thankfully had a website, so she began her search there. Cam found her a couple of minutes later.

"Nice," she said when she saw the band with the channel-set rubies Mackenzie was looking at. "Why rubies?"

"His birthday's in July. I looked it up on Facebook." Cameron smirked.

"Anyway, he said he's an eleven, but he was grinning. I hope he wasn't joking or anything. You know, like a scale of one to ten kind of deal?" Mac laughed.

"I doubt it. He probably figures I'll catch the reference, though. Either that or he's just happy I'm making wedding plans. Let me call them." Cameron waited while Mackenzie made the arrangements.

"I don't suppose you'll be able to do that for your clothes, huh?" Cameron wanted to know as soon as she hung up.

"Probably not. I can check out stock types maybe, but I still have to try things on. I was thinking maybe a sundress and some strappy sandals. They won't have much value later on, but I don't care. I want something nice to get married in. Maybe I can get a big, floppy hat that will shade my ridiculous face."

"What about flowers? You've got seeds for a flower garden, but haven't put one in yet, so you'll have to buy them. I should probably get something to wear, too."

"Good point. As stupid as I feel about doing a bunch of online shopping while the men-folk do all the hard work, let's see what we can find for stores in this town." A knock at the door had them looking up. Kelly was standing there, visible from the waist up through the half-door.

"Can I talk to you for a minute?"

"Sure. The ferrets are asleep, but watch out for their ninja escape tactics. Squeaker's very good at it." Kelly smiled as she came in, her eyes watching the floor until she closed the bottom half of the door again.

"Does he hide under furniture to sneak up to the door?" Mac smiled back at her.

"He sure does. Little bugger. He's the one we got from your shelter. We got Pickle through a friend of a friend. Something about attacking cats, though I originally thought they meant the cats were attacking the ferret. Until I got him home and realized just how feisty he was." Kelly was laughing by then.

"Ferrets are insane aren't they?" They chatted about the ferrets for a few minutes, before Kelly came to the point.

"Do you already have a wedding official? Like a minister or something?" Mac was surprised at the topic, but answered.

"No. I figured I'd ask for a list of locals when we picked up the licence in Parry Sound. Neither of us is religious. Neil hasn't said anything about it at any rate, and I would think he'd have done so by now with all my 'goddamnits.'"

"Don't forget the 'forchrist'ssakes,'" Cameron added.

"Oh, yes. Mustn't forget those. Why do you ask?"

"Well, if you need someone, and neither of you has anyone in mind, I'm a Justice of the Peace. It was a good way to support the shelter."

"I'll talk to Neil. He might have someone in mind, but I don't think so. I'll let you know." A quick grin had Mac smiling in return. Friends weren't always such a bad deal.

"How are your carpet sharks doing?"

"They're okay for now. It's safe. They all get along, luckily. They grew pretty used to one another at the shelter. These were ones that came in as bonded groups, so I never got them adopted out. I always felt so sad for them, but now I worry about the ones that were adopted. Anything could happen to them now."

"Well, you were as careful as you could be about sending them home with people who would love and care for them properly. Try to take comfort from that.

"I was working on a ferret run outside when I got this lovely tan. Neil and Billy are pouring a concrete base. It'll be fenced in with a bunch of soil piled on top, so they can safely dig like the mad things they are.

"We'll put in a couple of sheds for shelter, with lots of insulation and cubbies for sleeping. I'll have to work out temp controls right away. I know in the UK they keep them out year-round, but they don't have our temperature extremes. We've got more ferrets coming, too, so I may have to add space later."

"Where are you getting them from?"

"The shelter in Ottawa and the one in Sault Ste. Marie. There isn't any trouble up there yet, so I'm not sure how to convince them that it's coming. They'll have to see it for themselves before they listen to me, but I can't wait too long either. I need to have the fuel to get there and back, and we may run out down here before they do. Hard to say."

"If you need me to talk to them, let me know. We all sort of keep in touch in the shelter community."

"That's a good idea. They're more likely to listen to you. Do you know of any other shelters in Ontario?"

"Not that I'm aware of. Anyway, I'll let you get back to what you were doing. You know where I am if you need me." With a smile Kelly left them to their shopping.

24

KNOTTY BY KNATURE

Mac had finished her online shopping long before Neil and Billy were done working on the ferret run, so she had Cameron bring in whatever vegetables were ready to be picked. For once she was the one with dinner on the table for everyone, though she was more than happy to concede she didn't cook as well as Neil.

She'd confirmed with Kelly and Annette that they weren't vegetarians before pulling steaks out of the freezer to stick under the broiler. Mac had decided against buying a grill, since they would one day run out of propane, and outdoor fires might be a bad idea later.

She tossed fresh spinach into a salad with some chopped walnuts, snow peas, mandarin orange pieces, and a mild homemade dressing using brown sugar as part of the mix.

Neil told Billy to give him five minutes to shower when they stepped through the door, so Billy just talked to Mac while she cooked. He watched Cam the whole time, but Cam pretended she didn't notice. She was pretty good at it, too. Billy appeared to have no idea she was aware of his attention.

When Neil came out in his towel and told Billy he was good to head for the shower, he had to call his name a couple of times. Cameron still pretended ignorance. Neil went off to change into some of the clothes he'd brought back from the cabin that afternoon. Mac assumed he had cleared out his closet and dresser for Leigh.

Dinner was cheerful, even though Annette was mostly quiet. She still spoke up a few times, which Mac took as a sign that she was doing okay. Getting beat up was traumatic, but it could have been even worse. She wasn't mutilated, raped, or killed. Her minor injuries would heal. It was the sense of vulnerability she would need to recover from more than anything.

Kelly cleared the table, and they all went off to their separate activities once again. Mac talked to Neil about having Kelly perform the service. He liked the idea, so they let Kelly know right away that her services would be required. Then he filled her in on the progress of the ferret run.

Cameron went out to take care of the livestock, while Billy looked through Cam's game collection. They'd already decided on something a little less violent for the evening, since they just wanted to relax and be able to fall asleep. Neil and Mac had to get up early to go to Parry sound for the licence and for Mac to give her statement, but they were all really tired from the work they'd been doing lately anyway.

They decided to have the wedding by the river late in the afternoon. If anyone needed to shop for clothes, they could go with Cam and Mackenzie once the licence had been picked up. Neil and Billy both had suits they'd bought recently, so they were fine.

Mac was drooping by nightfall. Prolonged exposure to the sun did that to her, and the sunburn made her cranky. She wasn't snapping at anyone yet, but she figured she'd better head off to bed before she started. Neil kissed her gently when she leaned down to whisper goodnight.

"I'm not quite ready to sleep yet, honey, so I'll maybe stay up and play a game or two with the kids. You rest up. I've got big plans for you tomorrow." She gave him a tired smile. As long as those plans included a wedding, rather than her having to build anything out in the hot sun, she was there. She crawled onto the bed and didn't even remember falling asleep.

She woke up naked and very confused about it. The lack of clothing on the floor meant she hadn't undressed herself, and there were no signs she'd been having sex. Apparently Neil had stripped her, but she couldn't begin to understand why. She shrugged and started to drift back off to sleep.

"Oh no you don't, honey. We've got places to go." She tried to clear her throat.

"Gargh! What did you do to me? And why am I naked?" She

sounded like she'd been on a three-day bender, or had strep throat.

"Normally the answer to that question would be obvious, but sadly such is not the case today. Your clothes were dirty, and you were sprawled face down and crosswise on the bed. My guess is you passed out before undressing. I haven't done anything *to* you, because you're the approximate colour and temperature of a furnace. Do you have any aloe?"

Mac shook her head, the motion making her dizzy.

"Well, we'll have to remedy that. I've got a couple of plants that are still at my old place, though they're not really ready to be harvested from yet. Do you have something else for burns?" It took her several tries to answer him.

"Looks like you've got a little sunstroke. So long as you're of sound mind, however, I don't think they care how sound your body is at town hall. Up and at 'em, hot stuff!" Mac wanted to glare at him, but her face hurt too much to bother.

She had her shower with the spray on low. She wore another tank top, because she couldn't bear the thought of sleeves on her skin, but she slathered on the sunscreen. In addition to the Solarcaine and sunscreen, she wore a baseball cap, pulling her ponytail through the hole in the back. It was a Toronto Raptors cap with the brim curled perfectly. Neil thought she looked adorable, and was idiotic enough to tell her so. He got a poke in the ribs for it.

They arrived in Parry Sound right when the town hall was opening its doors, so they had to wait a few minutes for the computers to boot up before they could be seen. Soon they were headed back to the car with a bounce in both their steps.

The statement to the police took quite a bit longer, but she wasn't hassled. She figured Gilles had probably paved the way for her there. It made her feel guilty for not inviting Gilles or Chuck to their wedding, but the timing wasn't right.

Mac texted Kirk and Leigh once they were on their way back. Neither of them needed clothes for the wedding, but they still wanted to go with them. Neil gave her his truck keys so she'd have more cargo space, and sent Cam out when he got inside. They would pick up Cam's friends on the way. Kelly and Annette had already told them they didn't need anything.

Mackenzie gave Kirk and Leigh their money back as soon as they got in the truck. If they found something they wanted to buy, she'd feel like an asshole for keeping all their cash. She didn't need it anyway.

Mac stopped at a larger store to buy enough underwear for everyone for the next twenty years, and in fabrics that were the least likely to fall apart. She liked natural cotton for breathability, but it wouldn't last as long as nylon and other synthetics. She also made sure everyone had several pairs of sturdy shoes and boots.

It took only minutes in the jewelry store, since the ring was ready. Then they headed to the boutique for casual wedding attire. Mac stuck with her sundress idea, choosing one in a spring green, and Cam followed suit in a crisp, pastel orange that suited her offbeat tastes.

They didn't have the sandals she had in mind, though she did manage to get the floppy hat. The shoe store two doors down had something close enough to what she was looking for, that she made her purchases and they moved on. She bought a pair of metallic gold-coloured sandals with skinny straps for herself, and Cam chose a silver pair.

When she paused outside a casual clothing store, the others suggested they spend whatever they could on fabrics and sewing supplies next, and if there was anything left they could buy readymade items. There was no point in wasting money, so they moved on. A stop at a florist netted her a quickly-made bouquet that was nonetheless very charming.

The sewing store had a unisex sewing mannequin and some books on sewing and making patterns, so they could design their own patterns later. They also managed to find lots of fabrics that would hold up well, including some leather.

They bought quilt-batting, thread, needles of all kinds and even an extra sewing machine, along with parts. Mac already had knitting needle sets, and could create her own patterns, so she stocked up on some more yarn. She didn't know how long it would be before they had enough angora to make into something. Kirk and Leigh started hauling stuff out to the truck.

Mac had just paid for the last of the purchases when Kirk and Leigh came back in the store, completely out of breath and a panicked look on their faces. They ran straight over to her, and shielded her from the window.

"I think Gerry's outside, Mac. I'm sure it's the same guy from the gas station. You can use your phone's camera to look at him, instead of letting him see you." Mac's heart was pounding. She hadn't been expecting him. They'd gone to a town with better shopping, and Gerry's car was trashed.

"Good idea." When she looked at the screen, she saw Kirk was right. The clerk was giving them a funny look by then, but she didn't comment. Mac turned to her, needing her help.

"You see that kid out there with the long, greasy hair?"

"Gerry? Piece of sh...garbage. I went to high school with him. Why?" Mac wasn't surprised. The local high school covered a very large area.

"He's been bothering me, trying to follow me home, among other things. It didn't end well for him the last couple of times, so I guarantee he's not happy with me. Is there a back way out of this store that we can use?"

"You betcha. I'll be happy to show you the way. We're not supposed to bring people through the back, obviously, but my boss won't mind. Her husband used to beat her, until her family got hold of him. Gerry is just like him."

"Thank you." As the clerk led them through the back, Mac asked her name.

"Marian Taylor. Kinda old-fashioned, but I don't mind. I like old-fashioned stuff, which is how I ended up working here. And the last name really suited, too, even if the spelling is different." Mackenzie smiled at her as they went out the door.

"Thanks again. Really. I just don't want to have to deal with him today."

"No problem. Besides, you damn near bought out the store, so my boss is really going to want you to be a happy customer." Mac laughed.

"No doubt. I'll be coming back if I'm ever in the market for more stuff, though that won't likely be for a while. If I ever see you again, and there's anything I can do for you, don't hesitate to ask. My name's Mac. Short for Mackenzie. This is my daughter Cameron, and her friends Kirk and Leigh. Thanks again, and have a really good day!" Marian nodded and waved, and they watched her go back into the store.

Kirk scouted ahead for her, making sure the coast was clear whenever they hit a corner. They made it back to Neil's truck without running into Gerry, so Mac ducked her head a bit to avoid being seen and told Kirk and Leigh to finish up getting what they needed.

They were back in less than thirty minutes with heavily-laden shopping bags, and then they were all headed for home, Mackenzie flicking glances at the rearview mirror every minute or so. No one was behind them when she made the turn down their road, and they made it up to the house without incident.

"Alright, don't worry about unloading everything just now. Only the wedding stuff is really needed for the moment, and we have that here up front with us."

Mac used the bedroom to get ready, and Cameron took the bathroom. Kirk and Leigh could swap with Cam when she was done. There wasn't much Mackenzie could do about her face, other than adding more Solarcaine. She put on eyeliner, mascara, and tinted lip gloss, and considered herself presentable. She used sparkly bobby pins to hold back the sides of her hair at various points, leaving the length of it to stream down her back.

Both ferrets were milling about her ankles as she moved from one spot to the next, grabbing things from various places. She nearly stepped on Squeaker a number of times.

"Sorry, guys. I know this is irritating and stressful to you. How 'bout I put the harnesses on you and you can come out for the wedding? Would you like that?" Mac was already rolling her eyes at herself.

She knew ferrets had attended weddings before, since she personally knew several people who had brought their ferrets, and some who had even had them as part of the ceremony, like ring-bearers and whatnot, but she hadn't really thought about what she would do if she got married again. It never occurred to her that she would. By bringing them out with her, she would officially be a crazy ferret lady.

Cameron was waiting for her when Mac left her room with ferrets in tow. Kelly came out, already dressed, followed by Annette.

"That's a hell of a man you have there, Mac. It's beautiful what he's done in just a few hours. I can't wait for you to see it! For now, however, Annette and I wanted to give you a gift." Mac immediately started protesting.

"Annette might be dead were it not for you, so please let us give this to you. It would mean so much to us." Mac relented and took the box.

"You should open it now," Annette said quietly. "You can wear it for the wedding. It belonged to my sister. She died of leukemia several years ago, and I know she would really want you to have it. Then you just need something borrowed since your dress is new." Mac understood what she meant when she opened the box. It was an antique charm bracelet, and it had a deep blue crescent-moon charm dangling from it.

"Wow, this is really nice. Are you sure you don't want this to be 'borrowed' too?" Annette shook her head.

"I'm sure. Clarissa would be so grateful to you. She was my older sister and always protected me, so you doing the same would be important to her." Mac nodded, unable to speak, and tried her damndest not to let her eyes tear up. Even waterproof mascara had a hard time holding up to sentimental tears.

Mac had to have Kelly put the bracelet on her wrist for her. She was still holding the lead for the ferrets, in addition to her bouquet.

"Hang on, mom. I have earrings you can borrow that'll go really well with that." She ran off to her room.

"We've kicked her out of her bedroom haven't we?"

"Don't worry about it, Kelly. She'll have my room tonight, and soon we'll have the big house built. Neil and I already had plans to use the tent tonight. We've camped out in it before, and we wanted to do that for our wedding night."

"Hubba hubba," Annette joked, which startled Mac into laughing and dropping her bouquet. The ferrets were on it instantly. They only managed a sniff before she yanked it out of harm's way.

"Here, why don't I take the ferrets? I know what they're like on a lead, and Kelly will be busy marrying you two." Mac handed her the loop of nylon. They shared a lead, since they were connected by a Y-leash near their harnesses. It kept them from traveling six feet away from one another, and tying a person's legs in knots.

"I feel stupid bringing them with me, but they were awake and getting hyper with me getting ready. Before I knew it, I had them ready to go." Annette laughed and held up the hand without the leash.

"No explanations necessary. We're nuts about them, and we see far crazier people than you. Believe me!"

Leigh and Kirk came out of the bathroom just then, wearing much dressier attire, and walked over to join them. Cam came running out right after, and handed Mackenzie crescent-shaped earrings to go with the bracelet. Mac figured she was all set.

"Okay, that's it. I'm ready. Old, new, borrowed, blue. If anyone has any objections, speak now or forever hold your wicked tongue."

"We have something for the both of you, though it's not something you can get married with, so we'll bring it out with us, and you can open it together," Leigh said.

"I won't ask how you managed that one. Why don't we get going so my soon-to-be husband doesn't start thinking I've ditched the wedding and run off with a younger man?"

They set off as a group, but they spread out as they went, Kelly leading the way, followed by Annette with the ferrets. Kirk and Leigh went next, hand in hand. Cameron walked with her mother. It almost became a traditional wedding procession, except of course for the ferrets, who had no interest in walking a straight line.

Finally Mac saw the reason for Kelly's earlier comments about Neil. He had set up some chairs, as well as an arbor with pine boughs woven through it. There was a table to the side with food, wine, and beer, making her stomach growl and reminding her she hadn't eaten yet.

He stood there waiting for her, with Billy beside him. A portable stereo was playing the same type of music they had danced to. For the second time she was nearly moved to tears.

As soon as Mackenzie and Cam were in place, Kelly started the ceremony. Within moments Neil was speaking his vows and sliding a band onto her finger. She'd already done the same. Neither of them had looked down at their rings. Only at one another. When they finally had their first kiss as husband and wife, it was long, slow, and deep.

When Neil glanced at his wedding band and then looked up at her face, Mac squinted at him.

"Do *not* say it." Neil tried to look innocent.

"Say what?"

"If you say it's the same colour as my face, I'm going to commit spousal abuse even before our first dance."

"How is that fair? You said your ring matched my eyes. I have to come up with something at *least* as romantic. It's my job as your new husband." To keep him from seeing the laughter on her face, she looked down at her own ring. And burst out laughing anyway.

"How the hell did you manage to find a matching ring to the one I gave you?"

"I didn't, actually. Just a sort of great-minds-think-alike coincidence I guess. I wanted you to know I was wrapped around your finger."

"Aww. Alright, enough with the mushy crap. We've got paperwork to deal with." Neil poked her bare arm in response, making her yelp, but they went and signed the paper for the marriage registration. It was unlikely Kelly would even be able to get it filed, much less that they would have a chance to apply for a certified copy, but it didn't matter. The vows were spoken, and the paperwork signed. It was legal either way.

Neil whispered in her ear and Mac started laughing again.

"No, I do *not* want to be called Mac-Mac, thank you. You're right about that one. I'll stick with Thane. Not like I could change it to McKinnon anyway. We'd never get the legal paperwork in time."

"I know. I'd never ask you to change your identity. I don't understand it myself. Getting married doesn't mean you forget who you are."

"Yes! Exactly. But let's not get into the finer points of patriarchal society. We've got some old-fashioned dancing and sex on the menu, and I've been meaning to get me some of that!"

"A woman after my own heart."

"You keep saying that. I do not think it means what you think it means. I'm pretty sure I already caught it, or I'd very much like to know what I'm doing with Christmas wrapped around my finger."

"Christmas? Oh, yeah, I can see where you might get that idea. But does Christmas come early this time?"

"If you play your cards right, it just might. But only so long as I get my turn next."

"I doubt that'll be a problem."

"Not with you doing the work, no. Your manual labour skills are impressive. Speaking of which, this is all very beautiful by the way. You almost ruined my mascara."

"Did you get poked in the eye by a tree branch?"

"Funny guy. No, it made me a sappy fool for a second or two, however. It was perfect for us. Not overdone with a zillion flowers or anything. Good thing we're planning on kicking everyone back into the house soon, though, seeing as there's no lighting. It's going to get dark soon."

"What, you don't think I'm capable of ulterior motives?"

"The most devious, actually. It's one of your best traits."

"I thought it was my..." She gave him a poke in the ribs.

"Let's get something to eat so I can keep up with you tonight, and then we'll crank the tunes and have that romantic crap they call dancing. I kinda like it."

Once she got some food into her stomach they opened the gift from Leigh and Kirk, which turned out to be a large silver picture frame with their names and the date engraved on it.

"This is really beautiful, guys. Thank you so much!"

"I took a bunch of pictures while you guys were getting hitched, and Leigh took video, so we'll be able to put an actual wedding picture of you in the frame as soon as we print it off tonight."

Touched, Mac had a hard time hiding the tears that were on the verge of overflowing her lower lids. She grabbed them both in a quick hug, and then Neil did the same.

The younger generation wasn't done surprising them, though. Cameron turned off the music, and Billy brought out his guitar. Mac's mouth dropped open when he began to play a familiar tune and Cameron started singing along. They'd chosen Nat King Cole's *L.O.V.E.* and it took everything she had to keep from bawling her head off. She was just so damn proud of the two of them for doing something so meaningful for her and Neil.

When the song ended, Mac grabbed Cameron into a bear hug, while Neil did the same with his son. Then they switched, which embarrassed Billy and freaked out Cameron a little bit. She was not a hugger, and only rarely tolerated them from her mother, much less a man she'd just met, but Neil just laughed.

"That's what you get for doing something so wonderful for your mother and me. Thank you. Truly. It means a lot to both of us...as you might have noticed from the mascara running down your mom's face." Cameron let out a shout of laughter at that.

Once the ferrets had been taken back to the house, they all started dancing, with everyone using their phones to take more pictures. Neil seemed determined to keep most of the songs slow ones, so he could hold her in his arms, but the rest of them had something to say about that. They wanted to party and let off some steam.

By the time it got dark everyone was full, and laughter carried on the wind behind the six people heading back to the house, most of the food in their arms. Billy had offered to drive Leigh and Kirk back to the cabin, since Cameron would be there to open the gate, but they opted to stay over and play games. Kelly and Annette were talking about joining in, so it looked like everyone had a fun evening planned.

25

LET THE GAMES BEGIN

A couple of bottles of white wine were left in ice buckets on the table. One was a really sweet ice wine, while the other was a tart sauvignon blanc. Neil was poking fun at her so-called infantile taste in *vino*, but she wasn't having any of it.

"I'll have you know, ice wine isn't cheap stuff. They sold a bottle of it for thirty grand a few years back. Not that I'd pay that much for it myself. I'm generally happier with Molson Canadian. *Far* more infantile. I have eclectic tastes. At least we won't be stealing from each other's wine cache when the shit hits the fan. For that matter, I get the advantage there, I think. Not too many people go for the stuff."

"I wonder why. Of course, that's in an ideal world. People will go for anything if they're desperate."

"True enough. I mean, look at us." Neil growled at her, drained the last of his extremely tart wine, and yanked her empty goblet from her hand to set on the table that still contained the last of the food.

"Let's see about desperate, shall we?"

"I knew you'd see things my way eventually." Mac loved poking at him, because this was the usual result. Not that he wasn't aware of that.

"Be gentle with me, cowboy. It's my first time." He snorted.

"My ass."

"You want me to be gentle with your ass? Okay. We can go there."

"Yeah, we'll see how far you get with that. I meant you're nowhere near virgin status."

"Who said anything about virgins? I said it was my first time. First time banging you as a married woman. And I'm all injured and shit."

"You're a crispy critter, definitely. I wonder if you'll make a lot of crunching noises. Could be weird for me."

"You need to get out more. Well, maybe not. You start stepping out you really will hear some crunching, though that will be your bones. Alright, take me to bed, cowboy. And make it good. I've got things to do."

She certainly did plenty of them, though they all took place in the tent with her accomplice. Music continued to play outside the tent, and just under it she could hear the river and the wind. It might have been a short honeymoon out of necessity, but it couldn't have been a better one.

They woke up early enough to watch the sun rise, which was extremely rare for Mac. Normally she was still up at that time, not *waking* up. It was beautiful all the same, and more so with Neil beside her, the sleeping bags wrapped around them as they looked over the still-swift current of the river.

Oddly, she felt no sense of surrealism from having married someone she'd known less than a week. She smiled at the thought of Ian's reaction when he found out. He'd call her crazy and wish her well, whatever he might think privately, and no one ever really knew how well things would work out between people.

When the sun had risen they dressed silently in the clothes Neil had brought out with the camping gear, and headed into the house for breakfast. There was a lot of work to be done today. At least for anyone who would be allowed outside in the sun. Her floppy hat that looked so nice with her sundress was just not meant for daily use. Although the goats might enjoy chewing on the ribbons.

Neil got the morning chores completed, and brought in the stuff from the night before. Mac took care of breakfast. She was starving, so she made everything she could think of. Pancakes, bacon, omelets, toast, scrambled eggs, and even cold cereal, were put out for everyone.

They all dug in, though not everyone could sit at the table. Kelly and Annette took their heaping plates over to the futon and sat down. Mac decided she was going to have to make a bigger table for all of them, along with some more chairs. She figured there would at least be one more person once the shit hit the fan and she went to get Allan, but she would plan for more.

Leigh and Kirk took the rental car to the cabin to look after the animals there. Once Neil's truck was emptied, Mac gave him a list of things she needed from the hardware store. The additional insulation she needed for the sheds was at the top of the list. When she added mattresses to the list, Neil went out to hook up the horse trailer. He didn't argue with her, since he saw where things were going just as clearly as she did.

Mac got down to the business of cleaning up around the place a little bit. She had a bunch of laundry to do by this point, and when she was done Cameron started dumping her own clothes into the washer. Neil and Billy were back by then and finishing up the ferret run.

Kelly and Annette dealt with the ferrets from the shelter. Twelve ferrets created a lot of waste in one day, and the upkeep was pretty much constant. Annette began reading some of the goat and chicken anatomy textbooks that Mac had purchased, and Kelly got started on lunch.

Mac called Ian to let him know the latest news, and found out that the outages in Cleveland were getting worse. They were interconnected with Toronto, so she'd been expecting it. All the major cities were a backup for everyone else. And when one went the rest of them had a heavier load with less support. New York City was already down.

Ian had taken her advice on the insulin, as well as the most important items on the list she'd sent him, but he was still working to get the remainder. Lines in stores were long, power outages caused payment processing delays, and people were a hairsbreadth from panic. She hung up thinking it was time for a final run on fuel.

Everyone had lunch, and Mac told them the details of her conversation with Ian.

"Once we're finished eating, I'll set everyone up for access to the gate and doors. Billy and Neil should probably do the fuel run, and we can start battening down the hatches after that. Kelly and Annette, you should follow them and pull your money out of the bank, including anything you can borrow on your credit cards, if it's still possible. Buy lots of underwear, sturdy shoes, and clothes." She gave them the same advice she'd given Leigh and Kirk the day before, only adding deodorant and other personal hygiene supplies.

"This is about to blow up, I'm afraid, so we have very little time. I'm going to take a nap soon, so that I can go out after the sun is down and get some work done. We should pour a concrete pad and put a shed on it to use as a vet care building. I'll start on an exam table once I get Annette's input for it.

"Tomorrow I think we need to go get those other ferrets. I don't want to wait any longer than that. Can you call them and pave the way, Kelly?"

"No problem. God, this is really happening, isn't it?"

Mac nodded, plotting things out in her head. Neil spoke up to give his opinion.

"We should probably hit Ottawa first. The more urban the city, the faster people are going to run out of things and panic. Sault is a little more geared toward rural, whereas the capital city is necessarily more modern." Mackenzie nodded.

"You're right. We'll have to make two trips, though. We can't have ferrets confined all the way from Ottawa to Sault Ste. Marie, and then from the Sault home. We're talking fourteen or fifteen hours. The stress would be terrible for the ferrets." Kelly nodded her agreement.

"They can't be sedated for that long, for one thing. If they don't eat and drink four to six times a day, they get really sick, really fast."

"If there are dozens of them, we'll need to convert the truck bed or something, or make multiple trips. And that's something I don't want to do. When you call them, Kelly, can you find out how many there are so I know what to plan for?"

"Will do."

Neil waited for everyone to disperse before talking to Mackenzie in more detail about her plans.

"You don't have to take everything on all at once. We'll have plenty of time when we get back to build exam tables and a personal animal hospital."

"I need to feel productive, Neil. Sitting around and doing nothing while other people work is just not comfortable for me. You worked all day. I'll get some rest now, and you can sleep through the night. This damn sun stroke, or whatever it is, is making me really tired anyway. Either that or the fact that you kept me up so much of last night and we woke up at dawn." Neil stroked her hair and kissed her softly.

"Get some rest honey. I'll make sure everything is taken care of." Knowing that he would was the only thing that kept her from panicking at this point. She'd refused to let anyone else see it, but she'd been badly shaken by Ian's news. It didn't matter that it was what she'd been expecting. Now it was happening, and time was growing very, very short.

Neil wasn't fooled by it, she was sure, but he didn't say anything. Not everything needed to, or even should, be talked about. Reinforcing panic was never a good thing, and he did his best to soothe her fears without all the discussion.

When Mac finally fell asleep, her dreams were not pleasant ones. When she woke up things were even worse.

Sweat covered her body still when she left the bedroom to find Kelly sobbing and fear in everyone else's eyes. They were all seated around the table.

"What happened?" Her own panic skyrocketed, and she had to struggle to control her emotions.

"Ottawa is dark," Neil said softly, and pulled her into his lap to hold her.

"Obviously there's more to the story. What is it?"

"Civilians in Ottawa overtook parliament. They were in session to discuss the power situation in southern Ontario. A few members of parliament were killed, along with our prime minister. The military police couldn't stop the mass of people.

"We don't know all the details. Just what Kelly got from Lianne at the shelter there. Some is rumour, of course, since everything went dark there shortly after it happened, but Trudeau was definitely killed."

"Jesus. We need to get them out of there right now then. Can they get out of the city with the ferrets on their own? That'd be a better solution. The sooner they get outside the city, the better, and it would mean we wouldn't have to go into the city at all. We can meet them with fuel if they don't have enough." Kelly nodded and wiped at her eyes and nose.

"They were already planning to go, so I told them to leave and head this way with the ferrets. They have a van, though with all the ferrets it'll be pretty cramped. They *might* actually be able to get here on a single tank, so you may not have to head toward Ottawa at all.

"Sault Ste. Marie is a different story. It's barely even a shelter, so she doesn't have a van to transport a whole bunch of ferrets. Elizabeth said she was wondering if she was going to have to put them to sleep. She knows she can't stay in the city, and she has no way to move them. There are ten ferrets there, so it's not a lot, but she wasn't able to find fuel. She apparently ended up running out while she was looking for more, and had to abandon the car and walk home."

"We need a different game plan then. Looks like Lianne's

bunch is on alert status, rather than an emergency one, whereas Elizabeth's are our highest priority now," Neil said.

"Would Billy know how to get to highway 60?" Neil thought about it.

"He's been out that way any number of times, though I hate the thought of sending him out on a rescue mission. It's more the parent in me than anything else. I know he'd be fine, logically. I'd just rather keep him in a safe place."

"Tell me about it. I'm the same with Cameron. I'd say it's pretty low-risk, though. It's more that she doesn't know the area. Barely remembers living here when she was a kid. She does know how to handle a weapon, however."

"Billy, too. We don't have handguns, except for the SIG. Just long-guns. Should probably send them out with both a rifle and a shotgun, just to ease our parental misgivings. Of course, that's assuming there's a need for them to find the van in the first place. We'll send Lianne exact directions to this place, and tell her not to deviate from their route in any way, so if Billy and Cam do have to go looking they won't miss one another on the road. Hopefully they don't get lost.

"The real issue will be communicating with them. I doubt very much they have a satellite phone, and I would bet the cell towers will start going dark soon. If they can't call to let us know there's a problem, we'll have to set up a deadline for them to get here. If they don't make it by then, then the kids will have to go."

"You *could* stay here while I go to Sault Ste. Marie, but we both know that's not going to happen. It's far more likely we'll have a major problem on that trip, than there would be going a short distance to find the van from Ottawa."

"I'm glad you didn't put that suggestion forward seriously, or I would have to kick your ass. When we send them the detailed directions, we'll give them the timeline for when to expect a rescue. We'll leave one satellite phone with Billy and have the other one with us, just in case, though I'm not sure how much help we can be from that distance. We might be able to talk them through a situation, but that's about it.

"All the fuel containers are full, which is a damn good thing. Your timing was dead-on there, honey. I doubt we'll be able to refill them again even as late as tomorrow. Your car might be able to make the trip to Sault, one way, but it definitely won't make it back again.

"We'll have to strap every fuel container we can to the car, so we can completely refill the tank at least once, and then have fuel in reserve in case my calculations are off. The trip there takes just over five hours, plus any driving we have to do to find the shelter. How many people are we talking there, Kelly?"

"She's by herself. Lianne's got her husband, but they're in the van together. No kids other than the furry kind."

"How many ferrets does she have?" Mac was wondering if the run was going to be big enough. They already had a tally of twenty-two shelter ferrets. She wasn't counting Pickle and Squeaker, since they weren't going to be a part of the group.

"Twenty-eight." Mac whistled.

"This should be fun. Fifty rescue ferrets. We'll have to make some adjustments, because even with the run at the back we're going to start taking on the conditions of a back-yard breeder if we're not careful. And we're going to need more food for them. I bought a lot of kibble, but that won't last as long now. We'll have to start breeding chickens like crazy, I think." She looked at Neil.

"And here I thought we were going to have too many eggs." He smiled back at her.

"We'll have to start getting them used to eating eggs then," Kelly said worriedly.

"It can be done. Takes some patience, as you know, but a lot of times seeing another ferret eating something will get them curious. Both of mine love them as a treat, so we can start supplementing the kibble as much as possible. That's a problem for another day, though. We've got three more people on their way, which also means the big building is a major priority."

"We can get Billy and Cameron started on that while we're gone, assuming Cameron can tell Billy what to do." Mackenzie agreed, and set about creating a detailed list of instructions for them. Kelly and Annette volunteered to help with that, since their only jobs so far had been to look after the ferrets from Kelly's shelter.

Mackenzie wanted to close her eyes and hang her head in submission, but there was just too much to be done. She hated being unprepared like this. She'd spent so many years being anal about preparedness, with all her lists and sub-lists. It hadn't been a waste, but it still hadn't prepared them for the real crisis. If it had just been her and Cameron, things would have been perfectly fine, but that's not how it had worked out.

Now things had taken a horrifying turn. One she hadn't been expecting at all. At least not yet. Violence had erupted in the nation's capital, killing the person people would automatically be looking to for answers. They were abruptly without their most visible leadership, which meant the country could go into an immediate free-for-all. She found herself unexpectedly sad about Trudeau. He'd done a good job with the mess he'd inherited.

They strapped full fuel containers to the top of the trunk lid, and on the back of it, above the bumper. Having containers strapped to the roof would kill their aerodynamics, and they couldn't afford to do that now. They would also be limiting the number of ferret carriers to two, with five ferrets in each, so there would be room for Elizabeth to sit in the back seat.

This was not going to be a happy journey, even if it all went smoothly, what with Mac worrying the whole way there and back. Having Neil with her was really the only thing that would keep her from freaking out now. Impulsively she grabbed his hand as she walked by him during her final trip back to the house. He stopped and looked at her.

"It'll be okay honey. We'll make sure we get home to our kids safe and sound. We can take shifts driving. I'm not quite ready to sleep yet, but I will be soon. I can drive until we get past North

Bay and then you can take over. One person could do it in a day of driving, but we're already tired and stressed." Mac looked him in the eye then.

"Are you holding up okay? You've been looking out for me, but we've done a lot together the last few days where you've been drawing the short straw. You must be wiped." He smiled.

"I'm fine, really. Just starting to get a bit tired. It's your fault, though not for the reasons you just stated." Mac already knew where he was going with that, so she cut him off.

"Oh, no you don't. You're not going to blame me because a good wind gets you horny."

"While the wind is a pretty sexy thing, I really don't think that's what's been doing it for me lately."

"Probably the goats, then." She smacked his ass and moved on to the house, hearing his laughter trail behind him as he headed back to the car with the fuel can he'd been carrying when she'd stopped him.

Mac paused and looked at her truck then. It was parked in a different spot, and then it occurred to her that she didn't remember seeing it when she got back the day before. She'd been a bit distracted, what with getting married and all. It took her a minute to notice what was off about it. When Neil went to walk past her, she stopped him once again.

"How the hell did my truck get fixed?" Neil grinned at her.

"'Bout time you noticed it. I took it over to a friend's while you were gone yesterday and picked it up today. He's got a small body shop with a paint booth. Gave him a bonus to get it done right away. What do you think?"

"I think I married lucky. It looks like he did a hell of a job, considering. Good thing the truck is black, since it's a common colour to have in stock."

* * *

When they had been on the road for an hour, and the distance was flying by, Mac was grateful so many people had already run the stations dry. Otherwise she was sure the highways would be a mess. They saw the odd car that was still mobile, but more of them were abandoned than anything else.

As badly as she felt for the few people she saw walking along the side of the road, she didn't ask Neil to stop for them. It was too dangerous. These people were already afraid, and probably desperate enough to do anything. They couldn't risk being left by the roadside themselves. They not only had a job to do, but they also had to get back home when it was done.

Mackenzie took the wheel half an hour past North Bay, Neil not stopping until he was absolutely certain no one was around. She had already memorized the route that she'd need to take to reach the shelter. There would be no need to stop when she hit the Sault. It didn't matter to her who drove back, since she'd be anxious enough to get home it was highly unlikely she'd be sleepy.

Three and a half hours after she'd started her portion of the journey, Mac pulled into the driveway of the shelter. A woman came out and stood beside an old Camaro. When Mackenzie saw that it was packed and there were carriers inside it she started to get the feeling there might be some trouble.

26

MIDDLE AGES SPREAD

"Neil, wake up. We're here, and it looks like this woman thinks she's bringing her car. You brought that SIG with you right?" Neil was alert in a heartbeat. It was a skill she envied, since she was usually bleary-eyed for at least an hour after she woke up.

"Yeah. I haven't chambered a round because there's no holster for it, but it's in the moulded door pocket."

"Good. Get it ready before you get out, will you? I don't like the look of the situation here. She told Kelly she had to abandon her car when she ran out of fuel, so she's not looking like an upstanding citizen at this point. Maybe she has a second car, but I suddenly don't trust her." Mac set the parking brake after taking the car out of gear, but didn't turn off the engine, and then she got out of the car to introduce herself as politely as she could. She

362

wanted to start off on the right foot. There was no point in triggering a bad situation if she didn't have to.

"I'm Elizabeth. Thank you so much for coming. Thank God you brought extra fuel, because there was no way I was leaving my car behind." And there the shoe dropped.

"Elizabeth, we didn't bring any *extra* fuel. In fact, we were under the impression that you had already abandoned your car. We brought enough that we would make it back safely with this one, not enough to get back with two." The woman got a stubborn look on her face, and Mac prepared herself.

"Well, like I said, I'm not leaving my car, and the ferrets are already loaded and ready to go, so we'll just have to switch cars." Mackenzie crossed her arms, and Neil got out from his side.

"Your car wouldn't make it on the fuel we have," Mackenzie said quietly, her patience stretching unbearably.

"Well, sure it would. You just don't want to give up your fancy BMW!" Mac gritted her teeth.

"This car will travel five hundred miles on a single tank, and it cost me a grand total of a thousand bucks. I'm not so stupid that I'd buy a car for its coolness factor. Look, we came here to help *you*. More than that, we came here to help those ferrets. This is your only shot at a safe place right now. If you don't want to take it, that's your business. We'll load up the ferrets and go."

"You're not taking my ferrets anywhere without me, and I'm not leaving my car behind." Mac gave up on patience. It wasn't her strong suit anyway.

"Do you have enough food to feed those ferrets for the next ten years, or any way to get that much? Because if you don't we *are* taking them. The fact that you were already considering putting them down tells me that you don't. The fact that you're using them as a bargaining chip, rather than being concerned for their safety and survival, tells me you don't care about them as much as you care about your fucking car.

"I've tried to be polite about this. And I've tried to be logical. You basically want us to waste fuel on a car that won't make it to our destination, putting all of our lives at risk, and in the process pretty much guaranteeing those animals will die. You've just made my decision real easy for me with respect to leaving you behind. We don't need any more people at the farm, but I won't see an animal harmed for the stupidity of a human. So, they're coming with us. You're not."

"I'd like to see you try!"

"Are you mentally defective?" Mackenzie was stunned by the woman's cocky attitude, but then she understood when she saw her lunge toward a shotgun that was leaning against the wall. Neil fired into the wall of the garage, stopping the woman in her tracks when wood chips from the siding exploded out toward her.

"That answers that question, honey." Mac's lips quirked, but it really wasn't funny.

"Mentally defective and stupid to boot." Elizabeth started begging and gibbering at them, and Mackenzie sneered at her.

"Give me your fucking car keys. I'm taking the ferrets, and any kibble you have for them. You don't deserve to have any animals, and I doubt you ever did. From what I've seen of you so far, you're probably someone who used them to bring in money so you wouldn't have to hold a job. Fucking cunt." It was a word Mac almost never used, but she felt it was appropriate under the circumstances.

Elizabeth's hands shook as she took the keys from the pocket of her shorts.

"You're not really going to leave me here to starve are you? That wouldn't be very Christian!" Mac bared her teeth.

"I'm not a fucking Christian. And if you're any example of one of those, the world would be a much better place without them. Instead of getting religion, maybe you should get some morals instead. Not that you're likely to have time for that." Mac grabbed the keys from the ground where Elizabeth had dropped them, and started moving the carriers over to her car.

Once she started moving the kibble she noticed there was a bag of dog food in the garage, but none in the car.

"Please tell me you haven't been feeding dog food to these ferrets!" Elizabeth refused to answer.

"Or do you have a dog locked up somewhere in that house?" When she still refused to answer, Mac grabbed her by the ear and pulled her head at an unnatural angle to face her.

"I'm going to ask you this question one time. I want a full and complete answer, and if you forget a single detail I will make sure you don't live long enough to go through your food supply. Are there any other animals in that house, and by 'any' I mean dogs, cats, ferrets, birds, fish, gerbils, hamsters, mice, or pet fucking spiders? Are there *any* animals in there?"

"There's a dog, nothing else," she whispered.

"Why didn't the dog bark when the gun went off?"

"I knocked him out." Elizabeth cringed when she saw the look on Mackenzie's face. Mac couldn't remember the last time she'd been in such a towering fury.

"You were going to leave him behind, weren't you? We came for the ferrets, so they were your ticket out of here, but you didn't even care enough to ask if he could come with us. You're a fucking piece of shit. Christian my ass. Where is he?"

"Just inside the door. Tied up to the kitchen table." It wasn't until Mac opened the door that she understood why the dog had been tied up if he was unconscious. The smell of rotten eggs sent a shaft of fear up her spine. She propped the door open with the plastic dish rack from the counter to air out the room.

The dog was actually still conscious, but barely. He was a Doberman, and pretty big, too, which meant she'd never have been able to carry him, so she was very relieved when the dog struggled to his feet to try to do his job and guard the house. He couldn't even bark, though, and Mac felt tears of sympathy stinging her eyes.

She unhooked the leash from the choke-chain around his neck, careful not to let the metal scrape together, and briefly held the dog's face in her hands to let him sniff and lick at her. She wasn't sure how much he could still smell of her with the gas in the room, but he needed to feel a gentle human touch if she was going to convince him to come outside with her.

It only took a few seconds before he was amenable to her prodding. She left him standing in the yard, knowing he was too confused to go anywhere without being led, and went back in to turn off the gas, coming straight back out afterwards.

Mac knew it had been a risk, but she didn't want the house blowing up while they were still there, and she also didn't want to leave things like that when any of the surrounding houses might get blown up, too, or just catch fire. She didn't know what the situation might be with the fire department or other first responders, and something like that could rapidly get out of control.

She coaxed the dog over to the garage, but when he saw his owner he backed away and whimpered. Mac had already assessed the situation, and wasn't at all surprised. She walked around until she was face-to-face with her, and then punched her in the mouth three times before the woman saw the first one coming.

"Calling you a fucking cunt was giving you too much credit. I just don't have a word nasty enough." Mac watched the woman fall to her knees, her hands going to her face, and shook the blood from her hand. She'd broken the skin on her knuckles, she knew, but she'd worry about the pain later. Neil just raised his brow at her.

For the time being she got the antibacterial wipes out of her glove compartment, using them in hopes of avoiding a fight-bite infection. She'd rather not have to dip into their supply of antibiotics so soon, and she wasn't even sure if amoxicillin would be enough to handle an infection that vicious.

The fact that no one had bothered to investigate the sound of a gunshot was concerning. People were sleeping, sure, and probably wouldn't wake enough to understand what it was and get out of bed to check it out, but there were bound to be people who were still awake. If so, they were probably too afraid.

It was too late to get any information out of this woman, Mac realized. She should have questioned her before getting into the whole issue about the car, but the dog might have been dead by then. It didn't matter what the asshole on the ground had named the dog either. She'd be changing it. That boy needed a fresh start with people who wouldn't hurt him.

She had everything moved to the car a few minutes later, and took the precaution of removing the shells from the shotgun. Mac didn't want to leave the shotgun for the woman to reload, either, so she double-checked the barrels to make sure there was nothing lodged in them and stored it under the folded over seats. She found spare shells on a shelf only two feet from where it had been leaning.

"I guess she didn't read all those pesky requirements for the safe and legal storage of ammunition and firearms." Neil gave a dry laugh, though there was little humour in it.

"Alright, let's leave this terrible excuse for a human to her impending death. We've got better things to do." They got in the car once the dog had been coaxed into the back beside the carriers, and then Neil had a question.

"You going to check on the ferrets to make sure they're okay?"

"As soon as we're safely outside the city. They won't die without water or food for a few miles anyway, and I saw water bottles inside the carriers.

"Ah, fuck. No, I'm not going to trust it. Keep an eye on her while I get fresh water and food for those carriers. Then I'll tell you about the kitchen thing." Neil stepped out with her and re-aimed the SIG.

Mac didn't bother explaining to the woman why she was going back into the house. She was probably being paranoid, but after seeing a dog nearly gassed to death she wasn't sure. She sniffed the air as she went back in. It was better, but she was still cautious as she moved around, trying not to breathe too much.

She placed the bottles she was holding in the sink, found some empties and washed them out. Mac was even more careful when she placed the metal spouts on the countertop, even though there was no reason to think she could create a spark of any sort. The bearing inside the spout wasn't likely to do so.

She didn't see any poisons in the kitchen, so it was doubtful the woman had gone that far. It would have been hard to hide death-by-poisoning of two carriers full of ferrets, too.

When Mac had finished putting the bottles in the carriers, she dumped out the food in the dishes, threw the open bag of kibble on the ground, and then opened the fresh bag. It was this she added to the food dishes.

She took a look at the ferrets in the carriers when she put the food back in. They were huddled against the back walls. Once again Mac felt the sting of tears in her eyes. She let them sniff her hand in each one, but didn't have the time to soothe them. They had to start heading back home.

This time when they got back in the car, Mac released the brake and let the car roll back down the driveway. When she'd turned far enough, she depressed the clutch pedal, shoved it into first, and peeled away, leaving Elizabeth to die.

She was getting awfully sick of going to cities and dealing with bullshit like this, so she was relieved to be on her way. She stopped five minutes outside the city, and pulled over to put fuel in the tank. The car was starting to sputter. Then she got back in and started driving again.

"So, what was that you were saying about the kitchen?" Mac told him what she'd found when she'd gone in to get the dog.

"Well, it's probably better that you're the one who punched her in the face. I don't hit women, but I might have made an exception there, and she might not have lived through it. Not that this does her any favours. She'll be dead in two weeks, probably. I doubt she's made friends there. There sure as hell wasn't anyone rushing out to help her when I fired the gun."

"No, but people might not even know her. Not everyone talks to their neighbours. They're likely already terrified, though. That's the feeling I get at any rate." An electronic ringer went off then. It was the satellite phone. Something had happened at home.

"Hello," Neil said into the phone. Mackenzie waited impatiently to see what was going on.

"What do you mean they want gas to keep going? Don't they want to stay with us?" He paused to listen to Billy's response.

"Hmm. Hang on a second." He turned to Mac.

"Looks like they already had a place to go to, but no way to house the ferrets, so they want fuel to keep going. They only need half a tank I guess. They made it all the way there without Billy driving to meet them at least." Mac shrugged.

"We still have fuel even if we help them. They saved us the fuel we'd have used going to get the ferrets ourselves, and that makes two less people we have to deal with. Once we're hunkered in we won't really need it, and eventually it'll go bad. Might as well let them use it."

"Makes sense. Did you hear that Billy?" She waited for him to finish and hang up before asking what she already knew the answer to.

"So, the cell phones are down I take it?"

"Looks like. Not sure about the internet, since that didn't come up."

"I should touch base with my radio contacts. See how they're doing. You have a list of people you talk to, I take it?" Neil nodded, even though she could barely see his head move in the lights from the dash.

"Yeah, I'll talk to them once you're done. I'll teach Kirk and Leigh how to use my base station. I'm technically supposed to be there when they use it, but it doesn't matter now. Why don't I walk over once we get the animals settled, and everyone is up to date? I'll use my radio to contact everyone I know, and teach the two of them how to use it while I'm there."

"Good idea. Then we can keep in touch without having to go there all the time. It's one thing for them to have privacy, but I don't want them to be completely on their own either."

"We could also use their help if they're willing."

"They've been a big help already. I'm sure they'll be fine with helping us out a bit more."

"Alright. Let me know when you want to change seats. I'm happy to take over whenever you're ready."

Two hours later she stopped the car to let the dog water the roadside grass. Neil watered his own patch and then drove the rest of the way home once they were back in the car.

Mac almost felt like crying when she made out the tiny details that she had finally learned to recognize that marked the tree beside the gate. The sun had been up for a while, and the dog was now whimpering again in the back seat.

She felt like whimpering herself. She badly needed to pee. The last time she had gone was before they'd left for the Sault. She hadn't wanted to drip-dry on the roadside. Neil hadn't needed to show any such restraint, of course. She was wiggling in her seat when Neil pulled to a stop by the door.

"Can you tie up the dog in the shade with some food and water for now? We have no idea what he'll be like around all the animals, and I really have to go to the bathroom. We'll figure out what to do with him once everyone has had a chance to see him." As soon as he nodded, she bolted from the car.

Cameron stood up to greet her, but Mac ran on past her to the bathroom, while shouting for her to get the ferrets out of the car. Luckily everyone had been in the open living area at the time, so she didn't burst in on anyone using it, but at that point she was ready to pee on someone's lap if the toilet wasn't free. The relief nearly made her moan, but she managed to restrain herself. Neil was giving her an amused look when she came out.

"Oh, shut up. So, who knows what, about which parts, and whom?" She watched it play across his face as he ran her words back through in his head.

"Nobody knows anything, about any parts, or anyone. You weren't in there long enough to sink the Titanic or anything, even if it might have felt like that to you. Why don't you let Annette take a look at your hand before we get into any of it? Kelly and the kids are dealing with the new ferrets anyway. No point in running through it all more than once."

Mac could tell Annette had questions, but she held her silence for the moment. Mac just told her she might have fight-bite so she would know how to deal with it.

"When was your last tetanus booster?"

"I'm up to date. I've been getting the ten-year booster on schedule. Last was at thirty-five, so I'm not due for another five years."

"Alright. I'll have to irrigate it and debride the tissue, but it's best not to close it up. I'll give you antibiotics to stave off infection, but if it actually gets infected we should try to get you to the hospital. These bite wounds can get very serious. Ordinarily I wouldn't treat this at all, but things have already spiraled out of control out there. As a vet I'm sure I have far more experience with bites than most ER doctors, yet rarely ones that get as serious as human bites."

"I know. If I didn't realize how bad they were, I'd have been whining about all the fuss. I rarely consent to taking antibiotics, for that matter, but when I do I make sure I take the full course. That'll be even more important now.

"We need to make a list of vaccines we should pilfer as soon as the power goes down here for the last time. Maybe talk to a pharmacist about it. I need to get over to a pharmacy to talk to someone about another issue anyway. Neil, do you happen to know if a pharmacist lives nearby?"

"Yeah, I think so. I pass by a mailbox that has his last name on it anyway, every time I go in to the store. Since the landline phones have their own power supply, they might still work, so if we get him a phone that doesn't require power from an outlet, we can ask him to call us right away on one of the satellite phones if he needs someone to provide cold storage. I'm sure he'd like to preserve some of his stock if possible."

"There won't be much room in that medical fridge of Annette's, but we can bring his fridges here if necessary. I doubt a regular kitchen fridge would be precise enough, though it's better than nothing I suppose. If we have a bunch of fridges to power, we're really going to need to get the main PV panels and battery bank set up. That can be done before the house goes up."

"Everyone should probably get whatever booster shots are appropriate, myself included. Five years from now, when I need to give you a booster, those vaccines probably won't be any good," Annette stated.

"Agreed. Maybe you should make a list of your own, Annette. Like ways we should really be careful in our new circumstances, and then we can go over it all as a group. Some guidelines. We have to avoid overuse of meds for multiple reasons, but there must be things I'm not aware of, that will change now that we won't have access to readily-available medical attention.

"I get that we're a different species, but you've got the skill to go from one species to another, which is extremely valuable right now. What about dental care? Is that something you would be able to do if you had to?"

"In a very limited fashion. Animals don't normally need fancy dental work, even when owners have all the money in the world to spend on their pets. Mostly it's cleaning and removing bad teeth so that they can eat without pain.

"My tools for that are also limited. Mostly I have surgical supplies. If it came down to it I could, but we'd need to find equipment that's meant for human teeth."

"About what I figured. Still, *some* dental care is better than none. I remember reading about a man in the US who couldn't afford antibiotics and died from an infected tooth, so it's far more important than people know." Annette nodded her agreement.

"That's probably something we should have on that list you mentioned. People will really need to protect their teeth. No using them for things they're not intended for, proper hygiene to keep their hearts healthy...all that stuff."

By the time Annette had finished irrigating the wound on Mac's hand, and removed the jagged tissue, Kelly, Cam, and Billy were finished getting the ferrets cleaned up and settled inside the house. Everyone sat down to watch as Annette wrapped the hand in gauze.

"So, what happened to your hand, mom? It didn't look that serious or anything, and you usually ignore stuff like that."

"Punched a woman in the mouth a few times. The human mouth is filthy, and her teeth broke the skin. This isn't the time for me to be getting a nasty infection from some fucking cunt." Cam's mouth dropped open. She understood the significance of her mother using that word.

"Wow. Was it the woman with the ferrets?" Mac nodded, and explained the whole story to them.

"I'm sorry, Mac. I had no idea she was like that," Kelly said.

"She lied about everything. You couldn't have known. Anyway, what we need to do right now is make a plan. My previous plans kind of blew up. Nothing is the way it was supposed to go. People are all shifted around, and I have triple the number of furry, woolly, and feathery critters here than I originally intended. And the dog, of course."

"You brought the dog? Cool!" That was from Billy, who seemed thrilled with the idea of having one around.

"Yeah. I couldn't leave him there with her when she tried to gas him. He seems pretty sweet, which is surprising given the way he was obviously treated. I've always liked Dobermans, so now we've got a dog."

"Will he eat the ferrets and chickens, do you think?" Mac looked at her daughter.

"He's tied up right now. We'll deal with the introductions later. All of these animals are stressed right out, I'm sure, so they need a little time to get their balance again before we push anything new on them. He seemed calm in the car, though, and didn't bother the ones in the carriers."

"Why don't I try to get Kirk or Leigh to pick up the radio on their end, and have them come here? They should be part of all these plans. We can teach them to use the radio over here, and then start contacting the people we know. While I'm trying to reach them, you can check the internet. Check the phones for that, too, since the 4G network isn't the same thing as the GSM network the phone part operates on." Mac nodded at Neil and they both headed off to do their own thing, while Billy ran out to see their new dog.

27

SHORING UP THE DEFENSES

The news was disappointing on Mac's end. Her systems were all online, but it looked like major routing centres were down. She could still get to lots of sites, but it took a long time, which meant a large number of failed DNS requests. The 4G network was down. Her BlackBerry was mostly a storage device now, and a Wi-Fi enabled remote with access to her server.

Neil had gotten through to Kirk, so there would be eight for the breakfast Annette had started on. Cameron had gone out to deal with the animals, and Kelly was making coffee. Mac sat at the table, and Neil sat beside her, seemingly just as happy to let the work slide off his shoulders as she was.

"We're doing okay, honey. In a way we're all better off than we were *because* the plans didn't work out the way you and I intended. I know I'm happier because I have you, but strictly from a practical standpoint we've got a much better chance of survival with the group we've got now. We've got muscle, brains, skill, and a willingness to work."

"I know. I'm just really exhausted from all the changes. I'm used to a routine where I do the same things all the time, and this week has been complete chaos in comparison.

"One day I'd like to be able to just play a few hands of cards or something. Or maybe some board games, though I don't think any of the ones we have are for eight players. Or pool. I have a table in that pile of stuff over there, and I really want a chance to be able to use it."

"Well, the animals all have a place to be, even if things aren't perfect yet. The kids managed to get some of the arch segments in place for the other building, so it won't be long before we have our new home. For the moment I think we need sleep more than anything." Mac rested her head on his shoulder.

"Maybe, but more than anything I think we need to just sit here and decompress for a while. We haven't had any time to adjust to our terrifying new reality. People went crazy a lot faster than I anticipated, and I wouldn't have expected Trudeau to get killed. He should have been the most protected person in this country."

By the time the food was cooked and on the table, Kirk and Leigh were coming in the door. Billy came in with them, dog in tow. Of course, it only took the smell of food to convince him to come in. They were going to have to come up with a name for him.

They only had one dog around, so there wouldn't be any confusion or anything, but it was just disrespectful in her mind to keep thinking of him as *the dog*.

"What do you think of Gowan as a name for him?"

"As in *Strange Animal*? Scottish name for a German dog, but with the number of Celtic people around here I can see it."

"I considered a bunch of apocalyptic-type names, like Zombie, Geddy as short for Armageddon, Prism for their song *Armageddon*, and a few more. I've always liked that Gowan song, though, and the name fits for me."

"I like it. Now you've got the song stuck in my head, so I'll have to listen to it later. Let's see what everyone else thinks of the name."

When the suggestion was put forth, everyone seemed happy with it, so Gowan officially became a part of their family and celebrated with a big plate full of eggs. Mac couldn't help thinking it was a damn good thing dogs were omnivores and could eat basically what people ate. He hadn't been a part of their plans, but they could make a place for him.

As soon as breakfast was done, Mac went back into the bedroom to spend some time with Pickle and Squeaker, feeling as though she hadn't seen them all week, when that wasn't true at all. She just needed their love and warmth to ground her for a moment. Things were getting really bad and having her boys in her arms gave her the motivation she needed to survive in the face of all that.

As she sat cross-legged on the bed, both ferrets wiggling in her arms, she heard the opening vocals of *Strange Animal*. Soon she was humming, and then she had both ferrets dancing in front of her face while she sang the chorus to them.

"You're a strange animal, that's what I know," she sang. "You're a strange animal, I've got to follow." Neil walked in on her then, and chuckled at her foolishness.

He took Pickle from her and started doing the same thing, but Pickle was not impressed. He started wiggling his backside around to try to get out of Neil's grasp. Neil relented and set him on the floor. Then he gave Mac a look that she instantly recognized. Her breath caught in her throat, and she set the struggling Squeaker down beside Pickle.

"Now that I have your attention, wife, I was wondering how you felt about us performing some of our marital duties." She didn't need a second invitation. Suddenly she was starving for him.

"Maybe there are some private games we can play, cowboy, but aren't you supposed to be teaching Kirk and Leigh how to use the radio?"

"I asked the others to update them on our events last night, except for what happened with the couple from Ottawa, since we haven't gotten to that story yet. I completely forgot about them, until Billy started talking about some Mike guy I'd never heard of. Anyway, let's get busy here, honey. Before they come looking for us."

"Ooohh, cowboy. You really know how to turn me on with that

kind of dirty talk."

"I'm more of an action kinda guy." Once again Mackenzie found herself naked beneath him. The speed and strength he displayed had her arching toward him as he pressed himself into her. Her nails dug in as her excitement skyrocketed, which only seemed to urge him to move harder and faster. Within minutes she was flying, trembling, and trying not to scream. Her muscles gripped and clenched at him, triggering his orgasm.

They lay, clutching and panting, their skin slick, until Neil managed to draw enough strength together to roll off.

"I would really like to not have to get up right about now," she said haltingly, her breath hitching.

"To quote Jagger, 'You can't always get what you want,' and that's definitely on the list of wants rather than needs. We'll get up because we have to, since we already got what we needed."

"Who says? I don't think a really old rock star should be able to have a say in what I need or don't need."

"He doesn't. I do."

"Very funny. You don't get to make that determination either, cowboy. I'm the brains in *that* outfit."

"What outfit? Unless you're starting a new trend, you're not wearing an outfit. Granted, it would be a very fetching one if fashion dictated it."

"Oh, please. Hardly fetching, unless you count fetching your cock, because it seems to do that pretty well. I'm a forty-year-old woman who's had a kid, and spent a good portion of her adult life being sedentary. It's only been the last year or two that I've managed to take fitness seriously. I've got the usual scars and marks of any woman with that sort of history."

"Well, you'd be wrong on that front. Any guy who's seen real naked women, rather than the airbrushed and plastic variety in Playboy, could tell you that you're fucking hot naked."

"So I've been told, but I've never really believed that. Or why would men still want the magazines? You can't tell me it's for the articles, though Penthouse Forum might do okay there. No matter how ridiculously fake those letters are."

"Hey, we men will take what we can get. Just because they get confused about the value of real women, that doesn't mean men do. A bird in hand and all that."

"Isn't that what Brits call a woman? A bird?"

"Yeah, I think so. Not sure whether it's a compliment or an insult, but since it's not a term we use here I won't worry about it."

Mac was already rolling her body sideways and up, forcing herself to get out of bed. Want and need were in definite conflict in her body. Time for a shower, too, though she'd need help if she was going to keep the bandage dry.

"Come on, cowboy. We need a shower. Or at least I need one, and you need to help me reach all the naughty places."

"I'm your guy!"

"That you are. Husband." Neil gave a slow smile and dragged himself from the bed.

"Alright. Let's go shower. Probably not good to smell like sex while having our little end-of-the-world planning seminar."

*   *   *

"Okay boys and girls, here's what we're doing so far. Annette will be compiling a list of 'dos and don'ts' for us to read and adhere to. Not just for the animals, but for our own health as well. Without ready access to medical help, there are a lot of things that could prove dangerous for us, so when she has it ready we need to pay close attention. Things that were silly before will be things we need to take seriously. Let's not create problems where we use up our supply of meds."

She let that sink in for a minute, before continuing.

"Kirk and Leigh, we'd like some help from you if you're willing. For now we just need to get the enclosures finished to make things healthy for the animals. Particularly the ferrets. We've got fifty if you don't count Pickle and Squeaker, and they won't be housed with the other ones. Fifty in a small area means hygiene and health issues. Not to mention fighting. How are they getting along there?" Kelly shrugged and answered.

"Nothing we didn't expect. We've divided the run. The back door opens into the large part, and the gate opens to the other. We've got the twenty eight from Ottawa on one side, and mine on the other side, with the ten from Sault Ste. Marie here in the house." Mackenzie thought about it.

"Well we knew our current set-up wouldn't really work long-term, so we'll sort out plans for that in a little bit. Are you up for some more work you two?" She had directed the question at Leigh and Kirk.

"We've been given a great place to live, all the food we can eat, and safety in numbers. Meanwhile people out there are probably already starving. We'd be idiots not to help." Leigh nodded along before adding her two cents.

"Even if I were a completely selfish jerk, which I'm occasionally known to be, it's only to our benefit to make sure things work out. We wouldn't have a clue how to survive without your help, so tell us what you need done." Mac smiled at her.

"Alright, I need to prioritize the security perimeter. I've got a whole bunch of sensors we can put up still. I made sure I got tons of them."

Kirk and Leigh agreed to expand the chicken pen all the way to the garden, while Neil took on the new ferret enclosure. Kelly piped up to let him know he needed to keep it away from the other pen.

"We don't know anything about the medical history of those ferrets, and they could have infectious diseases. I don't want to risk the other ones." Neil told her he'd make sure of it.

Kelly and Annette would be doing examinations of the ferrets, in addition to handling their everyday care, so everyone would be really busy throughout the day.

"Billy, why don't you come with me to do the sensors? Cam can go with Neil. It gives us all some time to get to know one another better, since we haven't had much chance to do that." With that, everyone moved off to get things done.

The current sensors were wireless, which Mac didn't trust, so she and Billy grabbed a couple of spools of wire, lockable corrugated conduit, and Cat5e cable.

A direct line with Neil's cabin would mean she could set up sensors around their place as well, and connect the servers. Kirk and Leigh would have access to everything on Mac's server, like the hundreds of books stored on it, and both properties could be monitored for security breaches.

She still hadn't seen the cabin yet. It was always everyone else who had gone over there while she did other things, so she asked Billy what it was like.

"It's a nice place, though small like dad was saying. Kirk and Leigh might want to remove the wall between the bedrooms so they have more space to get around. It would be really nice for them that way. Dad wouldn't mind. As far as we're concerned this is where we live now, not there. You just kind of made everybody feel at home, even though you don't have the big house up yet." Mac looked at him in surprise.

"Really? I would have thought you'd be irritated with the lack of privacy. I worry about Leigh and Kirk being by themselves like that, though. Anything could happen. I hope there are weapons over there, aside from their bows." Billy nodded vigorously.

"Oh yeah. Dad left them a rifle and a shotgun, and gave them some instructions. Those bows are really cool, though."

"They really are. We all took archery lessons together a couple of years ago, and ended up buying our own equipment. We figured silent-but-deadly was a good way to go, just in case. They're not so good in really close quarters, but they certainly do the job from a distance. We've all got compound bows, except for Leigh. She liked the idea of the longbow. Probably a video game thing, but it still works."

"You think I could get one of you to teach me?"

"Sure. Your dad taught you to use a gun, so he's not going to have an issue with you learning archery. The silence is a big advantage. Gunshots might draw people here, which we don't want.

"If you're into the hunting thing, they're great for that, too. None of us hunt, though I know how on an intellectual level. Not just the killing part, but everything that's done after. I just have a hard time with the killing. That's why I didn't get any goats that were meant for meat. Eggs and dairy are enough for me. I have a thing about animals."

"My dad and I never hunted together, though he used to go with my grandma up in the mountains. He just didn't really want to hang out with any of the hunting types around here, so the closest he came to them was selling them their knives."

"There *is* a bit of redneck machismo in the ones around here, isn't there? I've known a few in my time. Guys that like to brag about killing over their limit and then leaving the animals to rot. Now people will be hunting at all times of the year, which is going to cause problems.

"Yet another good reason for us to get these sensors operational. We're far enough out that most people won't be able to walk here for hunting, but we might get the odd one. I still have to go over the land registry maps with your dad to see who might be around here, and who might be a problem neighbour."

It took a couple of hours to cover the area, setting up each motion detector. She screwed them to trees, but buried the wire inside the bark and in a trench inside the conduit. The longer it took, the more agitated she became.

She went back to the house for her bow, and to change into swimwear, so she could shoot the wires across the river, and then run the perimeter over there. It would have been easier if they had a bridge built, but she'd get to that later.

Having looked at the maps that showed Neil's property, Mac knew there was no way she could cover the whole perimeter with sensors. The best she could do was protect fairly well outside the buildings so Kirk and Leigh would have plenty of warning.

She'd need Neil's help with his power supply. She wasn't familiar with his setup the way he was, so it would be better if they went together. She didn't have any sensors left on her, either.

Mac wasn't at all surprised to see the changes when they got back. Neil and Cam had the new ferret enclosure well on its way, with a new concrete pad and a surrounding fence almost doubling their current space. The dirt would be put back on top when the concrete was dry.

The surgery area was well underway, with the pad poured and waiting for the shed to be put on top. She left Billy with Cameron to finish things up, and asked Neil to accompany her to his cabin.

They stopped at the house to grab more sensors, and four of the night-vision cameras. When she'd asked, Neil had told her he had a PC tower at the cabin that he wasn't using for anything yet, so she figured she'd strip it bare and set it up for cabin security. Neil said he had a monitor for the tower, as well as a keyboard and mouse, so Mac wouldn't need to bring those items.

They loaded the wire and conduit spools in the back of Neil's truck, and by the time they were done struggling with them Mac was extremely grateful the damn things weren't full anymore. They filled the truck bed, standing up side by side, and obscured the view through the rear window of the cab.

Despite her earlier shower and the brief swim, Mac was sticky with sweat and grime, and couldn't wait to get the job done so she could get home and clean up. Then she needed sleep. She only hoped she could stay coherent long enough to set up the server. It could take a long time to load software, never mind the actual setting up of the sensors and cameras.

She suggested that Neil install the cameras while she took care of loading the computer, one on each corner of the house to cover every wall, and most of the yard, too. She could only hope Neil wasn't as tired as she was. She stared at him for a minute.

"What?"

"Just wondering if I should be asking you to go up a ladder

right now. You've got to be pretty tired."

"I slept more recently than you did, honey."

"Maybe, but you didn't get as much sleep either, and it couldn't have been all that great since we were in the car."

"I'm fine. I drank another cup of coffee while you were getting stuff from storage. The one in the console is for you. I forgot to give it to you."

"Thank the tiny baby Jeebus!" Neil laughed as she snatched it up and started gulping.

"I'm guessing that means you need the boost right now?"

"God, yes. I'm heading perilously close to crashing, and I need at least *some* wits about me to set up this system."

"There's tons of coffee in storage at the cabin. I made sure I stocked up. Why don't I put on a pot before I do the cameras. We can drink enough caffeine to keep us up 'til dawn."

"Deal."

"So what did happen with those people from Ottawa? Did Cameron tell you anything? I completely forgot about it when I was talking to Billy and we were working on the sensors."

"She told me a bit. I guess the guy was drunk and leering at anything female. She said he gave her the creeps, so she was happy to see their taillights disappear."

"Fuck. I hope they like it where they are, and that we only gave them enough fuel to get them where they were going. They know where we live now." Neil gripped her hand.

"If they come back and cause problems we can deal with it. In fact, I'm pretty sure we can handle anything."

28

PARTING SHOTS

Gerry watched the interfering prick as he followed the snotty whore back into the cabin. He'd come here to show that fucker who he was messing with, ratting him out to his old man and getting him kicked out on the street.

"Family fucking emergency, my ass. Cocksucker," he spat, thinking of the sign on the door at the knife shop.

As a bonus he'd found out why the son of a bitch had stuck his nose in his business. Apparently he was getting it on with the city-bitch now. Well, they'd soon see about that. So far as he was concerned, he'd had dibs on her. Not that he wanted to touch her now. No, now he just wanted her dead. It was her fault his life was such a mess now, after all.

He had been standing there watching as the snitch put up all those cameras, sniggering about their stupidity. Did they really think the cops were going to come running if an alarm went off? Hell, the cops were busy in town trying to keep the stores from being looted. They didn't have time to worry about some dickhead out in the boonies. Considering how busy they were, Gerry didn't figure they would have much time to worry about one that was missing, either, much less some city-bred cunt.

After what seemed like forever, the fuck-face from the knife shop finally came back outside. Gerry put his rifle stock snug against his shoulder. He was sighting along the barrel, his finger tightening on the trigger, when something tugged at his shirt and pulled him just the smallest bit off on his shot. Still, he was pleased to see the stain spread across the asshole's shirt just before he went down. Now he just needed to put him out for good.

He became aware of the dampness running down his belly when he tried to operate the bolt on the rifle to load another bullet. He looked down in shock to see the arrow protruding at a severe angle through his chest. The end with the barb stuck out in such a way that it was blocking the movement of his right arm. That was when the pain kicked in and he noticed what a hard time he was having trying to draw breath.

He collapsed on the ground, only vaguely aware when the rifle was kicked out of his reach. The figure running past him was nothing more than a blur as Gerry's last remaining air made the blood in his throat gurgle. He didn't know or care who it was that had killed him, but he didn't think he was going out alone. That *was enough for him.*

*   *   *

The crack of the rifle had Mackenzie bolting from her chair. Hearing her daughter screaming for her sent ice through her veins. She ran out the door and launched herself from the porch, with no idea what she would find.

Cam stood over Neil's body, soaking wet and trembling from head to foot. Mac dropped to her knees beside him and felt for a pulse. It was racing, but it was there beneath her shaking fingers. Panic and hope mingled inside her. She whipped out her knife and sliced the front of Neil's t-shirt so she could peel it back and see where he'd been hit.

From the placement of the wound, Mac knew the shot had most likely gone through his lung. That meant she had to keep blood from compressing his good lung, so she rolled him onto the side that was damaged. Any blood filling the chest cavity would stay around the wounded area, instead of affecting the healthy lung. She checked his back. The second wound confirmed a through-and-through.

"Get me the satellite phone from the truck!" When she had it in her hand she unfolded the antenna and called Billy, who still had his dad's phone.

"Billy, get Annette over here right away. Tell her it's a gunshot wound. Rifle I think. Lung shot. Now Billy, now!" She ended the call to get him moving, and sent Cam into the cabin for the electrical tape she had in her backpack.

"Hey, cowboy. What the fuck do you think you're doing out here anyway? Getting shot and all that shit? You think we've got time for this?" He smiled up at her even though it was more of a grimace than anything else.

"You're too sympathetic," he gasped.

"No talking, cowboy. You've got a smart mouth on you, but this time use your smart brain. You need what air you've got. You'll be okay, though. You could survive on one lung, but that's not going to be necessary. We'll make sure you keep this one." He just smirked at her, taking her advice not to talk. Most likely because it caused him agony.

Seeing him struggle to breathe, Mac died a thousand deaths, but she knew he would be okay. Even without going to a hospital, a punctured lung could be dealt with.

Cameron came out of the house with towels and the tape Mac had asked for. It wasn't until then that it occurred to her to look around for the shooter.

"Fuck! Where is the fucking bastard? Why did he stop shooting when we're all sitting ducks here? We need to get him moved." Cam stopped her.

"He's dead, mom. It's okay." Mac dropped back onto her knees.

"Wait. What? Dead? How?" Her hands were shaking as she tried to get a patch of Neil's skin dry enough to tape over the wound. Neil's moan of pain drilled a hole through her heart that she had to ignore if she wanted to keep him alive.

"I killed him," Cameron whispered.

"Oh, Jesus." As much as she wanted to comfort her daughter, it would have to wait until Annette was there to take over. She had to cover the exit wound in his back, which was only slightly larger than the entrance wound.

By the time the truck pulled in and Annette and Billy jumped out, Mac was just finishing. Annette shoved her hands out of the way.

"Let me work here," she snapped. Billy tried to reach his dad, but Mac jumped up and pulled him away, wrapping her arms around him.

"Billy, look at me. He's going to be okay, but you have to let Annette do her job."

"She's a fucking vet!"

"Yes, and humans are actually easier to work on than a cat or dog. She has more medical training than you realize. It's okay, Billy. Your dad is going to be okay. We'll make sure of it."

Mackenzie gripped him tightly, but pulled Cameron to her as well.

"We're all going to be okay. I promise you. He can breathe. He's got a punctured lung, but they heal. I made sure his other lung wouldn't collapse and I covered the holes until Annette could get here. He's not going anywhere."

She kept the kids with her, one on each side, as they all watched Annette work on him.

"He's stable enough for now," Annette reassured them. Then she suggested they try to get him in to a hospital anyway, just in case. Mackenzie called 911, hoping they still had their phones up and running, and fuel in the tank of the ambulance.

Mac managed to get through to a dispatcher. When the police arrived ten minutes before the ambulance, Mackenzie was grateful to whatever supreme being was responsible when Gilles stepped out of the car. Between her husband being shot, and her daughter killing the shooter, she needed all the friendly faces she could get. They all did.

As hard as it was for her, she decided to let Billy go in the ambulance with his dad. She said goodbye to Neil with tears in her eyes, hating that she wouldn't be in the ambulance with him, but she knew there was no way Billy could drive right now, and he was the only person other than her who would know how to get to the hospital in Parry Sound. She knew Gilles would take her, but they would need their vehicle.

It killed her not to be able to follow right behind the flashing lights, but there were questions to be answered and Mac wasn't going to leave her daughter to answer them alone. Neil would be heading straight into the ER, assuming the hospital still had generator power. He wasn't going to need her until they were finished with whatever treatment they gave him, though Billy would be at the hospital by himself until she got there.

Her choices sucked. However she worked things out she was shortchanging someone she loved who needed her. Once a second constable showed up, and the coroner arrived, Gilles offered to take their statements at the hospital. Mac nodded her thanks and barely kept a handle on her emotions. Cameron didn't seem to want to go, but she didn't argue. Mac wasn't letting her out of her sight anyway.

Annette remained behind to give her statement so that she could head back home when she was done and let everyone else know what was going on. Mac could have radioed over to them, but she didn't want to take the time.

Gilles didn't argue when Cameron got into the truck with her mother, so Mac figured they were looking at it as a pretty cut-and-dried case of Cam defending the life of another human being. When they got to the hospital, Mac went straight for Billy. Seeing him rocking back and forth on the waiting room chair broke her heart. She sat beside him and pulled Cameron down with her.

"What have they said to you, Billy?" He was shaking, and his teeth chattered a bit when he answered.

"They haven't said anything here, but the guys in the ambulance said he was doing fine. I guess his oxygen levels weren't too bad, and his heart was beating normally. They said something about the blood loss being contained, but they put him on oxygen to make sure." Mac nodded.

"They would, yes. I'm not a doctor, but I can tell you that any blood loss would mean a loss of oxygen transfer, and with one lung not working properly they'd want to be sure his brain was getting enough. They just need to be sure there was no other damage.

"If this had happened even a day or two from now, the hospital might not have been able to do anything for him. At least this way we'll be sure he comes out of it perfectly alright." Gilles gave her a look, but he didn't argue with her.

While they waited, Gilles said he might as well get their statements, and then maybe they could go and donate some blood. He allowed her to sit with Cam while he took her statement, so long as she didn't interrupt. When he asked Cameron what had happened, she answered steadily even though Mac knew she had to be scared shitless.

"One of the motion detectors went off. We were outside working in the yard, but I went in to use the bathroom and saw the flashing message on the monitor for the server. Mom must have just finished setting up the sensors and cameras at Neil's cabin, because it was one of those that had triggered.

"I could see that guy watching the cabin, so I grabbed my bow and ran. I didn't even take time to tell anyone where I was going. I had to swim across the river that cuts through the property, which really slowed me down. Neil must have stayed in the cabin with my mom for a while, or I'd never have made it. I didn't even see the rifle at first. I knew he was going to do something, but I didn't know what.

"Neil came out and that's when he brought the rifle up to his shoulder. It felt like it took me forever to take aim, but I hit him as he was pulling the trigger. I saw him jerk a bit, so I might have thrown his shot off. I wasn't even sure if the arrow would go into him. I mean, I've never shot at a living target before."

"You have a .40 calibre Glock registered to you, right?" When Cam nodded he continued.

"How come you didn't take that with you instead? Most people would have grabbed a gun under those circumstances I would think." Cam shook her head.

"I didn't think I was allowed to. That's not our property, so I can't carry there. I mean, it's Neil's property and he's married to my mom, so I don't really know how that works, since my mom and I own our property together. It's kind of confusing, and I figured it would just be better if I grabbed the bow." Gilles nodded at her and patted her shoulder.

"It was probably for the best. That way there are no questions to be raised about whether or not you did anything illegal." He turned to Mac.

"You raised a damn good kid, Mac."

"Fucking right I did," she said, a relieved smile on her face.

"Okay, why don't I tell you my end of things so we can get this over with?" Gilles took notes while she gave him the rundown.

"You can ask Billy whatever questions you need to, but he wasn't there when it happened. I called him on the satellite phone so he could get Annette over there. She's a vet, so she's got enough medical training to deal with an emergency, and I've done a lot of studying on emergency treatments. Between the two of us I figured we'd be able to make sure he survived, even if we couldn't get him to the hospital."

"Yeah, about that. You mentioned something a few minutes ago about not being able to treat him at the hospital in a couple of days. What was that about?" Mac looked him in the eye.

"I'm pretty sure you already have a good idea what's going on out there, Gilles. You're a smart guy. The whole world is about to fall apart, and we've got front-row seats. Did you know they killed Trudeau?" Gilles' mouth dropped open.

"Are you kidding me?"

"No. It happened yesterday. I'm surprised you didn't hear about it from one of the other detachments. The power has already gone down in a lot of the major cities. Get on the radio if you can, Gilles, and find out every scrap of information that's available." He looked like he wasn't sure he believed her, but he knew her better than to think she'd lie about something like that.

"This is a lot to take in, but when things get really bad bring your family to Neil's. You won't be able to find my place, but you know where his cabin is. Keep enough fuel in your car to get there. Do me a favour and get on the radio to Chuck as soon as you can and give him directions to Neil's.

"I know you guys drifted apart, but I don't know if I can reach him now, and I want him to know he has a place to bring his wife and kids. You probably don't believe me right now, but the whole world is going dark. If you bring your family to our place, I'll explain the whole thing to you, but for the moment just keep what I've said in mind."

Gilles was still looking at her like he wasn't sure if she was crazy or not, but he sat there and thought about it for a minute.

"Maybe. We'll see what happens. If it's as bad as you say, I'll know soon enough and we'll all be seeing you. For now why don't y'all go donate blood. It sounds as if the hospital might be needing a lot of it." Then he looked at Cameron and waited until she was looking back at him.

"You didn't do anything wrong, kid. You did the right thing even if it might have been the hard thing. I'm sure your mother will tell ya that, but I thought you might want to know it from a cop. You've got nothing to worry about. Nobody will press any charges." He patted her shoulder and stood up. Mac walked him to the elevator so she could say goodbye privately.

"Thank you for saying that to her," she said quietly. Gilles just nodded and patted her shoulder too. Mac figured it was probably inappropriate for her to hug him at the moment, despite their long-standing friendship, so she squeezed his arm and let him go, hoping he would remember her offer.

Just when Mackenzie was about to ask the nurse where they could go to donate blood, he headed toward them to let them know Neil was in recovery. He said the doctor would be out to speak with them in a few minutes, but that it looked like everything was fine.

Mackenzie sat between the kids again and waited, relief causing her to sag in her chair. Even with logic telling her he was going to be fine, hearing it from the nurse seemed to make it sink in.

It felt like ages had passed, but finally the doctor came out to speak with them. Other than a chipped rib, antibiotics to stave off infection, and a chest tube to deal with a collapsed lung, it looked like Neil was healthy as a horse. Mackenzie looked the doctor in the eye as she went over everything, making sure she was telling them the whole story.

"You can go in to see him now, but limit it to one at a time. If he remains stable, it should only be a day or two before we release him." Mac thanked the doctor and headed toward Neil's room. Knowing how scared Billy was, she kept her visit brief so he'd be able to see his dad.

"You scared the shit out of us, cowboy. You know that?"

"Tell me about it. I'm okay, though. I love you, honey."

"I love you, too. So much. I'm going to let Billy come in now, though. He's terrified even though everyone is telling him you're going to be okay." Neil gave a small nod, obviously trying not to move his chest too much.

"Okay. Is Cameron here? I'd like to thank her after Billy comes in."

"I'll let her know." She kissed him softly on the mouth, her thumb stroking his jaw, and stared into his green eyes for a moment. It took every ounce of her will to drag herself away from his side.

After Billy went into the room, Mac looked at her daughter, and though she had some questions of her own she knew they would have to wait. As tough as Cameron tried to be, Mac could see she was a mess. Killing someone changed a person. Mackenzie knew all about that.

EPILOGUE

STILL WATERS

Brian Newman received the news of his son's death with a surface calm. After all, everyone had always told him that Gerry would come to a bad end one day. He knew they were right. It didn't change the fact that his son was dead.

Brian maintained his stoic demeanor, even on the rare occasions people felt they needed to extend false sympathies. Most of the time they were far too busy trying to deal with the issues caused by the power outage.

Brian didn't notice. After all, what parent would care about such petty issues when they were about to bury their only child? He was pretty sure there was more to the story than the cop had told him, and whatever he had to do he was going to find out the truth.

COMING SOON!

SALVAGE RIGHTS
Tipping Point Book Three
Author

For someone who wants to live a quiet and solitary life, Mackenzie is doing a terrible job of it. Somehow she and her daughter have managed to start rebuilding civilization on a small scale. But not everyone wants a return to law and order. There are those who look on the end of society as an opportunity, and they will stop at nothing to ensure Mac and Cameron do not succeed.

Sign up for Rain's mailing list so you get all the good stuff:

mailinglist@rainstickland.com

(If you have a problem, make sure you didn't put an 'R' in Stickland.)

Now available …

GROUND ZERO

Book Two of the Tipping Point Trilogy

The world went dark, but Mackenzie was one of the ones who had prepared for it. Not everyone is as fortunate. Prescription drugs are no longer available, and Mac's best friend is a type 1 diabetic. She manages to find someone who can make insulin the old-fashioned way, but she still has to get it to him before it's too late. That means leaving the safety of her hidden farm and travelling hundreds of miles to get there, without getting killed along the way. Meanwhile, her daughter is forced to contend with one disaster after another.

Paperback ISBN-13: 978-0994950031
Paperback ISBN-10: 0994950039
Kindle ISBN-13: 978-0-9949500-4-8

Now available ...

IMPƎRƎECTIOИS

Anthology
Editor and Contributing Author

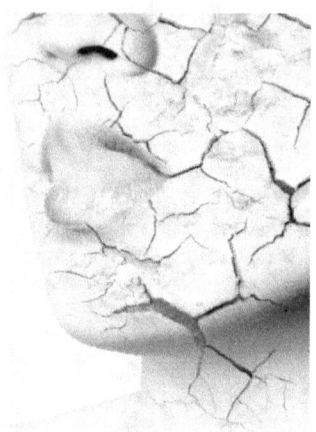

IMPƎRƎECTIOИS

Edited by
RAIN STICKLAND

Humanity goes to great lengths to do away with their perceived
imperfections, but where does the journey take them, and are they
any better for it?

Imperfections brings together some of the best up-and-coming
authors, for a veritable smorgasbord of fiction...and no genre is
safe. There's a taste of horror, a sampling of fantasy, a soupçon of
drama, and a dash of science fiction, all with a distinct dystopian
flavour.

Paperback ISBN-13: 978-0994950055
Paperback ISBN-10: 0994950055
Kindle ISBN-13: 978-0-9949500-6-2

ABOUT THE AUTHOR

Rain Stickland has been writing since the age of twelve, when the fever took hold and never truly dissipated. Despite two decades of interest in off-grid living, she was only recently introduced to the vast world of preppers. Her interest kicked up a few notches, however, during the Northeast Blackout in 2003, when the world went dark for millions of people, some for weeks.

Called the Canadian Tornado by friends, she's written and published nearly 400 articles on a wide variety of topics, including everything from stem cell transplants to the care and feeding of cats, dogs, and ferrets. She lives with her daughter in Ontario, Canada. You can find out more at www.rainstickland.com.